Conveniently in Bloom

LOVE IN FAIRWICK FALLS
BOOK THREE

ELISE KENNEDY

Copyright © 2024 by Elise Kennedy.

All rights reserved.

No part of this book may be reproduced in any form or by any electronic or mechanical means, including information storage and retrieval systems, without written permission from the author, except for the use of brief quotations in a book review.

CONTENT WARNINGS

See the end of the book for content warnings.

Also by Elise Kennedy

***Love in Fairwick Falls* Novels**

Accidentally in Bloom (Rose & Gray)

Wallflower in Bloom (Violet & Jack)

Conveniently in Bloom (Lily & Nash)

Unexpectedly Bookish (Pearl & Reed)

Falling at the Barre (Olivia & Luca)

Forever in Bloom - Summer 2026 (Allison & Wells)

∼

***Cozy Nights in Vermont* Novellas**

Fall Inn Love

Falling in Vermont

∼

***Only One Cozy Bed* Novellas**

Pumpkin Spice & Pour-overs

Apple Cider & Subterfuge

Hot Cocoa & Mistletoe

Snowed In & Snuggle Weather

∼

***Jingle Bell Springs* Novellas**

The Grump in Jingle Bell Springs - October 2026

To you.

May you find the safety you deserve.

August

LILY

Lily Parker threw open the windows of her studio apartment, preparing to watch the brewing storm. Trees swayed in the rolling sheets of rain. An old-fashioned summer thunderstorm was exactly what her soul needed after endless hours bent over arranging flowers.

She sat at the window overlooking Main Street, sketching flower arrangement ideas. It was an unusual approach, but her art background made her work unique. Bloom, the flower and plant shop she'd re-opened with her sisters earlier that year, had made a name for itself with her modern, chic arrangements.

Her cozy apartment sat above Bloom, and the stairs leading down from her apartment ended in the back prep room of the flower shop. She loved her thirty-step commute to the shop.

The smell of pencil shavings and summer rain drifted around her as she sketched her next floral line. The soundtrack of raindrops pelting the open windowpane made the work extra dreamy.

Bells clanged on Bloom's front door and echoed up through the doorway she'd propped open. Lily tossed her pencil and hustled down the stairs. "Hope you parked your rowboat outside," she called out cheerfully. "What can I help you w…"

A near-hulking 6'5" frame she was *very* familiar with came into view.

Nash Donnelly, cornerstone of the Fairwick Falls community, her older sister's best friend growing up.

And the one man she'd been in love with her entire life.

The man who starred in her most intimate dreams was now dripping all over Bloom's wood floor. His t-shirt and jogging shorts were plastered to every muscle on his body.

Thanks, universe. Just another vision to add to my Shouldn't Masturbate to Nash Donnelly But I'm Still Gonna spank bank.

"Nash, you're drenched." She grabbed a towel from the prep table to mop up the kiddie-pool-sized puddle surrounding him.

He wiped streams of water off his face with both hands. "The rain is brutal and you were the only one open. Sorry for the mess, Lilypad."

I hate that fucking nickname. Always Rose's little sister, not a fucking thirty-year-old adult with a sex drive in dire need of a tune-up.

"Thought about running home, but the rain was coming so hard I couldn't see two feet in front of me."

I'll be 'coming so hard' picturing you right now.

Fuck.

Focus, Lily.

Lily tossed him a towel and threw down more to mop up the water.

He ruffled his hair with it, squeezing water out of his thick brown hair. "Thanks," he said, now smiling.

Tingles of pleasure ran down her spine at having that smile directed toward her.

"No problem." Lily tried for a casual shrug but her eyes lodged on his clinging shirt that highlighted his sculpted arms and chest.

Nash had a muscular, wide frame. His towering frame dwarfed her five feet two inches, and she felt heat creep up her neck. Being the approximate height of a fucking oak tree, he was hard to miss.

But it was his soft, boyish smile that always did her in. The kindness in his eyes echoed somewhere deep inside her and settled there.

A loud *crack* and boom thundered through the shop, shaking the glassware and gifts, and Lily jumped. Nash smiled, still toweling off and wringing water out of his shirt. "Not a fan of storms?"

"No, I'm just..." *Restraining myself from climbing you like a tree and ripping your clothes off.* "...A little jumpy today. Too much coffee."

Nash pulled at his soaked shirt. "I hate wet clothes. I feel like I'm being suffocated."

"By all means, take them off." Lily's mouth twisted into a teasing smile, and he laughed, shaking his head.

Of course he'd never take her seriously. She was just 'little Lilypad.'

Always had been, always would be.

Good thing she'd go back to her life in New York in six months. She wouldn't have to think about how much she loved him. See him nearly every day and fall a little more in love with him.

She'd never, *never* ever admit her feelings. In her experience, that only lead to heartbreak.

And she'd seen the damage heartbreak could do.

No fucking thank you.

"Some of my dad's old t-shirts are back here," Lily said, walking to the back. She returned a minute later with an old red t-shirt in hand.

Nash held it at arm's length, reading it. "'Slap My Ass and Kiss My BBQ'?" He howled with laughter. "This is the most 'Frank' shirt I've ever seen. I remember him wearing it."

Nash removed his shirt right there in the middle of the shop. Lily's mouth went dry. He did that ridiculously sexy thing where he reached behind him and pulled off his shirt from the back.

Where did guys learn to do that? *Why* did they do that? Should *she* do that? Was it for strategic reasons or for sexy reasons?

All the thoughts left her head as she got an eyeful of pure, unadulterated male physique.

The wet t-shirt had highlighted Nash's biceps and broad shoulders, but it had hidden his brawny chest and firm, thick torso of sculpted abs. He didn't have a six-pack, but it was pretty damn close.

Close enough to haunt her dreams.

His chest was bare, but a small trail of dark hair near the bottom of his abs hinted at nirvana. She licked her lips as she stared, imagining what he might look like naked. He'd sure grown up since they'd all played in the pool together as kids.

He found the opening for the t-shirt and almost had it on when his eyes met hers.

Shit, you're staring. Heat rose in her cheeks and she turned away, needing to busy herself.

Normally, she had no problem making her interests known

to men. She'd had no shortage of dates in New York, but this was *Nash*.

He'd made his lack of interest in her abundantly clear the last eight months she'd been back in Fairwick Falls.

She'd try to engage with him, but then he'd find an excuse to leave.

His thick hair stood up sharply from his toweling, looking far too crazy for the always-buttoned-up Nash.

"You look like you stuck your finger in a socket." She perched on her toes, trying to reach the top of his head to smooth it down.

He ducked, his eyes cautiously watching her.

She had tried approximately one thousand times to put him firmly in the "love you as a brother" category, but his smell, his smile, and his voice just wouldn't let her do that.

She lingered longer than necessary fixing his hair, breathing in his expensive scent that always sent a jolt of desire down her middle.

"Much better," she murmured, stepping back. "We don't want the Prince of Fairwick Falls looking like he got mugged, do we?" A teasing smirk curved her lips as she leaned back on the checkout counter.

His eyes glinted with warm delight. "You *know* I hate that nick—"

But he was cut off by a bright flash of lightning and Bloom fell into darkness.

"Fuck," Lily groaned in annoyance as she looked outside. The street lamp was still on. "Why is our power out, but everyone else's isn't?"

A bright light appeared as Nash held his phone's flashlight over her. "Probably your breaker box. C'mon, we'll figure it out," and walked to the basement door.

Apprehension crept up Lily's spine as they stepped into the

dark, musty basement. "Remember when you and Rose hid down here and scared the shit out of Vi and me when I was like, five? I thought you'd both pee your pants, you were laughing so hard."

His laugh was quick and happy. "I have never, and I mean *never*, heard someone shriek that high."

"I think the circuit breaker is in the corner," Lily said, walking around a pile of dusty boxes.

The breaker box was situated in the back of the old basement in a tight cut-out hole. Lily had always pictured goblins hiding in the corner when she was a kid.

Hell, she kind of pictured it now, too.

"What do you think the chances are that my disorganized late father taped instructions to the breaker?" Lily asked, stepping over stacked lumber.

"Probably low, knowing Frank."

Her father had passed away in January, leaving the flower shop to her and her sisters. They'd been playing catch up to get the building in shape since then.

Lily stared at the breaker box full of labels with scribbles and switches, and stepped up on uneven, stacked bricks for a better look.

"Great," she sighed dubiously. "What now?"

"You've never flipped a blown breaker?" He lifted an eyebrow with a grin on that stupidly handsome face.

He looked like a prince who had trained as a warrior. Masculine, elegant, perfect.

"Normally I have a building super in Brooklyn who deals with crap like this," she said, smirking back.

And I'll be back there in six months so I don't get too attached,

"I believe in teaching to fish. I'll talk you through it."

He sidled into the small space behind her. *Gah. Why does his competence make him even hotter?*

His arms curved around her, one holding the phone's light and the other pointing to the list of switches.

His chest brushed her bare shoulders and she gulped. *Thank god for tank tops.*

"You see this? That's the first one you're going to try." His low voice rumbled pleasantly in her ear.

She tried to concentrate, but the scent of his cologne clouded her judgment. Goosebumps cascaded down her arms. Her nipples pebbled as his breath caressed her neck.

Her eyes closed slowly in pleasure, but she opened them quickly upon hearing Nash's sharp inhale, blinking hard in an attempt to stay focused.

"This one?" She asked, leaning ever so slightly back to chase the feeling of him against her.

His arm dropped but his chest now pressing against her back. "Uh huh," he said, his voice sounding strained.

Maybe he's more into me than I thought.

She flipped the first breaker, and nothing happened.

"Keep going," he murmured in her ear.

Her pulse spiked at the feel of him so close.

She tried the next one, and then the next. Each flip pulsed the tension throughout her body.

His breath was shallow next to her ear, his breath coming as fast as hers.

By the last one, her entire body was flush against his. The tops of his thighs against her ass, and her back against his abs and chest.

"No luck," she whispered.

She slowly turned in the small space, her hard nipples pressed against his chest that was heaving breaths, like she was.

The air crackled between them as she met his dark, intense gaze.

Nash didn't step back. His eyes dipped to her mouth.

What would he taste like?

A pull of lust made her eyes heavy.

A cacophonous boom rattled the building, and she jumped an inch in the air with a yelp, stumbling off the uneven bricks. He caught her, an arm wrapped tight around her waist.

"Hey, hey" he said with a smile, soothing her. "I got you."

She smiled against his chest and she could feel the rapid beat of his heart. His arm lingered around her waist.

Please don't move, please don't move.

She slowly lifted her head from his chest, looking up into his tortured face.

His arm tightened around her waist as his breath grew more ragged. She slowly licked her lips, dreaming of what he'd taste like.

His eyes traced the movement of her tongue and he gulped.

Ragged breaths pulled at his chest.

Please. Kiss me.

A roll of thunder boomed through the basement, and he swept down, catching her mouth in a deep, pressing kiss.

She sank into him, her stomach bottoming out as she finally, *finally* learned what Nash Donnelly tasted like.

Like cologne and spearmint and lust.

Like a needy, gripping desire to spread her thighs and pull him closer for anything he'd give her.

She kissed him with years of pent-up desire. She pulled him closer as he ravaged her mouth, and his arms tightened on her waist and back, pressing every part of her against him.

A curl of desire shot down her spine as he dragged his mouth across hers in unending, deep, needy strokes and *holy hell.*

Nash Donnelly could really fucking kiss.

His tongue ran across her lips, desperately, urgently, asking for more.

Yes.

With a moan at knowing what his *fucking tongue* felt like on her, her mouth opened.

And thank *god* he took the opportunity to kiss her deeper.

He licked into her mouth, and she met his tongue with hers, seeing stars as they connected.

His hand slid down across her back as he cupped her ass and gave it a hard squeeze, pulling her against him with a growl that didn't sound like the buttoned up Nash at all.

Fuck yes. Lose control with me.

A moan slipped out of her at how much he *wanted* her.

Her hands tangled in his wet hair. She raked her nails through it, and a needy moan sobbed out of him.

She needed more of him; his chest, his arms. *God*, his arms. She could come from fantasizing about them. She clawed at his bicep and groaned at how good he felt.

His mouth still feasted on hers, ravenously kissing her harder and faster, until he pressed her against the brick wall.

Desire made her dizzy and she met every kiss with a greedy, gulping one of her own as she slid her hands over him.

His hands roamed her body until one stroked her ribs, just below her breast, inching higher. She pressed into his hand, *needing* him there.

With his tongue brushing hers, he swiped a thumb over a hard nipple, back and forth.

Back and forth.

Back, harder.

Holy fuck.

And forth, harder still.

Her clit pulsed with every touch and she mewled in pleasure as he teased her nipple between his fingers, harder and biting her lip with need.

Just as she was about to *beg* him to fuck her, the lights came back on as suddenly as they'd gone out.

The shock of the brightness made them gasp, pulling back.

Nash stepped away as quickly as he'd started kissing her.

~

NASH

Pull your shit together.

Nash turned away to get his bearings and leaned on a basement post. He was currently sporting a class-A hard-on in thin, wet gym shorts.

Kittens. Your grandmother, think of anything to make it go away.

God, it's been too long since you've had a beautiful woman. You can't even keep your cock down when kissing someone you should not *be kissing.*

He knew, however, that it was no ordinary kiss. That was months—no, *years* of built-up tension and lust.

He'd known Lily all his life as Rose's little sister, until a chance run-in with her at a New York salsa club five years ago had changed everything.

He'd been newly single after breaking off his engagement, and his world tilted upside down as he realized the blonde bombshell he'd stared at across the room had been *her*.

Nash was seven years older, and it had been the first time that seven-year difference hadn't seemed so big. Something had shifted that night, seeing her out with her girlfriends—gorgeous, sexy, so confident.

Nash hadn't stopped thinking of her since, but he was born

to be the next leader of the Donnelly family, a financial bedrock of the Fairwick Falls community.

He was duty-bound to care for the community like his family before him.

Lily, however, hated anything with even a whiff of permanence.

He'd purposefully given her a wide berth, trying to stay away since she'd moved back to their hometown.

Temporarily, of course.

It would be the absolute worst idea to let his crush turn into something more. He'd be happy enough with his imagination and his right hand until she inevitably left town.

His body now under control, he turned around to see Lily dazed with lust.

The absolute picture of romantic beauty in front of him was a gut punch. Her full, red lips were swollen and pouted in surprise. Blonde curls escaped her hair clip and framed her heart-shaped face.

A thin tank top barely covered her, and her very short shorts revealed the curve of her ass.

That delectable, perfect, round ass.

Stop it, he ordered himself, *before you have to turn around again.*

Lily stepped closer with a warm, seductive smile. "I'd like to do that again." She slid her hands along his chest.

War waged within him. "Lily. Wait."

All he wanted was to carry her upstairs to her apartment and fuck her like he'd dreamed of doing for the past six months.

Hell, five years.

"This isn't a good idea," he said, hoping he sounded convincing.

A cat-like smile curved her lips. "Did you want to move this upstairs instead?"

Yes.

Fuck, wait, no.

He gently removed her hands from his chest and held them. "No, it's just..."

She'd leave soon, and he couldn't risk getting more attached.

Lie like your life depends on it. "You're just not my type, Lilypad."

There, that should stop things.

Instant anger flooded her face. *Oh shit*. He was in for a DEFCON-1 Lily tirade.

She ripped her hands from his. "I am not your" —she shoved him aside—"goddamn *Lilypad*, Nash Donnelly."

She stalked to the stairs but whirled around with a murderous glint in her eyes. "I am *thirty* years old. Thirty! Get your head out of your Fairwick Falls royalty, Ivy-league ass, and admit what you already know: You want me as much as I want you."

She stormed up the stairs, leaving a literal dust cloud in her wake.

Fuck. He rubbed his face in frustration.

"Lily," he called. "Come back here." Nash climbed the dusty stairs up to the showroom of Bloom and heard a door slam on the third floor.

Jesus, she's fast.

He took the spiral staircase two at a time and jogged up to Lily's studio apartment, calling up the stairs. "Lily, I'm sorry. Open up so we can talk."

A definitive "No" sounded from inside.

"Please open the door, I can explain."

"Try again," she called from behind the door.

"I didn't mean it like that."

"What exactly *didn't* your giant boner mean?" she taunted from behind the door.

"God*damn*it. Open—"

"Fine, have it your way." The door swung open with a dramatic flair, and Lily stood in a revealing, low-cut sports bra and tiny, hot pink thong panties.

Holy fucking hell.

All the breath left Nash's lungs.

Her breasts curved against the tight fit of the sports bra, giving her picture-perfect cleavage. Her hips were lush and round, and he thought they might feel amazing in his hands if she was on top of him. Her muscular legs flexed as she stepped into tiny, stretchy shorts.

"Shit," he muttered, coming to his senses and turning around. Some gentleman he was, ogling her while she was naked. "I didn't mean to open the door while you were...like that."

"It's fine, since, you know, I'm not *your type*," she said with venom. "You wanted to talk without a door between us. So talk. I only have ten minutes until my hot yoga class." Fabric rustled behind him and he peeked over his shoulder to see her pulling on a loose tank.

"I, uh..." He whipped back around. *Apologize, you asshat, then get out of here.* "I'm sorry. I didn't mean to insult you. You're very..." *Hot. Fuckable. Sexy. Perfect. Gorgeous.* "...pretty. Very pretty, Lily. But I can't date someone who can't stay in Fairwick Falls. I don't want to confuse you by starting something I can't finish."

She locked her door and brushed past him, then ran down the worn wooden stairs to Bloom.

"Nash, you're reading into this too much." She laughed, shaking her head at him as if he was being silly. "I was just hoping for a make-out session. Maybe a quick bang. A distraction. You don't have to get all emotional on me, 'kay? I'll happily find someone else to get my sexual frustration out with."

His brows furrowed.

What the hell? Just an outlet for her sexual frustration?

No, he wasn't crazy. There was *something* more between them. He knew it. It was why he had stayed the hell away from her.

She held Bloom's front door open with an outstretched arm. "Mark at the hardware store is single now. Maybe he can *change my lightbulb*." Her eyebrow quirked as she stared at him, tongue in cheek.

But a flicker of hurt hid behind her bravado.

Trying to ignore it, Nash swallowed his regret and stepped outside. He had to prioritize what was best for the Donnelly estate in the long-term.

"We're just not compatible, Lilypa—er, Lily."

She handed him his wet t-shirt. As he grabbed it, she caught his hand and yanked him down, meeting her nose to nose. "Then you won't care that when I use my vibrator tonight and come so hard I make the windows rattle with my screams...that I *won't* be thinking of you."

She slammed the front door to Bloom in his face and locked it, leaving him in the misting rain.

Well, fuck.

Next time, he'd run laps around his goddamn house before he'd suffer the temptation of Lily Parker again.

January

LILY

Lily Parker frowned at the most gorgeous bridal bouquet she'd ever made.

"Something's still missing..." she muttered to herself in the empty flower shop.

Feathery white peonies were flanked by white roses and surrounded with deep green leaves. Ivy was woven throughout.

It sat in between the *two other* most gorgeous bridal bouquets she'd ever made.

Why make one bouquet for your sister when you can make her three?

She'd always had a hard time choosing during important moments. What if she picked the wrong one? As a kid, she'd requested two birthday cake flavors (triple chocolate and lemon supreme, duh). As a teenager, she'd said yes to two boys for Prom (whoops!). As an adult, she never stayed anywhere longer than she could help it.

It was her fatal flaw.

And making something that would be in her sister's wedding photos until they all croaked in seventy years? That was pretty fucking important, and she was completely split on the decision.

The flowers *had* to be perfect.

"Maybe Rose can rotate between them during the ceremony," she muttered, picking at the colorful bouquet on the left. Pinks and oranges radiated out from the center of the bouquet.

But it still needs something. Lily jogged to the front of Bloom, her pride and joy. The flower shop had bright white walls with deep teal woodwork, modern brass accents, and greenery bursting from every corner. It was bright and crisp in the January morning. They'd shut down today to prep for Rose's wedding tomorrow.

Lily perused the shop's buckets of flowers. "There you are." She snatched a bundle of snapdragons. It would be the perfect complement to the peonies in the white bouquet.

Oh! Or maybe the third bouquet too.

"How's it going with the centerpieces?" Lily called over to Pearl, their new part-time help.

"Like I'm going to dream of daisies until I die." Pearl's black-painted lips were turned down with dread at the flowers in front of her.

Pearl's tough-looking tattoos and piercings didn't hide her outright fear at the daisies in front of her. "How do you know how to do all this?" Pearl asked in exasperation.

Lily stopped short. How *did* she know how to do this?

She'd been a freelance illustrator until she and her sisters had re-opened their late dad's flower shop. She'd never redesigned a store until she did Bloom's interior. Never sold a flower arrangement until they launched Bloom.

And here she was months later, living and breathing flowers as if she'd done it all her life.

"Uh...blind, ignorant confidence I guess?" Lily shrugged. She patted Pearl's shoulder. "You're doing great."

Her phone buzzed, and she whipped it out, getting tangled in the long scarf she'd wrapped around her neck to stay warm in the drafty old building. She felt like an icicle despite wearing fingerless gloves and an oversized beanie pulled over her ears.

> BRAD - GOOD WITH TONGUE
>
> u around? im back in the city for the night

Oof. Brad Good With Tongue was one of the *many* casual hookup bad decisions in eight years of living in New York.

Never dating. Never committing.

Always no strings.

She'd had a nearly twelve-month dry spell since moving back to her hometown of Fairwick Falls.

Aside from the one mind-bending kiss she'd had with Nash Donnelly four months ago.

She needed some distance from him ASAP before she lost her mind. It was only twenty or thirty times a day that she either saw him (yum), thought of him (when walking past Donnelly Park), or someone in the town mentioned him (get out of her head already!).

He was the only man she'd ever loved, and he could never ever *ever* know.

She wasn't his *type* after all.

Moving back had been temporary to sort out her late dad's estate, and then last May she'd committed to staying for six more months to launch the flower shop.

Her time was almost up.

Soon she'd be back in New York, a thousand lightyears away

from Fairwick Falls, Pennsylvania. Population: twelve hundred, three hours from anywhere.

> **LILY**
> nope - but check back in about a month (winky face)

The anxiety of betrayal somersaulted in her stomach. She itched to go back to New York *right now*. She'd reached out to a New York design agency on a whim weeks ago and finally got a response last night that they'd set up a call in the next week.

Her wandering lifestyle protected her. If she never stayed anywhere too long, she couldn't get too attached.

If you loved something too much, it could break your heart and leave you in pieces. And she was getting attached to her hometown again, with its festivals and town characters and all her favorite people.

Never a good sign.

> **VIOLET** 💜
> Mayday! Mayday! Bride incoming!

Shit fuck shit.

> **LILY**
> you were supposed to distract her today!!!!!! you know the peonies are a surprise from gray for tomorrow

> I'm sorrrryyyyyyyyy. I couldn't tell her noooo 😬

Ugh. She could never stay mad at her sweet-as-pie middle sister, but dammit Vi!

Lily scrambled to the back prep room. She couldn't ruin Gray's surprise of having off-season peonies flown in for Rose.

He'd planned the entire wedding so his overworked, type-A bride wouldn't have to.

The back door to Bloom flew open, and Lily launched her body in front of the bouquets. "They're not ready yet," she yelled defensively.

Rose, fashionable and lithe, strode in on five-inch heels wearing a happy smile. "I am bigger and older than you, Lily-bug. Move."

Violet fell against the open doorway, catching her breath. "She wouldn't stop once she knew you were making her bouquet and not teaching a goat yoga class."

Lily rolled her eyes as she tried to hide the bouquets behind her. "Oh that's a terrible lie, Vi. I'd never subject goats to a class of yoga students. Stop peeking," Lily said, hitting Rose's leg with her foot. "Gray will be *so* sad. These were a surprise for you for tomorrow."

"Move or I'll tell Mrs. Maroo, who's about to come in, that you used to write your name as Mrs. Lily Donnelly in your diary." Rose smirked, knowing she'd won.

"Damn, girl. You play dirty," Lily said, frowning. One whiff of gossip to Mrs. Maroo and the whole county would know. Lily stepped back from the bouquets. "Fine, happy now?"

Rose went still, her eyes filling with tears. "My favorite," she whispered as her fingers went to the pinkish-white petals of a peony. Gray had ordered ridiculously expensive hothouse white peonies as the base for at least one bouquet, knowing they were her favorite. "And these are gorgeous too." Rose cooed at the other bouquets.

Lily clapped. She loved seeing that misty look in her brides' eyes at her work. "You know me, I couldn't decide. So use any and all of them tomorrow. Oh! Or use one this evening at the rehearsal."

Rose wrapped her in a quick hug. "Thank you. They're extra special because you made them."

There was that churning of betrayal again in her stomach.

She squeezed her sister back, desperately wanting to tell her that her time was almost up in Fairwick Falls. *But you can't ruin it now.*

She'd wait until Rose was back from her honeymoon to announce she was leaving. No need to stress out the bride before her wedding.

"Hiya, kids." Mrs. Maroo rapped on the open back door, sporting neon green glasses and a winter coat that looked like a pint-sized circus tent. She was the coolest seventy-year-old lady Lily had ever met.

"There's the glowing bride." Mrs. Maroo squeezed Rose's arm affectionately. "And the newly engaged bride-to-be." She squeezed Violet's arm. "*And* the town gymnast." Mrs. Maroo winked at Lily with a mischievous smile.

"I can't help that I break out in handstands after five tequila shots," Lily said with a snort. Rose's bachelorette party had been a rager, and Lily had done *many* handstands.

Mrs. Maroo held up a to-go container. "I've brought payment for designing my business cards. Are you *sure* I can't pay you more than five cooked chicken breasts?"

Lily grabbed the container and opened it to check that the chicken was plain but gagged and slammed it shut. "This is more than enough. You know I can't bear to cook them."

"Aren't you vegetarian?" Mrs. Maroo asked in confusion.

"Vegan," Rose interjected. "Ever since watching the cow being lowered into the pit in Jurassic Park and then learning where our burgers came from. And she screamed"—Violet joined in with a smile—"'*You're all murderers! Murderers!*'" They teased in a dead-on dramatic impression of her.

"The chicken"—Lily stuck her tongue out at them—"is for Peaches." She grabbed two apples and walked to the back door with the container of meat. "She just had a baby and needs the extra protein. I don't inflict my moral code on others, you know."

"Not even rodents?" Rose asked with a smile.

"Possums are marsupials, you troglodyte," Lily called over her shoulder as she walked to the dumpster. *Honestly, no one would call a koala a rodent.* Poor possums, they did so much for the world and got very little thanks.

Lily tossed the chopped bits of apples and chicken breasts onto the plate she kept by the dumpster for Peaches and her babies.

"What on earth are you doing, dear?" Mrs. Maroo asked.

"One night I was out here taking a breather, and saw a cute little possum toddle over snacking on a rotten apple core. So I bring her snacks, especially when it's cold out. I always wanted a pet, but my life's been too unpredictable."

She checked the blanket in the box she put out for Peaches and her babies. "So I consider Peaches my free-range pet. She does her own thing, but I like leaving her little treats. Will I see you at the wedding tomorrow?" Lily asked, dusting off her gloved hands and standing.

But instead of turning to see Mrs. Maroo behind her, Lily was met with the man who'd haunted her thoughts since she'd fallen in love with him fifteen years ago.

"I'll be the one walking you down the aisle, I believe," Nash said, his eyes locked on hers. His eyes crinkled in the corners from his warm smile.

A long sigh escaped her, and her stomach did its normal flip-flop at seeing him unexpectedly.

Nash Donnelly was as much a part of Fairwick Falls as the town square gazebo, the strawberry shortcake festival, and Pop

Canon's decadent caramel apple pie pancakes at Canon's Diner.

Ooh, caramel apple pancakes and *Nash Donnelly. Now there was an idea.*

In her most private moments, she'd allow herself to fantasize about what a life would be like with him. How it would feel to be the recipient of all his thoughtfulness, his kindness.

Why do I have a thing for nice guys?

"Ah, yeah I guess we'll be paired up," Lily said, realizing Violet would walk out of the wedding with Jack, her fiancé who was the other groomsman.

God, she wanted to climb Nash like a tree. He had an expensive elegance that she simpered for. He was serious and earnest, and it made her day when she could make him laugh, breaking that all-business exterior.

Bonus points if she could make him blush.

That defense mechanism had hidden how desperately in love with him she'd been all this time.

"Is the Prince of Fairwick Falls exempt from decorating the reception hall with the other groomsmen?" Lily said with a smirk.

"I am not... Stop that." He chuckled, rolling his eyes. "You know I hate that name. Gray sent me to pick up the decorations for the reception."

"C'mon, they're in the cooler. See you at the wedding tomorrow, Mrs. Maroo?" Lily asked, tucking her hands around herself in the cold.

Mrs. Maroo slid her gaze from Lily to Nash with a growing smile. "Oh, I wouldn't miss it for the world, my dears. Can't *wait* to see you two walk down the aisle." She cackled as she waved a hand dripping with rings and crossed the street to her law office.

"Shall we?" Nash gestured for her to walk back into Bloom first.

His cheeks were ruddy from the cold, and a few hairs blew out of place in the chilly January wind. She wanted to walk on crisp alpine trails with him looking just like this. She'd pull him down by his scarf and feel the melting bliss of his lips as his heavy arms crushed her to him.

Like they had in August. Not that she'd thought about it *every fucking night since,* or anything.

Shaking away the vision of an impossible future, she mock saluted him like a weirdo as she headed inside.

Good thing Rose and Gray's wedding would be the last time they'd be thrown together before she left Fairwick Falls for good.

Chapter Three

NASH

Nash Donnelly daydreamed as Lily animatedly gave him instructions for Rose and Gray's wedding decor.

What would my life be like if I could date her? If I wasn't tied to Fairwick Falls?

He'd nursed a deepening crush on the pint-sized spitfire ever since she'd moved back last year. She was gorgeous, spunky, and his favorite one-two punch of funny and fierce.

His arms itched to wrap around her curves like they'd done months ago. Had it only been four months since he'd felt her under his fingertips?

"Are you even paying attention, *Nashly* Judd?" Lily threw her hands on her hips, her arched eyebrow leaping up to the beanie pulled low over her blond waves. She was bundled up in gloves, an enormous scarf, and a chunky bright yellow sweater that slouched around her curves.

Goddamnit, she was adorable. "The silk rose garland goes in a circle on Rose and Gray's table. Layer the lilies around it. Got it," he repeated. *Like I won't remember every word you say.*

He was man enough to admit he was incredibly attracted to

her curvy body. To her spritely shimmer of a personality that lit up a room.

He only regretted that they were two different people on very different paths.

After his willpower had failed and he'd kissed her in August, he'd kept his distance so his crush didn't get more serious. She'd never want the kind of stable life he was born, bred, and expected to lead. His future included being an active, permanent member of the Fairwick Falls community and raising the next generation in the historic Donnelly home.

The kind of stable life that all hinged on a very important, very secret fact.

That he urgently needed a wife.

He'd become president at the Fairwick County Community Bank after his father passed two years ago. The role had been handed down from generation to generation in the bank his family founded two hundred years ago.

He'd read the founding bylaws as a matter of due diligence when he'd taken the role and had been in a panic ever since. The bylaws required the president to be "a family man, for purposes unto community making."

Whatever the hell that meant.

The clock was winding down on his time to find someone before the bank's board caught on. They weren't happy about the updates he'd made the last few years—investing in updated technology for customers, more relaxed loan penalties—and would be happy to get rid of him. He couldn't let generations of his family down by not carrying out his responsibility.

He'd secretly worked with Mrs. Maroo for a year on a legal case if he couldn't get the board's approval to change them, but it had been slow going.

"While you're here, can you come to my studio?" Lily said,

pulling him out of his panic spiral. "The table cards I painted are finally dry and they're hung up high."

"Uh, sure." *I can probably keep my shit together in your apartment where I saw you in a thong.*

As he followed her up the steep stairs to her apartment, he allowed himself a brief ogle at Lily's curvy ass that starred in many of his one-handed fantasies.

Distract yourself. You cannot make another 'oops I can't help but kiss you' mistake again. You're a Donnelly; there's no room for error.

But she was adorable and sexy and so kind-hearted.

Even to possums.

"So why didn't you name her Apples?" Nash asked, genuinely curious.

"Who? Peaches?"

"Wasn't she eating an apple when you saw her?"

Lily shrugged with a mischievous grin as she unlocked her door. "C'mon, Nash. A possum named Apples? That's ridiculous."

She never failed to make him laugh, and her grin widened into a bright smile, framed by her plush, deep red lips.

Jesus. That sparkly smile of hers would be the end of him. Probably one of the reasons he'd developed a crush. Who didn't love it when someone pulled your head out of your ass and made you laugh once in a while?

His eyes adjusted to the dim light as they walked into her cozy studio loft. Chenille blankets were thrown over chairs, with stacks of books tucked in the corners. Her couch was covered in big pillows and more blankets. Twinkle lights hung in the eaves over a bed covered with—yep—even more blankets. Bundles of flowers hung from the beams, and art pieces lay against every surface in various states of being finished, creating an atmosphere that would make a Danish hygge expert jealous.

This woman lived out loud. Wherever she went, there was a trail of Lily that followed her—in laughter and smiles she gave people, her handmade gifts—usually one of her art pieces. In this case, it was the hand-painted wedding decorations drying on twine.

They were all echoing reminders that Lily Parker had been there, and the world was better for it.

Nash looked up at the rafters *he* could barely reach. "How on earth did you get these up here, Lilypa—" *Oh fuck.* He cleared his throat. "I mean...Lily. Sorry."

He cursed himself for almost using that goddamn nickname. In therapy, he'd realized it was his coping mechanism to remind himself she was Rose's kid sister.

She narrowed her eyes at him warily but replied, "I hung them using a creative combination of a stool on top of that table."

Jesus. A candle flickered behind her on her desk. "*And* you have a candle lit when you're not up here?" He crossed the small studio to blow it out.

She waved a hand dismissively as she dragged a stool under a low-hanging table card. "You worry too much. I'm in the building."

"How convenient. You can go up in flames with it." It was best he'd kept his distance from her. He worried about this woman nonstop as it was.

They worked in silence until all twenty table cards were down.

"There you go. Last one." He handed her the last painting and savored the quiet stillness as she looked up at him.

She looked so adorable today, bundled up in her winter gear. He'd give Rose a recommendation for a local insulation company for the shop. How did she expect Lily to work in a refrigerator?

She was usually a blur of ideas, activity, creation. In the cozy apartment, though, she was just a gorgeous woman who he wanted so badly it might break him in two.

"I should go," he sighed, even as he stood still, caught in her gaze.

Yes, there had been an attraction between them for a long time, but why did this thunderous crack of *more* keep hitting him harder and harder each time he saw her?

Her eyes sparkled with humor. "Busy day as Prince Donnelly, Bank President extraordinaire? Oh, oh, I know." She snorted with laughter. "Do you need to pick up those giant bags with a money symbol in case you get robbed?"

Nash's lips twitched in humor. *Don't look at her lips. Don't get sucked into those doe-like eyes, or her body that makes your cock hard with those fucking hips of hers.*

"Absolutely not." His hand drifted toward her gloved one, but he stopped himself before she noticed. "I expect robbers to come with comically large money bags."

She burst out laughing and he mentally high-fived himself like an absolute dork.

"Ah, while you're here." She turned and rifled through a stack of papers on her table. His skin crawled with the desire to organize it all. *How did she find anything?*

"Here." She held out a black-and-white photograph.

He took it in with surprise, eyes roaming every corner. It was a shot of him and his staff members laughing at the bank's holiday charity drive. Bloom had provided holiday decorations, and when Lily had dropped them off, he'd convinced her to stay for a while.

He stared down at the photo with delight. She'd caught him center stage, MC-ing the raffle to raise funds for the bank's toy drive and having a blast. His staff was doubled over in laughter at the ridiculous elf costume he'd worn. "Thank you. This is—"

"It's no big deal. Thought you might want it for your website or something." She cut him off and shrugged, playing off her gesture.

"Lily, it's not no big deal." He held her eyes with meaning. "Thank you."

She shivered as she smiled back. *Would pulling her into my arms to warm her up be weird?*

Jesus *Christ*, he had it so bad.

Nash always did the right thing, always said the right thing, never made a mistake. There was no room for error when the entire town had their eyes on him, and so literally the last thing he should *ever* do is lust after Lily Parker.

AKA Trouble on two legs.

"I better go," he said suddenly, mentally cataloging the rest of his errands so he didn't change his mind.

"See you at the end of the aisle," Lily called with a laugh as he walked down the stairs.

He walked next door to Fox & Forrest holding the large box of wedding decorations as he fantasized about what it would feel like tomorrow to escort Lily down the aisle.

She'd probably look gorgeous, and they'd probably have to take pictures together. Perhaps even wrap her arm through his, or touch her waist. Maybe they'd have to slow dance if he was lucky.

"There he is!" Nick announced from the counter, interrupting his thoughts. He lifted a box over the counter. "Here are the wedding favor cookies. Gray said you were coming."

"Great, pile them on top," Nash said, leaning down.

"Hey, thanks for suggesting we look into that 401k provider," Nick said with a smile. Nick and his husband Aaron owned the chic cafe and bakery. "It's been a game changer for our staff here."

It made Nash so happy to help local entrepreneurs that cared about the community, and their employees. "Good. Let me know when you're ready to talk Mega Backdoor Roths."

"Oooh." Aaron sidled up by his husband, slinging an arm around his shoulders. "Sounds naughty. I love it."

Nash burst out laughing. "I gotta go. See you guys tomorrow." Nearly the whole town was invited to Rose and Gray's wedding, and Nick and Aaron would be up front on Rose's side.

Nash turned around with the two large boxes and ran straight into Christina, who owned the hardware store.

"Hi Nash," Christina said, catching the top box before it fell. "Your cookie order came in from the fundraiser. Want me to drop it by the bank? It was so generous of you. Too much, really."

Christina's little boy had been shaking with nerves when he'd asked for a donation for his fourth grade basketball team. Nash had wanted to reward that bravery. "It's no problem. Next year if the team needs money, we can work something out so the bank is a sponsor."

"Oh my gosh, that would be so great." Christina beamed as she slid the wedding favor box back onto his pile.

His phone rang and he shuffled the boxes to grab it in time.

Gina. His matchmaker.

"Sorry, I've gotta take this, it's my uh…heart specialist," he said, fumbling for a better lie.

"Hi Gina," Nash said, his stomach tumbling.

"Sorry to call on the weekend but I need to double-check some screening criteria to meet your timeline."

Nash dodged people on the sidewalk, waving to every second person because somehow everyone in Fairwick Falls had picked fucking *now* to walk past him. "I don't have privacy right now to get into all the uh...details."

Of what kind of woman he wanted. *Brunette, definitely.*

How many kids that woman wanted to have. *At least two.*

Of what her professional background needed to be. *Finance or law.*

"I'll pull potential candidates and we can review later. Any deal-breakers?"

Nash thought back to the petite blonde in Bloom who was the life of any room she was in. Did she know the effect she had on other people? On him?

She was an electric current that lit up any room with vibrant energy. Her long sunshine hair had spilled out of a loose braid in the loft, and he'd thought about what it would feel like wrapped around his hand as he—

"Nash?" Gina said.

"Uh, yeah. Just, um..." He paused, looking back at Bloom. "Just no blondes."

That spot would forever be reserved for someone else.

He walked back to his car parked at the bank, with the photograph from Lily burning a hole in his pocket. He could practically feel it vibrating against his heart.

As he was crossing the street, he was shaken out of his thoughts when Agnes McBride, a long-time bank board member, exited the bank while talking to...wait, was that his *brother*?

Jeremy hated Fairwick Falls and rarely came back to visit. He had his arm around a young woman Nash had never seen. Hairs on the back of Nash's neck stood up as Jeremy walked toward him with slicked-back hair, skin too tanned, and eyes too beady.

"Hey, bro," Jeremy called with a cocky smile as he chomped gum.

Acid hit the back of Nash's throat. His brother was everything Nash hoped he'd never be: awkward, slimy, insincere, untrustworthy. Nash valued sincerity and duty above all else. Jeremy had cared far more about his trust fund and had blown through it in two years. Then tried several get rich quick schemes where he lost *other* people's money, all while convinced he was an 'excellent businessman.'

Cain and Abel had nothing on the Donnelly brothers.

"Jeremy," Nash said with little warmth.

A shiver ran down his spine. Jeremy showing up unannounced was a harbinger of doom.

"I'd like you to meet my wife," Jeremy said with a knowing sneer. "Becky Donnelly." Jeremy wrapped an arm awkwardly around the woman's shoulders.

The woman shrugged his hand off and barely looked up from her phone, completely disinterested.

"Congratulations," Nash muttered.

Fuck, it's happening. My worst nightmare is happening.

"Wait in the car, Becky," Jeremy ordered. She didn't spare him a glance as she walked to a bright orange sports car in the parking lot.

"What are you playing at?" Nash's eyes narrowed in disgust.

"You know *exactly* what I'm doing." Jeremy chomped on his gum with the same smug smile he'd had since childhood.

"What idiotic scheme do you have now?"

"It's not idiotic if it works, right?" Jeremy raised an eyebrow. "I've got a good connection now that wants to expand across Pennsylvania, and they're willing to buy us out. Think of the payday." Dollar signs practically gleamed in Jeremy's eyes.

Goddamnit. Nash had fought off acquisitions by large, corporate banks for years. Some members of the board wouldn't mind the big payday they'd get if the bank was acquired. Keeping the bank running and protecting Fairwick

Falls' interests felt like a way to memorialize his father. A large company would gut his father's legacy.

"Why do you even care? It's a small payday for the kind of schemes you run," Nash said.

"Maybe there's a finder's fee." Jeremy picked his teeth with his thumb as he scowled at Nash's car. "Or, you know, your job can't be that hard. Maybe I'll do it. Being president? A *married* president?"

"You're threatening me." The blood in Nash's veins ran ice-cold.

How the fuck did Jeremy know about the marriage loophole? His brother had the attention span of a ferret and would never have read the antique bylaws.

"Just think about it." Jeremy hit his shoulder as he walked away.

The hell was he playing at?

His schemes rarely worked, but Jeremy was no dummy.

The gauntlet had been thrown down, and it was pretty fucking clear: find a wife, or put the bank at risk of his younger brother selling to the highest bidder.

Chapter Four

NASH

The pulse of music throbbed through Nash's head as Rose and Gray's wedding guests mingled under fairy lights.

The bride and groom wandered hand in hand through the reception tent, chatting with guests. Gray was beaming with happiness, and Rose looked dreamily at her new husband. Nash had never seen either of them smile so much.

Nash willed his eyes not to look across the reception tent where a certain blonde bombshell held court with her senior-citizen yoga students. Lily had been adopted by every lady over sixty-five after she'd started offering free yoga when she moved to Fairwick Falls.

One more look won't kill you. No one will even notice you're staring at her like a lovesick puppy.

Well, lustsick.

He'd had a hard time ripping his eyes away from Lily all evening. During the pre-wedding photos, she'd descended the staircase in a clinging deep-sapphire dress. It had dripped off every single curve. Shining blonde hair flowed in silky waves over her shoulders. She'd looked like a deep, endless midnight sky come to life with a stream of stars pooled at her shoulders.

The vision of her walking down the aisle, floating like a breeze through a midnight sky, had clutched him by the heart.

Her bright smile beamed as she made a joke at her table. *Those lips.* He sighed thinking about them. They'd been tart and sweet like a ripe cherry when they'd kissed in August. She'd gone soft under his hands, her lush hips and breasts pliant against him.

His hands flexed thinking about the phantom memory. He'd spent, what, ten seconds kissing her? But that ten seconds had stayed with him ever since.

He resigned himself to looking for someone willing to stay in Fairwick Falls. Thus far, it had felt impossible. Yes, he needed a wife, but he needed the *perfect* wife. Someone who wanted the duties of the Donnelly family in the community, the fundraising, and the hosting. Someone who could help him carry the Donnelly legacy on for the next two hundred years.

No pressure.

"You know"—a British voice interrupted his thoughts—"you could ask her to dance. Instead of staring at her like a lecher." Jack sat down next to him and grinned as he drank his beer.

Nash slowly blushed as his new friend had pretty much nailed it. "I am not a lecher," Nash lied, sipping his scotch.

"No." Jack toyed with his glass on the table. "You're handsome and rich and kindhearted. The opposite of a lecher, actually. But you *were* staring. Admit it, old man."

Nash snorted as he took a pull on his scotch. "That would be a mistake."

Jack countered, eyebrows raised. "Sometimes mistakes lead to the best things. Trust me." Jack hit Nash's chest companionably as he stood up. "Now, if you'll excuse me, I have a fiancée to dazzle."

Violet blushed prettily as Jack pulled her out onto the floor.

Seeing Violet become her best self was one of Nash's favorite things last year. She'd gone from someone who couldn't meet anyone's eyes to confident and happy. Her relationship with Jack had started out as a fake dating scheme. They weren't supposed to fall in love.

Sometimes mistakes lead to the best things.

Taking a gulp of his scotch, Nash reconsidered as his eyes drifted to Lily.

What's one little dance between friends?

She was now squatting at a table with Alex, Gray's five-year-old son, giggling with him. She made farting noises into her elbow to make him laugh.

She got a particularly loud one that made Alex double over with laughter. Nash caught her eye with a chuckle, and she gave him a mock salute.

The DJ's voice boomed over the intercom. "Will the wedding party make their way to the dance floor for the last dance of the evening?"

Perfect. Nash downed the rest of his scotch and walked toward her. Just a dance between friends. Nothing romantic about it.

"Care to dance?" Nash helped Lily up and kept hold of her hand.

"I'm trying to convince Alex to dance with his new fabulous auntie," Lily said with a smile, looking down at Alex. "Whaddya say? Want to be my partner on the dance floor?"

Alex thought for a second. "I'd rather play trucks," he said and scampered off.

Lily pulled a comically exasperated face at Nash. "Chivalry is officially dead."

Nash squeezed her hand. "Let's see if I can change your

mind." He pulled her hand through his arm as he led her to the dance floor.

The soulful notes of Frank Sinatra's *I've Got a Crush on You* twined their way through the air as he pulled her to him.

The back of her dress was so low that his hand landed against her bare skin. The shock of it jolted him, and he avoided her gaze as they danced.

But he had to feel that velvet softness against his fingers.

"Lily, you look gorgeous tonight. Truly stunning," Nash said quietly.

A shy smile replaced Lily's bravado as she muttered a "Thanks" and shrugged one shoulder. "You look pretty good yourself. I'm surprised they could find a suit to fit your 'Superman meets highland warrior' frame."

She licked her lips, and his eyes traced the movement greedily.

What he wouldn't give to trade places with someone who could leave Fairwick Falls.

~

LILY

LILY WANTED to freeze-frame this moment: Nash looking dapper in a tuxedo with a rare dazzling smile, the one he reserved for people who truly delighted him.

A few hairs were out of place, falling across his forehead as they swayed. He looked like a Ken doll that had been roughed up a little. She liked seeing the always-perfect Nash rumpled from having a good time.

He stroked her waist as they swayed, and she sucked in a breath at the contact.

How did something so innocent, so undetectable as a gentle stroke of his thumb back and forth feel nearly pornographic?

He drew her into him with an air of experience and elegance, swaying her back and forth—perfectly on beat, of course.

Could this man do anything wrong? He was so out of her league, it was laughable. It would be easier to forget him, fall out of love with him, if he were a clod. She snorted at how unfortunately and irritatingly perfect he was.

"What?" he said as he spun them expertly in a circle.

"You. You're annoying." She gave him her best impish smile to soften the teasing.

"You have dancing notes, Parker?" Nash said with a slow, melting smile that made her gooey inside.

She liked this side of him. The one he rarely showed.

Loose Nash.

"You're, like, really good at everything and it's super annoying. Come on, name three things you're terrible at," she teased.

Nash huffed out a laugh. "I think you of all people could tell me what I'm bad at."

"Excellent point, Prince Donnelly. Loosening up, number one," Lily said, loving that she was making him smile. "Worrying too much, number two. Oh! Making mistakes. You're terrible at making mistakes; you hardly ever make them."

"Some of us can't afford to make mistakes," he said with a sad smile.

"Oh, yes, poor little rich boy," Lily said brightly, trying to get a laugh out of him. *Anything to make those sad eyes go away.* "Please, tell me the sob story that you cry into your money every night. Do you roll around on it first and then cry into it, or vice versa?"

That got a genuine laugh out of him, and she preened. She snaked her arm up around his shoulder as he drew her closer.

He leaned down to her ear. "I'll have you know I've never rolled around in money."

Her stomach jumped at his voice in her ear. "I thought that's how you went to Princeton. On a money-rolling scholarship." Delight coursed through her at teasing him.

"Almost right." He spun her out then tugged her back with practiced ease, catching her against him and whispering in her ear. "It was money *diving*."

A laugh burst out of her. If only he didn't keep this side of himself locked tightly away underneath the metaphorical *and* literal starched shirt he wore every day.

He gently pulled her in closer as the lyrics to *I've Got a Crush on You* hovered in the air around them.

Oh, if he only knew how big a crush she had on him.

She'd never been able to help how much she liked him. He was the ideal of everything she'd ever wanted: handsome, sexy, kind, honest to a fault, smarter than anybody else in the room.

And devastatingly *good*.

They both caught sight of Rose and Gray swaying in their own world, foreheads together, in the center of the dance floor. Rose looked stunning in an off-the-shoulder sheer neckline, clinging bodice, and small train. She'd decided to carry the white peony bouquet down the aisle and had used Lily's other two bouquets as her rehearsal and tossing bouquets.

"I've never seen her happier, you know?" Lily said, pointing to the bride and groom.

He nodded with a grin. "Same with Gray. He was *whistling* all day yesterday while we decorated. Your decorations are amazing, by the way. I'm always blown away by what you make." He stared up at the giant floral ball she'd made that hung above the dance floor.

His voice was matter-of-fact, as if she *was* amazing, no doubt about it.

"My arms and hands are limp from the last few days. Plus, I got into a fight with seven hundred thorns and lost." She held up her hand still clasped in his to show him the red marks where she'd been stabbed by those pointy little motherfuckers.

Nash examined the inside of her wrist and brought it to his lips for a soft, slow kiss.

Lily's brain went staticky as his lips held there for a moment.

Then two.

She desperately wanted to tug his shirt down so she could meet his lips with hers. It had been four long fucking months since she'd last been this close to him.

He startled, realizing what he was doing, and pulled his lips away. "I'm sorry. I...I shouldn't have done that."

The muscle in his jaw ticked as he hovered over her. His hand on her hip dug in, gripping the soft flesh there. She felt a fish hook of lust curve around her breastbone and tug her forward.

To do anything to be closer, to melt together.

The magnetic force between them was messing with her head. Lily took a slow step away from him on the dance floor.

Better to protect myself than lose something I want too much.

"I think..." she said, a small pant in her breath. "You should stay over there, and I should go get some air."

Nash didn't bother asking why as he held her gaze. They both knew whatever chemistry was between them couldn't be.

Yet she was drawn to him like a moth to a flickering, sexy lantern, and that felt very, very dangerous.

Lily walked toward the balcony that overlooked the art museum's gardens. She rounded the corner just as Pop Canon came around it, looking disheveled.

"Hey, Pop. You alright?" she asked the older diner owner. He had a lipstick stain on his cheek, and he kept his eyes down as he walked past Lily.

"Never better," he said quickly. A familiar giggle came around the corner. Lily peeked over to see Mrs. Maroo looking smugly satisfied.

"You crazy kids," Lily said with a chuckle.

"What can I say? We're still newlyweds and I love his little tush. What are you doing out here, my Lily of the Valley?" Mrs. Maroo ran a hand down Lily's arm, pulling her into a side hug.

Lily leaned into her. "Taking a breather. It was getting... crowded in there."

Mrs. Maroo rubbed her back. "You must be tired. You outdid yourself on the flowers. What's next on the horizon for our tour de force?"

"After Valentine's Day, I'll be interviewing somebody to take my place." She didn't share that she'd be gone much sooner unless she wanted everyone in the county to know.

"You can't leave." Mrs. Maroo said sadly. "You all just got started."

"You know me," Lily said, shrugging. "I don't like to stay in one place very long."

Mrs. Maroo nodded sagely. "I know. You occupy three pages in my address book."

Lily always looked forward to Mrs. Maroo's shirtless fireman Christmas cards each year.

"Why not stay? You girls have a good thing going now." Mrs. Maroo settled on a bench next to an outdoor heater and patted the seat next to her. Several blankets were draped on the bench for cozy night stargazing. Lily sat and wrapped one around their shoulders.

"I don't know," Lily said, feeling lost. "I never wanted to be like him, you know?"

Him. The unspoken ghost that traveled everywhere with Lily: her father.

He'd passed a year ago, and rarely a day went by where Lily didn't think about him.

They'd been close-ish. She'd call every few weeks, visit when she could. The loss of him still hurt though, and she didn't do pain.

It was easier if she kept busy.

She preferred to look forward rather than wallow in sadness. Almost a year later, she still hadn't opened the letter he'd left her in the event of his passing. Violet and Rose had both read theirs, but she hadn't been strong enough yet to deal with the pain.

Mrs. Maroo hummed in awareness. "Your father never did quite fit in here. He had the heart of a wanderer but was committed to you girls and the legacy that Ivy left behind."

Legacy was a nice way of saying her mother had trapped her father into owning her family business. He'd crumbled when her mother had died, and Lily knew from an early age that when you gave someone all that power, it could ruin your life.

She'd vowed to stay heartbreak-free and retain her freedom from that kind of pain.

"Lily, my dear," Mrs. Maroo said, squeezing her. "You have done a marvelous job with the store. I've known you since you were about two hours old and have rarely seen you this happy. *And* your hot yoga class kicks my ass."

Lily snorted.

She held Lily's eyes with a rare seriousness. "Just make sure when you're running, it's out of love, not fear. Make decisions with this"—Mrs. Maroo tapped her own chest—"and *sometimes* with this"—she pointed to the crotch of her sequined pants with a wicked smile—"but never, *never* make decisions based on the worst thing that could happen."

Unexpected emotion clutched Lily's throat. She'd never had a close relationship with her grandparents; that was Violet's thing. Her mom had died when she was a toddler. Her dad was flaky at best, being distraught and depressed during her childhood.

Grateful wouldn't even begin to cover what she'd felt for Mrs. Maroo throughout the years.

Funny how some people made themselves your family just by loving you so much.

"Noted," Lily said, struggling to get the word out through her emotion.

Mrs. Maroo stood and tucked the blanket around Lily's shoulders. "And don't be a dummy like my adorable new husband and wait thirty years to tell a very hunky someone you think he's pretty hunky." She winked as she headed back to the reception. "Time moves faster than you think, my dear."

Lily stared into the clear night sky, weighing how to avoid all the negative feelings creeping up on her. The loss of her dad. Leaving her sisters so she didn't get stuck in Fairwick Falls. How Nash would never love her as much as she loved him.

Future. Think about the future.

She'd schedule a call with KGM, the design agency, and hopefully knock the discussion out of the park. She'd look up apartments in New York so she could rip the news off like a band-aid when Rose got back from her honeymoon and move right away. Maybe even apply at a few yoga studios just in case KGM didn't work out.

There would be so many new things to start and do. It felt invigorating.

But there were also two weeks before she left. She considered Mrs. Maroo's advice as her mind drifted back to the man she'd been in love with for far too long.

I'm already in love with him, plus I'm great at compartmentaliz-

ing. What's the worst that could happen? Get more in love? Not possible. Maybe I can finally get him out of my system.

So if time moves faster than I think it does and I should make decisions with my lady bits...then ergo ad coitus facto...

She tossed off her blanket and marched back to the reception.

The only logical solution is to seduce Nash for a two-week fling.

Chapter Five

LILY

After doing a final sweep of the reception venue, Lily sat waiting in Nash's car. He'd volunteered to drop her off at Bloom on his way home after everyone else's cars were stuffed bringing back Rose and Gray's gifts.

All the better to start seducing him.

The driver side door flew open, and Nash slid in with practiced ease, looking like a small-town James Bond. "You warm enough?" He'd turned the car on for her earlier and now checked if the vents were pointed toward her.

She crossed her legs, letting the slit of her dress fall high onto her thigh. "On my way to hot and bothered."

She was happy to note his eyes were glued to her thighs as he gulped, but then he ripped his eyes up and shifted the gear stick into first drive without another word.

Of course he'd drive a stick shift. Such a control freak.

And why do I fuuuucking love that?

The console screen on his dashboard flashed as his phone's Bluetooth synced with the car. A list of recent contacts popped up. Gray, his mom, and...*what the hell?*

"Why the fuck are you talking to a matchmaker named

Gina?" Lily blurted out, staring at the contact on the car's screen.

His sigh was long as he stared straight ahead, winding through the parking lot. "Because I need to get married."

What the actual fuck? "Why?"

"Because..." He checked his blind spot as he pulled out onto an empty side road. "It's time."

Fuckity fuck. The window of sex-tunity—oppor-seduction?— was closing.

She still had a buzz from her last cocktail, and it was enough to loosen her lips. "Then we should have sex *tonight*."

He slammed on the brakes.

Okay, finesse has never been my strong suit.

"I...what?" He gaped at her as if she'd lost her mind.

Fine. I like a challenge. "We should have sex now before you find your...match thingy. I'm leaving Fairwick Falls in two weeks. No time to, you know, catch feelings."

His eyes fell to her lips briefly before he turned back to the road and took off.

He leaned on one elbow, moving his hand back and forth under his full bottom lip, pondering. His large hand stroked his stubbled, firm chin, and his eyes drifted off in concentration at her words.

Fuck, he needed to stop being so goddamn sexy or she'd insist he pull over so she could have her way with him *right now*.

"I thought you were leaving in a few months? You're leaving sooner?"

Okay, that's not an outright no. "An opportunity might come up for me in New York. Rose and Violet don't know yet. And in the meantime, we could have some fun."

He ran his tongue over his teeth, choosing his words slowly.

"I can't deny there's a certain...chemistry. But I'm too old for you and—"

"Bullshit." She laughed at his terrible argument. "You're seven years older than me. I'm almost thirty-one, not some virginal teenager."

"Lily, I'm not built for flings."

Her mouth curved into a smile as she settled in, happy to learn more. "You're telling me you lived in New York for five years and you *never* had a one-night stand?"

He looked horrified. "Never. My answer is the same as it was in August. You know I have to stay here. Plus, you're too important to me to lose. What if it became awkward?"

She bit back a smile. *Why do I love that so fucking much?*
Duh, because he's a good guy.

"You are talking to the *queen* of no strings. I know what I want." She'd been every Brooklyn fuckboy's dream, never wanting any commitment. Yes, her heart was hollow when she left their apartments in the morning, but she was satiated and her power was protected exactly like she wanted.

Nash maneuvered his car around the quiet, sleeping Main street. It was 1 AM, and the entire town was fast asleep. No other cars, no lights on. The sidewalks had been all but rolled up.

"And you want me?" Nash said with a challenging glint as he threw his car into park.

"For two weeks."

He opened his car door, apparently done with their conversation.

Ugh. Men. How unfortunate that I'm attracted to them.

She gathered her things, and by the time she turned to the door, he'd already opened it for her.

What the hell?

He held out a hand to help her out of the car. Why did that make all her lady bits jumble around inside?

Chivalry died at the New Jersey border. There was no sign of it in New York City, let alone among all the fuckboys she spent time with. All the better so she didn't fall for them.

He pulled her up with one tug, her stomach swooping along with it. She stood on unsteady legs out of the car. God, she fucking hated heels.

As she hefted her enormous gym bag full of hair tools and makeup, Nash reached for it. "Here, let me help you."

His voice was quiet and intimate, and she felt that same magnetic pull as when they danced. She willed her body not to melt against him.

Why did this man have to have her whole heart?

Why couldn't she love someone attainable and imperfect? Not a chiseled Greek sculpture with the heart of Lancelot, the manners of Danish royalty, and a bank account to match said Danish royalty?

"It's okay," she said quietly. He still held her hand from helping her up, and his thumb grazed over her knuckles. Her breath lodged somewhere in her chest as she grabbed her bag. "It's not like you were my date."

But oh, how I wish you were.

NASH

God, how I wish I were.

He looked down at Lily's heart-shaped face, her soft brown eyes reflecting back the moon in the clear, crisp night. He wanted to memorize exactly how her hair looked like melted gold against her skin. She'd be gone soon, and it would be all he'd have.

He sure as hell wasn't going to move his hand first, but he wouldn't allow himself any more than this.

For fuck's sake, he had a call with a matchmaker on Monday morning to find a wife.

She stepped away and hefted her bag higher. It was big enough to overtake her, but she was strong, if unsteady on her heels. He followed her to the back door of Bloom anyway. The Parker sisters had been threatened by a debt collector last spring, and he still hated the thought of Lily all alone on the abandoned street in the middle of the night.

"Plus, if you insist on helping me inside"—her voice was simmering and teasing now—"I'll think you're going to give in and take me upstairs for a quickie."

Yes, he thought instantly with a surge of lust. *No. Fuck. What is happening to me?*

As they reached the back door, she held his gaze with a challenging glint as if to say, *Are you man enough?*

Lust loosened his tongue. "There's nothing quick about what I'd do if given the chance."

A smile curved onto her face. "I see you're rethinking your stance on a two-week fling. C'mon." She ran her hand down his tuxedo shirt. "We're both adults. We've both had dry spells"—she had no idea how dry his spell had been—" and you *know* you want to try it."

The devilish look on her pretty face had him bargaining with himself. *Maybe if we just got it out of our systems, I'd stop thinking about her—*

A sudden rattle sounded behind Lily, and he stepped in front of her on instinct. "What the hell was that?"

"Peaches! Hey girl hey," Lily yelled in excitement. She

shoved his arm down to jog toward the rotund little possum with a tiny baby on its back. "Nash, come meet her."

"Lily, be careful." The blacktop was covered in patches of ice.

"Oh don't worry so much. Come meet her baby, Babc—" Suddenly Lily's heels flew out from underneath her as she slipped on ice, twisting her legs as she fell.

She cried out as she crumpled into a twisted heap, and Nash's stomach bottomed out in fear. He ran to her.

Lily lay on the pavement, sobbing in pain.

"Lily," he said through a tortured voice as he crouched down.

A low moan wrenched out of her until her sobs went silent with pain.

His hands reached for her. "Sweetheart, talk to me."

"My knee," she cried between moans. "I think something happened. I—"

She could barely form sentences, and his heart felt like it was beating outside of his body. He glanced at her exposed knee and the top of it was at an odd angle. *Fuck.* He'd seen this in too many basketball games. He wrapped a hand around her waist. "Let's get you to urgent care."

"No," she said suddenly. "It's fine. I'll ice it." She slowly sat up, and he moved an arm underneath her to support her. She cried out in pain as she moved her knee.

"Is it right here?" He ghosted his fingertips along the inside of her kneecap. She nodded her head while biting her lip through tears. "We need to get you to a doctor."

"No, it'll be fine. I'll take some Tylenol."

"Lily, Tylenol will not fix a dislocated knee."

She blanched. "I...I don't have insurance," she whispered.

His stomach bottomed out again. This whole night was feeling like a fucking roller coaster. "You didn't sign up for..."

She shook her head slowly, biting her lip in pain.

"It's fine. We'll figure something out." *He* would figure something out. He wouldn't let her not get treated. "We've got to," he said, urging her.

She started to shiver. Why didn't this woman have a jacket on? He took his suit jacket off and pulled it around her shoulders.

"I'll be with you every step of the way, okay? We'll figure something out."

She thought for a minute, sniffling through her sobs. "Okay," she whispered.

"Let's go slow, and you tell me when it hurts."

After a few false starts, he'd gathered Lily and her things up in a bridal carry and got her safely in his car.

He peeled out of the parking lot. "Here, hold my hand. Squeeze as hard as you need to, okay?"

She grasped his hand as tightly as she could.

It was only a ten-minute drive to urgent care, but it was ten minutes too many when this fiery warrior goddess was catatonic with pain.

"Lily, talk to me."

"Can't," she uttered through tight lips.

He needed to get her mind off the pain. "All right, you have opinions about how I live my life, so let me have them," he said, maneuvering them onto the highway, not even pausing before turning at the stoplight. "Don't hold back. Whatever will take your mind off it."

She squeezed his hand hard as they hit a bump coming onto the highway. "Fuck," she groaned.

His heart leapt up into his throat. "So sorry," he murmured, pressing her hand against his mouth for a quick kiss, not thinking until after he did it.

Shit. This night was going to be a minefield.

"You're too"—she ground her words out, huffing—"uptight."

"Great, keep going."

She squeezed his hand like the jaws of life. "You think you know what's best"—she gulped—"for everybody, even though they're *adults*." She slid a murderous glance at him.

He hopped off the highway and was happy to see the sign for urgent care a block away.

"Fair," he said, letting her say whatever she wanted without argument for right now. "But we'll revisit that once you feel better."

She scoffed, getting life back in her eyes. "All the women you dated..."

Oh fuck.

"...haven't been good enough for you." Her eyes were trained on the urgent care center, and her face drained of color.

What did she mean by that? But he was too distracted to ask follow-up questions as he slid into a parking spot.

He picked her up to take her in, and she wrapped her arms around his neck.

Her lip wobbled. "Don't tell Rose, okay? About the insurance. I told her I'd do it, but then I forgot, and tried one more time but the website didn't make any sense and I swore I was going to do it after the new year—"

"Sweetheart, it's fine." He kissed her temple without thinking as the automatic doors opened into Urgent Care. "I've got you. Let's just get you feeling better."

A wide-eyed Lily went uncharacteristically quiet and held him tighter.

Several hours later, with a reset kneecap, a pair of crutches in his back seat and a large pending charge on his credit card, Nash clicked a seat belt around a pain medication-filled Lily.

"You'll stay with me tonight," he said firmly as he drove away.

"Pssssh. I'll be fine at my place." Lily's words slurred together as the pain medication started working.

"There is no way you can handle two sets of steep stairs, including a spiral staircase, on crutches tonight."

"Don't need to be a burden. Drop me off at Vi's," Lily said with a yawn, already closing her eyes and leaning back in her seat.

"It's 3:30 in the morning. I'm not dropping you off at anyone's house except mine."

He heard a muffled *hmmph* from the passenger seat and saw Lily fully asleep.

Why did his heart feel so full at the idea of her in his house? He'd googled 'vegan foods' while he'd waited for Lily to come back from x-rays and sent Olga a list of groceries to buy in the morning. His housekeeper practically ran his life already, and that would be one less thing he'd have to think about.

Ten minutes later, Nash carried a zonked out Lily through his kitchen. She was groggy from the pain medication, and her head flopped with sleep as he carried her. He set her down on the bright white duvet of his first-floor guest room, and her head lolled to the side as she woke up.

"Why is your house so goddamn pretty? And fucking enormous?" she said, slurring with frustration. "Think of the *orgies* you could host."

He snorted. Apparently Pain Meds Lily had even less of a filter than normal Lily did.

Wait. What the hell was she going to sleep in? Her dress? He pulled his jacket off her. Her milky skin was marred with red marks where her dress had dug in. He couldn't stand giving her more injuries. He'd have to be creative.

"Don't move a muscle." He jogged to the laundry room where he grabbed a clean t-shirt. His old Princeton Basketball t-shirt would have to do for pajamas.

"Alright, arms up," he ordered coming back.

She swayed sitting on the bed. "Woo!" Lily dutifully threw her arms into the air like she was on a roller coaster. "This is fun. Why don't we have more sleepovers? Oh, I know. Because then we'd have *sex*. Are we going to have sex tonight, Nash?"

"Holy fuck," he grumbled. "Definitely not." This was not how he'd pictured undressing Lily after their make-out session months ago.

Or under the pool of lamplight earlier when he'd come too close to giving in.

He pulled his giant t-shirt over her arms and stomach. Luckily her dress didn't have straps, so all he'd have to do was pull it down without seeing anything.

She stared up at him, her face an inch from his with those big, brown eyes. "Hi," she whispered as he tugged it past her hips. Her sleepy smile was now one of his favorites.

Lord have mercy, his patience was being tested today. "Okay, now we're going to stand up." The t-shirt billowed around her hips.

"And *then*, we're going to have *sex*," Lily said with a sleepy, excited voice.

"Incorrect," he countered.

"Nash, you're wound so tight you might explode. You know, like a water balloon. You keep blowing up and up and up and up—"

"I'm going to unzip your dress now."

"Haha, I knew it." Lily threw her hands in the air with a loopy grin. "*Sex times*, it is. All aboard this *chugga chugga choo*

choo train." She wobbled her body until she cried out in pain from her knee.

"Stand still," he ordered.

"Oooo, Nash is using his sex voice," Lily whispered with a giggle.

"I'm unzipping your dress, tugging the shirt down so I won't see anything, and then closing my eyes while I take it off." He kept his voice dry, matter-of-fact, and straightforward to hold back the wave of lust at the thought of Lily undressed.

He'd think of baseball, his grandmother, the Chicago Bulls '95 lineup. Anything other than his fingers along Lily's hips.

He slowly slid the zipper of her dress down, which—thank god—started at her waist. He tugged the tight fitting bodice past her hips until it pooled on the floor. Still with his eyes closed, he tugged his long t-shirt down, and thank Christ it hit her mid-thigh.

He opened his eyes, and unfortunately, that was the moment the backs of his fingers connected with her thighs as he gave her shirt a final tug. Her skin was smooth and creamy, with a hint of the muscle underneath.

"You're no fun," she said with a pout. "Come ooooooon. Fate is conspiring to get us into this bed." She grabbed fistfuls of his dress shirt with her hands and pulled him in.

"Nope, nope, nope." He gently pried her fingers off his shirt and pulled back the covers.

They weren't good enough for you.

Her words echoed in his head as he gently maneuvered her to sit on the bed with her knee still in the immobilizer.

"Now you're going to lie down and let me know if you need anything, okay?" He placed her phone on the bedside table and glanced at the clock, 4 AM.

Lily flopped back into bed and was asleep before her head hit the pillow. Her face was a picture of bliss.

This had been the longest day that he could remember. And yet?

His heart felt fuller than ever to have Lily tucked in safe and sound where he could take care of her.

He'd have done it ten times over.

LILY

A throbbing pain woke Lily up from a deep sleep. Gray morning light filtered through unfamiliar gossamer curtains.

Why does my knee feel like I crushed a man to death with it?

Lily's brain creaked like a slow, abandoned merry-go-round.

She felt her leg. There was something on her knee. "What the hell? What am I wearing?"

Then it all crashed back to her.

She was in Nash's house. In Nash's shirt.

In one of Nash's beds.

Lily tried to piece together last night. Nash had been at the urgent care center, holding her hand, brushing her hair, kissing her temple, saying he was so proud of her.

How was yesterday her best-case and worst-case scenario all rolled into one?

A pair of crutches rested beside the bed within arm's reach. But more importantly, coffee and Fox & Forrest's vegan breakfast sandwich sat beside her phone.

She dove for the coffee as if it was a lifeline and noticed that yes, of course, he'd gotten her order exactly right. Two shots, oat milk, extra cinnamon on top, extra hot.

Nash Fucking Donnelly noticed things.

All that kind, genuine, Dudley Do-Right, 'I behave like a freaking Canadian mountie at all times' perfection would go to somebody else.

She shook her head to clear away the daydreams.

After inhaling half her coffee, Lily saw the note underneath the plate with a tiny folded napkin.

"Jesus, could he get any cuter?" she muttered through a mouthful of breakfast sandwich.

Call me if you need anything. - N

She snorted into her coffee. Was she a sociopath? Who *called* anybody anymore? She texted like a real human.

She snuggled into the silky soft sheets in the elegant, understated room, soaking in all this weird goodness.

This was his *guest* bedroom? This was nicer than any hotel she'd stayed at. The pillow was soft but supportive. The snowy white duvet tucked heavily around her legs with three extra blankets off to the side.

Nash Donnelly could host the fuck out of a broken woman, that was for sure.

Her knee twinged as she sat up. *Fuck.* How was she going to move back to New York like this? Or get up to her third-floor apartment above Bloom?

Her knee threw the absolutely worst-timed wrench in her plans. She and Peaches would have words about this later.

The caffeine hadn't yet cleared the haze of alcohol and pain meds from eight hours ago.

Why couldn't she think? Did she have any clothes with her that would go over a knee brace? She lifted the covers—no pants. How the hell was she supposed to get back to her apartment with no pants?

"Fine. I'll be a sociopath," Lily muttered as she hit the phone button on Nash's contact.

He picked up in one ring. "Everything okay?" he asked in a clipped voice.

"I need your help—"

"Be right there." Thundering footsteps came from somewhere above her. A wide-eyed Nash threw open the door. "Are you okay? Are you hurt? Do you need to go back to the doctor?"

"I'm fine," Lily said with a growing smile. She wasn't used to seeing Nash worked up. "I am currently pants-less and require your help. Unless you'd like me to shake my cheeks in my bright red thong as I hobble down Main Street."

His eyes narrowed as he gulped. "I'll get a pair of my pajama pants."

A minute later he handed her large black-and-red flannel pajama pants. "Do you, uh..." He scratched his neck. "Do you need help?" There was that pink blush on his cheeks she rarely got to see.

So. Fucking. Adorable.

"Just turn around." She swung her legs onto the floor, wincing from the pain. "In case I fall like an oak tree."

She wrestled with the enormous pajamas. "Jesus H. Christ, Batman. How long are your fuckin' legs?" she grumbled. She pulled them past her ankles for what felt like a solid five minutes. "Okay, I'm decent."

She reached for the crutches, and after a wobbling step, seemed to get the hang of it. "Hey, look at me goaaaaagh—"

A crutch slid out from under her as she lost her balance. Nash caught her around the waist before she plummeted to the floor. Her face had landed against the solid wall of Nash's muscular chest.

Not a bad way to be caught, all things considered. He righted her, hands on her hips until she got her bearings.

"First timer," she said with a sheepish smile.

She hobbled to the en suite bathroom two steps away without incident and managed to use the bathroom without falling.

As she slowly hobbled out, Nash was still in the guest bedroom.

He was big and imposing standing over her bed, all crossed arms and broody sexiness. "You need to stay with me."

He said it as an authoritative statement.

Lily paused mid-hobble. "Excuse me?"

"How are you going to get down the stairs from your apartment? What if you fall and no one is there? The shower in your studio is a death trap."

She loved her antique tub. And yeah, maybe she always fell in it, but she'd figure something out. "You worry too much, Nanny McNash." She hobbled across his guest bedroom and flopped onto the bed.

God, it had been a long twenty-four hours. Had Rose's wedding only been yesterday? She'd lived three lifetimes since then.

"I can keep you safe if you stay with me."

What a recipe for disaster that would be.

Seeing him every morning, or coming in from a long day at the office, his tie pulled down with a takeout bag in hand. *Yum, yum, yum.*

It would be impossible to keep her hands off him.

"I don't know." She couldn't meet his eyes. The unstated subtext was *"what if I want to jump your bones everyday?"*

"Try it for a few nights," he finally said.

"No nights," she countered.

She couldn't get too used to being taken care of. It would

hurt more when she left. "I don't need some duty-bound older-brother type taking care of me—"

"—I am *not* your brother," he interrupted, his tone laser sharp. He raked his hand through his hair again, tugging at the end.

"And what about that two-week fling?" She raised an eyebrow in challenge, wanting to outmaneuver him. "If I stay, do I get super sexy bedside Nash? Will my pain meds be delivered via your penis?"

"Lily," he moaned in frustration as he wiped a hand down his face.

People had a habit of doing that in her life—yelling her name in frustration because she didn't do what they wanted.

But, it turned out, she always knew what was best for her, and it was definitely *not* best for her to be within arm's length of Nash Donnelly if she couldn't have the fling she so desperately wanted.

Especially without her vibrator.

"There will be absolutely no sexy...anything. Just stay here for a few days. Please." His jaw clenched as he scowled with concentration.

There was no way she could go up the stairs in Bloom by herself in this state. Violet didn't have a downstairs bedroom in her house, and Rose and Gray didn't either. "For one day," she relented. "As a *personal* favor to you."

He stood taller, proud of winning. "Thank you. I'll get you some towels. I redid the guest bath last year and so the shower is easy to get in and out of."

This man thought of everything, didn't he?

"Nash." She grabbed her coffee, holding it to her chest as she cuddled up in bed.

"Yeah?" He turned around quickly.

She paused, biting her lip. "Thank you for everything." Her

voice was quiet. She had a reputation for being a wiseass, but she tried to give thanks where thanks were due. "For last night, for taking care of me, for not abandoning me. I'll figure out how to pay you back."

A shy half smile grew on his lips. "What are friends for, right?"

Dagger to her heart.

Right. *Friends*. Friends who talked in the car last night about the palpable chemistry between them.

Toooootally normal friendship.

A loud banging clattered at Nash's front door. "Lilian Grace, we know you're in there!" Rose yelled from outside.

"What the fuck?" Lily said, feeling betrayed. "Did you tell Rose—"

"I didn't," Nash said, hands in the air as he walked to open the door.

Rose stormed through the threshold of Nash's guest room. Her older sister scowled at her after wrapping her in a fierce hug. "I could kill you. Why didn't you tell me you were hurt?" Rose's face was full of concern. She loved her tough as nails older sister who was all bark and no bite, with a secret gooey marshmallow middle.

Gray, Jack, and Violet filed in after her. *Oh great.*

"How did you know?" Lily glared at Nash.

"Mrs. Maroo texted me to see if you needed anything," Gray said offhandedly.

They all stared at him curiously. "What? She's a poker buddy. Apparently she ran into Olga at the grocery store this morning."

Nash raised an eyebrow at her, as if to say '*See? Not a liar.*'

Lily turned back to Rose. "Aren't you supposed to be on a honeymoon?"

"We bumped our flight back. Where are you hurt? Are you

on meds? Who's going to take care of you? How are you going to work? Hold on, I need to make a list." She whipped out her phone from her back pocket like a wild west gunslinger.

Violet wrapped Lily in a hug. "I am so sorry that we weren't there for you. You went to urgent care? That sounds so scary."

"You okay, short stuff?" Gray said from behind Rose.

"I'll be fine. My dislocated kneecap has been re-located."

"She can barely walk," Nash offered.

"You are not helping." Lily glared at him.

Rose held up her phone. "All right, I made a list. When does your physical therapy start?"

"Uh, I haven't scheduled it yet," Lily said, wanting to deviate away from the topic of health insurance. She sent *help me* eyes to Nash.

He raised an eyebrow at her. "I'm trying to convince Lily to stay with me."

That's not what my eyes meant!

"Ooh, good idea!" Rose said, pointing a finger at him. "Lily... will stay...with Nash," she said as she typed.

"Wait, no. This is not a vote by committee. I'm thirty, goddamnit," Lily said.

"But still our little sister, and injured," Violet said, giving her another warm smile. "I'd offer for you to stay with us in a heartbeat, but we don't have a bedroom downstairs."

Lily put her head on Violet's shoulder. "Eh, you guys just want to have constant engaged-people sex," she teased.

"Astute observation," Jack said with a wink. "I'm sorry you're not feeling better. Can we bring you anything?"

"Thanks, but no," Lily said with a smile. "It was adorably ridiculous that all four of you rushed over, and I do feel very loved but now leave. Scoot. I should get back to Bloom after I pack up my things," she said, shooing them.

"The doctor told you to rest." Nash crossed his arms, knowing everyone else would agree with him.

"You were there with her?" Rose turned.

Gray wiped a smile from his face and glanced at Jack, who snorted back.

Ugh, she hated this. "Look, it's fine. I'll scoot on my butt down to Bloom when I need to work in the store, and then somebody can carry me back up. Nick and Aaron are strong, and they're right next door."

"*I'm* happy to do it," Jack said, raising a hand with a mischievous smile.

"I will do it," Nash cut in with a firm tone, glaring at Jack.

"It's no problem, mate. Our house is closer to Bloom than yours, and Lily can't weigh but, what, nine stone?"

"*I* will carry her if she needs carrying," Nash said firmly, fuming at him.

Jack swallowed a smile and looked at his feet. "Right."

Nash looked like a territorial bull ready to pee on her at any moment.

"Lily, what Nash says makes sense. You should stay with him," Rose said, pocketing her phone. "There. Done and done."

She didn't love that her loved ones were giving her no choice on how to live her life, but emotion felt thick in her throat. Having people who would drop everything, move flights because she got hurt, was a new feeling. She didn't have ride-or-die friends in New York, and it turned out...she kind of loved it.

"I think they leave you no choice," Nash said with a stern face.

She loved it when the little crease in his brow made an appearance. He was a man who would argue his way into taking care of you.

"All right, you wore me down, Mary-Kate and *Nashley*

Olsen." She threw her hands in the air in exasperation. "But only for a week or two. Or until I sprout wings out of spite so I can fly up the stairs of Bloom."

"Excellent," Rose said, clapping her hands together. "Now that I know you're in excellent hands—better hands, honestly, than normal—we are off to the Caribbean." She wrapped Lily in a fierce hug.

She loved that Rose had become a hugger since she'd moved back to Fairwick Falls. They'd all changed in the last year. Gotten better; closer.

But soon enough, she'd only see her during holidays once she moved back to New York.

"I'm going to miss you," she said, clutching Rose. It was silly, really. She'd see her in two weeks, but it felt like she was already saying goodbye for good.

"I know," Rose said, through a choked-up voice. "I'll send lots of sexy beach pictures so you're all very jealous."

A minute later, Gray and Rose whirled out of Nash's house as fast as they'd come in.

"Do you need us to bring you anything?" Jack asked.

"I can bring you some vegan snacks," Violet offered.

"It's already done," Nash said quietly, his arms crossed.

How the hell?

Violet smiled and nudged Lily's shoulder, fully aware that Lily had harbored a raging crush on Nash since forever.

"Olga's stocked the fridge with vegan options. It's no big deal," Nash said, brushing it off. "Should Violet pack a suitcase for you and bring it back?"

Lily Parker had never been so outmaneuvered in her life.

Chapter Seven

LILY

Lily wobbled on an unsteady leg, holding her DSLR camera up to her eye in Nash's bright white kitchen. Crutches were tucked under her arms as she focused the camera on a new arrangement she'd feature on Bloom's social media.

She'd pushed the conversation with KGM until after Rose got back. Things had been too chaotic with her injury, and she wasn't in the right headspace to wow them yet.

Over the last week, she and Nash had found a rhythm living together. They'd say a quick hello as they both went to work, and then another quick five minute conversation in the evening. She rarely saw him after he disappeared into the gym in the basement level of the mansion he called home.

It had still been cozy to have somebody to come home to every day, though. They made excellent platonic roommates.

Who had off-the-charts chemistry. No biggie.

She'd already gotten used to the comfy mattress, gorgeous shower, and all the benefits of Nash's house. Though 'house' wasn't a fair description of Nash's palatial family home. The Donnellys had lived in this house for over a hundred years, but

Nash had upgraded everything when he'd moved in. The finishings and appliances were all state of the art (she had yet to figure out the fucking microwave), and his designer furniture was comfortable.

Her jaw had dropped when she'd opened the fridge to find it stuffed full of oat milk, vegan butter, egg alternatives, fruits and vegetables, peanut butter, and all her favorites. When she'd tried to pay Nash for groceries, he'd waved her hand away. She honestly wasn't comfortable with being this spoiled.

It would be too easy to get used to it.

Tomorrow was her first follow up appointment for her knee, and her stomach was already in knots. She hated going to the doctor, but what she hated more was not knowing how on earth she was going to pay for all of it.

"Why couldn't I live in Canada?" she muttered as she leaned back to get a different angle of the flower arrangement. A crutch slid out from under her, but she leaned on the counter for balance, and *aha!* Got the shot she wanted.

"What are you doing?" Nash rushed through the kitchen toward her, holding her steady until she could stand up. "Why didn't you ask for help? You can ask me for things," Nash said sternly.

"I'd need a carrier pigeon to find out where you were first, Waldo."

He snorted as he handed her the crutch. "I do have a cell phone."

Lily hobbled to Nash's luxurious den beside the kitchen. She'd become best friends with his enormous cream couch after only one week.

She gestured with her camera as she checked her shots. "Sit down. Tell me about your week. I've barely talked to you the last few days. Oh! How did that matchmaker convo go? Was it wild? Did they ask about your preferred hair and eye color of future babies? What sort of cheesy lies did you tell them about the romantic things you do? When do you meet her? Is it going to be a video thing, an in-person thing? Will you meet her at the altar?"

Nash stared at her for a beat with a growing smile. "Which of those seventeen questions would you like me to answer?"

She pulled her camera up to take a photo, giving him the middle finger. He burst into laughter. She couldn't wait to look at the photo later.

"God, I don't even remember what you asked me." He ran his hands through his sweaty hair, looking like sex on a plate. Apparently he'd been downstairs in the home gym. She tried to drag her eyes away from the way his shirt stretched across his shoulders, the beads of sweat forming a V on his shirt, the definition of his arms that she wanted to sink her teeth into.

"I can make myself scarce if I'm in the way," Lily said. She never wanted to impose. Her skin crawled at the idea of overstaying her welcome. "For you know, your matchmaker dates."

He shook his head. "I moved the conversation with Gina. I wanted to make sure you were settled in, and she's been busy." Nash's eyes were on the ground. His jaw clenched as his hands ground together, his knuckles white.

What is he holding back?

"I don't get it," Lily said, cocking her head. "You're a handsome guy. You could parade naked through the center of town and have several offers of marriage by the end of the day. Though, I guess it depends what you're working with," she said, pointing at his crotch with a pontificating eyebrow.

"*And* we're done." Nash stood, his cheeks turning pink. She swore she saw him smile though.

"Oh, come on. I was teasing," she called from the couch.

"Yes, Lily. I've met you." He grabbed his nightly protein shake from the fridge.

"Oh! You can stand in front of Pop's and pass out flyers," Lily called with a snort. "Ooh, ooh, ooh! Or do a topless car wash in bikini briefs."

"Good night, Lilian!" he yelled as he ran up the stairs.

She flipped on the TV to take her mind off the buzzing that hit her heart whenever he was near. How hyper-aware she was of his movements. And how making Nash blush was one of her top five favorite things to do in Fairwick Falls.

∽

NASH

Nash pressed the bridge of his nose as he inhaled the terrible coffee from the break room. In a different universe, he'd have an Italian espresso machine installed, but the board had already roasted him over unnecessary expenses.

His father had emphasized the importance of mingling with his employees. They hadn't had much time together after his dad's diagnosis, but Nash had spent every day at his bedside, listening to his dad talk fervently about how best to take over the bank.

They'd both thought they'd have a lot more time together. That's what happened when you counted on things instead of proactively planning for them.

He wouldn't make that mistake again.

Nash chugged the silty, bitter coffee. He'd pushed himself the last week—going to bed late, waking up early, and, most importantly, working off all the unspent lust for his new roommate in his home gym.

The eight-thousand-square-foot house seemed like a camping tent with how often he bumped into her.

Walking out of the break room, he stopped by Maria's office.

Maria Lopez had been his right hand, his most trusted advisor, since he'd taken over. She'd been at the bank for thirty years, rising up through the ranks as a teller and putting herself through business school until she was VP of Operations.

Nash had felt uncomfortable stepping in as president, but luckily, she'd known him since he was a kid and they had a warm relationship. He knocked perfunctorily on her open door and was surprised to see Mrs. Maroo sitting across from Maria's desk.

Maria waved him in. "Just who we wanted to see. Close the door. We need to talk."

He leaned on the chair facing her desk. "You're not leaving us for Elliottsville Mutual, are you?" He made sure she was compensated so well she'd never want to leave. She was too important, the linchpin in his entire operation.

She rolled her eyes, sitting back in her large leather chair. "Hell no. Have you seen their predatory offers? Open a credit card and get a hundred dollars? Please. As if I would ever leave my home," she said with a kind smile. "We were talking about how things are looking…uneasy. Jeremy paid me a visit while you were out yesterday."

The hairs raised on Nash's neck.

"Even took her out to lunch." Mrs. Maroo raised an eyebrow.

His hand hit his heart. "You wound me." Maria had always seen through Jeremy's bullshit, even when he'd been a kid.

She waved him away. "I did it for intel, and let me say, Nash, you need to get *married*."

Maria didn't know about his matchmaker, but she knew the bylaws as well as he did. She also knew he and Mrs. Maroo, a surprising shark of a lawyer, had made little headway over the last year.

"Did you learn anything from the lunch?"

Maria leaned back, steepling her hands with a grimace. "He's courting Quantum Capital for a buyout. Promised me a prime position if I'd stay on after he takes over as president."

Rage boiled under Nash's skin. He'd heard horrible things about Quantum.

She continued, "He's hitting the pavement hard with the board to make a case for why you're unfit for this role. Quantum would be terrible for this town. They cut the staff in Cape Creek last year by two-thirds. Reduced hours for customers, put in new ATMs with crazy fees. Signed people up for predatory loans."

He couldn't bear the thought of someone laying off half his staff.

"Any luck with the special legal counsel you contacted for advice?" Nash asked Mrs. Maroo. He'd hired her to investigate potential legal loopholes he could exploit in case he didn't find a wife in time.

"Well, kiddo"—she leaned back, her gold lamé blazer flashing in the winter sun—"I'm afraid to tell you that is a gigantic negative. Your contract was by the books. The bylaws were clear. The president of the bank must be married or widowed. Other than arguing that the bylaws are discriminatory, which could take two or three years in court, there's nothing we can do."

"We have a month at most," Maria said, with warning in her eyes.

Nash rubbed a hand down his face. "Thank you for looking."

What would his dad say if he could see him? He'd had *years* to find a wife. Protect their family legacy.

He'd be so disappointed.

"Nash," Mrs. Maroo said softly, putting a bony hand on his arm. "You're not going to let him down."

He laughed at her reading his mind and shook his head. "If I'd been better with the board. Hadn't made the mistake of changing too many things—"

"Your dad made plenty of mistakes, so don't get all in your head about it," Maria said with a smile as she toyed with her coffee cup. "Did he tell you about the year the Big Christmas Bonuses were invented?" Her smile was wistful. "He'd meant to give everybody a six-*hundred*-dollar bonus, but wasn't paying attention when he typed the email. Therefore, the tradition of a six-*thousand*-dollar bonus was started."

"What?" Nash was shaken out of his thoughts. "He made it seem like that had been the plan all along."

"It was not." Maria laughed, rolling her eyes at the memory. "I was in charge of the ops budget and could have throttled him. Seeing the surprise and happiness on everyone's faces, though, was something I'll treasure forever. He couldn't bring himself to take it back. He took money out of his own paycheck for many, many months until everything was balanced again. He made mistakes like you'll make mistakes. No one expects you to be perfect."

His father had made mistakes like that? A simple typing error that could have ended a less profitable business.

An urgency gripped him to do his best for the place his father had loved. *The place I love.* "I need to make a call. See if I can get my situation rectified sooner rather than later. Thank you both."

"While I have you," Mrs. Maroo called as he opened the door to leave, "can I count on you to chair the food bank's Valentine's Day date auction again this year? No one does it as well as you."

"You know it," Nash said with a sad smile. *I probably won't be married by then anyway.* He was proud to say he'd commanded the highest price for a dinner and dancing with Mrs. Giordano last year. Though he got her lasagna recipe out of it, so he felt like he came out ahead.

"I don't know what we'd do without you around here," Mrs. Maroo said.

Nash waved as he walked out to call Gina to get an emergency meeting on the books. "Hopefully, you'll never have to know."

Chapter Eight

NASH

Hours later, Nash kicked his back door closed as he juggled too many grocery bags.

A sound sent a shiver up his spine as he walked into his kitchen.

Lily's crying.

Fuck. Did she fall? Is she hurt?

He tossed the bags down and sprinted to the end of the hallway, looking frantically in the guest bedroom, the bathroom.

"Lily?" he bellowed, ducking his head into different rooms.

Why is my house so fucking big? I'm only one guy. Who needs all this space?

He rounded the corner into the living room as she held up a pitiful hand.

"H-h-h-ere," she said through sniffles. She was holed up in her favorite position on the couch: pillow underneath her injured knee, other leg tucked at an impossible angle, given her hyper-mobility.

"Hey, hey, hey," he cooed as he crouched down in front of

her. His heart fell back into place knowing she was okay. "What's wrong?"

She shook her head. Her face was red and blotchy but still so fucking beautiful as tears streamed down. "I went to the doctor..."

"Are you hurt from it?" His hand skimmed over her leg.

She went still as his hand trailed her thigh, and he jerked it back. *This is why you normally hide in your basement gym, dumbass.*

She bit her lip as it wobbled. "I need lots of physical therapy, apparently. I have to wear this medieval torture device for four more weeks."

"Four?" Nash echoed in surprise.

She put on a brave face. "I'll find someplace else to live."

"No, no, no," he said, quickly. "Don't worry about that—" *'Sweetheart'* almost escaped his lips, but he bit it off in time.

He'd tossed his ass to hell and back when it had escaped his mouth so many times when she'd gotten hurt, not even realizing he was saying it. But he had a firmer lid on it this time.

Probably.

"And then six weeks of physical therapy."

"That's a lot." He had an insane craving to tuck Lily into his arms, pull her head onto his shoulder, and hold her while she cried out all her feelings.

That would be weird, right?

"*And* I don't have any time or money to pay for it." Her voice went watery. "My student loans have already been deferred. With all the stuff with Dad's tax debt last year, I've been pitching in to buy supplies—"

She wiped her nose with the sleeve of his sweatshirt she'd commandeered from the clean laundry basket. Was it weird he didn't even mind? He kind of liked seeing her in his stuff, in his place, taken care of.

"—and I don't have the money for physical therapy without insurance. I *have* to get it back in shape to teach yoga when I'm back in New York. Which means I have to sell my liver on the black market of Fairwick Falls so I can pay out of pocket because the world is a capitalist hellscape nightmare." She sucked in a big, ragged breath. "I asked if I could sit in the corner and watch somebody else do physical therapy, but they said no," she said with a sniff.

A smile crept onto Nash's face. Only Lily would think of a smart yet completely unorthodox solution like physical therapy auditing.

"They didn't want you to lurk outside the office and peer through the window with binoculars?" he said in a serious voice with humor in his eyes.

Lily chuckled into her fist. "It's a good idea, okay?"

"What insurance company does Bloom use?"

Lily rattled off a name Nash had never heard of. "I missed the enrollment period. I even looked at other options, but I missed them all. I'm just...such a fuck-up." A sob cracked through as she held a tissue up to her face.

"No." He grabbed another tissue from the box beside her and dabbed at her cheek. "You're not a fuck-up. Everyone makes mistakes."

Everyone at the bank—the tellers, janitorial staff, everybody—had access to the top of the line insurance. "Too bad you can't work at the bank," Nash said, his thumb running over her wrist. "I'm sure we could get you squared away."

Lily sucked in a breath. "I'm too busy with Bloom to get another job. I'll just pay through the nose and go into credit card debt. But enough about my shitty day." She straightened with a sniff and plastered on a smile. "How was yours?"

He held her hand, his thumb stroking back and forth. He wanted one more minute of this.

That moment of connection that spun into something different when they were near each other.

Nash reluctantly let her go and sat with his arms wrapped around his knees facing her.

"Maria and Mrs. Maroo and I chatted about Jeremy's surprise appearance in town." He'd run into him twice that week, coming out of restaurants with board members.

"Ew, yech." Lily made a face. "Does he want money? Or help burying a body?"

He loved that she immediately knew how much of a pain in the ass Jeremy would be. "Worse. He wanted me to meet his sham of a wife."

Lily threw her head back and cackled. "His *what?* That poor girl. Let's go rescue her immediately."

He rested his back against the coffee table. Even in a house with twenty rooms, half of which he never used, his favorite spot was right here: sitting two feet in front of one of his favorite people, cozied up into a tight little space in their own little world.

He liked seeing her smiling again. "Hopefully she gets a cut of whatever scheme he's pulling," Nash said, shrugging a shoulder.

"Scheme? What does that have to do with him getting married?"

Should he confess the situation? The real reason for the matchmaker?

Nash took the moment to consider as he shrugged out of his suit jacket and unbuttoned the cuffs of his dress shirt. He rolled up his sleeves, and Lily's eyes traced his movement with a quiet intensity.

She was a loose cannon, but she could keep secrets.

"There is an old bank bylaw that requires the president to be married."

Lily burst into laughter. "No way. I don't believe you."

Nash ran a hand down his face. "It's arcane and stupid, and if the board didn't hate me for trying to bring the business into the twenty-first century, I'd have already changed it by now. There's a lot of outdated, and frankly insulting, language still in there.

"Whoever runs the bank after me—one of my kids—I don't want them to have to be married. Could somebody use the phrase 'family man' against a woman? I need to make it right, but I've been trying to keep my head above water with the board."

Lily nodded. "I remember the whole hullabaloo around the ATM," Lily said, with a roll of her eyes. "You'd have thought you were the dark lord responsible for all evil in Fairwick Falls."

"And now they use it every day," Nash said, putting his head in his hands. "Earl even said it was *his* idea."

Lily smacked the couch. "*That's* why you need a matchmaker!" She pointed at him with glee at having put it all together.

He liked seeing the energy and excitement back in her face. "I haven't had any luck the old-fashioned way. Caroline was the closest I got."

Lily's eyes narrowed at the mention of his ex-fianceé. "I never liked her. She said shitty backhanded stuff. Like how your brand new car was 'cute' and 'economical.' You deserve a better wife than that."

His eyes met hers briefly as his fucking cheeks flushed. Why did he have to blush like a Jane Austen heroine? "She has to be willing to live in Fairwick Falls for the rest of her life."

"Has to be able to handle your mother," Lily said with a knowing smile. Karen Donnelly was a force to be reckoned with.

"And she has to want kids *and* raise them in this house."

"Sounds like such a hardship. Living in a gorgeous mansion with you," Lily said, rolling her eyes and smiling.

She stretched out on the couch, lying on her side, putting her face dangerously within reach of his hands. He wanted to push the lock of hair that had fallen in front of her eyes back from her face. Her sweatshirt gaped open, exposing her shoulder, and he wanted to let his fingers linger there.

Nash ran a hand through his hair instead. He tugged on the ends to relieve some of the tension. "I don't want to rush finding someone, but I can't let the bank fall into Jeremy's hands. He wants to sell it, and that would be a disaster for the town."

"Why?" Lily shrugged. "What's so wrong with the banks everybody else uses?"

Nash bit his lip with worry. "We're more forgiving on things like home mortgages and business loans. My father made me promise I would take care of Fairwick Falls." Nash sighed, leaning back against the coffee table. "When I was twelve, I was in his office doing my homework, and I overheard him personally step in to handle a situation with a loan officer. There was a family who did a lot for the community but had defaulted on their home loan for the first time. One of the parents had recently been laid off, and they had only missed one payment. My father acted as a personal guarantor on the loan without the family ever knowing.

"That night in the car, he talked to me about our duty to show up for others. How it was our responsibility because we were so lucky in having such a long history of prosperity. That was the first year I didn't make a Christmas list," Nash said with a sad smile. "Little did he know, he changed my whole life around that day just by being himself. And I can't let him down."

Lily's eyes were misty. "I miss your dad," she said with a watery voice. "He gave the best hugs."

Nash nodded, a lump of emotion in his throat. "I miss yours. He told the best stories."

"Me too," she whispered. A tear fell down her cheek. She wiped it away just as his hand moved to do it.

"I can't let the bank go to just anybody. It's too important. Too many people's livelihoods are at stake."

Lily toyed with the fabric of the couch. He wanted to tug her one foot forward so she'd fall into his lap, hold her as the emotion criss crossed her face. "I guess I'll watch you battle it out with Jeremy since I'll be in Fairwick Falls longer than I expected. I can't hobble through Brooklyn like this."

An idea crashed down onto Nash's shoulders, hard enough to make him dazed with it.

He couldn't marry just anyone to solve his problem. He needed somebody he could trust.

Who better than the woman with a heart of gold and a mouth as big as Lake Erie that he'd known his entire life?

The perfect solution in a stunning blonde package.

Did he dare ask?

But then it was all he wanted to know. Could she commit if there was a very clear expiration date?

He leaned forward, coming up to his knees. His heart beat like he'd been shot with adrenaline. "I know how to fix everything. Your therapy, my issue at the bank."

"And that is?" Lily said with an eyebrow raise.

He gulped.

"Marry me."

Lily bolted up in shock, a lock of hair falling across her pretty face.

The words hung between them as her eyes widened, and widened.

"Marry me, Lily," he said, his voice insistent and urgent.

God, now that he let himself think of it, it was all he wanted with every muscle in his body. "You'll get insurance. I'll make sure everything is covered. The board will see I'm married. We'll have been living together for a few weeks, so people might buy it. I can propose this week at a family dinner so we have witnesses."

"But we don't—I mean, you and"—she laughed with a shocked expression—"and then I'm...?"

I think I broke her.

A smile lifted the corner of his mouth despite the crazy words that had come from his heart.

This was a terrible idea, but he was going to do it anyway.

His heart beat outside his body with urgency. "I only need to be married for a few months. I have half the board on my side. I just need time to get the others to amend the bylaws. You do physical therapy in the meantime, and when you can walk again"—*right out of my life*—"we get a divorce. No one gets hurt, right?"

His eyes dipped to her mouth a few inches in front of him. She looked tousled and perfect on his couch, hair falling out of a messy bun, the too-large sweatshirt slumped onto her shoulder.

He felt drunk with lust for her as she bit her lip a few inches away from him.

He'd have to keep a tight hold on this.

"But who would believe we'd fall in love?" she whispered slowly, her voice lacking conviction as she stared at his mouth.

Her lips looked like a plush Cupid's bow. Soft. Inviting.

"I don't know," he replied, his voice barely a whisper. "Rose started a pool for when we'd kiss again. They must have thought there was something between us."

"Like we'd let that happen," she murmured as she stared at his mouth.

He could taste the cinnamon chocolate of her breath.

Wanted to gulp it down, close the two inch distance of their mouths.

"Marry me." There was a breathy need in his voice, and her eyes caught on his. "It'll fix everything."

Her chest rose and fell, complicated emotions passing over her face. "For a few months?"

However long I can get with you.

"Only a few months," he echoed back. Her pinky locked unexpectedly through his, and the jolt of want from that alone had him half hard.

But if there was one thing he'd mastered, it was self-discipline. He'd take a cold shower twice a day. Run ten miles to work out his lust.

He gulped. "We'd have to make it look real. No one can know. The board would do anything to have me out for a potential big payday like Jeremy might promise. Not even Rose or Violet can know."

His hand tightened, and he found their fingers were now tangled in each other's.

She nodded as if in a trance, staring at his lips. "We'd have to make it look real," she whispered back, her hand tightening on his. "We'd have to like...be a couple. Kiss."

He licked his lips, imagining what she'd taste like right now. That tart brightness? Or something lustier like musk and vanilla? "Whatever married couples do in public, that's what we'd do." His thumb stroked her other wrist, and he was so, so close to pulling her into him.

"I...I need to think about it," she said, blinking out of the moment and taking a big breath. "Insurance fraud is a big commitment."

He needed to pretend that his heart wasn't crushed at her potentially rejecting his fake marriage proposal. "Of course." He shook his head and released her hands, taking a step back. "I understand you need time to think about it."

She nodded as he walked out of the room.

Hopefully she'd say yes. Then he'd have an excuse to spend more time with her. See her laugh, keep her safe.

Fuck. I'd get to see her in a wedding dress.

That thought alone made his cock twitch with desire.

He could make this work.

He could get married for convenience to the woman he'd unfortunately developed a debilitating crush on.

It would be fucking *torture*.

And he couldn't wait for more.

Chapter Nine

NASH

Nash swept through his mother's stately home with a growing itch under his collar.

"Mother?" he called.

That's what she'd always been since he was a baby. Never Momma, never Mom, always *Mother*. The forty-minute drive to Elliottsville hadn't been long enough to figure out what he needed to say.

Mother, I asked the girl you said was a danger to good taste to marry me. Can I have your ring if she says yes?

Hey, remember the youngest daughter of the woman you hated? I'm planning on marrying her. But don't worry—it's only for a little while. I'll be divorced soon with no children, your worst nightmare.

Lily was still considering the arrangement, but he had a plan. If she didn't say yes, he'd move as quickly as possible with whomever Gina found.

Either way, he needed the engagement ring handed down through the Donnelly family for a hundred years.

"Nashford, I'm in the sunroom," his mother's regal voice called out.

God, he hated his full name.

She sat in a chic suit at the wicker garden table, sipping tea as she read from a book. Her ankles were crossed neatly, and she was wearing a smart suit as if she was heading somewhere. Always put together, always perfect.

That was Karen 'No room for mistakes' Donnelly.

Nash kissed her cheek.

"Have you come to rescue me from my terrible book club pick? I'm afraid Oprah's lost her touch; this book is insufferable." She gently closed her book.

Nash unbuttoned his suit jacket and sat.

"Has Jeremy been to see you?" she said with excitement. "He and Rebecca are staying here, and it has been so lovely." His mother's eyes went dreamy. "You know, I like that girl. Jeremy's always had excellent taste in women. She's quiet, well-mannered—"

Perfect for you to boss around. "Yes, they stopped by the bank."

"Oh, wasn't that thoughtful of him?"

Nash could hurl on her Chanel heels. He'd never understand the soft spot she had for Jeremy. She'd demanded perfection from Nash since he'd been born, drumming duty as the first-born of an 'important family' into every atom of his being. *'No room for errors, we're Donnellys, people expect more.'* But for Jeremy? There were always excuses.

She patted his hand. "What is it you wanted?"

"I need the Donnelly ring." He scratched his neck with discomfort.

She clutched a hand over her heart with a bright smile. "You've met someone."

"Maybe."

"Who is it? Oh, it's not that tawdry new teller at the bank, is it? The one with everything exposed?" she said with an eye roll.

"They'll never respect you if they can sleep their way to the top."

"Mother, it's not Trisha, and her work attire is fine." *God forbid a woman have large breasts in the workplace.*

"So, tell me about this special someone," she said with shining eyes. "How long have you been dating? Who is her family? Why hasn't she come to a family dinner?"

"It's still new"—he chose his words slowly, carefully—"but I have a good feeling."

She leaned back with a knowing smile. "You're not getting the ring until you tell me who it's for."

Fuck, she always knew how to play her cards right. How else would a girl from Possum Trot, Kentucky figure out how to marry up into an old money family and then proceed to reign over Fairwick Falls society for decades?

She arched an eyebrow at him as he stared at her in a battle of wills.

He blew out a breath. "Fine. It's Lily."

"Lily... Bakker? I thought she was married."

Christ.

"Lily Parker, Frank's daughter. You know, the family we were close with until you decided society standing was more important?"

Her face soured. "Oh, Nash," she tutted in disappointment. "She's not pregnant, is she?" She clutched her pearls around her throat.

Actually clutched real pearls. He couldn't wait to tell Gray.

"You know, I don't *technically* have to ask you for the ring since I know where you keep your jewelry." There was one safe in the house, and she'd given him the code when she'd moved to Elliotsville after his father's death.

"But Nash." She clucked her tongue, looking horrified. "She's so *unfit* for someone of your position. Of your standing in the community. We Donnellys cannot make mistakes, and you know her family tree is..." She grimaced. "There's a spotlight on us that your father and I trained you for"—*mercilessly*—"and I'm afraid she can't handle carrying the duty of this family. Being an example to the community."

"I love her." The words tumbled out before he'd checked himself.

It felt good to say it out loud.

Maybe it was the charade.

Maybe it was more.

"She's a perfect fit for me," he lied, knowing his mother was partially right. Lily would never want the society wife responsibilities that would come with being a Donnelly. Luncheoning, hosting charity auctions, fundraising dinners, being the mother of the next generation of Donnellys.

Lily would tell everyone to go fuck themselves while she buried herself in her next creative project. He kind of loved that, but it didn't fit with the life he'd had to live up to.

"Why the rush?" She asked.

"We've been dancing around each other for a year, trying to ignore this attraction." He let the truth slip through, finally honest with his mother for once. "I'd see her from across the room and a smacking stab would hit my heart, taking my breath away. She'd be laughing with a customer, and I'd think, 'That's my future. I want that with me all the time.' I feel like I'm finally alive when I'm with her."

A deep line formed between his mother's eyebrows as her face twisted with disdain. He hated disappointing her.

It's only for a few months.

"I do not give you my blessing," his mother said with a haughty voice, dabbing the corner of her eye as she walked to the kitchen.

"Wouldn't it be nice to bring the two families together like old times?"

The Parkers and Donnellys had been thick as thieves when Nash was a kid. They'd vacationed together and had endless BBQs. Lily had been a baby at that point, but he and Rose were inseparable. Jeremy was always in the mix, playing pranks on Violet.

"We can have dinner at my house," Nash offered. "Invite Lily's family. Rose will be back from her honeymoon. You haven't seen her in a while." His mom had always liked Rose, to her credit.

Her mother pouted. "Why couldn't you marry *her*? She's such a smart girl."

"Because Rose is already married?" Nash said in exasperation. "Look, I need to be across town, so either you can get the ring or I will," he said, finally stern so his mother would listen.

She clicked her tongue. "Fine, but I won't make this any easier for you. Get it yourself." She dismissed him with a wave of her hand.

He gritted his teeth, wishing he could tell her it was only temporary.

LILY

DAMN IT, why did I have to get the extra large latte?

And why hadn't she asked Aaron for a key to Fox & Forrest for emergencies like a late-night pee break?

It was well past 10 PM, and Lily was alone in Bloom. She'd decided to work late to process Nash's proposal.

A lullaby of Nash's angst-ridden voice repeating 'Marry me, marry me, marry me' had lulled her to sleep last night. It was everything she'd ever wanted and feared rolled into one: Her own Prince Charming proposing to her, but it was all hollow. Fake.

This is what you get for working late and avoiding the issue, she thought as a gotta-pee pang hit.

She considered the spiral staircase. Her leg had been doing pretty well today. Maybe she could manage the two sets of stairs up to her apartment.

She missed her studio with the desperate longing of someone whose stuff tended to explode wherever she went. She felt on edge in Nash's picture-perfect movie-set house. She didn't want to mess it up with her "Lilyness." That's what Rose had called it when they'd lived together in Violet's house last year, with all her little projects that she would leave half-finished.

"Fuck it. I'm a woman with ambition and brains and relative upper body strength." She hobbled to the spiral staircase. She sat on a hard metal stair, then slowly lifted herself up and sat her butt on the next stair with a thud.

"Only forty-seven more to go," she grumbled.

I'm gonna look like Popeye after this. All arm muscles, no nothing else.

As she rounded the top edge of the spiral staircase, sweat forming on her brow, she thought about singing a sea shanty. That would help, right?

"Heave *ho* this ass up the stairs," she sang under her breath as she lifted herself up. "Heave *ho–oof*, this ass up the stairs."

The clattering bell on the front door made her jerk her head up. Nash walked in with a horror-struck face.

"What the hell are you doing?" He quickly strode across the wood floor of Bloom, his long trench coat flapping behind him.

God, he looked so handsome. She wanted to tear off his expensive suit with her teeth. He'd looked so fucking sexy yesterday, kneeling in front of her on the couch with rolled-up sleeves, a loosened tie. She'd almost let herself get lost in the fantasy of it.

"Was I supposed to call you and say, 'Please, good sir. Might you come lift me over thine shoulder so I might use the little florist's facilities?"

He stopped on the spiral staircase so they were eye level and shrugged his coat off as he smirked, shaking his head at her.

She'd never get tired of lusting after him. His broad muscles, a wide back, all complemented by his kind face. "How did you know I was here?"

"Saw the light on." He squeezed past her up the staircase and tossed his coat over the loft half-wall.

He was overwhelmingly gorgeous today. A light dusting of snow was melting into his hair, and the cold had pinked up his cheeks.

He still had a suit on, apparently also having had a late night at the office.

A dark vest hugging his toned, thick middle, a dark tie, and a blue shirt apparently were the secret combination to her lady parts because she clenched every inner muscle with lust. The material stretched over his muscles as he put his hands on his hips, looking down at her with an arched, judgey eyebrow.

"I can get it." Her nonchalance didn't betray the desperate attraction she felt for him, she scooted backwards across the floor.

"You expect me to let you hobble up a flight of stairs, backwards, like a beached mermaid?"

"*Oh*, that's way better than Popeye," she said with a grin.

"Come on."

She sighed and raised her knees slightly so he could pick her up.

This was becoming a weird habit of theirs—him scooping

her up as if she weighed nothing and walking her wherever she needed to go.

The heat of his chest radiated against her, and she let out an involuntary shudder. "Soooo...how was your day?"

Warm up to talking about that whole getting married thing.

"Long," he sighed as he walked easily up the stairs with her in tow. "I had the pleasure of talking with my mother."

Lily gave him a sympathetic nod. "And you didn't go straight to the bar?"

She unlocked her front door and threw it open, breathing in the woodsy attic-y scent of her studio apartment. "Ah, good to be home. You can put me down now."

He looked around the entrance. "You don't have any crutches."

"Shit." Thinking ahead was not a strength of hers. The crutches were at the bottom of the staircase.

"I can at least drop you off." He crossed to her bathroom and slowly put her down in front of it.

The bathroom was a roughly built series of walls with no ceiling. She and Nash were going to get very familiar very quickly. "Bless you...but you need to leave."

"How are you going to get downstairs?" He ran a hand through his hair in frustration.

"I can't pee with an audience," she said, squirming.

"I can turn on the garbage disposal?"

"If the garbage disposal worked, that would be a great idea." *Don't think about rushing water.*

"Uh, I can hum loudly."

The gotta-pee pang hit again, *hard*. "Ugh, fine."

He started humming *Wrecking Ball* and she wondered if it was a commentary on the cleanliness of her apartment.

A few minutes later, she stood at the bathroom door with her hand on the doorknob for balance. She was decidedly ignoring the envelope in the center of her table with her father's handwriting. It had been almost a year since his death, and she still hadn't had the courage to open it.

I have more important things to think about, like whether I want a fake-but-real husband.

Nash was at her sink doing dishes, suit jacket off, sleeves rolled up. He hummed over the clatter. Was there anything sexier than a man doing your dishes? And holy mama, those muscular forearms that rippled with movement.

The last two times she'd climaxed using her vibrator, those forearms had played a starring role.

She smiled at the towel he'd tossed over his shoulder. "It just occurred to me that maybe you don't have a house cleaner and that you're a complete neat freak."

"Olga helps, but I do most of it." He grabbed the towel and wiped his hands off in that masculine way that made her think of doing dishes with him.

For the rest of her life.

She could be fake married and get this treatment every day, but could she guard her heart from ending up like her father's? Broken into a thousand pieces?

She'd only ever loved this man from afar. Leaving him after a few months might break her heart and her soul. Permanently.

"Do you think you'd be able to live with me for a few months, given this is how I normally live?" She gestured to the projects littering the space as she hopped to the bed and flopped down on it.

Her photography corner was half torn down. Prints dried in the window where she'd experimented with different painting techniques. Hung along the rafters were bunches upon bunches of drying flowers.

Nash ducked underneath a hanging batch of roses. "It's not

much different than my house now," he said with a teasing smile. She tossed a pillow at him for good measure. He laughed as he caught it and tossed it back at her.

He stood, leaning against a kitchen chair with his ankles crossed, creating a long, elegant line. *Sigh. Eat your heart out, Gregory Peck.*

"So, you're considering it? The queen of no commitments?" he asked.

Only thought about it every minute since last night.

"It's not committing if there's an end date, right? I'm great at compartmentalization. I'm a yoga teacher and an artist. I'm a sister and a business owner."

I'd marry you for insurance and also desperately want to jump your bones.

"So that's a yes?"

"I want to sign a prenup," she said, suddenly. She didn't want him to think she was a money-grabbing mole rat.

"That's ridiculous." He tugged on his hair that was already tousled. He stood with his hands on his hips, leaning toward her. She loved that he took up space. He was big and unapologetic about it. There was a swagger in his confidence that to others might look Ivy League, but she knew it was Nash being himself.

She hugged the pillow he'd tossed back at her. "I want you to be protected. What if I turn into a heinous bitch in the next six months?"

"I know you, Lily Parker." He walked toward her like a tiger stalking its prey.

Oh no.

Oh yes.

Oh boy.

He crouched in front of her so they were eye to eye. "Down to your bones. You are kind and trustworthy. The woman who insisted I re-home the spider in my kitchen rather than kill it won't become anything heinous. May I?" He gestured to spot on the bed beside her.

Goosebumps flooded her arms. *Sure. It'll be easy for me to straddle you and have my way with you.* But instead, she shrugged.

"Have you decided?" He sat beside her, looking nervous.

She really, *really* wanted to be fake married to him. Maybe this could be the perfect situation—she didn't have to choose.

Yes I'm in love with him and want it to be real, but I can still retain my freedom if there's an end date. No heartbreak required if he never loves me to begin with.

"Yes," she said, finally. It felt like a herd of rhinos thundered across her chest.

Don't freak out, body. This is fake.

Don't get your hopes up that this means anything to him.

The intensity in his eyes reflected her nerves. "Yes you've decided, or yes you want to get married?"

Chapter Ten

NASH

Nash's heart was in his throat, waiting on her final answer.

"Yes to all of it," Lily said in a rush.

Nash held her eyes as her words settled deep in his chest and melted there.

Staying with him.

"Yes to all of *what*?" he said slowly as his heart thundered, not wanting to get his hopes up.

He needed to double, triple, *however*-many check she knew exactly what she was getting into before he breathed a sigh of relief.

She bit her lip, looking nervous. "Yes. I will fake marry you until I'm better and you've fixed your weird bylaws issue."

"And there will be no prenup," he said with finality. *How could she even suggest such a thing?*

"There will *most* certainly be a prenup." She reared her head back with a look of horror.

"Maybe I *want* you to take half my stuff when we get divorced," he said, sparing a glance at her lips.

Her lips quirked in a smile. "So I'd have half a bajillion dollars?"

Nash snorted. "Not exactly." *Only ten million.* But they'd save that conversation for another day.

"Are there any"—he fiddled with a clasp on his watch, unwilling to look at her for this question—"jealous exes I should be aware of?" He darted a glance at her as he chewed his lip.

"Are you trying to figure out what my dating history has been, future husband?"

His cock surged with lust. *Oh, she really shouldn't call me that.*

He cleared his throat. "Trying to get the lay of the land."

"I'll happily tell you how my land has been laid." She raised an eyebrow in humor.

"And *there* she is, ladies and gentlemen." He wiped his hand down his face, laughing in spite of himself.

"A lot of fuckboys, no exes," Lily shrugged.

Nash felt a flood of relief, only for it to be followed by another layer of concern. *So it's not that she hadn't found someone.*

She's not even interested in more.

"What about you? How many Fairwick Falls bachelorettes will send me severed horse heads for stealing you?"

"I was so torn up after my dad passed, dating wasn't on my mind. And then, I was busy with the bank. Finally, I started thinking about it again..."

But then you moved back.

"...but then things got busy again," he said, clearing his throat. "First dates have been outside of Fairwick Falls in case it didn't work out. None did."

Lily arched her back, stretching, and her oversized flannel shirt fell off her shoulder, exposing the shoulder Nash dreamed of kissing. Biting. Leaving a territorial mark on.

He couldn't meet her eyes. God, how he wanted this to be real.

What a disaster.

He reached into his pocket. "I thought we should check if this fits."

The old leather box revealed a small antique velvet jewelry box inside as he opened it.

Her shocked breath rang like an atom bomb in the studio.

"I forgot I got a ring." She sat up with wide eyes.

He wanted to gather her up, do this all for real right now. But he didn't have that kind of margin of error in his life.

No mistakes, no room for errors. Not when you're a Donnelly.

"It was my great-grandmother's, the only piece they kept during the Great Depression. My great-grandfather wouldn't let her sell it even when the bank ran out of money. They had to sacrifice what they could to keep the town running. Unfortunately, all the other historic jewelry was sold off so people didn't starve."

Lily's hand came to her throat. He hadn't even shown her the ring yet, but her eyes fixed on it as if it was a rattlesnake ready to bite.

Just ease her in. "Obviously, you don't have to wear it right now. I'll propose this weekend at the family dinner. Your sisters and Gray and Jack should come, too. We can make a whole big spectacle of it. Lots of witnesses to show we're really getting married."

Lily chewed on her thumbnail briefly and then nodded, her eyes fixated on the meaningful piece of jewelry.

None of this feels fake.

He slowly opened the emerald velvet box with his heart racketing about in his chest.

This feels really fucking real.

Her eyes filled as it landed on the art nouveau masterpiece

his family had saved for generations. A wide gold band with filigree golden vines led to a starburst of turquoise surrounding a cushion-cut, two-and-a-half-carat diamond.

"Nash, we can't do this," she whispered with misty eyes. "That's real." Her eyes never moved from the ring.

His heart plummeted. "Sure we can," he said, panic in his voice. "It's just jewelry."

"It's..." Her voice faltered.

Oh no. Was she going to laugh at it like Caroline had? She'd called it 'hideous beyond compare.'

"It's..." Lily's fingers gently traced the edges of the vine-edged ring. "...it's gorgeous," she breathed reverently. "I can't. I'll ruin it somehow."

An electric shock strung through him as her fingers drew back.

"Let's just see if it fits," he said, urging her on. The ring felt heavy and meaningful as he pried it from the holder.

Ultimately, it represented the sacrifices his family had made. They'd liquidated their assets to make sure everyone in town had food. This was all that had remained.

The glass slipper after the ball as a hope for the future.

It felt heavy in his palm as he considered dropping it in her hand.

But no. That feels wrong. He couldn't just hand it to her.

He gulped.

"I'm sorry. I know this isn't real, but I have to—" He slid from the bed onto one knee in front of her, and she sucked in a breath.

He had to do it right. She deserved that.

She deserved everything.

"It's...I have to do it this way. I'm sorry. For practice," he said, stumbling, realizing he was probably making a bigger deal of it than she wanted to.

He might spook her if she knew his real feelings were quickly careening from a crush to something else.

This is just practice. "So, on Saturday, before dessert, I'll stand and say something, and then I'll get down on one knee, ask you to marry me, open the ring box. You'll gasp—"

"—That won't be hard to fake," she interrupted, gaping at the ring.

"You'll say yes, and I'll slide the ring on your finger. So...?"

She gave him her right hand. A smile quirked his lips. "Other hand, Lily."

"Oh, shit. Sorry, first time doing this." Lily laughed nervously.

Her hand shook as she held it out. He briefly met her eyes. "We're in this together," he whispered.

Her face was wistful and she nodded. "Together."

An electric current zinged through him when he touched her hand. This was like proposing to a live wire.

It hadn't been half as terrifying proposing to Caroline five years ago.

He slowly slid the ring on her delicate finger.

It was such an intimate gesture, making someone your fiancée.

The ring was exactly her size, and the peachy undertones of her skin reflected back against the gold.

"Perfect fit," he whispered. They were eye-to-eye as he kneeled in front of her. "And then..." His voice was low and hoarse. "It would be weird if we didn't kiss after getting engaged, right?"

His hand still held hers, but she'd stopped shaking.

She nodded. "We should practice that, too."

Nash gulped so loud, he heard it. He tried to keep his mind from imagining everything he wanted to do to her.

He'd pin her arms above her head while he ravaged her until

she was moaning and writhing. He'd do all the things he'd thought of since August—hell, since last year—when he'd been trying to get her out of his head.

"Nash?" she interrupted his thoughts.

The bed loomed in front of him with a siren's call. Picturing her throwing her head back in ecstasy as he buried his face in her pussy came too easily to his brain.

"No, it's, um"—he cleared his throat—"not here." He stood up and pulled her up with him to avoid temptation.

No room for failure; no room for mistakes.

"You okay like this?" He settled his hands on her hips. She stared into his chest and nodded, uncharacteristically serious.

The air grew thick between them.

Get your head out of your ass. This is an arrangement, a give and take. Both of us are getting exactly what we want, no feelings involved.

That's exactly how he should approach the kiss.

He lowered his head, grazing her lips with the sexual prowess of a wooden toy soldier.

Lily's eyes bugged out from her face. "What the hell, Nash? You're gonna kiss me like I'm your Great Aunt Agnes?" Spunk was back in her voice.

He couldn't help but smile. *There's my firecracker.*

Nash swallowed, not meeting her eyes. "I don't think they'll notice."

"We want them to think it's real, right?" Lily said with her hand on her hip. "I mean, if you *want* your brother to catch on..."

Fuck, she was right. It had to be believable.

She can't know how much you want her. How much you've dreamed of her.

"But my breath. I had a lot of coffee today," he stammered. His hands dropped from her hips as he plotted his escape.

Why am I such a fucking coward?

"C'mon, just do it." She smacked his chest playfully, not picking up on his panic.

"I don't..." He ran his hands through his hair.

Why was this room so small? Why did she smell like a bouquet of flowers? Why was her bed *right fucking there?*

Why did he want to haul her against him and *not* give her a chaste romantic kiss, and *claim* her instead?

Her face was bewildered as she quirked her eyebrows at him, unaware of the internal war waging inside. "Nash, just kiss me like a man who wants to *bang his fiancée.*"

"I can't," he snapped finally.

His voice echoed in the studio as she reared her head back in the silence.

Fuuuuuck.

Her eyes went wide with surprise. "What do you mean?"

I want to savor you.

I want to bathe in the luxury of your lips and drown in how much I want you.

I want to kiss you so perfectly, so completely, you'll never want another soul as long as we both shall live.

"Let's just go home," he said with frustration.

He turned away to grab his coat. Otherwise, every part of how much he wanted her would come flowing out.

"I'm staying here." She hopped back to the bed and flopped down.

Jesus, he did not need this right now. He was on a hair trigger as it was. "You can't stay here by yourself," he said with exasperation.

"A, you're not the fucking boss of me. B, I'm home. I'm going to stay here where all my stuff is." She crossed her arms resolutely and raised an eyebrow.

A pixie with a permanent attitude.

Why was *this* who his heart and his cock longed for?

"What if you get hurt?" he said, irritation coursing through him. "Do Rose or Violet even have a key?"

"No," Lily said slowly. "Why would they need one?"

"No one has a spare key, you're injured, and *I'm* the crazy one for wanting you to come back home where you belong?"

God, he sounded like a controlling husband from the 1950s. What he really wanted to say is '*I worry about you when you're not with me. I always want to make sure you're safe,*' but that felt too real right now, so demanding 1950s husband it was.

"I like having my own space. I'll be here even while we're fake married."

His teeth grit on the word *fake*. "I should have a key to make sure you're okay, or somebody should. Give it to Rose or Violet if you don't trust me." He was growling. he knew. But it was better than the alternative of giving in.

She sat up with a fiery look. "Why do you even care so much now? You barely talked to me the first eight months I lived here. I can manage on my own. I've *always* managed on my own. I depend on no one, ever." She sounded indignant. "Plus, if I'm here, I won't clutter your space and take over your fridge. What a win for you, not having to deal with your chaotic fake wife."

Goddamnit he hated that f word.

"Who was it?" he said with unchecked anger.

"Who what?" she asked, confused.

"Who convinced you that you were too much? That you didn't deserve an easy life with someone who cared for you? I swear to god, Lily, I will *end* them for making you think because you're loud and funny and real, you deserve anything less than the fucking moon." He towered over her petite frame, knowing exactly what she was doing by pushing him away. "You're not going to shove me away. Let me make one thing clear: I am not one of your New York fuckboys. It's not cute when you distance yourself. I'm not relieved when there's less of you in my life. I am marrying you, Lillian Parker, because I think you would be an excellent, albeit temporary, wife. Now"—he tugged on his suit jacket with a vengeance—"I'll get your crutches so you won't fall to your death stumbling in this godforsaken studio."

He thundered down the steps, steam coming out of his ears.

He could see her ploys, how she kept him and everyone else at arm's length. Never committing. Just funny Lily, silly Lily, here for a good time Lily, but he saw through all that shit.

He saw how kind and funny, caring and smart she really was.

He strangled the crutches in his hands as if they'd called his mother a whore and thundered up the stairs.

She wouldn't let him into her life? Fine. They'd have an ice-cold roommate-ship for three months. He crossed into the studio, prepared to set her crutches down and storm out.

But Lily stood a few steps inside the door, leaning on one foot with tears in her eyes.

Shit, he was too harsh with her. She'd walked on her bad knee and gotten hurt. "Lily, I'm sorry—"

"Here," she said quietly, holding out a key. "I want you to have it. If you want."

A key to her apartment.

The key no one else had.

He saw the olive branch she offered, letting him in where no one else had been before.

She looked like she was nervously offering him her heart. Her long hair swept over her shoulder, cozy sweater over leggings. Her lower lip caught between her teeth as her eyes were wide with nervous vulnerability.

And god help him, his iron will finally broke.

He dropped the crutches as ragged breaths pulled at him.

Swiping the key with one hand, his other hand dove into her golden hair.

He pulled her in, kissing her as a wave of lust and need inside him crashed through. He breathed her in, felt her soft lips kissing him back, and his knees almost buckled.

He groaned as she melted into him, ripe-cherry brightness bursting into every inch of his body.

He kissed her again, and again, and *again*, gulping waves of her scent and her soul. Gathering her up, needing her closer, hungry for her to stay right fucking here.

She whimpered as he opened her mouth with his needy, urgent, desperate kisses. His hands framed her perfect face as their tongues met, and he pulled her closer, craving, needing, *longing* for her.

Desire made him hungry, territorial. Every dark part of him wanted to take her.

Have her, *make* her his.

His brightness.

His firecracker.

He needed her closer. Fuck, he needed to be *in* her.

His mouth invaded hers as she met him match for match. Desire for longing, a sea of want and lips and tongues as his hands raked through her hair.

His cock was steel, and holy lord, why hadn't he fucked her yet? She'd offered months ago, and he could've had her mouth a thousand times.

Her hips, his obsession, called to him. He mapped the curve of her waist with hungry strokes, grasping at the softness of her hips. The curves he wanted to consume, trace with his tongue. She thrust against his leg and *fuck*. His cock throbbed feeling her moving under his fingers.

She arched into him, moaning, and he slid his hand to her

perfect, round ass. He grabbed it territorially, fingers digging in hard as she bit his bottom lip ruthlessly.

Fuck yes. His spitfire would ruin him.

He was so hungry for her. He'd been fasting for years, and now he wanted every inch of her. She took it so well, writhing for more under him. Mewling as his thumbs hooked under the band of her yoga pants and he felt the soft skin of her ass.

His cock demanded he feel every inch of her. The lusty memory of her tits had kept him company for months.

His hand slid up, and she arched into him, pressing her tits into him. *Fuck yes.* With a groan, his thumb found her nipple as his fingers claimed her breast. Her tongue licked into his mouth greedily as he rubbed her nipple in slow, agonizing circles. Her low moan was a siren call to him. Calling him home to her.

His other hand cupped her jaw, keeping her exactly where he wanted her. He teased her up and up as her breath sobbed out between their kisses. Her heartbeat raced like a wildfire against his palm as he thought how easy it would be to unbuckle his pants and fuck her right now. Make brutal, feral love to her like the beast that he kept locked inside craved.

Too real. Too much. His hand stilled on her breast as he finally wrenched his mouth away.

He pulled back, both of them gasping for breath. His thumb traced the bottom of her lip as she stood in stunned silence, looking gorgeous and ferocious and just as hungry as he was.

No more. You were too close to losing control, Donnelly.

"That was for practice." He turned to go without another look at her.

Too dangerous.

"Lock your door!" he called over his shoulder. "I'll lock the front door of Bloom when I go."

If she barely whispered for him to stay, he'd have been on his knees at her mercy. He'd suggest every single position he'd dreamed of for a year as he fucked his hand, thinking only of her.

As he thundered down the stairs, the enormity of what he'd done hit him like a crashing wave.

That was a mind-numbingly stupid thing for them to do, but god, he already missed the taste of her.

Chapter Eleven

LILY

Lily - We're happy you're feeling better. Let's set a meeting up to talk about a partnership later this week.
   Rachel Mercy, Creative Director at Large, KGM.

Lily stared at the email. Could she have her cake (Nash's mouth, holy lord) and eat it too (still work with a New York agency)?

Yes, she decided wisely. *Why not both?*

Rose was going to flip her shit. A partnership could mean national recognition for Bloom.

"You look like you just ate a canary, Lilybug." Rose sauntered past her with gardening supplies through Bloom. They were prepping the store for filming the next episode of Violet and Jack's *Plant Parent SOS* show. They had unexpectedly created a hit last year that had been picked up by a cable network and often incorporated Bloom into episodes for 'maximum PR opportunities,' as Rose called it.

"You've heard of KGM, right?"

"Uh, *yeah*. I tried to work with them on my last media project in LA, but they never returned my calls."

"Apparently they return mine." Lily shrugged, flashing her phone to Rose.

Rose—the calm, cool, collected sister—shrieked. "What? How? What...how? *How* did you do this?" Rose said, wild-eyed.

"I asked if they would consider a partnership with me or Bloom or whatever because I've always admired their work. I linked to our recent projects, like the viral videos with Violet, our product lines with local businesses." Lily tossed her head to the side, pretending to play it cool.

"Well, fuck yeah, we want to chat," Rose said. "This could be huge. They can get a Bloom product line into stores all over the country. They're tastemakers for women ages twenty-five to forty-seven."

"Okay," Lily said, wiggling in place with excitement. "I'll email her back and say I would love to chat this week."

Now would be a good time to bring up *The Mission*, as she'd coined it in her head. Operation: Trick My Nosy Sisters into Believing Nash Wants to Marry Me.

It had been approximately seventy-two hours since The Kiss to Be Remembered on Her Deathbed, and in traditional Nash form, he'd pretended nothing was different when she went back to his house the next day.

They'd agreed to start dropping relationship details so their proposal on Saturday wouldn't come out of the blue.

Rose straightened a display as Lily drafted a reply to KGM. "How goes it in Chateau de Donnelly?" Rose asked.

Lily pocketed her phone and went back to arranging the plant corner so everything would look perfect for filming the next day. "Wouldn't you rather hear what happened in my apartment a couple of nights ago?" Lily said, snorting to herself, knowing exactly how she was leading Rose on.

"Hey, are these chunks of Swiss chard for something?"

Violet called from the back, holding up a container of leafy greens.

"They're for Peaches when I leave tonight," Lily called back. Despite her injury, she'd decided Peaches had earned a special treat after accidentally creating a situation where she got to kiss Nash again. "C'mere. You'll want to stay for this news."

She knew Violet would feel left out if Rose found out about the 'relationship' before she did.

"Uh-oh. Bad news or good news?"

"I bet it's sexy news," Rose said, sitting on a side table, eager to hear some gossip.

"Ooh!" Violet clapped her hands together. "I knew it, I knew it, I knew it!"

Well this is taking all the fun out of it.

"So...Nash and I may have kissed again."

Violet threw her arms up and laughed, and Rose smacked the table. "Damn, I was a month off."

Lily rolled her eyes at the fact that they'd kept their bet from August.

"It's been very whirlwind, even though we're keeping it on the down low. You know his mother. But we were hoping—"

"We? They're already a 'we'," Rose said, elbowing Violet.

"—you could join us for dinner this Saturday. His family has a monthly dinner tradition, and he invited all of us."

"So, what does this mean? Are you staying in Fairwick Falls?" Rose said, getting out her phone.

Lily knew the very specific swiping gesture and feral look in Rose's eyes that meant she was starting a new to-do list. "Should I cancel the candidate conversations we have lined up to be your replacement? Maybe you should start looking for a bigger place. Oh no, you'll move in with him full-time obviously. I'll start a sub-bullet list to get the rest of your things moved over to his place because you're injured."

"Wait, wait, wait, wait," Lily said, throwing her hands in the air. "You're like a fucking steam train. Don't cancel the interviews yet." She still needed to leave in a few months. She could get someone in place who could eventually replace her, and then Bloom would be set once she went back to New York.

"But you're dating Nash. It sounds serious, right? You don't date…anyone," Violet remarked, confused.

Shit. Uh… "If the KGM partnership goes well, maybe we'll need an extra set of hands. That person can take over the day-to-day creative operations here."

"Hmm." Rose waggled her head in thought as she did the mental calculation. "We could maybe swing it. You're right; we'll keep the interviews on. Damn, no more to-do list needed." She pocketed her phone.

"So what's he like to be with as a boyfriend? Is it everything you ever thought it would be?" Violet said, taking Lily's hands with a dreamy sigh.

Oh shit. Right. Girl talk.

"Has he balanced your bottom line?" Rose said with a cocked eyebrow.

"Hey, I'm the one who's supposed to make the dirty innuendos in this family. And, uh, yes," she said awkwardly, remembering she needed to tell a compelling story because they knew her. If she liked a guy, they would have been in bed ages ago. "Ten out of ten in the sex department." *Ugh, I need to get better at lying.*

"What happened to 'no commitment necessary, Lily Parker's guarantee'?" Rose narrowed her eyes with suspicion.

Turns out, it was *annoying* having somebody who knew you so well.

"You know Nash is different." Lily shrugged, hearing the kernels of truth in her voice.

"That's true. You've been in love with him since you were, what, fourteen?" Rose asked.

"Thirteen," Violet corrected. "Wait, no, it was younger. Weren't you super little when I saw his name in your diary?"

Twelve, but who's counting?

"That was just a crush." *I didn't really fall in love with him until I was fifteen and dazzled by his good looks when he came back from college.* Lily went back to her camera, fussing with the settings. "Anyway, you know he's different."

"He's your white whale," Rose said with a sage nod. Violet agreed.

Ha. She was so good at this. "We've already started to use the 'l' word."

"The 'l' word? You mean love?" Violet said with a surprised smile.

"Yes…love." Lily said the word like she was coughing up glass. She *never* used the 'l' word with anybody. She barely used it with her sisters.

"Nash told you he *loved* you?" Rose looked as serious as a heart attack. "Nash is a serious guy. He doesn't say stuff like that unless he really means it."

Lily cleared her throat but clasped her hands behind her back so she didn't chew her nails, trying to stop the nervous tells her sisters knew. "Yep, that's what he said to me."

"Was it during sex? Because I don't think that counts," Violet said.

"*After* sex totally counts," Rose countered.

"Oh, uh, no. It was not." But Lily wouldn't even let herself think about what it would be like to have sex with Nash. To belong to him.

Not just bang it out, but to actually wallow in all the big feelings she'd kept deep down for so long.

"Definitely *before* sex," Violet and Rose said at the same time and burst out laughing, clutching each other.

Lily rolled her eyes with a smile and went back to finishing the plant corner. *Sisters.*

At least she had them fooled.

∼

"Olga, are you sure there's not something I can do?" Lily wrung her hands with nerves. "I'm shit in the kitchen, but I'm pretty good at measuring things."

The elderly woman who had worked for the Donnellys for ages said nothing but waved Lily out of the kitchen.

Lily chewed her lip. Only twenty-five minutes and the family dinner, aka the ruse, would begin.

She and Nash had successfully avoided spending more than five minutes together over the last week. Lily was up to her eyeballs prepping for the Valentine's Day onslaught as well as a wedding that weekend. He also worked long hours and at home, he'd bolt whenever she would enter the same room.

They hadn't talked about the logistics of when they would get married, but she assumed it would be soon.

"If he would spend more than two fucking seconds in a room with me," she muttered, re-arranging the dried pine bows and candles she'd artfully placed along the table, "then maybe we'd have a plan."

Nash pushed through the swinging door to the dining room as he fixed his cufflink. He looked like he'd stepped off a photoshoot, slick but with a touch of grit. Nash wasn't a pretty boy. He was sophisticated and masculine with an air of elegance that spoke of generations of good breeding.

The dark charcoal of his expensive suit shone luminous in

the low light of the dining room. It had to be tailor-made for him, wrapping around his long, muscular arms and wide back.

He stopped when his eyes found her dress. She'd worn the only one she had that wasn't formal wear. It was awkward with her knee brace, but it wrapped around her, clinging to her curves, dipping at her cleavage, with off-the-shoulder sleeves. "You look so nice," she muttered flatly. "Is this good enough?"

"You're exquisite," he murmured. His eyes wandered up, tracing a slow line along her body. She clenched at the stoked heat in his eyes. Thankfully, that made the butterflies in her stomach less raucous.

Normally she'd pace in this situation, but she could barely walk, so she opted for biting her nails and flapping her hands with nerves. "What if they figure us out?" she said in a panic.

"It'll be fine," Nash said calmly. He checked his other cufflink and then walked around the table straightening each place setting by a millimeter.

Lily glanced at the clock. Almost time. "Do you think I should eat a snack now or closer to dinner?"

Nash straightened with a confused look. "We're eating dinner in twenty minutes. Why would you need a snack?"

"Well, you know. I like carrots and dinner rolls, but I can't always make a full meal out of whatever vegan options there are. You don't want wine-drunk Lily on an empty stomach while we deal with a fake proposal."

She'd gotten used to making do for the last twenty-five years, after she'd realized the positive impact being vegan had on the world. She couldn't bear the thought of eating an animal or having it locked up and unhappy. She'd gotten used to eating what she could at shared dinners and having a snack later.

Trying not to take it personally that no one cared enough to make something for her.

Nash shook his head as if remembering something. "The

meal is vegan, Lily." He brushed past her, walking to the bar cart. He pulled out a martini shaker.

"The...whole meal?" Lily asked, her stomach plummeting for some reason.

He searched through the liquors in the cabinet. "You're vegan. Why would I have something my future wife can't eat when we get engaged? I need to make sure you have enough."

My future wife.

She wanted to tuck those words away and carry them with her always.

Her voice came out a whisper. "But what about you?"

Nash shrugged. "I won't have food made that you can't eat, if that's what you're asking."

"So, *you'll* be vegan?" She scratched her head, completely thrown by this. Nash had never exhibited interest in animal welfare or the environmental impact of the meat industry.

"I wasn't sure how comfortable you'd feel"—he poured a martini into a chilled glass—"if I smelled like meat when we kissed. As long as we're together, I'll be vegan."

He handed a martini to her, and she took it, dumbfounded.

Granted, her experience with actual dating was minimal, but she was pretty sure other people didn't do this for their partner.

"You don't have to."

"It's fine. I want to," he said, pouring another two martinis. And right at seven o'clock, the doorbell rang.

Nash let out a long-suffering sigh lifting the second martini in his hand. "That would be my mother."

Lily locked eyes with him and downed the martini as he sent his eyes heavenward. "This is going to be a disaster."

Luckily, soon after Nash's mother arrived, Violet and Jack strolled in.

Violet, whose self-appointed job was to make everyone

around her feel comfortable, and Jack, who could charm the pants off a concrete gnome, managed to keep Nash's mother entertained so Lily could sit in the corner and try not to blurt out curse words.

She had to be the perfect girlfriend for Nash tonight. No dick innuendos, not too many cocktails.

Keep your shit together, Lily. Just for one night so everybody can believe he really would love you.

Even though every woman with a pulse in a three-county radius will want your head on a pike for nabbing the most eligible bachelor.

Good thing you don't even want all that relationship stuff.

But cracks started to form around those old, worn thoughts. Whispers calling from somewhere inside made her question... was that all still true?

She shook her head, willing herself not to think about it tonight.

Nash sat dutifully beside her as his mother prattled on about some garden club. He snaked his arm around her waist as a boyfriend would do, and it was all she could think of. The heat from his hand pressing into her hip, the gentle, absent-minded stroke of his thumb along the fabric of her clinging dress.

His touch was an aphrodisiac. She clenched her legs together so she didn't squirm. His thumb strokes felt like licks of desire along her spine.

She felt enveloped by Nash as he sat beside her. His broad shoulders tucked behind her body with his arm wrapped firmly around her. He made a joke, and she barely registered the words, still in a lusty daze.

Maybe chugging the martini was a bad idea.

Had she eaten today? She'd had fruit for breakfast but had skipped lunch because she was so busy. *Great, I inhaled a martini on an empty stomach.*

"Sorry we're late," Rose said, striding in, holding a bottle of wine, followed by Gray.

Nash checked his watch. "I think it's time for dinner." He squeezed Lily's waist and kissed her temple.

As they stood to move into the dining room, the front door opened again.

Nash looked confused and turned to her. "Did you invite Aaron and Nick?"

"No." Lily swayed as she stood, wobbly from the martini hitting her all at once.

In walked Jeremy, quietly followed by a woman who looked bored beyond reason.

"Looks like we're in time," Jeremy said with wide open arms. "Lily. I haven't seen you in years." His outstretched arms gathered her in an awkward hug.

Yikes.

Nash pulled her away from Jeremy's embrace.

"Mom said you'd left town," Nash said through gritted teeth. He stood so ramrod straight with fury, he looked like a walking two-by-four.

"I moved things around so I can hang out with my brother's new girlfriend." He threw an arm around Lily's shoulder that she shrugged off.

"I'll find two other place settings…somewhere," she muttered under her breath.

After a peek into the kitchen to let Olga know there would be nine, not seven, for dinner, Olga silently threw her hands in the air, looking heavenward.

Lily turned back to the dining room to face her fake engagement. "Couldn't have said it better myself."

Chapter Twelve

LILY

Thus far, the night was going great.

They made it through appetizers, and the martini buzz died as her stomach was filled with spring rolls.

"So, how long have you been dating?" Jeremy asked with a sneer as he reached to grab another spring roll.

She and Nash locked eyes as they both answered.

"A few months."

"Weeks."

Oh shit, they hadn't talked about their backstory.

Violet and Rose's eyes narrowed and a gleam shone in Jeremy's.

"Which is it?" Jeremy said, dipping a spring roll aggressively in the peanut sauce.

Somehow everything this man did irritated the fuck out of her.

Nash beamed and grabbed Lily's hand. He looked perfectly at ease, unlike her stomach that was a B-52 bomber of nerves. "You tell it best, my darling."

A somersaulting stomach was a great way to start off lying to all of your friends and family.

"It only *felt* like weeks"—Lily smiled nervously, trying to recover—"but it's been on and off for the past few months."

Not *entirely* a lie after their kiss in August.

"After he was kind enough to take me in, I finally wore him down." She sent a sparkly smile to Nash as if they had a secret joke.

"Is that what started all of this? You moving in?" Rose asked.

Why didn't they have a plan? Or a backstory?

"Uhmmm..." Lily faltered, panicking as she looked at Nash.

She hadn't even thought through what a wedding would mean. Would she get a dress? Would they get married in a church? Or swing by the courthouse on a Tuesday in yoga pants? She'd been so pre-occupied after the best kiss of her *fuck.ing.life*, her brain hadn't been able to focus on anything else.

"Actually, honey." Nash squeezed her hand. *He really needs to be consistent with his terms of endearment.* "I think it's time we bring out the entrees. Would you help me?"

She followed him into the kitchen, and he tugged her away from the door. He bent low, whispering into her ear. "We need to get our story straight—"

"We could have talked this week if you'd hadn't bolted every time I saw you," she argued.

"We dated but told no one," he whispered fervently. "We've already said I love you, have had our first major fight, and things are getting serious as we've talked about our future. Deal?" He stood back, his hands on his hips.

She nodded. "Deal." Though she wished there were about another twenty steps to that plan so he'd keep murmuring in her ear.

He ran a hand down his face. "I'll do the thing before dessert."

Great, like she was supposed to eat something and be normal. *Not feel like a popcorn kernel about to burst as I wait to be proposed to by the only man I've ever loved.* "Fantastic."

Olga peered over her shoulder with a raised eyebrow.

Nash grabbed the serving dish of coconut curry and rice. "You ready?" His back was to the swinging door, his eyes locking with hers.

This would be the last time they could talk before they went through with it: the irreversible fake proposal that was a real proposal.

But was fake.

But also real.

Lily kept flip-flopping in her head but nodded anyway with a groan.

She held up the mango and peanut Thai salad as they walked into the dining room. "I hope everyone likes Thai food."

Karen frowned as if noxious gas had invaded the room. "This is highly unusual. Usually we eat roast chicken or duck."

"Lily's vegan, Mother." Nash set the dishes on the table.

"I adore Thai food," Rose said, jumping in, reaching for the salad.

"Me too." Violet nodded, trying to set an encouraging tone.

"I don't like coconut," Becky whined like a leaky balloon.

"I know, dumpling," Jeremy said, pulling a face at her. Jeremy scooted his chair back with a gleam. "I'll see if Olga can heat up some frozen chicken tenders for us."

"There is no meat in this house," Nash said, his voice icy.

Holy lord. He'd cleared out the freezer for her too?

"You are welcome to eat dinner or seek accommodation elsewhere." Nash turned toward the end of the table. "Vi, could you pass the curry?"

"Rose." Jack broke through the tension in his *I'm a charming Brit* voice. "Tell us all about your *gorgeous* honeymoon, and don't skip the tawdry bits," he joked, and the mood loosened.

As dinner wound down, Nash caught Lily's gaze as she and Jack bantered about the next product line Bloom should do. Lily's idea: floral scented candles. Jack's idea: an endless assembly line of Violet's chocolate chip cookies.

"Shall we adjourn to the library for dessert?" Karen stood with an expectant face.

"Actually"—Nash interrupted—"I'm glad you're all here. It's good to have both the families together." He found Lily's hand underneath the table and squeezed it.

For her benefit, not for everybody else's.

"Our families have a long history of friendship," Nash said, speaking very formally as a dumbfounded look came over her sisters. "I hope that this can be the restart of that close relationship"—he beamed at Lily, nervousness gone—"because we'll be spending a lot more time together." He winked at her.

Was that for them or for her? Either way, it was *working* for her as she reminded her vagina to calm the fuck down.

"Lily, the last few months have been the best of my entire life. Your sense of humor and genius are only outmatched by your beauty. You've made my life better in every way imaginable."

He now held their hands above the table as he scooted his chair back to kneel.

A muttered curse echoed across the table from Jeremy.

Nash's eyes never wavered from hers. "I never meant to fall in love with you. It was the *last* thing I tried to do." The world could have exploded around them, but it wouldn't have mattered. She was safe and sound as long as she was connected to him. "But I'm so glad my heart had other ideas and chose you."

He opened the ring box.

"Lillian Parker, please do me the greatest honor of becoming my wife."

She indulgently tried to memorize the picture in front of her. How the candlelight hit Nash's face, casting a glow that softened his chiseled features. The vulnerable quirk to his eyebrows that looked as if he'd flayed his body apart for her, showing his deepest depths.

There was something real in how he asked. In how he knelt in front of her.

She smiled at him slowly, hoping he would know what it meant. A smile that said *"I'm so glad I'm doing this with you."*

A "Yes" burst out of her, and she launched herself at him.

Nash caught her by the waist as he knelt and placed a brief kiss on her cheek. She held out her left hand.

A gasp and cheer circled the table, but suspiciously missed three people. The Donnellys sat back with stone faces and furrowed brows.

A very secret part of her desperately wanted to wear that ring again. It felt fated, like it was made for her. Like it *belonged* with her, connecting her to Nash.

Nash stood, and Lily knew that this was the moment for the big kiss. He pulled her to him, and her breath caught.

Note to self: Try not to dry hump him this time.

Nash leaned down with a smile as she reached on her tiptoes to meet him. A simple brush of lips. Nothing too intense.

But his hand on the small of her back pulled her in as the other hand held her chin, caressing it. She breathed him in as he kissed her, letting herself melt against him.

He'd catch her if she let herself get carried away like last time.

She nipped at his lip, wanting to prolong this sugar-soaked bliss. The sweet moment of their mouths meeting.

For them, *and* for show.

Her heart pulled her toward him, not wanting to let go. A blanketing sensation came over her when he held her. Her stomach relaxed, and she could just *melt* into him. Like she was supposed to be there. She was safe.

Maybe for the first time in a long time.

He drew back, slowly releasing her lips. He was still so careful though. His touch was gentle on her cheek, stroking it.

The world saw her brash personality, her blunt humor, and thought she didn't need that gentleness.

But she craved it.

She'd rarely experienced it, and he was her sole supplier.

She pulled back, trying to regain her wits. She'd let herself get lost in the dream of him really wanting her.

I am marrying you, Lillian Parker, because I think you would be an excellent, albeit temporary, wife.

She might as well have that tattooed on her thigh because she'd remember it until the day she died.

But Nash's eyes never left her lips as she pulled away. God, she hoped that they did that a lot more in public.

She turned around with a smile, remembering they had an audience. Rose's mouth was open in shock, and Violet gathered her in a fierce hug.

"This is...so unlike you," Rose said, her mouth still hanging open.

"You know me," Lily said with a shrug she hoped was convincing. "I can change spur of the moment."

"Oh, stop being so negative." Violet tapped Rose's arm and gave Lily another bear hug and squealed. "You know she's had a crush on him since she was a kid. Nash is different."

Gray and Jack grabbed Nash in a bro-hug, teasing him about *finally* joining the family, but his eyes met Lily's with a questioning glance.

Ah, fuck.

Rose enveloped Lily in a tight hug. "I'm so happy for you, Lilybug."

Lily noticed that the Donnellys all sat at the table, staring into their uneaten coconut curry.

"When I wore that ring"—Karen swirled her glass of white wine—"it complemented my olive skin tone. You might need to tan a bit, dear, so the gold doesn't look gaudy." She chugged the rest of the glass.

"I'm so shocked. Are you absolutely stunned?" Rose said, shaking Lily by the arms.

"Oh my gosh, it was so romantic the way he got down on one knee," Violet gushed and grabbed Lily's hand. "Holy clover, this ring is absolutely stunning. I can't even imagine what it must be like to wear a family antique like this. I'm *so* jealous."

Their excitement rang hollow in her ears, knowing that in another lifetime, she would have wanted to be Nash's *real* wife. Had she wanted to settle down in Fairwick Falls, have a family, and never leave.

But that wasn't what she wanted in this life, right?

Nash poured a round of celebratory drinks, and they all settled in the library with dessert, except for Jeremy who had gone to make himself a coffee.

"So, when did you two really start dating? Tell us the whole story." Violet wiggled in her chair. She was a complete romantic, and Lily didn't want to disappoint her.

"Well"—Lily looked over at Nash—"you tell it so well, honey bear."

Nash choked on his champagne, caught off guard by the nickname she'd invented. He dabbed at his mouth, recovering. "Lily and I had a run-in at Bloom—"

"He couldn't keep his hands off of me," Lily said with enthusiasm, perching on the arm of Nash's chair.

His hand landed on her hip and squeezed. "That's not exactly how I remember it, poodlekins. I was a perfect gentleman, as always."

Poodlekins? The fuck?

"Except when no one else was around," she interrupted. "You should see the little love notes he would write me, signed from 'Your Smoopiest Lil' Cuddle Bear'."

Nash squeezed her hip, biting the inside of his cheek as they both tried not to laugh.

Violet cooed with wide eyes. "Love notes?"

"Yes, with little construction paper cards he made himself. He even made a replica of Bloom out of construction paper that said 'Where love *blooms*'." She swallowed a snort of wicked delight.

"Uh…" Nash sat up straighter. "It was a very manly construction paper project."

"*Then* he asked me to be his girlfriend by serenading me with a Celine Dion classic, wearing only a red bow tie, and carrying a bouquet of roses in front of his giant—"

Karen gasped.

"All right, that's enough," Nash said, clearing his throat and pulling Lily onto his lap. "Don't believe a word this one tells you," he said, squeezing her to him, kissing her cheek.

Heaven. Pure goosebump-y heaven to have his lips and the scratch of his five o'clock shadow brush her cheek. She leaned into him so he lingered, and she wiggled her bare feet with happiness.

"Why didn't you say anything?" Violet said with large eyes. Thank god for Violet's baby deer-like naïveté. Lily was sure Jeremy and Becky were on to them, but at least she had a couple of people fooled.

"And what changed your mind to stay in Fairwick Falls?

Violet's been awfully upset at the idea of you leaving," Jack asked.

"Yes, what changed your mind?" Jeremy echoed with a mocking voice.

Violet gasped. "You're not pregnant, are you?"

"*Fuck* no," Lily barked out with a laugh and then caught herself. "I mean, no," she said primly, as Karen's face turned a fetching shade of beefsteak tomato.

"Why aren't you wearing shoes?" Karen demanded, unable to contain herself anymore.

Lily's bare feet wiggled as everyone stared.

"Then you couldn't see my new pedicure." She wiggled her toes with an impish smile. "Had to replace the Christmas green and red. Went with neon orange this time." The silver toe ring on her middle toe winked in the evening light of the library.

"This is a shoe family," Karen said, firmly setting her after-dinner dessert on the coffee table, sputtering. "We do not walk around barefoot with toe rings in January in a house that predates the Pennsylvania Constitution. You will not bring this historic family down with your hippie dippy, no meat, no shoes, no problem attitude. We Donnellys have a responsibility to this community, and you are not cut out for it."

Nash lifted Lily onto her feet and stood up. "I think it's time for you to go, Mother. We'll see you in two weeks."

Nash escorted his mother out of the library, but she turned around in confusion. "What's in two weeks?"

Nash locked eyes with Lily. "That's when we're getting married."

Holy poodlekins.

Chapter Thirteen

LILY

They spent the next hour talking about wedding details over drinks, until Lily excused herself. Her stomach was tied in knots from the anxiety. She needed a minute to figure things out after lying to her two favorite people in the entire world.

Lily hobble-walked to her bedroom. Just needed a minute to get her head on straight in the safety of her own room.

But she stopped short when she saw Jeremy standing in the middle of *her* bedroom.

"What the fuck are you doing in here?" she barked.

The ball of hair gel and bad choices turned toward her, wearing an almost-human grin. "An unusual arrangement for adults who are dating. Sleeping in separate rooms."

"I keep an odd schedule." *Somewhat true.* "Nash gets up early, so we sleep apart. It doesn't mean anything about our relationship."

"Hmm." He wandered around the room, making himself at home even though it was *her* fucking space. "Part of me thinks this is all *too* coincidental. You're a pawn being used for his little game."

"*You're* a giant bag of *dicks* that needs to get the fuck out of my room," Lily said, raising her voice. Red tinged the corners of her eyes.

Jeremy held up a neon purple vibrator that was lying on her messy bed. "See, it's things like these that make me think you and Nash aren't quite so happy."

Lily was about to launch herself at him, nails aimed at his eyeballs, when a loud voice thundered behind her.

"What the fuck are you doing?" Nash's voice called out from behind Lily as he rushed into the room and, in a flash, wrenched the vibrator out of Jeremy's hand and had him pinned against the wall by his neck. Nash fumed at him, murder in his eyes. "How fucking dare you, you little weasel. What are you even doing in here?"

Jeremy sneered with cold hatred. "Your little sl—"

"Shut up," Nash spat, cold and hateful. "You will never set foot in this house again. You will never *touch* anything in this house ever again."

She'd never seen him so furious.

"Okay, okay." Jeremy tapped Nash's arm. Nash let him fall, and Jeremy rubbed his throat as he walked out of the room. "I'll be around, though. And I'll definitely be watching for any slips." Jeremy walked past Lily with a chilling smile. She shuddered.

"Are you okay?" Nash said, running his hands along her arms.

"I guess, but I'll need to set fire to that vibrator now." Lily shuddered. It registered that Nash had now seen her vibrator, maybe even touched it. "This has been a weird night."

He nodded, looking dazed. "Good thing we only have to do it once."

Lily pulled Nash into a hug and whispered in his ear. "Two weeks?"

"Like I said"—he kissed her cheek as he pulled back,

glancing at the doorway—"I can't wait to marry you." He cupped her cheek, running his thumb slowly back and forth.

Nash bent to her ear. "Keep pretending this is real until I say otherwise. I want to check something after everyone leaves." He brushed his nose along her cheekbone. "Okay?"

She nodded. Shivers ran down Lily's arms, even knowing this was all a show.

Why did she always get tongue-tied when he did that? Usually she was quick to joke, make others laugh, but he overwhelmed her with his size and his scent and how much she desperately wanted him.

They saw everyone out after lots of squealing from Violet. Rose had already sent an itinerary for the next two weeks to get everything ready.

As Lily picked up the glasses and plates in the library, Nash strode in but stopped suddenly. "You've been on your feet all day. Didn't the doctor say to rest? I don't want my wife injured on our wedding day," he said loudly.

Why was he being so weird? "Doctor Ali said I should strengthen it, the bastard. I'm going to get the dishes started."

"I'll be there in a minute."

Lily had made a valiant effort on the first third of the fancy china dishes by the time Nash came in. He pulled up a stool for her.

"Sit. I'll wash, you dry," he said, rolling up his sleeves. "I looked at the camera feed in my home security system." He whispered in her ear over the clatter of dishes and she felt that sizzling pull toward him.

"You have cameras installed?" *Uh-oh.* She thought back to all the times she'd hopped around the living room not wearing pants.

"I don't check it regularly, only when something seems off."

Noted. No more underwear parties in common spaces.

"I don't have one in the guest room. Just where anything valuable might be, and in the exits." He handed her a large serving plate to dry.

The rush of water over the sink covered their low voices. "What were you looking for?"

"I wanted to see where Jeremy wandered. Wouldn't be the first time he planted bugs or cameras to blackmail someone." He picked up another dish to scrub. "He wandered around the first floor before he went into your room. But I can't know for certain if your room has a camera or mic in it because—"

"No cameras in there," Lily said, already understanding the risk.

He scrubbed at a stubborn spot on a plate, putting all his meticulous focus into it.

I bet that's how he'd have sex. Not missing a detail. Being thorough with every single ounce of his six-foot-five attention. Kissing him earlier had turned her brain into a permanent, ongoing, sexy slideshow.

As she clenched at the thought of what a very attentive Nash might do to her, he interrupted her thoughts.

"So you'll need to move into my room tonight."

Lily reared around in surprise, spinning on the stool. Sleep next to her walking spank bank? *No way.* "I will not."

"Yes, you will." He glowered at her with authority, brows furrowed.

Oh fuck, why is that hotter? Go away, lady boner.

"We don't know what he put in there. He could be watching you sleep or undress," he whisper-yelled at her over the running water, his jaw clenching.

Lily stood to whisper-yell back, her nose next to his chest. "Then he'll get a *free show* because I can't make it up to the second floor yet."

"I'll carry you," Nash said as if it was the most obvious solution in the world.

That is a dreamily dangerous idea. "Every time I need to go upstairs to sleep, you're going to carry me?"

"Or I can have a lift installed. Should only take a couple days."

"Absolutely not." Lily went back to drying the forgotten plate in her hands.

"He already mentioned he'd try to catch us in a lie. At this point, we'd be sleeping together."

"Nash, I'm not going to sleep in your room," Lily puffed out in a fierce whisper.

"Why?" His voice raised in irritation.

Because I'd lose every ounce of my fucking sanity. I'm having a hard time remembering this is all fake as it is.

"Because then I couldn't masturbate myself to sleep," she yelled finally, setting the plate down with a clatter.

He let out a low growl as he straightened and busied himself with another plate. "We'd make it work. You can fall asleep first and I'll go in, um, after the fact." He ground out the words, his eyes never left the serving plate he scrubbed.

"I will not be told what to do, and when to do it." She snatched the next plate from him.

"We need to move you," he said in a whisper again, turning off the water.

She spun away from him and hopped off the stool. He could do the rest of the dishes if he was going to pretend he ruled her life.

"Lily," he said sternly.

If she ever gave in to every single one of her fantasies and pounced him, she was going to specifically request that voice.

He caught her around the waist as she hobbled across the large kitchen, leaning into her ear as if he was nuzzling her neck. "We have to pretend as if we are a couple on the first floor. He might be trying to blackmail me."

Lily stopped in her tracks, staring ahead, panting from her frustration and the nearness of him, at the heat of him along her back.

"Fine," she said with a bite in her tone. "So like I told you"—she said loudly and slowly, as if talking to a class of kindergartners—"my knee hurts tonight, and I can't manage the stairs without you in the morning. I'm going to sleep in the guest room, but don't worry." She sent him a cheeky grin, whirling around. "I'll think of you the *whole* time I'm trying to fall asleep. Unless you'd like to watch?"

She raised an eyebrow as his cheeks turned pink. She'd never get tired of making this man blush.

A low growl of irritation sighed out of him as he locked eyes with her. *Ha*.

"Have a good night," he said, kissing her cheek slowly and going back to the dishes.

Lily changed into comfortable clothes and came back to a text from Nash.

> **NASH**
>
> I don't like the thought of you in there and him watching you.

Lily turned off the light. *No red or green lights blinking that I can see.* She flipped the lights back on.

> **LILY**
>
> don't be such a worry warthog
>
> it wouldn't be the first time i've slept on camera with a strange man watching me

A pile of plates crashed to the floor in the kitchen.

> kiiiiddiiiing
>
> god you're so easy to rile up

That was the fun of him. Just by being her full Lily-ness, she endlessly caught his attention.

> I'd really prefer you sleep upstairs.
>
> It's a large bed. You won't know I'm there.

Ha, right.
She'd read that romance book.
She'd definitely end up dry humping him in her sleep. Sleep Lily was absolute trash for tall, stern, *g-g-g-good to the bone* guys.

> don't worry, if there's a mic, i'll put on a great show for him

> I'm afraid to even ask.

Lily opened the side drawer of the bedside table and perused her vibrators. She needed something *loud*.

She took out a teal bullet vibrator and turned it up all the way. Just for good measure, she added out loud for any mics in the room, "If I can't sleep with him, I can fantasize about my future husband."

Lily moaned loudly, doing her best impression of an adult film star. She turned the vibrator up even higher. "Oh Nash," she moaned loudly.

> NASH
>
> Stop that right now.

Ha.

> you, dear sir, are not the boss of me

She moaned even louder, longer, and fuck it. This was all kind of turning her on, so she let the vibrator drift over her nipples, enjoying the sensation.

"*Yes*, Daddy Nash," she laughed as she said it, knowing how much he'd hate that.

> WHAT did you just call me?

"Yes, yes, *ughn*," she yelled out. "Right there." She hovered over her clit, teasing it. "Nash, more," she pleaded.

> Lily, you should stop right now.

She paused to text him back. Wanting to play a dangerous game.

> maybe i like torturing you 😈

She pictured Nash's face glowering at her as she closed her eyes. The moans felt real as she thrust against the vibrator over her sleep shorts.

He'd probably be stern and unyielding. Thrusting into her hard and fast as his usually perfect hair flopped in front of his face. He'd *claim* her, biting into her shoulder.

"Please, Nash, fuck me," she cried out, in the moment.

The door to her room slammed open as Nash stormed in, still wearing his dress shirt and slacks.

Before she could register what was happening, he threw her over his shoulder, the vibrator still buzzing in her hand, and thundered up to the second floor.

"You don't want your future *wife* fucking her—"

"I said"—his hand slapped her ass as she bounced on his shoulder—"stop being a brat."

He tossed her on the bed and she landed in the pillowy duvet, ass first.

He looked mad and horny as hell, like he'd finally snapped.

He knelt over her, forearms caging her in as he caught the vibrator that nearly bounced out of bed. "If you're going to moan my name, I'd prefer you do it in our bed, *wife*."

Oh.

God.

Damn.

She whimpered at that word, biting her lip with need. His *wife*.

There wouldn't be any cameras or mics up here. This was all just for *her*.

For them.

The vibrator buzzing in his hand landed on her nipple, and she arched into it. He lay panting over her, not moving his hand.

His face was a war of emotions, fighting desire and anger, as he stared down at her from an inch above her face. She moaned, trying to bite it back as the vibrations on her nipple were winding her up and up.

She didn't want any of this to stop.

His eyes were transfixed on her lips. They were caught in a moment that felt outside of time.

Don't stop. Don't go.

His forehead met hers as she licked her lips, desperate for him. Desperate for any other part of himself he'd share with her.

He'd planted his knee between her thighs. Her fingers grazed up his inner thigh along his expensive slacks, and his cock was mouthwateringly hard. She clenched at the outline of it.

At how much he clearly wanted her.

Fuck she wanted him so badly.

"We shouldn't do this," he ground out, his nose grazing hers with longing. He moved the vibrator, teasing her nipple back and forth, back and forth.

She moaned, arching into his touch.

She grazed his cock again, matching his rhythm, teasing it back and forth. Her eyes were full of challenge. "Tell me to stop."

"I can't," he panted against her cheek, looking tortured.

She moaned on purpose, rubbing her hand along his cock as she stared straight into his amber eyes.

She reached for him, but he was lightning-quick, pinning her hands above her head.

She arched into the vibrator on her nipple as his steely glare pinned her. He lay panting over her, watching.

"Need to protect you. But all I want is..." His nose drew a line along her cheek as she closed her eyes, leaning into him.

He pulled back, moving the vibrator down her stomach, over her sleep shorts, and landing straight on her clit.

"This," he sighed against her cheek.

She arched, moaning and thrusting against it.

"Say my name, Lily." He caught her lobe between his teeth, and pleasure showered down her spine.

She fought to keep her eyes open. Her hips ground against the vibrator. "Yes, Nash, more."

She let herself drown in the impossibility of what was happening. Nash making her so wet she'd soaked her panties through. The hard plane of the vibrator against her clit as he teased her with it.

"Eyes on me," he ordered, and his square jaw was set in a firm line. "Look at me when I make you come."

Fuck yes. That stern voice was back.

Her shirt had bunched up her stomach and he lowered to her stomach, biting at it softly.

She was so wet, she knew it had come through her shorts.

"Lily," he sighed as he kissed her stomach, lapping at her skin between nips. Her hands ached to wring through his hair, push his head down farther between her thighs. "Can't stop thinking about what you sound like when you come."

He drove the vibrator up and down her pussy outside her shorts.

"Oh fuck, oh fuck," she moaned, arching against him. His hand still held her wrists as he nipped his way up to the underside of her breasts.

Locking eyes with her, he nuzzled her shirt out of the way, exposing her breasts to the air. The buzzing teased her clit, and she was about to lose her mind.

Nash looked like a wolf about to eat his sheep dinner. His tongue ran a circle around her nipples, and she cried out his name. He sucked hard, flicking it with his tongue.

He pulled the vibrator away and she moaned at the loss of it.

"But since you were a brat, I'm not letting you come," he murmured against her chest, "until you scream my name properly. Until you *beg* me." She bucked her hips, missing the vibrations.

What...what did he want? She'd already said Nash. God, the pleasure of his beard scratching her breast was too much. Too him.

He laid the vibrator so the end barely touched her clit. Another wave of pleasure built as his fingers stroked along her seam.

"What...I don't..." She writhed her head from side to side in pleasure. "What do I call you," she panted.

His fingers dipped under the side of her sleep shorts, under her panties, as molten-hot pleasure poured down her spine.

He slipped a finger in her, and heady, lusty pleasure wrapped around her as she clenched around him. He groaned.

"You're a smart woman," he ground out. He slid two fingers inside and crooked them. Her breasts arched as if on command.

He was playing her like a fiddle.

And she *needed* him, wanted to fuck every part of him.

His fingers slid up to her clit, circling there slowly as she moaned, locking eyes with him.

"Fuck me, husband," she pleaded.

He moaned at her words, closing his eyes in pleasure with a tortured smile. He leaned over her, whispering in her ear. "Good girl."

Goosebumps flooded her arms and she threw her head back with a sob as he drilled into her clit, fucking her mercilessly with his fingers.

Lily saw white blotching stars as her entire body spasmed against his hands. He didn't stop as she screamed *husband*, with wave after wave cresting on her orgasm, soaking up every drop of pleasure.

Fuck.

Me.

She connected into her body, pulsing with pleasure as she rode the final wave of the best orgasm she'd ever had.

She slammed her eyes closed as aftershocks twitched her body, recovering from a literal dream of Nash's hands and mouth on her.

As her heartbeat came back inside her body, she fluttered her eyelashes open and saw the vibrator beside her, now off.

She was lust-drunk and wanted to do that seven more times. Wanted to take him into her mouth and taste him.

Nash stalked through his bedroom. His cock was hard, and he looked torn as he searched through his dresser.

She lazily turned on her side with a cat-like smile. "I think your turn is next." She patted the space next to her.

But then she registered his expression.

He looked tortured. "That was a mistake. I'm sorry—"

Panic shot through her body, replacing the feel good sex hormones as she shot up. "If you say I'm not your type *one more time*—"

"It's not that," he interrupted. "I just...we can't. That was a mistake. I shouldn't get—" He cleared his throat, not looking at her. "I can't get attached. I'm going for a run."

He walked out of the room without another word. A minute later, the treadmill in the basement started.

She flopped into bed with frustration.

This was going to be the longest two weeks of her goddamn life.

Chapter Fourteen

LILY

A sea of white tulle surrounded Lily as she sat, dejected, in the bridal shop dressing room.

Maybe I should throw on the next one that fits and be done with it.

But who didn't love wearing the shit out of a pretty dress?

Okay and a tiiiiiny part of me wants to impress Nash.

She groaned as she looked at the pile of dresses. Nothing against Cooperstown Bridals-R-Us, but they didn't exactly have the gown of her dreams.

As she grabbed a random dress to get it over with, a knock sounded on the dressing room door.

"We found one more. Are you decent?" Violet called.

"Eh, enough." Lily had on a corset bra that went to her navel and yoga pants.

Violet opened the dressing room door. "I think we found the one," she said with a mischievous smile.

"I can't do this anymore," Lily whined in exasperation. "Just duct tape some white taffeta around me and shove me down the aisle."

"Close your eyes!" Rose yelled out as Lily rounded the corner into the bridal shop boudoir.

She clamped her eyes shut as Violet tugged her forward. "If it's another dress that makes me look like a stumpy cupcake, Violet has to bake me pumpkin muffins for six months."

"Ready? Aaaaaand surprise!" Violet and Rose called out at the same time as Lily opened her eyes.

A gorgeous, chic, and bohemian dress hung in front of her.

"Whoa," Lily whispered slowly. "I didn't see this out here."

"Doesn't it look familiar?" Rose said with a knowing smile.

Lily walked around it, taking the dress in. "Kind of."

The dress had long, flowing silken sleeves and an empire waist that would suit Lily's small frame while still being generous enough to accommodate her curves.

She touched the fabric. It looked old, like it was vintage. The satin wasn't bright white anymore but had turned to a cream that would look good against her peachy skin.

As her hand connected with the silk, a picture flashed back to her.

"Oh my gosh. This is Mom's," Lily whispered.

She barely remembered her mother, but she'd memorized her face from poring over her parents' wedding pictures.

By the time Lily had come around, her mother was in the deep throes of her demons. But she'd always remembered the striking beauty of her mother on her wedding day.

"I've had it since we cleaned out Dad's house." Violet sniffled as she wrapped an arm around Lily's waist. "I brought it to surprise you. The owner said she could do the alterations if you wanted this instead."

Rose ran her hand down Lily's hair. "We want you to have this."

"But..." Lily whispered, her fingers catching on the gauzy sleeves. It was a touch hippie and bohemian, like her.

A mist clouded over her eyes. The last person to wear this would have been her mom. Violet and Rose had actual memories of their mom, but she could have this one thing for herself. "You don't mind?"

"Bell sleeves aren't my thing, anyway," Violet said with a teary smile. "I want to be a princess goddess on my wedding day."

"You'll look stunning in it. Go try it on." Rose nudged her with her hip.

As the cool lining slid over Lily's curves and the silky sleeves whispered against her skin, she knew this dress was the one.

She stepped out to show her sisters.

Violet's eyes misted over as tears ran down her cheeks. "You look so much like her."

"No, I don't," Lily scoffed. "I'm blonde. I'm short. Look at these hips." She shook her hips from side to side.

"But you have her vibe." Rose closed the tiny buttons on the back of the dress. "Her *Screw the world, I'll do what I want in a gorgeous dress* vibe."

Lily stood on the pedestal and looked at her sisters in the mirror. Her stomach turned at the thought of lying to her two favorite humans on the planet.

"He is going to drool when he sees you in that," Rose said, arching an eyebrow. "Your boobs look great."

"Are you guys taking a honeymoon?" Violet fussed with the train of the dress.

"Uh," Lily stalled. *Shit, we haven't talked about it.* "I'm not sure. He's really busy with work right now."

Not a lie. Let's see how many of those I can rack up.

"And it would be hard for me to travel right now with the knee brace." Also not a lie. *Great job, me!*

"What's all the rush, anyway?" Rose asked, playing with Lily's hair as though she was doing a wedding updo.

"You're going to beat me to the altar, and I've been engaged three whole weeks longer than you," Violet said, wiggling her own engagement ring.

Fuck. Fuck. Fuck.

"You know Nash, he wants to get everything settled. Very no-nonsense. Plus, I'm not really into all the fuss of a wedding."

"It was kind of worth it to see Karen's face turn into a self-righteous steaming peach," Rose said, snorting. "I've already talked to her *three times* this week. She won't believe me that you don't want the country clubhouse. At this rate, though, it might be in Pop's Diner if you don't decide soon enough."

"Why not do it at the store?" Violet said.

Lily almost laughed it away but...*There's an idea*. It'd be great for their social media posts.

"It would be a hell of a lot prettier than the Fairwick County Municipal Courthouse," Rose drawled with an arched eyebrow in the mirror.

Violet clasped her hands in excitement. "We can move all the tables, put in chairs, you can get married in front of the floral wall. It'd be like our family was there with us."

Lily always felt the ghosts of past generations of her family surrounding her in all the best ways when she was in the store.

"And it's available, and we can make it look cute." Violet clapped her hands together, the top knot of curls on her head bouncing from side to side. "Oh my gosh, this is the best idea I've ever had."

"But remember, there's no pressure. Just have fun and make it what you want," Rose said as she played with Lily's hair.

Violet and Lily stared at her.

Lily leaned in, waiting for the catch. "What just came out of your mouth?"

Rose fussed with her train. "It's your wedding. Not everything has to be about showcasing Bloom, Lily."

"Are you ill?" Lily said, cocking her head at Rose.

"No, I'm feeling some feelings." Rose wiped her eyes. "I don't know, seeing you in our mom's dress is making me feel all sorts of things and I hate it and let's change the subject."

"Rose is a human after all," Lily cooed as Violet snickered.

"Next thing you know, she'll be saying she loooooves us," Violet teased.

Rose shook her head with a smile. "You guys are the worst. I'll go get the owner and have her stab you extra hard with the fitting pins."

"I'll put the other dresses back," Violet offered.

Lily was left alone in the dressing area, and she finally allowed herself to take in the sheen of satin against her skin—and the one thing she could finally have that nobody else had with her mom.

This wedding was starting to feel real rather than like a sham of convenience.

Did she want it to be real?

Lily Parker—the queen of indecision, of temporary everything, of hit-it-and-quit-it, mistress of "let's keep it casual, no contract"—was going to marry the man she'd loved for fifteen years.

And maybe, just maybe, she wanted it to be real.

NASH

White lilies.

Nash rubbed his fingers across his lips, smirking. Of *course* she included white lilies in arrangements the bank bought from Bloom every week.

He'd been staring at the white lilies across from his office for an hour, imagining Lily's face as she arched under him. Of the perfection she looked like when she came. Of her scent that he'd hated to wash away.

It had been a week since *the incident*. Work had been busy, and Lily's schedule was endlessly crazy, so they hadn't seen each other except in the bed at night. He'd taken to punishing himself in his home gym until she was asleep.

Less temptation that way.

What would she look like naked? He'd pictured it a thousand times, but now he couldn't *stop* thinking about it.

He could *not* get involved with her.

She was leaving as soon as the ink dried on their divorce papers. He knew her. She could barely make a choice for dinner, let alone be a permanent resident in a small town four hours from anywhere.

And then there was the unending question mark that was his brother. He seemed to be around every corner. Nash had spotted him having coffee with one of the board members yesterday.

The bastard.

Enough of this mulling. He needed to talk out his frustrations today, and he knew the place to go.

But first, he'd indulge himself with a pit stop at Bloom. He'd have to see Lily, given she was always there. They'd have to kiss and pretend to be a couple. *But some things can't be helped*, he thought with anticipation.

He bundled his wool pea coat around him, blocking the late January chill as he jogged across the street to the Fairwick Falls town square.

He grasped the cold brass of Bloom's antique doorknob and yanked it open. He stepped into the fresh springtime smell of the flower shop.

Nash's eyes roamed the empty store, and Pearl, Bloom's new employee with enough tattoos to make a longshoreman jealous, sat at the counter reading a book, not looking up.

"Welcome," she called with little enthusiasm, her eyes never leaving the book as she flipped a page. The spring-scented air that he now associated with Lily surrounded him. That herby spring green scent that smelled like hope.

"Is Lily here?"

"Your betrothed?" Pearl said in a bored voice, flicking her eyes up from her book. "Wedding dress shopping. Can I help you?"

"Oh, right." He'd completely forgotten about her plans. "Just picking up a couple of bouquets."

The bright coolers were full of beautiful arrangements. He opted for two smaller bouquets of daffodils and lilies.

As Pearl rang up his purchase, watercolor sketches along the counter caught his attention.

"These are nice. Are they new?" Bloom sold handmade gifts on consignment from local vendors, but he hadn't seen art like this before. He picked one up, thinking Lily would like it. It reminded him of her.

"Yeah. Lily finished those last week."

Nash startled, as if she had read his mind.

She'd used bright watercolors to create sloping wildflower fields. Gorgeous, colorful wildflowers placed this way and that like an English garden on steroids.

"She said she missed wildflowers most in winter. That they were her favorite flower." Pearl shrugged. "Wanna buy one?"

"No," he said, putting it down but then thinking better of it.

"Wait, yes. I'll take a couple, but let's keep it a secret between us."

He tucked the cards in his pocket, a plan formulating in his head. Wildflowers *are her favorite flower.*

Go figure. She didn't love the stunning roses or lilies or dahlias that featured in all of her arrangements, but the flower that was free and wild and gorgeous beyond compare.

Just like her.

A SHORT DRIVE LATER, Nash pulled over on the low sloping hills of Fairwick Fall's cemetery. He liked to clean off his dad's headstone and have a heart-to-heart every few weeks.

The frozen grass crunched as he walked to his father's grave.

"Hey, Dad," he muttered, laying one of the bouquets on the headstone.

Leaves had accumulated there, and he wiped them away, shining it up as Bob Donnelly would have loved.

The ache inside of him was almost too much. He crouched, running his fingers over his father's name etched into the granite.

"Man, I wish you were here." He bit his lip to keep it from wobbling at the overwhelming loneliness. "Jeremy's up to something. You could always set him straight."

A shudder ran through him as a hard burst of wind came through.

"I'm getting married," he said suddenly. "Not sure if it's a good idea, but seems like my only option to not let you down and, uh"—he wiped his mouth as he laughed in spite of himself—"and I can't wait. It's Lily. You always liked her, I think. Called her 'that spunky kid of Frank's.'"

He stood. "Well, anyway. I still miss you." He put a hand on the granite and squeezed. Nash wasn't sure what the afterlife held, but it had to mean something that he felt closer to his dad when he was here. That he felt like he wasn't alone in all of it, and there was someone somewhere helping him shoulder the burden.

He tapped the headstone. "See you next month, Dad."

Nash walked fifty feet from the Donnelly section of the cemetery, toward more modest gravestones, and stopped in front of where his friend lay.

"Hey, Frank," Nash whispered.

Bouquets were placed along the modest headstone. Probably Lily, or one of the other people in town that had adored her father.

Frank Parker had been the life of any room he was in. He'd always offered a non-judgmental set of ears when Nash was getting his bearings at the bank after his dad died. Made him smile when he needed it most.

Nash dusted leaves and ice off of Frank's headstone. "I wish you'd come into my office with your Hawaiian shirt and flip-flops and yell at me about how more people in this town needed help. About how my dad would have been proud of whatever I'd done that week, even though I knew I could do better. I wish you'd trick me into buying you a piece of pie at Canon's Diner." Nash's voice caught with emotion. "It's been a sad year without you, but having your girls back in town has been a consolation."

Why was it so much easier to talk to your friends, to tell them how you really felt, once they were no longer there?

A twinge hit his heart at remembering the last time he'd seen Frank.

He'd stopped by the bank to talk with him, but Nash had been late to a zoning meeting for a new ATM.

I should have stopped.

He should have made time for him—like Frank made time for everyone else—but he'd been in a rush. Frank had waved him off with a carefree smile, saying he had a question about his finances but it could wait.

That was the last time he'd seen him alive.

Guilt churned through Nash's stomach. He should have known something was up. Frank never asked for help.

"I'm so sorry I didn't stop," he choked out. He wiped away a tear. "I could've helped, you know." His voice came out in a whisper.

He fiddled with the bouquet in his hands, his eyes filling. "Would've lent you all the money I had. You just had to ask."

A tear fell off his eyelash and dropped below as he blew out a long breath of regret.

Instead, Lily, Rose, and Violet had inherited an enormous tax debt after Frank had died suddenly in his sleep that night.

"But you always wanted to teach me lessons"—a hollow laugh shook his shoulders—"and I guess this was a good one: always, *always* make time for those you love."

He cleared his throat, suddenly nervous despite talking to a ghost. "I'm, um...I'm going to marry Lily?" He said it as a question, waiting for some sort of sign around him.

Frank would have thrown his head back in laughter, knowing what a spitfire Lily was.

But shockingly, the cemetery remained calm and quiet in the gray morning.

Nash crouched beside Frank's headstone, careful to stand beside, not on, his friend. "I don't believe in asking for permission. Lily's a grown woman with enough strong opinions to power a Dutch windmill." Nash laughed to himself. "But part of me thinks..." He looked around suddenly, worried somebody might overhear him.

"Part of me thinks maybe..." He chewed out the words. It felt important to at least be honest here. "Maybe it might be longer than a few months. Or I don't know, maybe I want it to be. Lily's gorgeous and smart. So funny and so big-hearted. I want to protect her, even though she's the last person that needs it." He set the bouquet of flowers on Frank's headstone. "She doesn't need protection. But she deserves it. Anyway..."

Nash chewed his cheek. "I wanted to ask if it was okay with you if I married her. And if it is, give me a sign. If it's not, well, let me know and I'll see what I can do."

He waited for something—lightning, a voice, anything—but he only heard a gust of whistling wind blowing over the lonely tombstones.

"I'll assume you're thinking about it. You never did like to be rushed," he said, smiling at the engraving along Frank's headstone.

Strands of ivy were engraved onto the sides around Frank's birth and death dates. Underneath where some people had "father" or "loving husband," Frank had arranged for an engraved sentence: *Don't worry, he's back with his love.*

Nash looked next to Frank's headstone at Lily's mom, Ivy, who had the same pretty bouquet as Frank's. Frank had changed after Ivy had died. He'd been a shell of a person for over a decade. It was only after many years that he'd finally gotten back to the gregarious man Nash remembered from his childhood.

"I don't know if I'm cut out for this love business, Frank, but I promise you I'll take care of her...however long we're together. And even after that, if she'll let me."

Nash walked to his car slowly, pondering how the loss of one person could make someone crumble.

Did he want that? Did he want a soulmate who took part of his soul with them?

He already felt lost when he wasn't with Lily, and this was only a temporary arrangement. A marriage of convenience.

Would he be strong enough to withstand her inevitably leaving him?

LILY

Makeup on point? Check. Hair on point? Check. Adorable floral wall with Bloom's neon sign perfectly framed behind me in the video? Check.

Lily stared at herself in the video preview on her laptop. She fluffed her long blonde waves, perfectly styled for her first call with KGM. Violet had a filming conflict, and Lily had assured Rose she could handle the call solo.

The glint of her engagement ring caught her eye in the camera preview. It felt good to take a break from the constant drumbeat of thinking about Nash, the wedding, or—*gulp*—the wedding night.

So she'd poured herself into work when she could.

She'd wow KGM with her charm, her humor, and they would brainstorm what a design partnership could look like.

KGM specialized in taking everyday household goods and elevating them. Their product collaborations had been featured in international press and viral social media accounts. Chic influencers used their gold-plated water glasses, or showed off their ottomans that looked like gigantic fluffy clouds. What they made led the home goods industry trends.

Lily had always crushed her kickoff calls with her freelance clients before she'd dedicated her last year to Bloom. She could charm the pants off the stuffiest corporate project manager.

The sound of someone joining the video call on the other end made her blood pump.

This was it: showtime. The chance to launch the biggest phase of her career yet.

A conference room full of disinterested, chic-looking creatives stared back at her. Her face looked garish in the video preview compared to their lounging in a brightly lit, high-end conference room.

Lily's smile grew brighter as a defense mechanism. "Hi, everyone!" she said in a bright, warm voice.

These are my people. We're all creatives. I can win them over.

"Lily. So glad we could chat for a few," a clipped British voice sounded out at the far end of the table. "I'm Rachel. We emailed."

"Oh, yes. It's so nice to meet you," Lily said warmly. "I'm coming to you from Bloom Headquarters in Fairwick Falls, Pennsylvania." Lily gestured to the Bloom sign behind her with a sparkling smile.

Unimpressed silence greeted her.

Rachel shifted in her seat as she checked her phone. "Yes, we're so excited to see the concepts you have for our discussion."

The blood ran cold in Lily's veins. "I'm sorry, the what?"

"That's why we scheduled this twenty-minute call, so we could talk through your ideas and then see if they're a good fit for our fall lineup."

Oh fuck.

"Oh," Lily said slowly. Rachel hadn't mentioned any of this. "I like to work collaboratively with my partners," Lily said, a spark occurring to her. "I'd rather come up with something together, so there's not too much Bloom in the mix."

She hoped her smile hid the spin cycle of nerves in her stomach. Three coffees this morning had been a bad idea.

Rachel blinked quickly and sat straighter. "Oh. I suppose if that's part of your process. I wouldn't have scheduled an entire cross-functional kickoff."

"Lily, give us a minute," said a man with a thick European accent, maybe Swedish. He muted the speakerphone as they leaned together, heads bent over the conference table. The rest of the room typed away on laptops, not meeting Lily's eyes on the video screen.

The impossibly European man in all black and circular glasses finally reached for the speakerphone. "You know what? It's fine. We'll have a smaller creative kickoff next week."

"I can have some concepts ready in a couple of days if you'd like me to take a first stab at it. Then we can chat about it," Lily offered, starting to panic.

"You can Jammr it to me or Joanna, or send over a preptock, if that's easier for you," another young woman said into the speakerphone.

"For sure, I can...um..." *What the fuck is a jammer or a preptock? Am I having a stroke right now? Are they saying real words?* "I can share them in a couple of days." *Fuck, fuck, fuck.*

"Great, talk then." Rachel hung up the video call without another word. Lily stared back at her own face on the video screen.

What the fuck just happened?

She needed to jammer something? What the fuck was a jammer?

How has so much changed in the one year I've been out of the corporate design world?

And she was supposed to come up with a whole product line by herself that met their standards in a couple of days?

"I can do this, I can do this," Lily whispered in a shaking voice to herself as she slammed the laptop screen down.

The backdoor of Bloom opened and Rose's click-clacking heeled footsteps echoed through the store. Rose checked her watch. "You're already done?"

Rose had sent her about a million and a half prep texts this morning, double checking that Lily would be okay to handle the call alone. And like a dummy, Lily had said, *"Of course I can handle it. I'm a creative talking with other creatives. I know what I'm doing."*

Boy, was the vegan egg substitute on her face now.

"Yeah, you know. We wanted a quick 'get to know you' call." Lily shrugged, lying.

She already had a million and a half things to do today. What was one more?

Lily glanced at the empty flower coolers that needed more arrangements. She felt this unending pressure to be a factory instead of refilling her creative well. Pearl was an okay helper in the shop, but Lily didn't trust her with the artistic side of the business. *I'd somehow end up with all black arrangements.*

Rose tapped away on her phone, half listening. "Good to know it went well. What were the next steps?"

"They are very interested to see my ideas," Lily said with a proud smile.

"Great. Don't forget we need that garden concept for the *Plant Parent SOS* shoot in a couple days."

Fuck. She hadn't even started that yet. Plus KGM now, and the wedding, and the shop arrangements.

"I can't do everything around here, Rose," Lily snapped. Panic came through in her voice. "I feel like I'm doing every fucking thing. *I'm* the one doing all of the planter designs for

Violet's show. *I'm doing the arrangements for the store that are getting so fucking boring.*" Tears pulled at the edges of her eyes. "Plus all the stuff we sold last May at our fundraiser that I have to deliver for Valentine's Day—the busiest time of a florist's year. Plus the social media, *plus* a whole new fucking product line for the biggest company we could ever partner with."

She panted as Rose looked at her with wide eyes. "That's a lot, Lily. You're doing a lot."

"Fuck right, I am," Lily said, hitting her hand on the table. "No one works as hard as I do."

Rose was uncharacteristically soothing as she rubbed Lily's back. "I thought you liked having lots of projects to keep you challenged."

"Now it's keeping me exhausted. And you know, there's the whole, like, fucking...wedding next week."

"You're dealing with a lot." Rose sounded like she was talking to a spooked horse. *Which is kind of how I feel, honestly.* "How about we bump up the interviews for your second-in-command? We'll do them right after the wedding. You're handling a lot and our business is expanding. We're going to need somebody to fill your shoes on the day-to-day."

I'll be leaving in a few months, anyway. Better to find someone to take her place now. "I think that's a good idea."

"Consider it handled," Rose said with a smile, running a hand down Lily's hair. "Can I help you with anything today?"

A gleam hit Lily's eye. "Just—" Her eyes floated toward the door.

"An oat milk latte and a vegan lavender donut from Fox & Forrest? Got it," Rose said with a knowing smile as she lovingly pinched Lily's cheek.

Having your older sister for your boss sometimes came in handy.

NASH

In the last week, Nash had found himself coming home earlier and earlier when he knew Lily would be there.

Because, he could admit, he enjoyed pretending to be a couple on the first floor with her. He'd searched the first floor, but there was still a chance a hidden mic or camera was placed out of sight.

"Stop beeping at me, you pestilent Swedish douche canoe!"

Lily's voice rang through the house as Nash entered from the garage. "Is that my future wife's dulcet, sweet voice I hear?" He chuckled. He walked past three paintings drying along the hallway and a pile of fake flowers that had been beheaded.

"I hate your microwave," she called as he entered the kitchen.

"I know, sweetheart. It's not the first time you've called it a douche canoe." He tapped the 'stop all the beeping button' on the microwave, and walked toward her.

His favorite part of coming home. An excuse to kiss her. Touch her.

Anything.

She was in overalls and a lacy bralette, her hair tied back with a handkerchief and paint streaks on her face. He reached for her, but she put up a hand. "Careful, I'm covered in paint."

His hands framed her face. "I think this should be safe enough."

Her mouth curved into a simpering smile as he bent to kiss her. He already thought of her as his wife, despite the fact they weren't married yet.

It's why it had slipped out during *the incident*.

He let himself linger as his lips met hers, breathing in the floral cloud that followed her. They melted against each other when they kissed, and Nash angled her head so he could take more. She sucked his bottom lip into her mouth and ran her tongue along it. Lust surged into his cock. A little moan escaped her mouth as he ran his fingers up into her silky sunshine hair.

A mental flash of her under him, coming from his fingers two weeks ago, had him pulling back. God, it was like defusing a bomb every time he touched her. He was a hair trigger from blowing up and hauling her upstairs again.

"Hi," she sighed against his lips.

"Hi," he echoed back with a dopey grin on his face. In many ways, First Floor Lily and Nash felt real to him. More like himself.

In their bedroom on the second floor, they were in a strange limbo of wanting each other, but keeping their distance.

"How was your day? Apart from fascist microwaves? And why did you murder a bunch of fake flowers?" He pointed to the random pile of flowers.

She stretched, looking tired. "I've been working all day on these concepts for a potential partnership with a big company. I'm all in my head about it. Everything I've made has been shit."

She waved a hand to a stunning mixed media painting on an easel. Fake flowers burst out through the canvas as if coming to life in bold unearthly colors. "See? Reductive, uninspiring," she huffed.

"What painting are *you* looking at?" He walked toward it to get a better look. "This is...cool. I'm sad I can't think of a better word. People would love something like this."

"It's not cool," she groused. "It's inspired by a 2023 fashion line theme featured in Vogue combined with a Rauschenbergian mixed media take on florals. Reductive."

She said it as though *she* was reductive.

He leaned against the kitchen counter, blown away by her. He pulled her between his legs.

"Hey," he said, forcing her to meet his eyes. "You are an artistic genius, Lillian Parker. The best part of seeing your work is not knowing what you'll do next." He kissed her paint-covered wrist. "Whose idea was it to first have Jack and Violet film together and then edit the video into a viral sensation?"

He paused, knowing the answer.

She rolled her eyes. "Me."

"And who not only redesigned a flower shop, but had multiple magazine articles about the excellent design of Bloom's brand?"

A smile snuck onto her face. "Me, I guess. But they were local."

"And who, pray tell, has made *every one* of her brides cry when they saw their bouquets?" She'd been so proud when she'd told him.

Her cheeks were wide with an embarrassed grin. "Oh fine, fine. Me."

He kissed her cheek. "You are Lillian Fucking Parker. Don't forget it."

She blushed as she nodded to herself. "I won't."

He'd started seeing a new side of her, shyer, more vulnerable since they'd decided on their scheme.

He was sad to say it only made him want her more.

"Ready for bed?" He was wiped after the longest, most boring conversation with two board members over racketball. He'd almost gotten them on his side to change the bylaws.

Lily stretched, cat-like. He wished she wasn't wearing paint-covered clothes so he could crowd her and kiss her like he wanted to. Press her curves against him.

"Yeah, I guess. My brain is fried for today. Plus, tomorrow is the wedding rehearsal," she said with a nervous wiggle.

She took the steps up to their bedroom slowly, but was more stable than yesterday. "The doctor said I should schedule physical therapy for next week."

He followed behind her so he could catch her if she fell. "You're doing great," he said, trying to avoid staring at her ass. His hands itched to pinch it, like a neanderthal.

Normally he went downstairs to run and work out his lust, but he was absolutely beat today.

Once their feet landed on the second floor, a switch flipped between them. They knew they didn't have to pretend.

Didn't *get* to pretend.

"I'm not going to run tonight," he said, as she came out of the bathroom in her pajamas. "Should I leave? So you can...?" *Masturbate without your future husband nearby?*

"Take a self-guided tour? Visit the safety deposit box? Finger paint at the oyster bar?" She waved her fingers to emphasize her point with a wicked smile.

A smile crept on his face even as he shook his head. "Never heard that last one." He tossed his watch onto his bedside table.

"That's because I made it up. I don't know if you heard, but apparently I'm Lillian Fucking Parker, artistic genius." She flopped back into bed. "Nash, I was joking when I said that. Your bed is easy to fall asleep in."

"I should have expected that." He pulled back the covers on his side of the bed. "Since you snore when you sleep."

She turned in mock outrage as she put lotion on her hands. "Libel! I do *not* snore."

He leaned on his arm with a smile, enjoying being awake in bed together for once. "Okay fine. You don't snore, but you *do* snuffle. It's adorable."

She cackled as she snuggled under the covers. "Like a little piglet hunting for truffles? That's worse."

He flipped off his light, and the room was cast in dim moonlight.

"Are you ready to be married in two days?" he asked into the darkness.

A long sigh sounded from her side of the bed. "The flowers are almost done. So I suppose. I decided to go with dahlias. "

He smiled in satisfaction, thinking of the surprise he had for her.

"You?" she asked.

"It's nice sleeping next to someone again," he answered, fully knowing that wasn't really an answer. "Next to you," he finally admitted. "And you don't really snuffle that much. Plus, I like that it's one more thing I've learned about you."

A silence settled between them in the dim light.

Probably best they went to sleep.

Two big days of keeping a tight leash on his feelings were ahead of him.

"It's because I shared my peaches with her," Lily said quietly.

Nash's brows crooked together in confusion. "What?"

"The reason her name is Peaches. I was outside that night eating a snack, trying to clear my head. In August. The night after you and I..."

Our first kiss.

"Well, you know," she continued. "And here was this sweet-faced little possum, drenched from the rain with a moldy apple core. She started to sniff at a jagged can and I just...I didn't want her eating trash. She deserved better. So I shared my peaches and they made her so happy."

Nash's heart melted into a buttery pool. He loved the secret soft underbelly behind Lily's spunky exterior.

What was she capable of if she let herself fall in love?

He couldn't wait to show her the second surprise he had in

store. "Someone asked about a honeymoon," Nash said suddenly. "We hadn't talked about it, but I said we were taking a day trip after the wedding. We can reschedule if it doesn't work for you."

"A trip?" Lily smiled, leaning up on her pillow.

"It's nothing big," he said quickly. "I know you can't take time away from Bloom right now, and I have commitments at the bank. But it would give us an opportunity to take pictures, make it look like the real thing."

The glimmer went out of her eyes. "Oh." She turned over to go to sleep. "Sounds good."

He could feel her disappointment.

Why did every move he made with his future wife feel like the wrong one?

Chapter Sixteen

NASH

Warm water ran over Nash's shoulders as he stood in his tiled shower, trying to think about anything other than the past six hours—the rehearsal for his wedding.

It had been exquisite torture to let his real feelings show through at the rehearsal.

Fawn over Lily like he always wanted to, but never let himself get too comfortable.

He would *not* think about how perfect she'd looked in her simple, elegant cream sweater dress. Wouldn't think how it had hugged every single curve. The low dip of the neckline framed her breasts. Two lush mounds he tried not to stare at as he watched her practice walking down the aisle toward him.

Wouldn't think about her hips that swayed toward him and made his mouth water. Her generous round ass that his hands itched for. If she was really his, he'd grab it as he slid past her in the kitchen on a cozy Sunday morning.

He palmed his hard cock as the water rushed across his face.

Lily was staying at Violet's tonight, having a sleepover before the wedding. No risk of her overhearing him.

A thrust against his slippery hand felt so fucking good. Two more pumps. *Just focus on the sensation. Don't think about her.*

He pumped body wash into his hand and ran the slickness over his cock. *Think of the warm water hitting my cock, feeling so slick.*

Just like her pussy would feel like if I slid in.

Goddamnit. "You know what? Fuck it."

Might as well take advantage of being alone tonight. He could cry her name out a hundred times.

He leaned against the glass wall of his shower, letting the water run along his shoulders. Gripping his cock, he tugged hard, picturing her on her knees, mouth open and waiting for him. *She'd look so gorgeous with those wicked, plush lips around my cock.* "Fuck yes," he muttered.

She'd beg him to fuck her. He'd toss that tight sweater dress up over her head and fuck her hard as she begged for more. "You want more, don't you, sweetheart? My wife begs for all of this cock," he ground out through gritted teeth.

His hands would map her curves, caressing, licking anything he could reach. Inhaling that permanent spring scent as he slid in and out. Her wicked smile teasing him over her shoulder as he took her harder and harder from behind.

He pumped hard, again and again, into his fist. Imagining her tits bouncing as he thrust against her. At her moans. God, that fucking *dress*. He couldn't get it out of his head. "You wore that dress for me, didn't you, Lily," he groaned.

A thud sounded in the walk-in closet connected to the bathroom. Wariness crawled along his spine as he stilled, listening for more. The closet door was cracked open and it was dark. *Is someone in the house? Someone Jeremy sent?*

He wrenched the water off and grabbed a towel to wrap around him, dashing to the walk-in closet connected to his bathroom.

As he was about to pull back the door, a lump fell forward, throwing the walk-in closet door open.

"What the f—*oof.*" Nash caught flailing arms and legs covered in a cream sweater before they hit the tile. "Lily?"

Water dripped down his chest as he held her. Beads of water landed along that cream sweater dress that haunted his thoughts.

"Uh...oops," she said, eyes wide and cheeks flushed in embarrassment.

He stared in amazement, trying to piece it all together as he lifted her to standing. The walk-in closet had two entrances, one to the bathroom, one to their bedroom.

But the closet was dark. And she'd clearly been leaning on the bathroom door.

She pulled away but he grabbed her waist, holding her in place against the doorframe.

"Lily, hold on." He tried to catch his breath. His eyes searched hers in the dark doorway of the closet. "Did you...did you hear me in the shower?"

She looked down, cheeks blushing harder.

Oh fuck, she did. He leaned over her, caging her in.

She shoved at her hair. "I...I just came in to grab something I forgot." She turned but he blocked her with his other arm.

"With the lights off?"

"I came up to get my shoes, but..." She licked her lips in the heavy silence, staring at his chest only a few inches from her face. "Then I heard you talking."

She still had the cream dress on, and he wanted to rip it off of her. Bury his face against her.

Just once. Take her one more time like you both want. Only one more time.

"Lily, were you watching me in the shower?" he asked darkly.

She lifted her chin defiantly, fire in her eyes. "What if I was?"

Oh fuck. His cock pulsed under his towel. Her skirt was lifted on her left side, hitched up high along her thigh.

Like she'd been reaching under it.

"Give me your hand," he growled.

She ground her teeth as her chest rose and fell and handed him her left hand reluctantly. He brought her palm to his lips as their eyes locked.

He inhaled as he kissed her palm and *fuck,* her scent was right there. His eyes closed, savoring it. The beast burst out of the locked cage inside of him.

He wanted her. *Now.*

His eyes flashed open. "You were joining in, weren't you? Rubbing your clit while you watched me fuck myself?"

Color rose along her cheeks as she bit her bottom lip.

Eyes locked on her, he sucked her two fingers into his mouth. He moaned, closing his eyes. Her scent landed on his tongue like ambrosia. "Fuck, Lily. You taste so good. Even better than I imagined," he said with a dark smile.

"You imagined it?" She panted.

"Every fucking day for a year, firecracker." She gasped as he sucked her fingers again, getting every drop of her. He ran his tongue between her two fingers, riding up and down the V of them, until he heard a small moan from her.

He popped them out of his mouth. "Such a naughty girl."

She eyed his towel around his waist with a challenging glint, running a finger along the top of it. "What if I want more?" She tugged his towel so that it fell to the floor, and he stood naked and dripping, cock jutting out.

He palmed his cock, still leaning over her, tugging up and down for some relief. "I think you like being a brat. Being told exactly how bad you are. Being punished for pushing me too far," he said, his voice low and cocky.

She wasn't used to men pushing back, he could tell. But he wasn't afraid of her games. "I should take you over my knee. Maybe that's what you've wanted this whole time."

He wanted to touch her. To feel the sting of his hand on her perfect ass. To make her come.

Just one more time, then I'll stop.

She nodded, breath caught.

Fuck yes. His eyes darkened as he lifted her chin to meet his eyes. "Beg for it, wife."

Her eyelashes fluttered as she stammered in surprise. "Pl-please. Spank me," she whispered.

"Hmm," he murmured and caught her earlobe between his teeth, tugging. She sucked in a breath and he could feel her nipples against him. "Beg harder, my little brat."

She moaned as he ran a thumb over one nipple. His cock was weeping, screaming for attention.

Just one last time.

"I..." She moaned as he bit her earlobe again. He swirled his thumb around and around her tits. "*Fuck.* Please. Please. Please." She moaned in time with his strokes. "Spank me until I"—he pinched her nipple—"oh fuck, until I come," she gasped.

A slow smile curved his face as he sat on the bench in the darkened walk-in closet. She stood in front of him, backlit by the bathroom. His eyes never leaving hers, he pulled her leggings down with a vicious tug. "You'll tell me to stop if it's too much," he murmured against her stomach.

"Yes," she moaned. He ran his hands along her bare thighs, under her dress. His cock pulsed as he skimmed over her hips and found her panties, ripping them down.

Fuuuuck, her scent. She was so wet he could smell her. Were her panties soaked? Was it from when she watched him in the shower?

Don't come like a teenager the minute you touch her.

What he *really* wanted was to rip every piece of clothing off and fuck her until dawn.

He ground his teeth, and patted his thigh. "On my knee, wife. Since you want it so badly."

Lily lay across his thighs, her injured leg resting on the bench.

Her wet pussy was hot against his leg and he rocked her against it, giving her friction on her clit. She moaned, head dropping onto the bench.

His hands ran along the back of her thighs. He slowly slid the edge of her sweater dress over her ass, leaving her exposed.

"I stared at this all night," he said as he rubbed a hand over her bare, plump cheeks. His fingers dug in, wanting to claim it. See it jiggle under his hands.

"I wanted you to," she whispered.

He thrust his cock into his fist. "Such a teasing little brat," he murmured, rubbing a hand on her ass. "How many swats should you get?"

His hand came down hard on her ass with a stinging spank. Lily's low moan nearly made him come into his hand. "One, for peeking at me through the closet." He rubbed the sting away, grabbing her ass, jiggling it. "*Fuck*, you're so hot."

He rocked her against his leg to give her the friction she wanted.

He loved seeing her perfect ass in the air, tits pressed against the bench. His hand came down again on her other ass cheek. "Two, for being a brat." She threw her head back with a moan, lip caught in her teeth. His cock pulsed in his hand. Fuck, he wanted to see that again.

"Three"—he swatted her harder and she gasped in pleasure—"for making my cock hard as you walked down the aisle with your tits bouncing."

He could feel her rocking her hips against him. Her scent was his undoing. He needed one more taste. He smoothed a hand over her pinked skin, sliding his hand between her legs. She looked back with anticipation, those caramel eyes molten with lust. He dipped his fingers into her and she clenched around him, sighing out a groan. "You're so wet, Lily."

He pulled out his fingers and licked every drop. She toyed with her nipple as she watched him, wanting relief.

His eyes never leaving hers, he pulsed into his cock with one hand and spanked her harder with the other. "Four, because you love it so much." He rocked her against his leg, wanting to watch her come again, and she ground against him, desperate for release.

"Five"—he spanked again—"so I can see my favorite shade of pink on my wife's skin," he murmured.

"Oh fuck." She moved against him. His leg was slick with her. "Say it again," she moaned.

He dug in, rocking her against his leg. "Come on me, wife," he growled, and spanked and rocked until she was a moaning, wet mess.

He tugged at his aching, weeping cock as her screams grew higher and higher, until he slid two fingers into her pussy and rocked her hard against his thigh. "And I'll come all over this pink, round ass."

"Nash," she screamed, throwing her head back as his balls

tightened. He mercilessly rubbed his cock against her, coming in long, hot spurts, painting white streaks of cum over her ass.

They panted, not looking at each other.

He'd slipped. One more time.

What the fuck had he done? How had he let himself go that far?

Nash slid off the bench, moving her forward. "Wait here."

That was a mistake, but aftercare was still important. He ran a washcloth under warm water and stared at himself in the mirror with self-loathing.

You're better than this. Self-control is the one thing you have control over.

He could *not* get more involved with a woman who would leave in a few months. His life was here. His duty was here. His cock needed to stay far away from her from now on.

Nash ran the washcloth over her, cleaning up their mess. "You okay?"

She smirked at him coyly. "Good thing I'll be standing for most of tomorrow."

Their wedding.

Shame washed over him at his lack of control. "I'm sorry for slipping. Again." He stood, grabbing his towel and wrapping it around him. "We...can't do this again. I'm sorry I wasn't strong enough to keep myself in check. I'll do better."

She blinked quickly, processing what he'd said. Standing, she pulled her leggings up and tugged her sweater down.

Lily lifted her nose in the air with a hard stare. "I guess I'll never learn, will I?" She shook her head in disbelief. "Push me away once, shame on you. Push me away *three* times?" She grabbed white heels from her side of the closet and laughed to herself with disgust. "Shame on me."

She hobbled out the closet door and down the stairs.

His stomach turned at the idea of hurting her feelings. He

hated to push her away, but she was already nearly fucking perfect, and his crush was morphing into something he didn't want to think about.

He had a feeling Lily Parker would be a forever kind of love if he let himself fall.

Chapter Seventeen

LILY

Lily's soul was hovering somewhere outside her body as she considered what she'd be in approximately twenty minutes.

A married, wife of convenience.

She concentrated on not fainting from nerves in the back of Nick's SUV as he drove to Bloom with her sisters in tow.

Nick hit a pothole, and Lily clenched as she bumped up and down. Her ass was still sore from her Very Bad Decision yesterday.

Was she in love with Nash? Obviously.

Was she going to marry Nash? Definitely.

Could she stick around and make it a real relationship beyond sex? Absolutely not.

She thought about making Nash wait at the altar. Letting him squirm after he'd pushed her away *yet again*.

Why couldn't they just have a little fun while she was there?

Nick slowed to a stop in front of Bloom. "Go get 'em, tiger." Nick's happy smile met hers as he threw the SUV into park.

"I'll settle for not barfing from nerves," Lily said with a wobbly smile.

Rose and Violet beamed at her. They both held smaller versions of her dahlia bouquet. Wildflowers would have been her ideal bouquet, but it'd been impossible to get them on the short timeline in early February.

Violet squeezed her shoulders in a side hug. "It's going to be great. C'mon, you have a husband to marry."

Lily opened the SUV door and Aaron held out a hand for her.

She slid down from the SUV, but her dress caught and she heard a rip.

No!

To save it from ripping more, she landed on her high heel sideways and a shooting pain bolted up her leg. She cried out and nearly tumbled to the ground, but Aaron caught her elbow to steady her.

"Oh, fuck. Rose, come here," Aaron called.

"It's fine. I'm fine," Lily said, biting her lip to get through it. She wouldn't look ridiculous.

Supporting her on either side, Rose grabbed one arm and Aaron grabbed the other. Lily hobbled and hopped the short walk from the curb to Bloom's front steps.

"Can you make it down the aisle?" Rose said.

"Here. I have to..." Lily toed off her heels. "Ah, much better." She sent a tight smile to Aaron and Rose.

Aaron frowned with empathy. "I could get a rolling chair from the cafe."

"Over my dead body," Lily muttered. "I'd rather army crawl down the aisle."

Aaron shrugged and opened the front door to Bloom where her wedding guests sat waiting.

She looked stupid and ridiculous in no shoes and the end of

her mother's dress ripped. *Just like me, chaos.*

But this time it's not so cute, she thought with shame.

Violet's eyes were full of concern. "Are you—"

"Violet," Lily snapped. "I am shivering in old silk chiffon in Pennsylvania in early February. Get your ass down that aisle."

"Okay, okay, okay," Violet said, walking through the door confidently into the wedding ceremony.

Rose squeezed Lily's arm. "I'm proud of you"—*Oh god, could this get any worse?*—"for not running away." Rose kissed Lily's cheek, wiped a bit of lipstick from it, and walked into Bloom.

Lily did a mental check before she walked in. *Bouquet, hair, flowers, scribbled piece of paper with my vows on it.* They'd decided that writing their own vows would help sell their relationship.

The end.

Time to get married.

She handed her heels to Aaron, who took them graciously, as she hobbled across the threshold of Bloom.

The stunning sight of Bloom filled with her friends and family was overshadowed immediately.

She couldn't believe it.

How?

Hundreds of wildflowers lined the aisle on either side. Bright oranges, yellow, purple, whites, bright spring green, all tucked together in planters so they sat stretching upward as if she was walking through a wildflower field.

This had *not* been in the plan. She didn't even think she could *do* something like this.

She heard the shutter of a camera click over the scraping of people standing.

Gray whispered from behind his camera. "It's a surprise from Nash. He thought you'd like them."

Lily's eyes shot to Nash's at the end of the aisle. He looked entranced, like he'd been handed the most precious jewel and wasn't quite sure what to do with it.

Her heart melted and she blinked back tears at the sweetest man she was going to marry.

The string quartet sitting in the loft re-started her walk-down-the-aisle song for the second time.

Better get a move on. She took a hobbling, small step but her knee ached.

Don't curse obscenities, don't curse obscenities. She winced as she took another hobbling step, biting her lip.

"Lily, stop," Nash called out.

She'd been staring at the floor in front of her, willing herself to take another step. By the time she looked up, he was in front of her.

Oh no.

"You okay?" he whispered.

She let out a sigh of relief. She thought for sure he was going to call the whole thing off. Change his mind that the loud, mouthy girl was too terrible of a choice for a temporary wife.

"My knee...I'm fine—"

"Here, let me." Suddenly, his arms were underneath her legs as he swept her into his arms with ease.

A bridal carry for the bride.

A collective gasp let out from their friends and family.

"Remember to find me dashing and be in love with me," he whispered in her ear as he walked them down the aisle.

She was too dazzled for any snappy comeback. The man of her dreams was carrying her down the aisle through thickets of wildflowers.

It was too perfect for her to make fun of.

"Yeah, like that," he said with a slow smile.

They reached the end of the makeshift aisle. Lily had

replaced the neon Bloom sign with a white floral installation. Nash sat her down under it.

Mrs. Maroo stood behind a small podium. "Well, I'll be writing about *that* in my diary later tonight. You may be seated. Now, the couple has asked for the ceremony to be short and sweet, which is too bad for them because I have things to say."

Nash's lips twitched with humor as his eyes connected with Lily's. All the hurt feelings and awkwardness of last night was gone.

They were in this rollercoaster car together.

He looked so handsome it almost hurt to look at him. The tux stretched across his broad shoulders. His jaw had just a touch of stubble, just the way she liked. His eyes that always caught her by the heart looked back with warmth.

Mrs. Maroo continued, "I've had the pleasure of knowing these two their entire lives, which makes me feel old as hell."

Lily burst out laughing, and even Nash couldn't contain a chuckle.

God, his mother probably hates this, she thought with glee.

"In fact, *I* was there when Miss Parker was moony-eyed after being rescued by Nash when she got stuck on top of the Town Square gazebo ten years ago."

Nash's eyes lit with humor and their guests chuckled.

"And any fool saw Nash staring longingly at Lily when she moved back last year. She was blissfully unaware of how obviously in love he was."

What?

She has to be wrong, right?

Nash's cheeks went pink, and a pained look crossed his face for a flicker of a moment.

"He stared after her, as if she held the secrets to the universe in her little round—"

"Okay, that's enough," Nash interrupted.

"Annnywhoodles." Mrs. Maroo's wicked smile made their guests laugh. "I, along with the rest of the town, am so glad that you two finally, *finally* got together," Mrs. Maroo said with exasperation. Nods and whispered *yeses* sounded in the crowd.

Lily shook her head at Nash with happy disbelief as he beamed back at her. *These people.*

She loved them so much.

"So, let's hear those vows and get to the cake. Nash?"

Gray put his camera away and now stood behind Nash as his best man. Nash grabbed the rings from him.

He pulled out a small piece of paper. "I'm going to keep this short, spicy, and sweet, like my future wife. I'm positive every guest here has set me up on a blind date." A chuckle rippled through their guests. "And the only fault of all those lovely women, is that...they weren't you."

He looked up from his paper, and she felt a *boom* in her chest as his words landed there.

"I spent years looking for the perfect wife with a checklist, thinking it would be simple to find someone who checked every box. But I shouldn't have been looking for the perfect wife. I should have been looking for the *right* wife. The right wife for me is the gorgeous, spunky woman who loves to do things her own way, and who is brilliant beyond measure. She's fierce and cares more for everyone around her than they'll ever know. I'm sure to others, our relationship may look rushed."

A forced cough sounded behind them, and Jeremy sneered behind a fist. Thank god she'd very specifically instructed Mrs. Maroo to omit the *anyone object* part of the ceremony.

"But," Nash continued with a glance at Jeremy, "what they don't know is that I've been falling for you for five years."

Five years?

Her eyes fixed on his. *The salsa club.* Where they'd danced and he'd protected her from a creep.

He paused, biting his lip, looking like he'd admitted the worst thing in the world. "I fell for your kindness, concern for every living thing, your humor, and not the least of all, your brilliance. Lily Parker can do anything she puts her mind to, and I can't wait to see what our life together will be like. You are my own wildflower. Rugged, raw and bright, and the most gorgeous thing nature has made. I am hopelessly in love with you and I plan to remain that way. I—" he cleared his throat with emotion, "I...I cannot *wait* to call you my wife."

Five years? This whole time?

He slid her ring onto her finger, and she sighed at the familiar, happy weight of it.

They stared at each other, time seeming to stop as Nash's cheeks grew pink. How much of what he admitted was a lie?

How much of it is real?

"Lily?" Mrs. Maroo said. "Lily." She shook her arm.

"Oh, sorry." Lily grabbed for the piece of paper wrapped around her bouquet.

Her fingers trembled as she held the paper, all of this suddenly feeling Big and Important.

Here goes everything.

"It might seem silly to get married in a flower shop, but I love Bloom because it's where I feel closest to all the people I love. To my sisters, my parents, and most importantly, the boy I first fell in love with."

Nash's sharp inhale made her glance up through watery eyes. She guessed today was a day for confessions.

If you couldn't say it when you were getting married, when else could you admit you'd loved someone forever?

Her lip trembled, but she went on.

"That boy was handsome and strong, smart and caring. Everyone said you'd go places when you got older, but I only wished it would be somewhere I could go too." She bit her cheek, trying not to cry. "Everyone was surprised how tall you were, but I thought the size of your heart was more remarkable. Everyone knew how generous you were, but I thought the rippling impact of your simple kindnesses was more impressive.

"I've watched you my entire life, and loved an impressive man from afar. Since I've fallen in love with you...now I *see* you." She cleared her throat through a shaking voice.

"You're soft yet brave. Fierce yet sweet. Cunning yet honest. Flawed..." She flicked her eyes up at him, and he looked back at her with thunderstruck wonder. "...yet perfect. I fell in love with the good-hearted man I knew you'd be a long, long time ago. My heart has found its way back to you again and again, and I know it always will."

She slid a simple gold band onto his finger, and she blinked up at him with a shy smile.

He mouthed *Lily* almost as if he wasn't aware of it, his chest heaving up and down with anticipation.

"Well," Mrs. Maroo said through a teary cough, "this short and sweet ceremony isn't turning out so short after all, so let's move it along. Nash, do you?"

"I do," he said immediately, never taking his eyes off of Lily.

"And Lily, do you?"

She paused, waiting.

Should she do this? Was this the *right* thing to do? To get married for convenience to the man she really loved?

Could she lie to *him*?

She glanced out to the guests. Would she lie to all of these people that she cared about?

Nash took her hand and squeezed it, winking at her with a hopeful smile.

Butterflies floating around her midsection settled at that one ounce of reassurance.

"I do," she said with a mischievous smile.

"By the power of the Holy Mackerel Online Ministry and the state of Pennsylvania, I happily proclaim you husband and wife. You may—"

But Mrs. Maroo didn't get a chance to finish.

Nash's hand grasped Lily's elbow as his hand slid into her hair, his lips capturing hers.

Lily leaned into the kiss, pliant against him. She kissed him back, wanting to him to know he had her whole heart.

Nash pulled her against him tighter as the sounds of clapping faded away. It was just his lips, his taste, that were her world.

She opened for him as he slanted his mouth against hers with a groan. He wrapped his arms around her and held her tight against him.

All the air left her as she yearned for him, kissing him back.

The heavy feel of his arms around her, holding her safe, was a counterpoint melody to his lips plundering her mouth. Her tongue ran along his bottom lip. His sharp inhale of breath at the contact made her stomach drop.

God, she wanted this man.

She wanted her *husband*.

As Nash pulled away, Lily felt the haze of realization start to fall over her.

She was someone's wife now.

Fucking bizarre.

"Ready?" he whispered over her mouth with a smile, his dazed lusty eyes still staring at her lips.

Right. They had a party to throw.

"Ready." She could do it as long as she was with him. He picked her up again.

She'd honestly forgotten about the pain in her knee with the swoony, life-altering last 15 minutes of her life.

Guests tossed white flower petals at them as he carried her down the aisle.

Lily murmured in his ear. "You know, the number of times you've picked me up—"

"Swept you up, I believe, is the right phrasing," Nash said back with a smile.

She rolled her eyes with a beaming grin. "It's starting to get ridiculous, husband."

Chapter Eighteen

LILY

Jazz and low, candlelit tables surrounded Lily as she and Nash held hands walking through Fox & Forrest. They'd rented the cafe for their reception, keeping things intimate and as low-key as the Prince of Fairwick Falls could make them. His mother had tried to talk them into the country club, but Nash had finally put his foot down.

"I still can't believe you got Karen to relent to Fox & Forrest." Lily whispered to him, sipping champagne. His hand never left hers. She couldn't remember a time in the last two hours when Nash hadn't been touching her.

"I threatened her with never seeing her unborn grandchildren if she didn't agree."

Kids? She hadn't even thought about that with Nash.

What if she got pregnant?

Wait, that was ridiculous. He said that he wouldn't slip again. She could keep it in her pants for the next few months, probably.

Maybe.

But Nash looked devastatingly dashing—like the sexiest,

tallest, most honest James Bond there ever was—and she desperately wished for a few minutes alone with him.

Lily turned to speak to Pop, looking absolutely adorable in a polka dot bow tie, but she felt the gentle brush of a kiss on her shoulder. Nash squeezed her waist and whispered in her ear. "I'm going to check on the first dance. Can I get you anything?"

"A white wine and one of those tortellini things."

Nash winked and kissed her cheek as he left. Her stomach swooped.

This was going to be a really dangerous few months.

"Guess you think you've won now." A slimy voice sounded behind her.

Jeremy had elbowed his way past Pop and stood too close to her. His smug smile didn't hide the hatred in his eyes.

"Of course I won," Lily said with a bright smile. "I married the sexiest man in the room. The only thing that would make today better is if you got the fuck out of my wedding reception." Her blinding smile contrasted with the hatred in her eyes.

Jeremy snorted as he jangled the change in his pocket. "Such a lady," he said, but his eyes weren't even on her. He tracked a man that walked behind her. "Hey Josiah." Jeremy slapped his back as the man walked past. "Hell of a squash game this morning."

Nash appeared at her elbow. "It's time for you to go." His voice was ice-cold.

Jeremy's smile grew wider. "That's fine. I've got a hot tip back in New York. Big opportunity. I don't need to waste my time here"—Jeremy downed the glass of champagne he was holding—"for now."

A shudder went down Lily's spine as Jeremy turned with a slimy smile and left.

A glass of wine appeared in her hand. "Are you okay?" Nash whispered in her ear.

She reveled in the nearness of him. "I'm very glad he's not my permanent brother-in-law."

He leaned back with a chuckle, his eyes darting to her lips. They were married, right? Brides and grooms kissed at their reception.

"Better kiss me again to make this believable," she whispered.

He nodded, his hand sliding along her waist. He leaned in, brushing her lips with a gentle kiss that went and went as he gripped her hip possessively.

God, she'd let him run her over with a forklift if he just kept doing that.

"I think that's our song," Nash murmured against her lips.

She was in a lusty daze, and all she could think about was his fucking *hand gripping* her in the best way possible. What would *two* hands feel like? "We...we have a song?" She shook her head to clear it.

He held out his hand to lead her to the dance floor. "It's what we danced to at Rose and Gray's wedding."

We have a song. Little heart emojis fluttered around her head as Nash led her to the center of the floor.

Without guests to distract them, Lily became too aware of Nash. Too aware of how handsome he looked. How good he smelled.

How very *married* they were.

"You look absolutely stunning," he said suddenly, looking at her with concern. "I can't believe it's taken me this long to tell you that."

She smirked up at him. "Eh, we've been busy pretending."

Nash cleared his throat, pulling her closer. "Yeah."

"Hey," Lily said, wanting to make him laugh. "You look very

handsome. If you weren't my fake husband, I'd totally hit on you and then try to drag you back to my place."

A warm light danced in Nash's eyes. "Good thing we're heading back to the same place anyway."

A gooey sensation pulled at her heart as she got lost in his smile. Her head was already clouded from his kisses and his caresses and his warm, tender looks. This was all pretend for him, but still.

She couldn't help but flirt with her husband.

As they rolled away from the cheering crowd outside of Fox & Forrest in a decorated car, the silence between them was deafening.

And it stretched.

And stretched.

The warm and tender looks they'd shared in front of everyone else vanished with the click of the door lock.

Wow. He *was* a good actor.

Get out of your fucking head, Lily. He was acting, you were acting, none of this is real except the legally binding union.

"So you're okay taking a road trip tomorrow?" He pulled into his garage a few minutes later.

It occurred to her that she now semi-permanently lived at an enormous mansion.

"Holy fuck, this is my house. Well, I mean, *your* house," she said, correcting. "I mean this isn't...you know."

"Lily, this is our house. It would be best for you to call it that from now on. Stay there."

"Don't tell me what to do," she replied with little heat, but she was tired and in pain. Nash opened her door and pulled her up to standing.

She winced. She'd done pretty well walking on her hurt knee, but it was all catching up to her now that the adrenaline had worn off. "You don't have to...you know," she said through clenched teeth.

"Lily," he said sternly. "I am tired. I lied to a lot of people today. My brother is still eagerly awaiting my demise. My mother is barely speaking to me, and—" He cut himself off, swallowing his words. He clenched his jaw. "And it's been a long day, so please. Let me do this one thing."

She relented, throwing her arms around his neck at seeing the tension on his face.

He picked her up so she avoided the steps up to the door and kept walking into the kitchen.

He felt warm and solid under her arms. She tried to memorize the feeling of him holding her like this, knowing she might not feel it again.

He still hadn't put her down as they stood in the dim kitchen and their eyes slowly connected.

Hot and cold, cold and hot.

And when she was in his arms staring at her mouth like he wanted to plunder it again, *very fucking hot.*

Would her sanity last after another few months of this?

"I think we're inside now," she said quietly, unable to take her eyes off of his lips a few inches from her face.

He licked his lips. "I thought it was..." He cleared his throat. "I wanted to savor the tradition, carrying the bride over the threshold. I'll carry you up."

My heart. She hadn't even considered that he'd carried her over the threshold. That he'd care about that.

She was learning that Nash, despite all appearances, was a sentimental man.

He walked up the staircase leading to their bedroom.

The tension felt thick between them. *Make a joke. Say*

anything. "I guess it's fitting for a husband to carry his bride to the most important room of the night." *Oh fuck, why did I say that?* His eyes flew to hers as he stumbled on the top step.

"Not that I mean we have to—" she said, suddenly.

Their bed had never loomed larger in the center of the room than at that moment.

"No, no, no. It's not—I wasn't expecting. That we wouldn't," Nash said quickly, as he set her down and backed away, rubbing his eyes in frustration.

He walked past her as he tugged his bow tie off.

That was going to live in her fantasies for a while—the unbothered heavy tug on satin as he shrugged out of his jacket. The ends of the bow tie hung on either side of his neck.

As Nash removed his cufflinks, the totality of what they'd done struck her.

They were *married*.

She'd married the man she was secretly in love with. A wave of anxiety turned her stomach. She needed to get back to normal immediately. Put everything about today behind her.

Try to not get attached to all of it. She looked down at her dream of a dress.

Oh no. It had taken an army to get her ready that morning. *I can't get undressed by myself.*

Lily turned in the mirror to see the tiny buttons down her back. Impossible for her to reach, and she couldn't rip her mom's dress.

Just ask your sexy husband of convenience to undress you on your wedding night.

You know, the night after he spanked you and made you come so hard you were sore the next day?

No biggie.

"Can I ask a favor?" She turned around and pointed to the buttons.

"Oh," he said slowly. His face looked pained, as if he was holding something back. "Uh, sure."

He furrowed his brow, leaning down. The ends of his bow tie hung from his neck, dangling in the air. She wanted to pull him into a dark corner by the black silk. Taste him again with a desperate urgency.

He never kissed her during their 'slips.' And she wanted to ravage him when he looked like this. Wrap her legs around him and feel his cock against her as she feasted on him.

She felt the tug on the back of her neck as one button was finally free. *Right, back to reality.*

"I hope you don't have any plans tonight"—he murmured in frustration at the tiny buttons—"or for the rest of this week." His breath puffed along her neck, making goosebumps stand along the edges of her arms.

Put him in the friendzone, girl. This is the same boy who super-soakered Rose, Violet, and you with ice water when he was a kid.

This is the nerdy (swoony) teen who'd had braces.

Don't think about how this man swept you off your feet and walked you through an aisle covered in wildflowers shipped in from god knows where.

"Thank you," she said suddenly, remembering the surprise at the wedding.

"Well, you can't sleep in this." He tugged another button free.

"I meant the wildflowers. Thank you."

His eyes met hers over her shoulder with a soft, embarrassed smile. "Pearl mentioned they were your favorite."

There was that somersault again in her stomach. He'd learned that wildflowers were her favorite, filed it away for the perfect moment, and now he was undressing her on their wedding night.

She was in uncharted territory.

She looked over her shoulder at him bent over the row of buttons. "I never really thought about what people did on their wedding night."

Nash slowly raised an eyebrow at her.

She squinched her eyes together in embarrassment. "Oh god, you know what I mean." *I might as well just slingshot myself into traffic.* "I meant when the party is over and you de-wedding yourself."

"It's a very pretty dress," he said quietly as he unbuttoned the dress, taking his time with each button.

"It was my mom's," she said quietly, caressing the skirt.

"I'm glad she could be there in some way," he said with a sad smile.

He would have been nine, like Rose, when her mom died.

"Do you, um..." She bit her lip. "Do you remember her?"

Nash furrowed his brow in thought as he unclasped another button. "She had this air about her. She was gentle and earthy, like you could tell her anything. Pretty unlike my mom," he said with a snort. "One time Rose and I were playing in the back of Bloom. I must have been about seven. I spilled a pot of red paint all over the floor. I felt awful, and being a kid, did a terrible job cleaning it up. But she wiped my tears and told me not to cry. Told me floors were meant for making messes. She was gentle and bright," he added with a smile.

Lily huffed out a sad laugh. "I guess I couldn't be further from her, huh?"

He'd worked his way to her waist. At this point, she could slip the rest of the dress over her hips. The back of her dress gaped open and she held it to her chest.

He stood and opened his dresser to grab pajamas. "You have the same twinkle in your eye that she did. She was quick to make a joke, even if she was quieter. She saw the funny parts of life like you. Didn't really care for pomp and circumstance, and knew how to have fun. So, in a lot of ways, you're exactly like her."

Lily blinked back tears, trying not to let the emotion show. That he'd given her one of the best gifts of her entire life just then. She turned around, grabbing her clothes. "Thanks," she said quietly.

"Have a good night," he said, walking out of the room.

She whirled around, surprised at him leaving. "Where are you going? It's two AM."

Their eyes connected. *Don't leave me. Stay,* she wanted to ask.

His smile was sad and hollow. "I don't think I can sleep just yet. You go ahead." He went downstairs with his clothes in hand. She knew exactly where he'd go: to that damn treadmill he went to every night until she fell asleep.

She stood alone in their bedroom on their wedding night, desperately in love with her husband.

LILY

Bare trees swished past as Nash's car barreled along the highway at the crack of dawn.

AKA 8:30 AM.

He'd barely spoken two words to her that morning—their first day as husband and wife. They drove in silence toward their honeymoon day trip.

He seemed off in another world. Distant. Could she take months of this?

She closed her eyes, exhausted from the last week. She'd pulled late nights working on her KGM pitch and hours on her wedding flowers. She'd fallen asleep as soon as her head hit the pillow last night.

Lily sighed and put her forehead against the cold glass. A lullaby of barren fields swirled past her as Nash drove down the highway.

She fell into sleep with fitful dreams. Every tenth face was Nash's, staring at her like he'd done the first night they'd shared a room: with lust and need, unable to help himself any longer. Finally giving into whatever it was that they had between them.

A bump jostled Lily awake, and the car slowly slid onto a gravel road. She sat up, wiping the sleep from her eyes.

Their honeymoon was in a cold, empty field?

Nash pointed to a sign ahead on the long gravel drive. "You, um." Nash cleared his throat, shifting in his seat. "You follow them on social media."

The entry sign welcomed them to Paws & Plow Rescue Ranch.

"Wait, I *know* them," Lily said, spinning back around, gluing her face to the window. She adored the work they did rescuing farm animals from slaughter. "I didn't realize they were close."

"I thought you'd want to see them in action," Nash said with a smile.

Lily's heart melted.

Black and white lumps loped through the fields. "Do you see those adorable cows?" She clapped her hands. Three cows in a field rolled a big yoga ball, playing like gigantic, half-ton dogs. "And they have best frieeeeends," she cooed as two cows nuzzled each other.

Nash drove down the winding gravel road through a thicket of pine trees and parked in front of a giant barn. Chickens roamed unhurriedly through a cute fenced area.

Lily leapt out as fast as her leg would allow, and a farmer in a heavy flannel jacket waved hello.

"Mr. and Mrs. Donnelly." The man waved as he slowly walked from the main building to their cars.

Whoa. That was the first time she'd been called Mrs. Donnelly.

"Ms. Parker, actually," Nash corrected and took her hand.

They'd decided she wouldn't go through the hassle of changing her name since they'd only be together for a few months.

But she'd sort of *liked* the sound of Donnelly as her last name.

"Oh, my apologies. I'm John, the founder of Paws and Plow. But you can call me Farmer John," the man said with a smile as he shook their hands. "Excited for your special tour?"

Lily wiggled her hips with excitement at the prospect of petting some cows. "I'm *such* a fan. Will I get to see animals up close?"

"Definitely. We have a special surprise to thank you for your amazing donation," the man said, taking off his hat and scratching his head in wonder.

"Donation?" Lily said, looking up at Nash, whose cheeks had turned an interesting shade of pink.

"It's nothing, really. No need to mention it," Nash said dismissively. "I think Lily wanted to see the cows."

Farmer John's bright smile wouldn't let it go. "Of *course* it's worth mentioning. Your donation saved a whole truckload of baby goats."

Lily stared in confusion up at Nash. "Did he say a *truckload* of baby goats?

"Um—" Nash cleared his throat. "I wanted—I mean, um… the donation was a wedding present. For you," he said finally.

She *loved* that this suave and sophisticated man got all stutter-y and bashful when he was embarrassed.

"When Nash called us two weeks ago"—*two weeks ago?*—"I thought we were being pranked with how much y'all wanted to donate to our little sanctuary. Here, follow me." Farmer John waved them through into the fenced area. "And watch your step. The pigs roam free, which is great for them, but not so great for your shoes."

Lily hobbled through the muddy pasture as Nash held the gate open for her and offered his arm for stability.

John smiled over his shoulder. "Your timing couldn't have

been better. There was a hoarding case a few counties over, and the little guys were too malnourished for any farm to be interested. They were going to be put down, but luckily, we had your influx of cash for medicine, feed, and hired a couple extra people to handle them."

Visions of bouncing goats raced through her head. She was completely bowled over with the fact that: A, Nash would care about what she was interested in; B, that he'd get her a wedding present; and C, that it was the most perfect gift. Something that she truly believed in, that would make the world a better place.

So like him.

"You saved a bunch of baby goats for me?" she said, turning to Nash, whose eyes were fixed to the ground. His cheeks were now an adorable shade of magenta.

Still, my beating libido.

"Watch it." He caught her around the waist right before she stepped in something gross. "Lily, like I said, it's nothing. A little token. A present."

"I think you and I have different meanings of token, husband," Lily said jokingly in a sultry voice.

"Don't," he said suddenly, his eyes flashing.

Of fuck, right. That was what she'd screamed when she'd come all over his hand.

He stared at her for a moment, but then broke away.

Tension between them boiled over, but they kept walking.

Farmer John was oblivious to the sexual showdown in front of him. "Why, we named the whole barn after you, Lily." He pointed to a small plaque on a picturesque red barn covered in climbing vines.

She walked closer to look. *The Lily Donnelly Barn.*

Her stomach plummeted to the ground.

"We can have that changed to Parker, if you prefer," Farmer John said.

"No, it's fine," Lily said with a distracted smile, unable to take her eyes off of it.

What world had she stepped into when she'd said "I do" to this man? She turned to Nash with her eyes suddenly full of misty understanding. "You did this for me?"

Nash's mouth lifted in a lopsided grin. There was that thunder of understanding, of respect, of something that felt like a lot more than a marriage of convenience.

"You haven't even seen the best part." Farmer John grabbed the sliding barn door and pulled with all his weight.

Fifty tiny baby goats bleated as they streamed out from the barn.

In tiny Hawaiian shirts.

She instantly dropped to the ground, needing to pet them *immediately*. She was already crying at the cuteness.

"Oh my god," she sobbed, overcome with emotion. "These are the cutest fucking things I've ever fucking seen," Lily yelled through her tears. "And they were going to put you down. But then they didn't because—" She choked up, shaking her head, unable to finish it.

One particular little goat was extra curious and stood in front of Lily to get close enough to pet.

"And they have little Hawaiian shirts. Like my dad used to wear. Did you see?" She turned to Nash, needing to share this miraculous moment with him as tears streamed down her face.

He looked like he'd seen a ghost and ran a hand into his hair. "I don't know if this is a good sign or a bad sign."

Signs? What was he talking about?

Farmer John laughed. "We're doing one of those viral video things, and a volunteer wanted to dress them up."

"Well, you look very dapper," Lily said, scratching two goats that were chewing on grass near her knee. "My dad always loved Hawaiian shirts. He practically lived in them."

"Do you want to hold one?" Farmer John grabbed one in a bright red-and-green shirt.

"Yes," she whispered, too excited for more.

It nuzzled in as Lily pressed its little body against hers. She ran her cheek against its scratchy little whiskers. "You guys need to get back in the barn. Aren't you cold out here?" The goat let out a tiny little bleat in response. "Okay, okay. Time for you to go back inside and get all warmers and toasters."

A volunteer started shooing the baby goats back into the barn. Lily peeked inside. They all had little cozy nests of blankets and hay.

"Your donation helped us to get this barn back online. We'd had some roof problems, but we were able to get that fixed so we could house all the little guys. They'll live here for as long as they need to, and the friendlier ones will come with us to school events."

Several had hopped back in their warm piles of hay. Space heaters blew in warm air. "But they'll all be safe?" Lily said with a teary voice.

"Until they're old and gray. They'll always have a place with us."

"Can I, um—" She bit her lip, trying not to burst into sobs. "Can I come and visit them?"

"My dear, you can come every day if you like and feed them with your own two hands."

Nash had hung back along the outskirts of the fence and spared a head pat for a straggling curious goat who stared up at him.

"I take it you're not a goat person?" she asked over her shoulder.

His mouth quirked. "I'm not a livestock person, but I'm glad they will be 'warmers and toasters.'"

Lily felt a chill run through her and shuddered.

Nash took off his jacket and wrapped it around her shoulders. "Speaking of, maybe we should head out. You're cold."

She happily wiggled at the weight of his warm coat on her shoulders. "We haven't even done the tour yet," she said, looking back at the barn with regret.

Farmer John drove around the corner in a golf cart. "All aboard our Loco-*moo*-tive."

"And we'll see the cows?" She clapped her hands together.

"You can even toss them one of the balls."

"This is the best present ever!" She shook Nash's arm, throwing her arms around his waist in a fierce, tight hug. His arms wrapped around her, hugging her back.

She felt a kiss on the top of her head and peered up. Nash looked sweet and wistful.

"I'm glad you like it," he said with a soft smile. "Come on, let's finish the tour so we can get you all warmed up."

An hour later, Lily waved to the Paws and Plow Rescue Ranch staff as Nash backed out of the ranch's driveway.

"I thought on our way back we could visit an art museum and grab lunch," Nash said as he pulled onto the highway.

"Um, we're not going to talk about the forty-three baby goats still living in this world, too cute and too pure for it, because of you?"

"Lily," he sighed. "It's no big deal."

"It's a big deal. Hey," she said, putting a hand on his arm. "Thank you," she said earnestly. "It means a lot you would even get me any present, let alone the best present I've ever gotten."

Nash clenched his jaw, looking pained rather than happy, and stared straight ahead. "You're welcome."

And then the silence between them stretched.

And stretched again.

Sighing, she settled into her seat, trying to get comfortable. Maybe someday she'd figure him out. Why he'd go cold right as she felt that tug of *more* between them.

"There's an exhibit on Fauvism at the museum that I thought you might enjoy," he said quietly. "Thought it might be good to give you a break from sitting in one place and stretch your leg."

Oof. Those flutters started again.

"Nashford Robert Donnelly," she said in a slow, amazed voice. "How do you even know what Fauvism is?"

"You go on enough first dates with art history majors, you learn a few things. But I guess I won't have to have any more first dates. One of the benefits of being married to you," he said with an absent-minded smile.

Fake, fake, fake. This is all fake.

Keep him in the fake box.

He's not that swoony. He only just gave you the best fucking present ever.

Don't think about his hand on your ass two nights ago. Of how hard you came rubbing against him.

An unexpected blush tinged her cheeks, and she unwrapped her scarf from her neck, needing to cool down. "I've missed going to museums to get inspired. I practically lived at the MoMA when I first moved to New York."

He stole a glance at her as he drove. "I would have pegged you for a Met girl; all of those textures, dynasties, different art styles. Reminds me of what you do now. You take inspiration from everywhere and turn it into something your customers will enjoy."

He said all these things as if they weren't the most groundbreaking, sexiest things she'd ever heard from a man. Somebody who actually noticed what she did, not how her ass looked in a pair of jeans.

She was still shocked though, that he'd nailed it. "Yeah, that's exactly what I wanted to do. That's why it's really going to suck to leave Bloom."

He rubbed his lips in thought for a while. "Do you ever think you'll stop moving around once you finally find your place?" He said it in a carefree tone, but the hidden weight of the words still clouded her thinking.

"I don't know. I never wanted to be like, you know, *him*."

"Who? Matisse?"

She snorted, taken out of her melancholy. *He is a trip*. She could count on one hand the number of men who knew Matisse founded the Fauvism art movement, and they'd all gone to art school with her.

"No, my dad. Trapped in a small town, unable to leave, trying to make the best of a bad situation."

"I thought Frank liked Fairwick Falls. He seemed happy enough."

"Aside from the 20 years where he mourned his wife," Lily muttered as she stared past the empty fields and bare forests hurtling past her window.

His letter sat on her kitchen table under a pile of papers, but she always knew where it was. Before she'd moved to Nash's house, she'd feel it staring into her wherever she moved in her apartment. The last part of her dad waiting to be shared with her. She didn't want to feel the pain of his loss all over again.

She was still mad at him, even though she missed him so much. He'd finally gone to therapy once she was in college and mostly returned back to his old self, according to Rose and Violet.

But she'd had to grow up with a melancholy father who rarely paid her attention unless she was making him laugh.

That was where she'd perfected her comedic timing, and her outlandish blunt personality. She'd taken endless swings at seeing a light in his eyes. How she'd yearned for the dad that Violet and Rose had talked about. When he was funny and silly and warm. Not lost and distant, caught in a mist of missing her mom.

She sighed against the window, painting a heart in the fog against the glass. "I guess that's the danger of giving your heart to somebody. You can lose yourself. Which is why I absolutely refuse to."

Probably not the thing to say to your new husband who you've actually been in love with for fifteen years.

What if she told him and ruined everything? What if she opened up and admitted he was perfect in her eyes? That she'd been hopelessly in love with him ever since she was 12 and he'd made sure she was okay after a hard fall at the Frost Fest ice rink? He'd been a cool older boy and he'd been kind, and handsome, sitting with her as she iced her elbow until Rose got there.

"You never plan to fall in love?" he said with an incredulous look back at her as he pulled off the highway.

"Not if I can help it," she lied, her smile not meeting her eyes.

Switch the subject before he asks you about your childhood crush on him. "So is there anything I should keep in mind now that we're married? I'm not sure what kind of rules you rich people have. I'm sure your mother has about a hundred I've never heard of."

"You mean *us* rich people," he said, absent-mindedly picking goat hair off his sweater at a stoplight.

She cocked her head in confusion. "I'm not rich."

He turned into the art museum parking lot. "You're married to me and you have full run of my bank account. I thought that would have been clear. I have credit cards ordered for you. Use whatever you need."

He parked and turned off the car as if he hadn't just said the craziest shit to her.

Fourteen separate thoughts crashed in her head. *I'm rich? I have his credit cards? He planned this already?* "Nash, that's not why I did this."

"People will expect you to live a certain kind of life if you're married to a Donnelly. Plus, you'll need new outfits as we host people or go to dinner to charm board members," he said, straightening his collar in the rearview mirror. He cracked open his door and looked back at her. "Ready?"

For a life where I'm married to you? Not remotely.

Chapter Twenty

NASH

Nash forced himself not to stare at his wife's ass as he held the art gallery door open for her.

The last 24 hours had not gone to plan.

The wedding was *supposed* to feel fake.

And yet he felt *very* married to the woman whose smile was a permanent resident in his every dream.

The farm was *supposed* to be a cute thing.

He wasn't supposed to get a gigantic fucking *neon sign* from her dead father that he approved of their marriage.

Or maybe disapproved.

Nash wiped a hand down his face. *Leave it to Frank to send the message through a goat.*

Lily pointed to the bench at the center of the museum lobby. "We should get a photo. So we can prove we're all honeymoon-ish. Honestly most of my photos at the farm were of the cows."

He reluctantly sat. As she sat on his lap, flashes of her bent over his knee had his cock hardening.

Fuck. Think of anything other than her tits bouncing as you spanked her.

His hands draped by his sides, even though they itched to snake around her.

Shit. He screwed his eyes shut, thinking of the smell of pig manure at the farm. *There. Hard-on gone.*

"We have to look married and happy about it," she said, elbowing his chest.

He wrapped his arms around her waist and pulled her against his chest. He covered her hand with his, loving the feel of it in his palm.

She sighed against him as she took endless selfies with the museum entrance behind them. She looked adorable in her cropped sweater and cute jeans today. Her hair fell in curled waves, and he could admit they looked so fucking good together. Like they were *supposed* to be together.

"Think we should get one where we're kissing?" she asked quietly.

He'd savored the taste of her yesterday and already missed it. He'd get lost there if he let himself. Lost in taking her mouth, letting his lips wander along the column of her throat. Who could blame him?

He nodded silently, bringing her chin slowly to him. He brushed his lips against hers as her hand tightened in his. Their eyes never closed as he pulled her in.

It was like she saw into his soul.

He brushed their lips slowly, trying to keep everything PG. But it was like asking someone stranded in the Sahara to only have a sip of water.

He craved her, nearly gasping with the strain of holding himself back.

He pulled back, remembering his promise to not mess up again. He nodded to her phone. "Get a good shot?"

She blinked in surprise. "Uh, yeah." She swiped through several. She hopped off his lap and wiggled her leg as though it hurt, but she still held his hand. "Are you ready for a guided tour by a loud-mouthed art major?" She favored her injured leg as she stood in front of him.

"Why don't I get you a wheelchair? Your knee will get worse if you keep walking without the brace."

Lily rolled her eyes with humor. Her smile was sparkly and charming as she swung their interlaced hands. "Do you worry this much at work? I'm surprised your employees haven't mutinied. Made you walk the financial plank."

He laughed, shaking his head at her. "No, I only worry about people that—"

—I love.

Oh no.

Oh fuck.

A thousand tiny puzzle pieces clicked together from the last four weeks.

Her teasing, her laughter, her tears. How she made him laugh and how her smile lit him up from inside.

How he'd kept wanting to make her happy, like finding the farm thing, and the art museum. He wanted to make her life as joyful as she made his.

He was so hopelessly in love with his wife that it hit him like a punching bag to the chest, nearly knocking him sideways.

I'm in love with Lillian Fucking Parker.

She narrowed her eyes playfully. "You only worry about people that...are left-handed? That...have a penchant for possum care? That...swear *Die Hard* is a Christmas movie even though it's obviously not?"

Christ, she wasn't helping by being so adorable. His chest felt tight, realizing he'd been falling for a long time. Maybe since the moment he'd slid the ring on her finger in her loft.

She squeezed his hand, still interlaced in hers, with a look of dawning concern. "You okay? You look like you might barf. Need to go to the car?"

He laughed with hollow sadness. "No, I just need a minute. I remembered a phone call I need to make. You go ahead; I'll catch up."

She shrugged and grabbed her purse with a playful smirk. "If you can't find me, I'll be at the gift shop where I'll start a *large* tab with your name on it."

He took out his phone and stared at the black screen as his brain fritzed with panic.

I'm in love with my wife.

But this can't change anything.

She still wants to leave once she's better. I still have to stay.

She'd literally *just* said she would never fall in love with anyone.

And yet, here I am. Such a fool.

He took time to cool down and get his head on straight. He wandered through the large gallery, lost in thought and trying not to think of Lily. He enjoyed the arts and, in another lifetime, would have been a professor. One where he didn't have a life plan laid out before him from birth.

Twenty minutes later, he turned the corner into a side gallery and found Lily meandering along a wall of 19th century artists.

The paintings showed fantastical settings in deep, rich colors. A depiction of Romeo and Juliet professing their love caught his attention. Juliet's blonde swirling locks floated in the air, reminding him of the blonde that wouldn't leave his thoughts.

Romeo looked up adoringly at his Juliet, gobsmacked with the surprise of her. At how utterly impossible and ill-fated their match was.

I can sympathize.

Oh god, was his life a Shakespearian romantic tragedy?

"Look at you, studying art." Lily's bright voice appeared beside him. "Ooo, this is one of my favorites."

He glanced at the description next to the painting. It was depicting Act 2, scene 2. "This is the part where Romeo is telling Juliet that his devotion is so great, he could share everything together if they could only live happily ever after."

"Hmm. I don't remember that, *but* in fairness I slept through freshman English," she said with a laugh. "Is that the part where he says 'Whot light through yonda' win'ow breaks'?"

Nash chuckled at her comically terrible cockney accent, and she looked delighted at making him laugh. She was utterly romantic and perfect with her face upturned to him in the dim light of the gallery. Big brown eyes he wanted to sink into, like swirls of caramel. Hair like spun gold flowed over her shoulders.

"'*My bounty is as boundless as the sea, my love as deep. The more I give to thee, the more I have, for both are infinite,*'" he said quietly, staring down at her.

Lily's face went still with surprise.

Fuck, that was the wrong thing to say. *Don't quote Shakespeare at your new hot wife who you've fallen for.*

She blinked rapidly. "Did you just make that up?"

"That's Romeo's line in that scene," he said offhandedly, needing to escape. "Come on, let's grab lunch." He pulled her out of the gallery. *And hopefully she'll forget that little slip of the tongue.* "The museum cafe has a great vegan selection."

She stared at him in disbelief as he pulled her along. "Wait, do you just, like, *know* Shakespeare?"

Fuck. "Not really, though I read it to fall asleep sometimes. I was Romeo in high school."

"Of course you were. Because it's not enough that you were

an all-state basketball player valedictorian, you also had to be a perfect romantic hero."

"Holy fuck," he whispered, stopping short.

"Is that another Shakespeare quote?" she said as she slammed into his side with a smirk.

"No, that's Al Binghamton,"—he pointed across the open cafe of the art museum—"and his wife. He's a board member who I've had a rocky relationship with."

"Oh, let's go say hi," Lily said, now tugging his arm. "Old people love me. I'm very charming."

And a loose cannon. "No, it's fine. I don't want to bother them."

"Oh, come on. You look hot, I look hot." She tugged him across the cafe as if they happened to be walking past. Nash made eye contact with Al and waved.

"Well, hello!" Al said, standing up. "If it isn't the newlyweds. What are you two doing here?" He shook Nash's hand with a firm grasp that didn't portray his 80 years.

"We couldn't get away for a long honeymoon. You know how Nash is so dedicated to the bank." Lily placed her hand on Nash's arm so her wedding ring caught the light. "He still insisted though that he take me away for a day of art appreciation. It's my passion."

A pretty older woman stood next to Al. "Isn't that lovely? A young couple appreciating art on their honeymoon. More people should be like you two instead of gallivanting in a tequila-fueled haze."

Al smiled at his spunky wife. "Meet my wife, Cheryl."

"Oh my gosh, I love your scarf," Lily said, turning on all her charm.

"My granddaughter got it for me for Christmas."

Lily's brilliant smile sparkled back at her. "That color really suits you."

Ugh. Small talk. My actual personal hell. "Well, we don't want to interrupt," Nash said, steering Lily away.

"Oh, nonsense. I'm so sorry we didn't get to come to the wedding," Cheryl said. "But we'd already volunteered to watch our grandchildren."

"Maybe we could host you at our house for dinner," Lily said brightly.

Holy fuck. Invite Al Binghamton over for dinner? It was like introducing a wolf into the baby goat pen. He'd been trying to get golf time with Al for the last seven months.

Cheryl clapped her hands. "That sounds lovely. Albert, what do you think?"

"Whatever you want, dear." Al grimaced out a smile as he glanced at Nash.

"Well, then it's settled. I'll call next weekend and we'll set something up. It was so nice to meet both of you," Lily said warmly and waved to their grandkids.

Nash placed a hand around Lily's waist and guided her to the hostess stand. He'd made a reservation for them in the quiet, private dining area overlooking the misty gardens.

"Well done," he murmured into her hair and placed a kiss there.

Tried not to linger over the scent of flowers in her hair.

"See? People aren't so scary," she said brightly as she limped to their table.

"Are you sure you're doing okay? We can head home."

"And *not* eat the vegan club sandwich I saw on the menu back there? You're out of your goddamn mind, husband."

Husband.

Rein it in. Not the place to get an erection at her calling you her husband. Honestly, why did that have to be his kink of all kinks? Why couldn't it be bondage? Or breath play?

But no, I have to get off on my dream woman calling me her husband.

He pulled her chair out for her. "Eager to start physical therapy tomorrow?"

"You mean torture I pay for? Yes, I'm thrilled," she said, sitting. "But I will be excited to eventually be able to walk up a staircase without having to take a break."

He stilled, thinking about the night when he'd hauled her up over his shoulder, the vibrator ricocheting in his hands.

Don't think about her naked. Don't think about her under you. Or on top of you. Don't think about any fucking thing other than what's on this menu.

Lily seemed oblivious to how her words affected him. He'd just shut these feelings down. Simple as that.

Just stare straight ahead, grit through the next few months of his life.

∼

LILY

Lily hobbled into Nash's house. She'd slept the entire way back from the art museum, and her body felt stiff and achy now. He'd been Stonehenge silent after the art museum, responding to her with one-word answers, so she'd finally given up and used the drive back to rest.

It was like he'd turned into another person after lunch. Being with this man was like withstanding the tundras of Siberia. Glimmers of sparkles on the sloping snow taunted her, and then bam—bitter nothingness.

Nash walked through the kitchen with a pile of mail, setting it neatly in a stack on the edge of the counter. Without another word, he left the kitchen.

She looked through the mail. The familiar gut-twisting logo of her student loan company stared back at her.

"This day is already pretty weird. Let's make it worse." She opened the letter assuming she'd see the standard message. *'You owe a fuck ton of money, pay us immediately.'* All red letters, all caps.

Instead, she was met with something completely different.

"What the fuck?" she yelled. She scanned the page, flipping it back and forth, and checked the front of the envelope to see if it was a joke.

No. No one could be this cruel. Her eyes scanned it again.

It's all been paid?

All $70,456.28, paid in one lump sum. The letter was congratulating her on being done repaying her loans, finally.

Okay, they didn't have to add that last word.

But was this a mistake? Did the financial aid fairy grace her with a computer malfunction? She wasn't part of any loan forgiveness program.

Holy fuck. Wait a minute.

She dialed his number and he picked up in one ring.

"Meet me in the kitchen, now." She hung up. God, she wanted to pace so badly.

How dare he. He didn't even ask.

Thundering footsteps came from the third floor and then the second floor as Nash ran down the stairs. "Are you okay? What's wrong?"

She whirled on him, seeing red. "Did you do this?" She threw the letter across the counter.

He straightened, his face a wall of granite again. "You said it was stressing you. I took care of it. It's no big deal."

"It's $70,000 worth of a big deal. I should be consulted. This is my life, my future, my problem."

His jaw clenched as he stared at her. "It's really not a big deal for *me*, Lily."

Ugh, what a pompous, rich asshole. "Oh, I'm fully aware cash spurts out your ass whenever you want, but some of us have to work for a living. Some of us work really fucking hard, actually, and have big fucking bills and we don't need you spurting your cash everywhere uninvited."

His brows furrowed as he somehow grew even taller, more rigid in quiet anger. "I thought you'd be happy. You didn't know how you were going to pay. I took care of it."

She drilled her finger into his chest. "You didn't even *ask*."

He bent to her eye level. "Fine, I'll ask now. Lily, would you like me to pay off your student loans?"

"No!" she yelled immediately into his face. "Maybe. Probably, *Idon'tknowshutup*," she said all in a rush. "The point is I'm an adult in this relationship."

Nash crossed the kitchen to go back upstairs. "You had a problem. It was easy for me to take care of."

Lily screamed her rage up at the ceiling, finally releasing the frustration from the day. All the feelings that swirled around as she reached out, tried to connect with him, and was met with a confusing cocktail of lust and granite.

He looked back at her unfazed, the fucker.

Why couldn't he at least be scared of her? "How much did you spend?" she called.

He halted. "I thought that would be obvious, $70,456."

She hobbled toward him. "No, you condescending ass. At the sanctuary. How much?"

He wouldn't meet her gaze. "It's not important."

"How much money do you *have*?" She tried to catch his eye, but he looked away.

The silence landed between them.

...*Oh fuck.* "Do you have, like, *a lot* a lot?" Her brain

zip-zapped a million miles an hour. *How had they not talked about this?* "But you're like...a relatively normal guy."

He, again, stared straight back at her with a stone-faced expression. "I *am* a normal guy."

"With either really poor spending habits or a fuck ton of money," she countered, coming up close to him, drilling a finger into his chest. "Are you *hop on your plane, go to your private island, hunt white tigers for fun* kind of rich?"

His nostrils flared as his facade cracked with irritation.

Ha, she was getting to him.

"No. I am, however, the product of generational wealth. I made excellent investing decisions when I was young *because* of said generational wealth and I spend money on things that matter to me."

She wasn't buying it. "But your clothes. They're just normal clothes."

"Clothes don't matter to me." He tried to walk past her, but she stepped in front of him.

Her eyes narrowed. "Your car is nice, but it's nothing extravagant."

He looked over her head, not meeting her gaze. "Cars don't matter to me."

"Then why would you spend your money on me..." Her voice fell as she finally put two and two together.

Those things don't matter to him.

I do.

"Why is it such a problem that I paid it off?" Nash said, stepping closer to her.

"Because," she countered.

Such a great argument. Good job, Lily.

"I'm happy to take one thing off your plate and it doesn't hurt me that much, so tell me why. Why is it a problem?" He looked down at her with those fucking eyes. The ones she got lost in.

She started backing away, needing space to think clearly. "Because you already did the thing with the barn," she said defensively.

"Why is *that* a problem?" he asked, getting heated.

"*Because*," she spat back. Her back hit the kitchen cabinet, and he stood toe to toe with her.

"Because why?" he said, towering over her.

Her heart beat hard against her ribcage. "Because I can't get used to this," she yelled, finally admitting a deep truth she didn't even know was buried inside of her. "I can't get used to this," she repeated quietly. "It's all too..."

Dreamy. Perfect. Luxurious.

"...much," she lied.

Her head was getting too crowded with him. With this lifestyle. She'd only been 'with' him for two weeks, but already she'd gotten used to having heaps of avocados in the kitchen. Not thinking about her monthly budget for coffee, art supplies.

Not feeling desperately alone in the middle of the night as long as he slept right beside her.

She needed distance from him. It would be less painful later if she didn't get more attached. Even more lost in the fantasy she let herself believe when they were in public. "Since we're married now, we don't have to sleep in the same room. Right?" She followed his Adam's apple as he swallowed.

He cleared his throat and stepped back, fidgeting with his watch. "I suppose not."

She could breathe again without his cologne clouding her thoughts of what forever safety might feel like.

Nash finally met her eyes, his face emotionless. "I had an engagement ring budget. Since you were willing to wear my family's ring, I used the money for your loans. You are welcome to pay me back."

He walked past her without another glance.

"Fine, I will," Lily spat. She'd felt cornered and threatened by how much he might like her despite all the conflicting signs. The marathon tango of hot to cold that she'd danced in the last 48 hours was fucking exhausting.

He walked upstairs with thunderous footsteps, and he called back, cold and unfeeling, "I accept checks, PayPal, or cash. But only if it spurts out of your ass."

"You *wish* you could see cash come out of my ass!" Lily spat back.

Definitely a great thing to yell at your husband/roommate/childhood crush/current crush/dude you were hopelessly in love with on day two of your marriage.

Chapter Twenty-one

LILY

Lily would give everything she owned to never see a red satin heart ever again.

She stuck a *Forever and Always* sign into a heart-shaped arrangement of red roses.

Barf.

Love can go suck a big fat one, she thought as she stabbed another sign into a silk rose arrangement.

Valentine's Day was only a week away, and she'd been injured-knee deep in roses, teddy bears, and chocolates as Bloom stocked up for the big day.

Every hour she was awake, she was at the store prepping for Arma-love-geddon.

She'd also made headway with KGM in the last week. They liked her initial ideas and would mock up a Bloom home goods-inspired line to see if any national chains would be interested. Now she just had to prototype her ideas and see if they'd work.

And on top of the mountain of work, she hadn't spoken to her husband in almost a week.

She'd barely seen Nash, given she'd moved back into the

first floor bedroom. He practically lived in his office, and, to be fair, she lived at Bloom's prep table.

They really would be man and wife in name only.

The bells on Bloom's front door clattered, and a few minutes later, Pearl popped into the prep room with a confused arch in her pierced eyebrow. "There's a lady here who said she's interviewing for a job. Is this because I played *Love is a Bitch* in the store the other day?"

Lily threw her head back with laughter. "No, you're not getting fired. Plus, Mrs. Maroo added it to her playlist. Send the candidate back. It's for my second-in-command." Pearl shrugged a shoulder and went back into the store.

Lily stretched and a groan wrung out of her. Pain shot up her leg as she lifted herself off the stool. Physical therapy had been a bitch that morning.

Let's hope this candidate doesn't cry like candidate number one, doesn't mansplain like number two, knows how to work a computer unlike number three, and isn't an airhead like number four.

Her second-in-command (actually future replacement, unbeknownst to Rose and Vi) had to be perfect. Thus far, the odds were looking slim at finding someone she could entrust the store to.

She turned around and came face to face with Allison Gordon, owner of Cooperstown Florals.

"Hi," Lily said with surprise. She and Allison had met at a *Women in Stems* floral networking event a few months ago. They'd talked about grabbing coffee, but Rose's wedding had popped up, and the debacle since then had kept her busy. "Sorry, I almost didn't recognize you with the new hair."

Allison was tall and curvy with peachy pink hair that had been blonde the last time Lily had seen her. Her nose ring winked in the shop's light.

"Hi." Allison waved warmly. "Yeah, trying to get back to my

old self after a long time being blonde." She hefted a tote on her shoulder. "Is this where we'll do the interview?"

Lily shook her head to clear it. "Wait, *you're* the Allison that's interviewing?" She'd been expecting an Allison *Styles*.

Allison nodded and pushed up her glasses with a shy smile. "I go by Styles, my maiden name now. *Finally* got everything changed back." She raised her eyebrows as if it had been an ordeal.

"And you're interviewing for *this* job? Don't you own your flower shop?" *Oops—not the most tactful way to ask why someone wanted the job.* She smacked her forehead. "Sorry, I mean...make yourself comfortable. I'll be your *very* professional interviewer today, I promise."

Allison laughed, looking less nervous as she set her things down. "So I own Cooperstown Florals, but I have this great store manager who runs the day to day so I'm not really needed. I'm so impressed with what you've built since last year. The way Rose described the role, I could operate at a much higher scale with all the exciting things you're doing. Violet's cable show, the physical products you've done with local companies, all the big weddings you've booked. We've even talked about bringing my store under the Bloom brand."

Lily really needed to talk to Rose more often. Or read one of the five thousand emails she sent. This was all news to her.

Pearl trudged into the prep room in her heavy combat boots to grab her coat. "I'm heading out." She pulled on her heavy black puffer coat decorated with safety pins and patches of local bands. A concerned look came over her face though as she leaned on the back door. "But, like, don't stay too late, okay? It's supposed to snow a shit-ton tonight."

Interesting. Who knew there was a soft girl under all that black cat energy? "Aw, Pearl. I didn't know you cared so much. We won't."

Pearl rolled her eyes with an embarrassed smile. "I just don't want you to break, like, your other knee. Or whatever. Have a good night," she called as the back door slammed shut.

Lily waved goodbye with a laugh as Allison opened up her laptop on the prep table. "The role has changed recently. This will be more of a creative partnership. But you'd still run projects independently sometimes. Are you sure you'd be interested?" She didn't want to waste anyone's time. She'd seen Allison's work and it was great.

"Honestly, the past two years have been kind of crazy personally." Allison tucked her bob-length hair behind her ears. "I need a change, and something like this could benefit both of us. Can I walk you through my portfolio?"

She was firm, but gentle in her explanation. Kind and strategic. *Pretty much the opposite of me, ha.* This could be great. "Let's see that bad boy," Lily said with a smile.

This could be the perfect situation. Have someone experienced and competent take over when she left in a few months. *Hopefully she likes possums.*

Allison's portfolio was full of photography and graphic design projects. She had a solid eye for details and kept up with the trends.

"Oo, oh! I love what you did for this wedding. Using clouds of baby's breath for that huge impact," Lily said. She was loosened up and chatty as she pointed to Allison's screen. "I remember seeing it on social media and being so *jealous* I didn't think of it first!"

Allison laughed. "Then it sounds like we could be a great team."

Lily glanced at the clock and was surprised to see it was almost 7:00. They'd talked for almost two hours. She'd forgotten what it felt like to gossip over a shared love of design choices, nuance, and craft. She felt energized and happy.

"Oh my gosh." Allison blanched as she looked at her phone. "I'm so sorry. I didn't realize it was so late. I talked your ear off."

"No." Lily waved a hand to swat away her concerns. "Honestly, it's been the highlight of the day. It's just been me and these accursed Valentine's Day arrangements." Lily gestured to the pile of red and pink roses. "I can walk you out."

"Or..." Allison smiled with a hopeful grin. "I can do a free trial. Lend you a pair of hands for a little while."

"I can't ask you to do that. The road will be treacherous back to Cooperstown if it gets snowy," Lily said.

"Nah." Allison put down her things. "My parents moved to the outskirts of Fairwick Falls. They'll be thrilled if I spend the night." Allison picked up a bucket of roses with a questioning look.

"Then you are my absolute new favorite person on earth. Don't tell my sisters." A sigh of relief escaped Lily at finally having help from another artist.

They lost track of time, gossiping over shared acquaintances, Allison's background in design, Allison's messy divorce (god, she wanted so many juicy details, but it felt inappropriate to pry during a job interview), and of course, how to make the Valentine's Day arrangements even better as they worked together. Lily hadn't had this much fun while she worked in ages. *Maybe since college.* She'd always worked alone.

The snow had stayed away for an hour longer than originally anticipated, but thick flakes started to flutter down. Lily looked at her phone as they finished up the last batch and found a string of texts from Nash.

> NASH
> You walked to work today, right?

> When will you be home? There's a big snowstorm starting soon.

Then twenty minutes later.

> You're not walking home are you? It's 8 degrees outside.

> Oh god you would do something like that.

She snorted. *He ain't wrong.*
Then ten minutes later.

> Is Violet taking you home?

Then two minutes later.

> Just talked to Violet, she said you're at the shop.

> I'm driving to Bloom to pick you up.

Lily glowed inside. She'd never been septuple-texted before. It was an odd feeling having someone constantly worry about her. She projected self-confidence and capability, but all she really craved was to have someone care for her. She'd tried to enter her soft girl era in New York, but damn, it was hard to do that when it felt like the world was against you.

She started to respond, but the front door of Bloom unlocked and she heard familiar footsteps as Nash walked to the back.

Their eyes connected in a silent conversation. He seemed worried and maybe still a little mad. Would their fight go on forever? She was new to this relationship crap.

She stuck on a friendly smile as he walked toward her.

"Nash, meet Allison. She's made the mistake of interviewing for Bloom, and I've already put her to work. Allison, this is my... husband." *Weird, weird, weird.*

His stern expression melted away and a friendly smile replaced it as he stuck out his hand. "Nice to meet you. The snow is getting bad out there. I hope you're local." The large floor-to-ceiling windows were full of fat falling snowflakes.

Allison grabbed her coat. "I should get going. My mother's going to be thrilled to have a surprise visitor."

They said their goodbyes, and Lily gathered her things to go.

Nash fiddled with a rose petal on the table. "I forgot you'd be slammed right now."

She pulled on her coat. "For some reason only red roses could declare your undying love. Why do they all love fucking roses so much? You know who doesn't stab you? Daisies. *I'd* much rather have a flower that didn't have gigantic spikes on it."

"Like wildflowers?" Nash said, meeting her eyes.

Oof. A Mack truck hit her heart with longing.

He carried a bundle of fabric under his arm.

"Get a new scarf?" she asked.

He shrugged. "It's an old blanket. It's going to be really cold tonight. I thought—" He cleared his throat, not meeting her eyes. "I thought Peaches might need it. I'll drop it in her box."

He brought a blanket for my possum?

She couldn't form words in response as he went out the back door to the garbage bins. Her heart melted and apparently had taken the power of speech with it.

I guess our first fight is over?

He came back inside and locked the door behind him. "Ready to go?"

A sketch she'd worked on earlier in the week caught her eye

as she grabbed her things. She'd started sketching it even before her brain knew what she was doing. She'd cleaned the sketch up, adding layers of watercolor to it.

"This isn't 70,000 dollars coming out of my"—she swallowed with a smile—"wallet. But it's just a small gesture to say sorry for not being more gracious for all your gifts. And you know. For Valentine's Day."

She shrugged and handed the small painted sketch to him. "It started out as a warm-up sketch one day, and took on a life of its own."

Nash's eyes widened and unexpectedly filled as he frowned at it, full of emotion. *Oh no. Maybe this is the wrong thing to give him.*

"That's my dad," he said in a choked voice.

"It's a memory I had of him when I was in high school. I was at the bank putting up a flyer for a fundraiser. A little kid had dropped his teddy bear and the mom was frantically looking for it. Your dad had found it and kept it tucked safe away."

Bob Donnelly had been a big man, like Nash. Lily painted her memory of him crouching down in his three-piece suit with a bright smile, holding out a worn teddy bear. His bright, warm spirit contrasted with the stark background of the bank. She'd tried hard to capture the joy on his face when a little kid ran toward his outstretched hand with the teddy bear.

Strong arms wrapped around her as Lily registered that she was being hugged a split second later. Nash held her tight, and she hugged him back, their fight apparently over now.

He pulled away and dropped his arms, but stood close. "Thank you. For the painting and the memory. I'll ask in the future about big stuff."

Lily was moved. She hadn't thought he'd care that much. "Thank you for thinking of Peaches. And I'm sorry for not being more grateful."

His eyes flitted to her mouth, and she wanted to crystalize the moment. All that possibility of tasting him again. She'd been dreaming of his lips for a week and was becoming addicted to the whole body feeling of his kisses.

He stepped back with a subtle shake of his head as if admonishing himself.

Right. Lily grabbed her purse. "Welp, time to brave the roads to your house, I guess."

"Our house," Nash said, correcting her as they walked to the front of the store.

If only it was my house and my real home with you forever.
If only.

~

NASH

The soft tinkle of piano notes floated through the quiet restaurant as Nash listened to Al Binghamton drone on about his racketball game. Candlelit tables surrounded Nash, Lily, and the Binghamtons as they sipped after-dinner espresso.

They'd just finished dinner at the only four-star restaurant within a fifty-mile radius. Lily sat giggling with Cheryl in their own conversation. They'd hit it off immediately, and Nash sensed they were kindred spirits.

Nash hadn't been able to take his eyes away from the vision beside him at the table all night. He'd purposefully kept his distance from her when they were home together. After their fight, she'd moved back to the guest bedroom. It was for the best. Less of a chance to blurt out his feelings or do something stupid.

When she'd come into the foyer that evening, he'd felt like he was married to Cinderella. She wore an ice-blue clinging dress in a classic cut, but it hung on every perfect place on her body. The material had a slight sparkle to it, and her hair was loose in long, curling waves. She'd never looked more beautiful.

He was married to a fucking princess in disguise.

"And I've lost him," Al said with a chuckle, sipping his coffee.

"Sorry," Nash said, dragging his eyes away from Lily. Al slapped his shoulder with a friendly pat. This was a far cry from the cold man who'd joined the board a year ago.

Al grabbed Cheryl's hand. "It's honestly refreshing to see a young man so in love with his new bride."

"And then *I* said," Lily said, in the middle of an animated story to Cheryl, "I'm not paying for lilacs that belong in a Salvador Dali painting."

Cheryl threw her head back with laughter.

"They were practically *melting* on the floor, Cheryl." Lily burst out in laughter. "One was literally draped over a tree branch. I'm not making that up."

Cheryl wiped at her eyes. "Oh stop, I can't take it. Oh, you're gonna make me tinkle."

Lily's bright, charming personality could win anybody over. His wife practically glowed in the middle of the cozy restaurant. A warm wave of wanting hit Nash's chest.

Maybe that fucking bylaw was actually a good idea.

He reached for her hand. She glanced over her shoulder, and he brought her knuckles up and brushed them against his lips. Lily's ability to connect with people never ceased to amaze him.

"*I* used to paint when I was young," Cheryl said, sipping her coffee with a mysterious air. "Before life took me off onto a different path."

"It's time for you to get back on your artistic horse. Try painting again," Lily said with an energetic smile.

"Oh, I don't know," Cheryl said, waving her hand away at Lily.

"Come on," Lily said, encouraging her. "What does it hurt to get out some paints? I could loan you my easel. I hardly ever use it."

"You should do it," Al said, putting a hand around his wife's shoulders. "Our life has changed so much in the last few years. Things have settled down. We don't have as many commitments anymore. You should pick it back up again."

"I'm so glad you agree, Al," Lily said with a glint in her eye that Nash recognized.

Uh-oh.

"Change is such an important part of life, don't you think? Us adapting to it," she continued.

"Of course. If you don't adapt, you wither away. It's important to keep changing to keep up with the times," Al added.

What the hell? Al was the single biggest proponent of *nothing* changing in Fairwick Falls.

"You are so right," Lily said with an only slightly placating tone that Nash recognized because he knew her so well. "I think it's important for any institution—Bloom, my flower shop, for example—to adapt to the changing times. Even, say, a bank should keep up. Like all of the updates Nash wants to make to the bank's bylaws. Removing outdated language about gender and expectations that don't apply to the 21st century."

"Well." Al sat up straighter, not wanting to be outmaneuvered by a pint-sized hot blonde, if Nash had to guess. "I've always believed in preserving important things, Lily. Some things can change on the surface, but tradition is important to remember where we come from."

Cheryl leaned forward with her silver-streaked hair glinting in the candlelight. She smiled and rested a hand on her husband's arm.

"You would never know it now, but in the 60s, those words would have been the last thing out of his mouth." Cheryl's voice lowered with a mischievous tone. "He had hair to his waist, tie-dye shirts, bell-bottom jeans." Her eyes sparkled with mischief as Al scoffed.

Nash and Lily exchanged surprised glances. It was hard to imagine the stodgy Al Binghamton as a free-spirited hippie in the 60s.

Cheryl's mouth quirked. "Didn't you used to say that change was the only constant? Of course, that was after he rolled up a very large—"

"Anyway." Al cleared his throat.

"It sounds like you were a chic trendsetter, Al." Lily sipped the rest of her wine with a warm smile. "I bet you still are."

Al looked at his wife, who shrugged back at him. "I'll consider it. You're very persuasive, young lady."

She was a hell of a lot more than persuasive. Gorgeous, fierce, absolutely perfect, and sand through Nash's fingers with every passing day.

The four of them walked to the restaurant's coat check, and Nash's stomach sank. Jeremy walked through the front door of the restaurant with two other board members in tow. Nash and Al exchanged pleasantries with the men as Nash glared at Jeremy.

What the fuck was he playing at? This was over. He was married to Lily, things were going well with the bank, membership was up, profits were up. The fact that Jeremy was still playing a game he'd already lost showed how stupid he was.

As Cheryl and Lily chatted off to the side, Al talked to the other board members about their golf weekend plans for April.

Jeremy spoke low next to him. "How's your sham of a marriage going?" His weaselly eyes slid to Lily. She hadn't yet put on her coat, and her creamy skin practically shone in the golden light of the restaurant. She turned, giving a view of her back as Jeremy's eyes lingered on her.

"You wouldn't mind if I took your hot little gold digger for a spin, would you?" Jeremy said with an evil smile growing on his face.

"What the actual *fuck* did you just say to me?" Nash saw red. He restrained himself enough to keep his voice calm, but his hands had already balled into fists at his sides.

"Oh come on. Word in New York is that everyone's had a turn in her—"

Nash hadn't even realized his hand had come up for Jeremy's throat until he heard the shocked yell of Lily behind him. He'd slammed Jeremy against the nearby wall without thinking.

"That is my *wife*." Nash gripped the throat in his hand harder. "Speak of her again, even fucking *look* at her, and your smug face will be buried into the concrete."

Jeremy's face was turning red, but an evil grimace slid onto it as the board members went to intervene. Nash shook them off as he let Jeremy down.

"Let's go, Nash," Lily said, pleading at his elbow.

Nash turned around, finally registering that everyone in the restaurant, including the board members, stared at him in shock. He grabbed Lily's hand and, without a backward glance, walked out of the restaurant.

She was his *wife*.

He'd do whatever it took to protect her.

Chapter Twenty-two

LILY

Okay, we're going to die here.

That was all Lily could think as another foot of snow fell outside on the lawn.

The snowstorm they'd expected a few days ago had only been flurries. Then, unexpectedly, an unending downpour of snow had started over Valentine's Day weekend and hadn't stopped since.

It was day three of being snowed in with her husband, who never stayed in a room more than five minutes with her.

She walked into the kitchen to get a snack? He left.

She was in the living room reading a book? He would walk in, grab a blanket, and practically run out.

The chardonnay currently loosening Lily's libido thrummed through her veins and swirled in her glass. She stared at Nash's office door that had been closed since 9 AM that morning.

Seventy-two hours together in this house and she'd spent less time with him than with her gynecologist at her annual exam.

Honestly, between the two, she'd gotten far more action with the gynecologist.

But things weren't adding up.

The kisses were explosive. The honeymoon was cotton candy sweet. That one time with the vibrator they hadn't talked about, and the hottest orgasm of her life being spanked until she came all over him. He nearly defenestrated Jeremy defending her honor (so fucking hot) and constantly touched her when they were out in public.

And he didn't want to spend time with her at home.

She took a sip of wine and furrowed her brows. *It doesn't add up.*

They were adults. Why couldn't they just bang it out?

Maybe I'll finally seduce him.

Wine glass still in hand, she rifled through her underwear drawer. She unearthed her swimsuit to take advantage of the deliciously huge hot tub in Nash's backyard. Luckily, her physical therapy was going well, and she didn't need the cockblocker, AKA knee immobilizer.

She slipped into the bikini. It was tiny, pink and made her boobs look fantastic. Grabbing the wine bottle and another glass, she knocked on Nash's door with a smile.

It was well past five o'clock, and they'd both been working nonstop for the last three days at home. She'd killed the KGM conversation today. Things were going well with the new product line. Once she got back in the studio, she'd be able to photograph some of the ideas she'd prototyped.

Nash opened the door, and surprise overtook his face.

"Hot tub time!" she said, dancing with the wine bottle and glasses in hand.

"Uh–I, uh…" he said, stuttering, unlike himself.

Ha, the bikini is working.

"Come on, you've been working for three days straight. Come help me christen the hot tub. It'll be my first time hopping in it."

"No, I can't do that," he said, refusing to look at her directly.

"It's almost six o'clock. Come on. I won't bite, I promise."

"I have things to do, Lily," he said, finally leveling his gaze at her. "Not all of us are free-spirited artists. Some of us have to pay the bills."

Nope, not gonna let him give me the cold shoulder. "Um, your giant pile of money squirreled away in a vault somewhere is what pays your bills."

"I have to keep making more of it so everyone can keep a job at the bank, so everyone's investments stay sound, and yes, so I can keep my vault happy. I don't have time for childish activities," he said, getting haughty.

He always did this when he wanted to distance himself.

"Um, *hi*. Hot tubs are the least childish thing you could do. They're very sexy and adult," she said, gesturing with the wine glasses.

Her tits were barely contained in the bikini, and she was getting cold. It was February after all, even if she was inside.

He raised an eyebrow, impatient to get back to his work.

"*Fine*. I will go have very adult fun times by myself."

Without saying a word, he closed the door in her face.

Except now the hot tub only made her mad.

One more glass of wine in, she'd changed out of her swimsuit into silk sleep shorts and a tank top. She'd been slowly pacing for an hour in her bedroom, replaying every conversation they'd had for the last three days. Hell, the last four weeks.

When they kissed, it was like her soul intertwined with his. They had fun together when they were out in public. So why the fuck didn't he want to spend any time with her?

They'd even made good partners at the dinner with Al. She hadn't said one inappropriate joke all night, and it had been *torture*. Al talked about his racketball score, saying 'I just can't get it up' again and *again*. She'd had fifteen jokes on the tip of her tongue and nearly broke a rib keeping them all in. She'd made Nash listen to every single one on the way home.

Finally, her willpower broke, and she wandered through the house to go find him. It was after six, so she knew *exactly* where he'd be after he drank his nightly protein shake. Honestly, did this man have any fun?

Lily needed fun to breathe, to create, to be herself. He seemed to live in a world of Spartan self-discipline. He punished himself in the home gym in the basement regularly, especially on nights where they'd had a run-in.

She slowly hobbled down to the finished walk-out basement. A wall of glass windows showed sparkling snow falling over the rolling hills of the backyard.

The gym was clean and spacious, taking over the entire basement of the enormous house. There were weight racks, a treadmill, and every type of machine she could want.

He can't escape me here if I'm also here.

She'd chase that motherfucker through his own goddamn house until he finally broke down and told her what the hell was going on.

~

NASH

A FAMILIAR STILTED rhythm echoed on the stairs as he heard Lily walking down to the basement. He increased the speed on the treadmill and focused on the financial podcast blaring in his ear.

He clenched his teeth, trying to scrub the image burned into his retinas. He'd opened his door and seen his every fantasy in front of him: Lily in a barely-there bikini with a happy, bubbly smile and glass of his favorite chardonnay.

Just focus. No room for mistakes.

He sucked in air through his nose and out through his mouth as Lily talked over his podcast. Honestly, Kai Ryssdal and a volatile market could take his mind off of most things, except the blonde waving her arms like a traffic conductor in front of him. He paused the podcast, popping one earbud out.

"What?" he said sharply. He needed to keep a lock on everything. He couldn't look at her, couldn't engage with her. Otherwise, the boiling pot of lust and need he kept locked tight would explode.

Again.

It had been a long three fucking days in this house trapped with her. You'd think in an 8,000-square-foot house, it would be easy to avoid her, but no—she was everywhere. Popping around every corner now that she was more mobile. Bored, wanting to hang out, looking so soft and huggable in her pajama pants with her messy bun on top of her head.

He'd forgotten what it was like to really live with a woman. One that you found irritatingly and distractingly adorable and, in his case, shouldn't touch.

You're a Donnelly. Do your duty. No room for mistakes.
Breathe in the nose, out the mouth.

"What is it?" she said, stepping in front of the treadmill.

"I don't know what you mean," he said quickly, pressing the incline of the treadmill. If he worked harder, he couldn't focus on her.

Perfect form, engage the abs, loosen the shoulders.

She held a glass of wine as if it was her prop for her interrogation. "Did I do something wrong? Did I piss you off?" she yelled over the noise of the treadmill.

"What? No," he said suddenly, keeping his eyes straight ahead, not looking at her in her sexy silk sleep shorts that rode up to reveal the long expanse of upper thigh. She wore a soft tank top, and if he allowed his eyes to linger, he'd be sure she didn't have a bra on.

Snow fell in gentle waves in front of the window, and he tried to focus on every single flake in front of him.

"Come on. We've been trapped for three days. You've barely spoken ten words to me. I try to be nice, I try to be friendly, and you just dash away. It's like you're married to this treadmill and not to me. Nash, just tell me." She stepped up to the lip of the treadmill, getting in his eye-line so he couldn't avoid her anymore. "Tell me what I did. Talk to me. You can't run away from me in here."

He slammed the stop button on the treadmill and hopped off. Raising his arms behind his head, he tried to catch his breath. "I'll go run outside."

"There's a hundred feet of snow," she said, slowly hopping off the front of the treadmill.

He walked in a slow circle, trying to slow his hammering heart.

"What did I do wrong? Why won't you talk to me like a human?"

"I can't," he said, puffing, and started toward the stairs. He'd run through two feet of snow before he gave in.

"No," she said, blocking his exit.

Damn, she was faster now. "How many glasses of wine have you had?" he said.

"Fuck you, none of your business. Two." She took another sip defiantly.

He tried to dart past her. She slammed a hand in front of his face in the stairwell. "No, you have to tell me. Why are you avoiding me?"

"It's not that, I'm just..." He backed away, trying to catch his breath.

"You can't trap me in this house and not talk to me. Just, for the love of God, *tell me what is going on*. Are you in love with somebody?"

"No." He puffed out a laugh. *Yes, sort of.*

Why wouldn't his heart stop hammering? He hadn't run that hard.

She got in his face, sounding exasperated. "Am I boring? Do you think I'm stupid, and you don't want to talk to me because I can't keep up? I read things. I sent you that article on environmental influences on the stock market."

"Of course I don't think you're stupid," he said, trying to put some distance between them. He looked everywhere but in front of him. She was too sexy, too smart, too alluring, too *right fucking there*.

He backed away in the gym, but she kept following him. "Is it that I'm not good enough?" He couldn't contain it much longer. Her eyes went teary as she blinked furiously to keep from crying. "You want to spend time with somebody else? Some...some other woman?"

Finally, he broke.

He fell to his knees, gasping as the truth rushed out.

"It's because I *want* you," he yelled, letting the admission finally, *finally* fall off of him. He gasped as it all rushed out. "Because I need you like my next breath. I've wanted you ever since my soul found yours and I feel like I'll break in two if I don't have you. I want *every* part of you and I'm tearing myself to shreds to keep my sanity. Because the minute I give in, you'll be gone. And I'd rather suffocate than know how good it could be between us. I just..." He panted, rubbing his chest, as the world tilted around him. "...*Goddamnit*, I just *want* you."

He rode a rollercoaster as feelings shuttered by him. Relief. Joy. Fear. It felt so good not to hold it all in anymore

To finally let part of himself be free.

He panted, staring at his hands, finally raising his face to see her. She looked like a fuckable dream standing above him, biting her lip.

"Then have me." Her tone was sultry, challenging.

Christ. If only it was that easy. "I can't," he said, looking back down. He'd give in completely if he looked at her curves and her peachy skin that begged him to bite into it.

"You can."

He had to maintain some sanity. Or he'd lose himself completely in her. "I *cannot.*" He stared at the ground, willing her to go away.

She pushed back as much as he did. "Nash, I *need you to fuck me,*" she argued.

You know what?

Fuck it.

He pushed up in one movement and picked her up. His mouth was on hers before he pressed her against the brick wall with her legs wrapped around him. He feasted on her mouth. *Fucking finally.* His tongue met hers, finally not holding himself back.

She'd pushed him to the brink, and now she'd see how much he wanted her. His teeth grazed her lips as she moaned under him. She rolled her hips into him and bit down hard on his bottom lip. *Fuck*, she might have drawn blood. He growled, sucking harder, finally enjoying that brightness he'd missed for so long. Claiming it as his.

His cock was hard against her heated middle, and she ground against him as he pressed against her, needing every inch. He *wanted* this woman.

Wanted all of her. Her messes. Her lusty kisses. Her best days. Her worst.

And she just wanted his body.

He pulled away from her mouth, like a magnet leaving its mate unwillingly. He rested his forehead on hers, trying desperately to gain a foothold in the last two minutes of honesty.

"I can't," he panted. "I won't. I won't be one of your fuckboys." He saw a flutter of recognition in her eyes.

He'd caught her in the game she was trying to play with him. "I don't *feel* like this for people. Except when..." *When I'm in love with them.* "When I have feelings for them. So I cannot do this with you. Because it would be one-sided. I'm not a release valve. I don't just want your body, Lily. I want *you.*"

He dragged his eyes from her pouting, swollen lips. Her chest rose and fell like she'd sprinted a mile. Like she was panicking.

He slowly put her down but never took his hands from her waist.

She shook her head. "You don't mean that. This can just be fun. Then later, you'll forget it and find someone who's a better wife for you."

He wanted to roar in frustration, but instead, he pulled her in. She had to understand.

He'd *make* her understand.

"Goddamnit, Lily. There isn't better for me. You are perfect right now. When you leave your art projects every-fucking-where, like a trail of your soul. When you cry over baby goats because you're the sweetest person I know. When you're a goddamn foul-mouthed artistic genius. I want to devour you whole. I want you enough to crawl through hot coals. You are the last thing from forgettable. You are *everything*, Lily, and I want all of you."

She swallowed, looking like she was fighting with herself. "No one..." She wouldn't meet his eyes. "People don't feel like that about me."

"Or maybe you never let anyone get close enough so they could crave you like I do. I know every single nook and cranny of your baggage and your joys." He caught her eye. "*I* feel like that for you."

He put every single card he'd been holding on the table as he waited on the precipice.

"Tell me," he pleaded, nearly losing his mind. "Tell me you feel this *more* between us."

Would she pretend like this was nothing?

Her chest moved up and down with ragged breaths, but her eyes were fixed to his. She looked like a deer about to bolt.

Fuck. Please don't run from me, sweetheart.

If he'd blinked, he'd have missed it. But, no.

There it was again.

A tiny nod.

And another one as a tear slid off her lashes. "I lied," she whispered through wobbly lips. "That day in Bloom last August. I wanted the kiss to be more. So badly."

"Thank *Christ*." His lips landed on hers as he gathered her into his arms. He wasn't letting her go.

Tonight or otherwise.

Chapter Twenty-three

NASH

Nash kissed his wife with every atom of his soul, crushing her against him. He was hungry for her, but he'd take his time.

He'd waited too long.

Slowly, so slowly, he slid his hands down and grabbed her hips, pulling her against him. "I've stared at your curves for over a year," he growled. "Thirteen months of torture."

She smiled against his lips. He kissed her cheek, her jaw, licking each bit he could find that was new to him. Her throat was a work of art, delicate but strong. Like spun copper.

He raked his teeth along her skin, feeling feral. She moaned out his name, her nails scratching up and down his arms.

He wanted to fuck her hard. Needed to feel the press of every part of her against him. Needed to taste her. He'd thought of it a thousand times in the last week. Since his slip before the wedding.

He grabbed her ass and gripped each cheek as she ground against him. She was fierce and small and luscious, and he wanted her so badly his teeth ached from self-restraint.

"I don't want to scare you," he panted. "I'm a bigger guy and I feel *crazed* for you—"

"I trust you," she said without even a pause. "Always."

The pink glow in her cheeks was perfect. She was perfect. God, if he could have one woman for his life, he wanted it to be this one. He wanted to bend her over. Make her scream his name. He wanted her dazed and lusty and writhing and moaning, and happy.

His cock pulsed with the thought of her in every position.

"The things I want to do to you." He ran his nose alongside hers. "They're...unspeakable."

She growled as she kissed him. "God you *are* perfect." She climbed him like a tree until her good leg was wrapped around his waist, and she pressed herself against him.

Never taking his mouth from hers, Nash walked them to the bench press. He wouldn't wait one minute longer to have her.

His fingers dug into the soft flesh of her inner thighs. She was so fucking hot. And he needed every inch of her thighs, her ass. He was going to devour it all.

He threw his leg over the bench press and slowly bent over to lay her down gently, never breaking his mouth from hers.

His hands framed her face as he bent over her, kissing her as if she held his last breath. "Birth control?" he muttered.

She nodded. "IUD. Last test was fine. Haven't been with anyone since"—he sucked on her neck and she gasped—"I moved back last year. I'm good."

He huffed out a breath. It had been five years for him. "Same," he said, not needing to freak her out over the fact that he hadn't fucked anyone since his ex-fiancee.

He kissed along her stomach, moving fabric out of the way, needing to taste her soft, milky skin. He kneeled in front of her and took a moment to breathe in her scent once he got to her shorts, rubbing his face there shamelessly. Her scent had haunted him for weeks. He'd dreamed of what she'd taste like, look like, as he ate his fill of her.

He growled, raking his teeth along her thighs. "I've thought of eating this pussy a thousand times."

He pulled off her shorts and panties, savoring the view of it. Wicked delight made his cock throb as he found it drenched for him. He nipped the soft flesh of her inner thigh, licking each nip as he went. "I want to feast on you. Lick, bite, suck. Anything." He rubbed his stubbly cheeks along her thigh as she sucked in a breath.

Her bare ass cheek hung over the side of the slender bench press, and he slapped it, loving the jiggle of it.

"Oh my god, I feel so..." She sighed out a breath. "Bad."

He inhaled her, holding back the beast inside for one second longer. Lifting her legs, he placed them on his shoulders, making sure her knee wouldn't hurt.

He slapped the other side as she moaned. "Good. Now spread your legs, wife."

He pulled her hips up to his mouth as she yelped, diving his mouth onto her like a starving animal. He licked and sucked, tasting each part of her. His tongue ran hard laps from her entrance all along her ridges. Up and down, up and down. His arms wrapped around each thigh, locking her in place as he feasted harder and harder.

He bit her clit and she cried out in pleasure, arching her back. In the mirror behind her, he could see her tits fell heavy onto her neck with cock-hardening cleavage. Round breasts spilled out of her loose tank top as he held her ass in the air, feasting. He'd come from seeing her tits bounce if he wasn't careful.

She was tart and sweet, tasting like ripe cherry goodness

that was *his*. His tongue stroked hard circles around her clit, slamming into it again and again and again. How could something so small be his undoing? He'd do anything, be anything if he just could keep eating this feast *right—fucking—here.*

Hands dove into his hair, clutching at it, urging him on. He ate her like a man starved. Biting, licking. He'd feast until she had no more to give.

"Don't stop, Nash."

He looked up, meeting her eyes, loving the weight of her legs holding him down. As if he'd happily be there for all eternity. The obscene feeling of his face buried between her legs.

"Arch those tits for me, firecracker. I want a view while I make you come."

She rode his face, thrusting against his tongue as she played with her tits. He'd die a happy man as of right fucking now. A picture-perfect blonde, his wife, in his favorite position: soaking his face.

He slowed, not wanting her to come too quickly. Taking each lick along her dripping pussy, he etched his name into her with his tongue.

He inhaled her shamelessly. "I knew you'd be gorgeous, but I never guessed it would be this good."

She moaned and shoved his face down harder. He reveled in it, smashing his face against her, drowning in all of her.

She cried out and bucked against him. "Fuck yes, more."

His tongue moved in and out of her entrance, and he murmured as he held her gaze, "You know how to get more, sweetheart. Beg."

She tossed her arms over her head, grabbing the bench behind her. "Please. Please fuck me, husband. *Please.*"

His cock throbbed at the words. At her pleas. He needed to be inside of her. Coming over and in her.

Nash lowered her legs to the ground, careful of her injury,

while sucking her clit as she screamed higher and higher. She rattled the windows with her cries. He wouldn't stop until she asked, sucking on her perfect clit. He flicked back and forth in his mouth until her back arched as she pressed up, grinding his face into her until she came with a shriek, and collapsed on the bench.

He pulled her up to sit, capturing her mouth.

She kissed him back with abandon, not caring that his face was soaked with her taste. So fucking hot, his firecracker.

He pulled away, licking the taste of her from his lips. "Now bend over. You're going to watch me fuck you."

She panted as she bit her lip, looking like she couldn't believe the words coming out of his mouth. "Say it again," she said in disbelief.

He stood in front of her face as he pulled down his gym shorts and boxer briefs until his cock bobbed out. He grasped it, giving it a hard tug of relief.

She stared at his cock with delight. He was lucky he was proportional for his height.

"Happy three-week anniversary to me," she whispered as she licked her lips.

No way. He'd come in two seconds if she sucked his cock.

He held her jaw with his hand, forcing her eyes up to him. "I *said*, bend over, so you can watch me fuck you, *wife*."

She bit her lip with a breathy moan. She scrambled around so her good knee was on the weight bench, and she faced the mirrors on the wall.

Her hair had fallen out of the messy bun and fell along her shoulders. Her loose tank top showed the swell of her breasts, but he wanted more. He pulled her shirt down until her tits popped out. He'd buy her a thousand shirts as long as he got to see her bounce for him tonight.

He slowly pushed in, not wanting to come too fast. "Fuck." He breathed through his nose. "Lily, you're too tight."

She grabbed a breast, playing with her nipple. "You're so…"

Oh fuck, I'm really not going to last long. He inched in further, and she cried out. "You're so big. So full," she panted.

He looked down at her stretched around his cock. "C'mon sweetheart, you're doing so good. Almost halfway in."

Her jaw dropped as she met his gaze in the mirror. He reached around, finding her clit. It was swollen and sensitive, and she clenched around him as he slowly rubbed her, getting her used to his size.

She pushed back into him, taking a few more inches. "So good," she whispered, closing her eyes.

This was the vision he'd dream of. Lily lost in pleasure. Pleasure of his making. He grabbed her hip, digging his fingers in with a growl, and pulsed into her slowly until he bottomed out. She put both hands on the bench for stability and clenched around him, moaning.

Mine. He pulled out and pulsed into her hard, her tits swinging from the force. "Say it," he growled, forgetting she wasn't in his head. "Say you're mine."

She sobbed as he fucked her, grinding against him, meeting him pulse for pulse. Harder and harder. "I'm yours. All of me."

"Fuck. I need all of you." He thrust and pressed her forward until she was underneath the racked bench press bar. He dove his hand back between her legs and slid the other into her hair. He raked his fingers through her scalp and gripped it, pulling her hair back as he fucked her hard.

She moaned, throwing her head back. He tugged again and slammed his hips into her. "Say it again, wife. Who wants all of you?"

"You," she screamed as she sobbed out the start of another climax.

He released her hair and grabbed the bench press bar. He leaned close to her ear, still staring at her through the mirror's reflection as he rubbed her swollen clit. "Your husband"—*thrust*—"wants his wife's tight"—*thrust*—"soaking wet pussy."

She clenched around his cock in rippling waves as she came. He managed to swallow the '*I love you*' on the tip of his tongue. He fucked her hard, coming into her in hot, crazed spurts, instead of admitting how gone he really was.

∼

LILY

LILY MET Nash's gaze in the mirror, panting.

Holy mother of all sex gods.

Nash Donnelly just wife-fucked her with his enormous cock.

And judging by the smile on his face as he pulled out of her slowly (ow, Jesus Christ, how big *was* it?), he wasn't bailing on her this time. Wasn't pushing her away.

She'd have to talk about the dreaded F word.

Feelings.

Gross.

He walked to get a hand towel at the water station in the gym as she sat still, getting her equilibrium back. As she closed her eyes, a gentle hand rubbed the towel along her inner thigh, cleaning the mess they'd made.

Of course Boy Scout Badge Nash was two steps ahead of her, caring for her so gently. He pulled her into his lap, careful with her leg.

This man had fucked her *hard*—hair-pulling, gripping her hips hard enough she'd have bruises tomorrow—and yet had kept her injured leg perfectly safe.

She nuzzled in. "That thing you did? With the hand in the hair?" She sighed into his shoulder.

"Not okay?"

"You should teach an online course. Spread your talents to the masses. It's like being fucked by a caveman who is a masseuse."

He squeezed her tighter. "I'd like to be clear, since I know the last two times..."

"You ran away upon gaining post-nut clarity?" she helpfully replied.

He laughed. "Yeah. That." He rubbed her arms, her thighs still bare since he'd tossed off her shorts. "I meant what I said. I have feelings for you. I'm not running anymore. But I know this type of thing is...new...for you."

She'd felt like she was skydiving when she'd admitted to wanting their August kiss to be more. "I don't know how to navigate this. Technically, we're married. I mean...what happens next?"

He pulled her close, kissing her cheek slowly, and soothing pleasure cascaded down her shoulders. "I just want to be with you. To kiss you whenever." He kissed her neck, and goosebumps trailed down her arms. "To sleep next to you at night and *finally* spoon you."

Oh god, she was going to melt right now. "You wanted to spoon me?" she asked with surprise.

He laughed and squeezed her. "So fucking bad. Every night next to you was torture. That's why I started sleeping with that body pillow."

She threw her arms around his neck suddenly, feeling like her heart might break at the sweetness. He'd lain there for weeks cuddling a fucking pillow imagining it was *her*.

"So," he murmured into her hair. "Do you want to go on our first official date?"

Could she do this? She really, really, *really* wanted to try. *It's just dating. It's not permanent. Nothing to be terrified of.* She nodded finally.

"I'd love to date my husband."

Chapter Twenty-four

LILY

Lily's stomach was tied in knots. T-minus five hours until her first date with her husband.

She was still sore from the two additional rounds of heart-palpitating, head-thrashing, moan-inducing sex they'd had last night and this morning.

And yet he insisted on a traditional first date. *So like him.*

Her stomach jumbled at the idea of a date with feelings. It had been a long fucking time since she'd had one of those. He knew that she *liked him* liked him.

Good thing he didn't know she loved him. How mortifying would that be?

Back to work. The clatter of Lily's DSLR shutter sounded like a shot in the quiet flower shop. Heaps of frothy purple iris petals covered bare winter branches on a white drop sheet.

Hustling as fast as she could to her computer, she downloaded her photos and manipulated them in Photoshop, putting neon green streaks over the photo.

Was this corny? Did it look cool? She angled her head from side to side. Cold panic tingled at her fingertips. Was she a gigantic fraud? "Uninspired" was the word that Rachel had used on the call this morning, giving her notes on the latest designs.

"This cannot look like your grandma's mumu." She brightened the color on-screen so it was overblown. The gentle purple and organic texture of the branches was interestingly at odds with the neon green.

This had to be different and fresh, a new take on modern florals. "Spring is badass," she muttered. Nature had to fight its way out of the cold against all odds.

And as she'd learned recently, being vulnerable was *fucking terrifying*.

So yeah, she was going to double down on her theme of Punk Rock Spring. As long as Rachel and the seventeen thousand stakeholders at KGM agreed.

The back door to Bloom was wrenched open, and Rose popped her head in.

"Let's go," Rose said quickly, barely taking her eyes off of her phone as she typed out a message.

"Oh fuck, it's three already?" Lily shoved her laptop and camera into her bag.

They'd hired Allison immediately after her interview and would likely merge their stores together under the Bloom brand if everything went well after the first two months of having her on board. The snow had cleared, so they were driving to Allison's shop to collaborate on an upcoming wedding. Lily was so excited for a reprieve from the four walls at Bloom and her case of the 'not good enoughs'.

"How's Punk Rock Spring going? And our new best friends at KGM?" Rose said, opening her car door.

Knowing she'd eventually move back to New York, Lily had initially insisted she manage the relationship with the creatives at KGM.

Like a dummy.

"I'm not used to so many politics. I mean"—Lily flopped into Rose's car—"as a freelancer I'd talk to one person, they would deal with all the political shit, and I could just do my thing."

"That's what you get for being good at things. They get harder," Rose said.

"I know, I miss the simple days." Lily rubbed her temples.

"So no pressure, but the KGM partnership is a big deal for us." Rose interjected as she hopped on the country highway to Cooperstown.

Lily growled at her. "I don't need more pressure, Rose."

"I said no pressure."

Lily rolled her eyes. *Sisters*. "It doesn't work like that. You can't say no pressure and then *apply pressure*."

"But," Rose interjected, "this is our big way in. We could be in Omaha or Phoenix or Denver or whatever little podunk town is outside of Denver. You can't get cold feet and bail."

"Ugh," Lily groaned out. She hated that her sister knew her so well. "I know. I don't want to let you down. You're building a dynasty."

"*We're* building a dynasty," Rose said, squeezing Lily's good knee.

"I need a couple more weeks to charm them and make sure what I'm producing isn't crap." She'd worked so hard her whole life to get to this point. She couldn't let the fact that KGM was petty, lazy, and full of infighting delay her journey back to New York.

But do I even want to go back to New York?

She shook her head to clear it. *You're just dating Nash. It's not a permanent commitment. Maybe we'll do long-distance if KGM works out. I can have both.*

She always did hate choosing.

They walked in the back of Allison's pretty flower shop. It

had a 'fun rich aunt' vibe that Lily liked, but it could definitely use some updating.

"Hi there, bosses," Allison said with a smile. She was rocking a grandma-core chunky sweater made of crocheted afghan squares with oversized wire-rimmed glasses. She looked cozy and totally in her element.

"You two do your artistic thing. I'm going to sit quietly and make some spreadsheets for us," Rose said with glee in her eyes.

"I don't get how we're related," Lily said. "Oh my gosh, that looks so good." Lily beelined to the wedding decorations.

They'd taken on a small, last-minute wedding, and it was Allison's first solo project for Bloom. The bride was a hipster folk artist who was marrying an organic apple farmer. Rustic twine was artfully wrapped around burlap with a bouquet of local early wildflowers, thick, lush greenery, and delicate daisies.

"I think you completely nailed it. I can see the wedding pictures of them standing out in the middle of a field now," Lily said with a wink.

"Yes, exactly!" Allison said, pointing at her. "I was thinking we could do something simple and organic for the table decorations." Allison showed two options, one using beeswax holders with fake battery-operated candles and apples as part of the decor.

"Oh my gosh, perfect. I love that the groom will be included, too."

Lily waited for the smart sting of hurt pride, that she wasn't the smartest one in the room, but instead she was so excited to see the Bloom brand come to life. What she made was growing beyond her, taking on its own life. She was there if anything went wrong, but she was so proud of what Bloom was becoming.

Her eye caught colorful images on the wall of Allison's workroom. Paint swatches and pictures of new lighting fixtures were tacked onto an idea board.

She darted across the room like a kid in a toy shop. "Are you starting to think through how we'll redo your store?"

Pictures of new display shelves, paint chips, and a store layout sketch were taped next to each other. Lily's eyes roamed the board, trying to piece together Allison's vision.

"Oh, it's not ready yet. I know everything's not official yet with the store merger, but I got excited at the idea." Allison nervously twisted her hands. "I was just playing with some ideas. But something isn't feeling quite right."

They'd talked extensively about Bloom's brand promise, how her Bloom-ified store could be funkier, more modern, more Lower East Side than Upper West Side.

She peeked out into Allison's shop. It was a historic older building, but unlike Bloom, it had low ceilings and a cottage vibe. The layout of her shop was smaller, with nooks and crannies for displays.

Lily glanced back toward the board. "I think I see the problem. You can't do something that doesn't work for the space. Your building"—Lily walked into the front of the store—"see how cozy it is? You have low ceilings, warm undertones in your wood; you're like a magical garden cottage. You can take the modern, clean lines of Bloom, but change up the fixtures and the layout so that it feels cozier, more lived-in. Instead of a big floral wall, maybe your feature would be a magic garden seating area."

"I freaking adore that"—Allison clutched Lily's arm with bright eyes—"but that doesn't go against the Bloom brand?"

Lily tapped her chin in thought. "Bloom's brand is chic, and larger than life, and... unexpected. So yeah. It totally fits as long as we have gigantic purple *Alice in Wonderland*-style blossoms in our magic garden seating area."

"Oh my gosh, yes, and maybe like teacups. I have a whole collection in a dusty corner. Honestly, I'm a grandma at heart, if you couldn't tell." She gestured to her outfit and floral teacup in her hand.

"Yes, and maybe the whole concept of the store is that it keeps getting crazier. It starts out clean, like Bloom in Fairwick Falls, and gets more imaginative and crazier the further back you go until you're in this 'down the rabbit hole' feeling."

"Oh!" Alison squealed, wrapping Lily in a hug. "This is so much more fun with you."

Rose raised her eyebrows, impressed. Lily knew that look. Rose was already jumping three steps ahead. Maybe they'd make Allison's store part of Bloom sooner rather than later.

Joy and happiness bubbled out of Lily. This *was* fun.

Why couldn't this be her whole job?

"Since you two are so in sync, maybe Allison has some thoughts on your product pitch," Rose offered.

"I will owe you one thousand favors if you do. Take a look. Tell me what to do." Lily opened her laptop and shoved it at Allison.

Allison widened her long legs, settling in to stare at the screen with quiet determination, putting a hand under her chin. "Oh, that's great. It looks so cool," Allison said in a serious, quiet voice. She pointed out a different technique to apply effects Lily was using to get an even bolder print. They talked for fifteen minutes about different techniques.

"Let's hope KGM likes it, too." Lily slammed the laptop down. "Enough of that. Let's start planning *Allison's* wonderland."

She dragged Allison by the hand through her own store as

they brainstormed. Lily lost track of time, enjoying her own imagination, co-creating a better future for Bloom.

OF COURSE, her hair wouldn't cooperate the first time it actually mattered.

Lily pulled a traitorous curl out of the curling iron, her hand practically shaking with nerves. "I swear I will chop you off if you don't behave," she muttered at her wonky curl.

This is why I don't go on normal dates. They're too intense. Too important.

I want it all too badly.

A strange chime sounded in the living room and echoed into the first-floor guest bathroom where she was getting ready. *What the heck was that?*

She pulled out the curl, finally behaving now, and clicked off the curling iron. Now just a final pass on her makeup and she'd be ready.

Her phone buzzed.

> **HUSBAND**
> Ready for our date?

Of course he's ready at 7 on the dot.

> **LILY**
> You're too perfect. Be late next time!
> I'll be ready soon.

> Could you be a little more specific on when?
> It's cold out here.

What?

The strange chime rang again.

Oh my god.

She hurried to the front door, opening it to find Nash smiling with a big bouquet of flowers.

"I'm here for our date." His smile was a mixture of pure excitement and, if she had to guess, nerves.

Her insides melted at the sight. "I've never gotten flowers on a date," she whispered, probably staring like a love-drunk goober. The bouquet was a bundle of bright dahlias framed by thick green leaves.

He stepped in and kissed her on the cheek. "Since we're doing a traditional first date, I thought we'd do the full experience. You look gorgeous," he said, lingering as he placed another kiss on her cheek.

His cheeks were pink from the cold, and he looked masculine and elegant in his designer coat. A soft blue sweater curved into all her favorite places on him, many of which she'd licked that morning.

She couldn't take her eyes off of the flowers. He had bought hundreds of wildflowers for their wedding, taken care of her student loans, made a sweeping donation to her favorite charity. So why did this feel different?

She'd never been *romanced*, she realized, shaking her head at the realization. "I should go put these in water."

"Already set it out." He pointed to a vase filled with water on the foyer table.

A cavalcade of butterflies stormed into her stomach. Nash Donnelly missed no tricks.

Definitely uncharted territory.

Fifteen minutes later, they sat discussing their days over wine in the low, flickering light of Fox & Forrest. She couldn't stop talking about how much fun she'd had with Allison. "It's been so great to have another set of really capable hands while I deal with the product line."

"Has KGM pulled their heads out of their asses?"

She smiled at him using the exact phrase she'd uttered that morning as they'd gotten ready for work. "I might have to go to New York. It's gotten rockier as they show the concepts to the *many* layers of middle management."

"Why wouldn't they love what you made? You're brilliant." Nash squeezed her hand with a proud smile.

"That's what *I* said." She laughed with him. "But they are more focused on moving up in the company than the project. I'm collateral damage."

"Sounds exhausting. I know you'll make something amazing anyway, despite all that."

The server delivered their vegan pasta, and Lily realized her body felt *settled*. She was able to just be herself with him. Not having to perform or be outlandish. She was calm, and happy.

"How about your day?" she asked. *This is what people do on real dates, right?*

Nash cut the long noodles on his plate with precise movements. "The board vote is in a week. I think I have enough people on my side for a confident majority. I played squash with Josiah Whetstone today to make sure he was on board."

"Did you throw the game so he won? I'm assuming with a name like Josiah he's one thousand years old."

Nash nodded. "I did. And you're right. He's approximately old as balls."

Lily choked on her wine in surprise. "I think I'm rubbing off on you."

He bit into his pasta with a wicked smile. "If I recall correctly, you already did the night before our wedding."

Her cheeks flushed at being on the receiving end of naughty teasing. "Nashford Donnelly. Behave yourself." She'd never expected this side of him.

His eyes were full of warmth as he placed a slow kiss on her cheek. "I hate my first name, but"—he met her eyes—"I like it when you say it."

After sharing the best vegan cheesecake Lily had ever eaten, Nash held out her coat as they got ready to leave. It was stuff like this that she was so unused to—having someone that took care of her. Nash pulled her hair out from under her coat collar, and she tried to savor the jolt of swooniness from it.

Life achievement I didn't even know I wanted: unlocked.

They walked straight into the Frost Fest that had kicked off while they'd been in the cafe. The yearly festival lit up the town square, covering it with a twinkle light maze. In her younger years, Lily had made fun of sappy couples kissing and walking hand in hand in the tiny maze. Mostly because she never thought she'd be one of them.

Nash pulled her arm through his. "I thought we'd go through the twinkle lights if your knee is okay."

They passed the bank's logo listed as a sponsor as they entered the sparkly maze. *Of course he would sponsor something so adorable.* "Depends. Did you take your *other* first dates through the twinkle lights?"

"I would never share something so close to my heart as the Frost Fest with anyone but you," he said, squeezing her hand with a laugh. *Swoon.* "Though Margie was my backup if you said no," he joked.

Margie was an ancient waitress at Canon's diner who said exactly what she thought at all times and absolutely adored Nash. Lily snorted. "God, I love her. When I first moved back after Dad died, I'd sit and gossip with Margie while we rolled silverware. It made everything seem less lonely."

"I think that's when I really started falling for you," Nash said out of the blue. "How you were with Margie. She and Pop were both so sad after your dad passed. But you have this magnetic energy that lifts up the people around you. I saw you trying to make them laugh, even as you all wanted to cry together. I tried to ignore what I felt, thinking you'd leave soon. But I could never get your kindness out of my thoughts."

It was like a bomb went off in her heart. She was thrown by the honesty of his words, and she stopped in her tracks, thunderstruck. "Wow." She puffed out a breath of surprise. "You just...say what you feel. Like a crazy, emotional stuntman."

He put an arm around her as they walked. "I've been waiting a long time to tell you how much you mean to me."

This was new for her, having somebody be this open and honest about their feelings. What on earth did someone say to that?

He waved to friends wandering through the bright maze but kept his attention on her. "You never had someone tell you all the things they liked about you?"

"I mean, usually, the plan was to meet up in a bar, suss each other out, and then have a ton of sexy fun. So, they didn't tell me important things and I didn't tell them anything either. Being that vulnerable...it's terrifying. I never exposed all my soft underbelly to people who didn't care about me."

But Nash cares. Maybe I can be an emotional stuntman too. He deserves it.

Be brave.

Nash stopped with a sad smile as they reached the end of the maze. "You don't have to say anything ba—"

"I think it's super hot that you're so nice," she blurted out. "Oh god, is that weird? Sorry, I'm new at this." She shook her hands with nerves and breathed through a surge of panic at being so honest. "It's so attractive that you're the most trustworthy person I know. I'm like...I'm like horny for your goodness."

She started to hyperventilate. This was *terrifying*. "Oh my god I'm so bad at this. It's like jumping into the deep end of a pool of jello without floaties."

"Hey." He brought her in for a hug as a rumble of laughter rolled through his chest. "You're doing great."

She wallowed against the comfort of his chest, hoping she'd never have to look him in the eye again. *I'm horny for your goodness??*

Jesus H. Christ, Parker.

He pulled her chin up to look at him with a smile that made her gooey inside. "You'd make a great emotional stuntperson." They'd stopped smack-dab in the middle of the gazebo, and Lily just knew everyone was staring.

"I never expected to be one of the sappy couples that got all gooey at the Frost Fest," she said, biting her lip as he held her close.

"I don't know." His eyes roamed her face like a caress. "I've been falling for a long time. Seems pretty expected to me," he whispered before capturing her mouth. She sank into the kiss as he pulled her closer. Her tongue swiped over his lip, tasting him and wanting to claim him as hers.

Claim that heart she loved so much.

She wrapped her mittened hands around his lapels, urging him to keep going.

Wolf whistles sounded behind them, and they broke apart with a chuckle. They were holding up the selfie line in the gazebo.

She slid her hand into his as they walked out of Frost Fest. "We should make this a yearly thing. See how long we can make the selfie line next year," she said with a laugh.

Nash's eyebrows rose.

Wait. Fuck. We may not be together next year. "Or, you know. No pressure." *Oh. Em. Fucking Gee. Who even am I? You're letting this go to your head. This was* one *date.*

He wrapped his arm around her. "Next year sounds nice. Your knee okay enough to walk home?"

She almost said yes, but then...their agreement would be that much closer to ending if she was completely healed. Then they'd have to decide what to do. "Uh...it's hurting...some," she lied.

He bent down in front of her. "Hop on. We need to make sure you can use it when I get you home."

Delight coursed through her as she hopped on his back. Her stomach swooped as he lifted her to his full height. "Nashford Donnelly, are you going to have *sex* on the first date?" she said, sounding scandalized.

"Nope."

Her hopes fell.

He peered back at her as he walked to their house. *Nash's house,* she reminded herself.

"We're going to move your stuff back into our bedroom where it belongs. *Then* have sex on the first date."

She squeezed her thighs around him and sighed.

Where it belongs.

Chapter Twenty-five

LILY

Four days later, a cold wind chilled Lily's bare legs. She walked along Main Street to the bank with barely a limp in her step.

A gust of wind whipped at her as she walked by Canon's Diner. Her hands flew down to her thighs to shield herself.

She'd planned to surprise Nash with afternoon delight in the most inappropriate place and currently wasn't wearing any underwear.

Their second date as husband and wife had been takeout and breaking in his hot tub a few nights ago, which he'd shamefully never had sex in. He'd asked her what she wanted, and she'd been honest. Just time with him in his luxurious house, and an all-access pass to his mouth.

She had a million things to do today (remake the presentation deck that KGM had comments on for the third time, set up for Violet's filming tomorrow, make a test bouquet for a new bride), but she wanted to make Nash feel special. He'd done so much for her, and he'd been so stressed the past few days. She wanted to enjoy him while things were still uncomplicated. Just dating, no pressure.

That would all change when the board voted and they'd finally need to have *the talk.*

The *what the hell do we do now* talk.

She shook snowflakes off in the bank's lobby. She knocked on his door and heard a muffled "Come in" as he peeked out from the private bathroom tucked into the side of his office.

A bright, happy grin of surprise shot across his face.

Danger, Lily Parker. You are in danger of never leaving Fairwick Falls because of how much you want this man.

"What are you doing here?" He grabbed his shirt from a hanger on his bathroom door and shrugged it back on.

"Thought I'd surprise you," she said coyly.

"I'm sorry I can't talk. I have to listen in on my next meeting." He shrugged into his shirt and bent down for a slow, simmering kiss.

He already had her gas burner going, and he didn't even know why she was there yet.

"Oh, that's too bad. I was hoping we could"—she waggled her eyebrows—"break in your office next." She closed his office door and locked it.

"You are trouble," he muttered, pulling her back to him for a kiss. "But I can't."

"Why were you shirtless?"

He buttoned up his dress shirt. "I needed to work out some frustration between my meetings. I was doing push-ups."

"Ooh, sexy." She trailed her fingers up and down his chest.

"Thoughts of murder aren't so sexy. I caught Jeremy trying to bribe a loan officer to give him numbers on the bank's business. Plus, I'm stressed trying to get everything ready for the board." He wiped a hand down his face, looking like he was carrying the weight of the world.

Lily sat across from him, already plotting. She knew exactly how to de-stress him. "What do you have to do in this call?" She looked at her fingernails, covered in green stain from building the magic garden concept in Allison's store.

"I'll listen. Williams is the point person but still new. I want to ensure he can handle the relationship with Capital Investments."

"Gotcha, so you're *nannying*." Lily poked, knowing she would get a rise out of him.

He grinned, knowing *exactly* what she was doing. "I am doing my duty to ensure the bank is taken care of."

Lily pulled a face as if to say, "*I think I was right.*" "All right, I'll sit and listen."

"Suit yourself. It's going to be boring."

That's what he thinks.

Lily plotted her moves as the call started. Nash's webcam faced him. No reflective surfaces behind him. Window shades were drawn.

Lily scooted her chair back with a screech. *Oops.*

Nash glanced at her over his computer monitor. "It's okay, I'm on mute."

"Excellent," she muttered under her breath. She stood in his eyeline but behind his laptop camera so no one could see but him.

"You're going?" he asked.

"Nope, but pretty soon you'll be coming," she said with a wink.

She made a show of untying her wrap dress as Nash's eyebrows leapt to his hairline.

"Lily," he commanded. His cheeks turned pink. "Stop that," he said under his breath, though it had no bite to it.

Her wrap dress was now fully untied, but she held it together.

"Stop what?" she said, letting it fall open, exposing a bare breast and the fact that she had no underwear on. Nash jumped out of his seat but then quickly sat back down.

"What are you doing?" he whispered, trying not to move his mouth while he stared straight into the camera. An older man droned on about APRs and long-term capital gains.

"Why should I stop when this is so fun?" She let her other hand fall so that her front was completely bare, both breasts out and a sinful smile on her face. She drew her hand up and down the center of her breastbone.

His jaw clenched, and his knuckles were white, gripping the edge of his desk.

"Lily." He clicked furiously with a mouse. "I've turned my camera off for now. You need to get dressed. I shouldn't do this."

"Pshh. You can totally do this. You said it was what's-his-face's job anyway, right? You're micromanaging him."

"I'm not a micromanager," he said, taking offense and forgetting that she was naked in front of him. So she grabbed her breasts, and his eyes instantly darted downward.

"What do you think, Nash?" a voice asked on the call.

Lily chuckled. She could bet her life on what Nash was thinking about. He scrambled for the unmute button.

"Sorry, Bill. You cut in and out. Can you repeat the question?"

A complicated finance question was repeated to him, and Nash, never taking his eyes off of her tits, answered using words that sounded like a foreign language.

"I'm going to be off camera, given my connection's not so great." His mouth hung open as he muted himself.

She pouted with a wicked smile. "You're not going to tell me to go away, are you?"

"You are a very bad influence," he said, shaking his head with a dark smile.

"I forgot to tell you one thing before we got married." She grabbed a pillow from the chair beside her

"You're a troublemaker?" He looked hungrily at her.

"I adore," she leaned forward, her breasts hanging over his desk. "And I mean, *adore*, sucking cock."

He ground his teeth together with a low growl as she stood there, but what was the fun in that? She slowly lowered herself down to the ground in front of his desk.

"This is a bad idea," he sighed out.

Lily climbed under the desk on all fours, grateful that her knee was nearly healed.

Her head popped up on the other side between Nash's legs. His cock was standing straight up in his slacks, and her mouth watered at the sight of it.

Someone else asked him a question, and he unmuted to answer it, while she *so* carefully unbuckled his belt.

As he responded to another complicated financial question, she slid the zipper down. The black fabric of his boxer briefs was tented.

She tugged the fabric down, grabbing his hot, hard cock. She could barely close her fingers around his shaft. He'd been talking about interest rates, and his speech stuttered only for a moment as she wrapped her hand around him.

As he finished his response, she looked up at him, making eye contact as she ran her tongue along the head of his cock. He slammed the mouse button, hitting mute, and looked down at her with a wicked smile. "You are going to get punished for this, my little brat."

She smiled in response as she slid the whole head of his cock into her mouth. A bead of pre-cum gathered on the end, and the salty taste swirled in her mouth. Giving head wasn't for everyone, but it made her feel debauched and wicked when she bobbed her head up and down on a cock. Catching all that power as she sucked on him with such little movements. Like she could do anything and his knees would buckle for her.

His hands dove into her hair, and he pressed her head down onto him, wanting it so bad. *Yes.* She relaxed her throat, trying to take all of him. Saliva ran down the shaft as he inched further in. "God, your mouth feels so good," he murmured in a whisper, despite being muted.

She pulled back, using her hands to rub his shaft. He sucked a harsh inhale through his nose at the contact. "Are you going to be a good girl and take all of it?" he murmured, his hand raking through her hair and urging her on.

She responded by sucking the head and sliding back down on it, taking all of him as he threw his head back in pleasure. "You look so gorgeous choking on my cock." He thrust into her mouth, and she could feel herself go wet at his possessiveness.

He grabbed one of her breasts, claiming it. "You're doing so good. Look at you taking all of it."

She clenched in response, wanting him between her legs.

He found her nipple and rubbed it back and forth, teasing her with his thumb and forefinger.

She sucked harder, wanting to make him come so hard down her throat.

But he pulled her off of him suddenly as he panted to catch his breath. He pumped his cock in his hand and captured her mouth. "Stand up, wife."

Yes. She loved it when he got possessive and command-y.

His hand grazed up and down his shaft lazily as she stood in front of him, her back to the camera. He clicked a button and the video call ended.

He towered over her, leaning so he crowded her space. A knuckle brushed the underside of her breast as he whispered in her ear. "I'm going to come on your gorgeous pussy while you keep your hands on the desk. Then you'll use it to make yourself come. Understood?"

She nodded, too turned on for a smart comeback. She wrapped her hands on the lip of Nash's desk. Her dress fell to either side of her body. The heat from him felt like a furnace against her bare skin. He rubbed the head of his cock against her clit, and she bit her cheek, trying not to moan.

"Fuck, you're so perfect. It's like this pussy was made for me," Nash panted next to her ear. "I've dreamed about bending you over this desk. Fucking you any time I want." He rubbed her clit around and around with the head of his cock. She moaned, but he wrapped a hand around her mouth. "Shhh."

Fuuuck. Why was it hotter that way?

She reached up, desperate to touch him, but he stilled and raised an eyebrow. "I said you're in trouble, Ms. Parker. Hands on the desk."

She clenched. Fuck, he was good at this. She arched her tits, wanting the friction of his shirt. "Eyes on me," he commanded, and she fluttered her eyelashes open.

His hard brown eyes held her in a steely glare until he'd fucked his cock in his hand again and again, brushing against her sensitive clit. With a strangled curse, he came all over her pussy. Hot cum ran onto her clit, sliding down her thighs.

He leaned against the desk, catching his breath as he kissed her shoulder. Sitting back down with his pants unbuttoned and cock out, he took her in with a sinful smirk.

"Now, use all of what I gave you."

Every inner muscle clenched at that command.

She reached between her legs to feel how he'd covered her with his cum. She fingered herself, rubbing it against her clit that was begging for attention.

"Spread your legs, wife. I want a good view."

The image of Nash in a suit and tie, perfectly buttoned up

except for his cock that was growing hard again, telling her to be so bad was enough to send Lily over the edge too fast if she wasn't careful.

She leaned on the desk, hitching a leg up to spread her legs wider. She arched her back, enjoying the feeling of being so bad for him. She rubbed her clit with wet, slippery noises of his cum against her fingers as she fucked herself for him.

His hand wrapped around her thigh as he watched her. A show just for him.

He leaned forward, his voice low and serious. "When was the first time? The first time you came thinking about me."

Oh fuck. She wasn't ready to be *that* honest. That he was the first man she'd ever thought of like that.

She scrambled, thinking of when she'd first thought of *this* incarnation of Nash. Grown, serious businessman. "After I saw you in New York at the salsa club," she admitted. She'd almost texted him the next day but had talked herself out of it. "You were so hot." She ground against her hand, holding in a moan. "I pictured you fingering me on the dance floor," she panted.

She met his eyes as his nostrils flared. He released her thigh and slipped one finger in her, then two. "Like this?" His cock was hard again, and it pulsed as he slipped his fingers in.

"Yes." She threw her head back, about to climax, rubbing faster. His hand covered her mouth, and he pulled her onto his lap.

She slid down onto his waiting, hard cock without a word. She knew what they both wanted.

"Your leg okay?" he murmured against her cheek. His chair was so high that her legs didn't reach the floor.

She nodded. "Though I'm not much help in this position," she panted.

He looked down to her bare breasts scraping against his dress shirt. "You are perfect." His voice was reverent—a complete contrast to the carnal lust she felt, to how dirty they'd been.

His hands lifted under her ass, and he moved her up and down as she ground against him. He captured her lips, and she clenched, wanting all of him to stay with her.

"Sweetheart?" he murmured against her lips.

Ooooof. A punch right in all my keep-him-forever fantasies. "Mmm?"

He pulled back with a wicked smile. "Since my hands are occupied, pinch your nipples."

She grabbed her breasts as she rode him, grinding against him as he slammed her ass up and down against him.

Foreheads meeting, he locked eyes with her as she whimpered, on the edge. "I told you you'd be in trouble. Now you have to say you're sorry before you come."

She clenched around him, loving being bad. Being caught by him. "Sorry." She pouted with a smile that wasn't sorry at all.

He pulled her close, whispering in her ear, "Say you're sorry for bringing this tight, dripping wet pussy for me to fill."

Holy. What.

Desire curled around her core and beckoned her to orgasm. "Sorry for bringing my dripping—"

"Tight, sweetheart." He caught her earlobe between his teeth and bit down hard.

She whimpered. "Tight, dripping pussy for you to fill," she moaned.

He sucked on her neck, and she bit her lip to keep from screaming *more more more*.

"Sorry I rode your cock like a needy brat," he growled.

"Sorry I rode"—*Oh god, I'm going to come*—"I rode..." He slammed into her, bouncing her tits out of her hands as she grabbed the chair behind him.

"More," he growled.

"Sorry, I rode your cock..." *So good, so good. Yes.* "Like a needy brat. Oh god—"

And she came around him as he fucked her mercilessly, spilling into her for the second time.

She panted as they stilled. Her heart hovered outside her body between them. She looked into his eyes. Surely he saw—he had to see—how much she loved him right there.

How much he'd been hers for far too long.

Chapter Twenty-six

NASH

"All those in favor, say aye."

Nash heard eleven ayes in the room.

"All those against?"

Silence.

"The new bylaws have been approved and will be ratified in two weeks, pending legal review."

A cascade of tension flooded off Nash's shoulders. He'd changed the language.

He no longer had to be married.

Provisions were now in place, so it didn't matter what the race, gender, orientation, ethnicity, or marital or pregnancy status of the leadership of the bank was. He'd removed all gendered language from the bylaws and put in additional measures so in an emergency, the bank would sacrifice itself to give customers their money back.

After shaking hands with the board members, he sat back down in the empty conference room, his legs feeling wobbly.

He'd done it. He'd finally done the impossible thing.

So why did the win feel so hollow?

He wasn't renewed with vigor for the future at the bank.

He'd simply done the right thing, and in doing the right thing, he no longer needed a wife.

He had a primal urge to see Lily in that moment, to savor every last second with her before admitting he didn't need to be married anymore.

Would there be a dust cloud from her running when he told her the news? Would she stay for him?

Could he even ask her to do that?

He loved her as she was. He'd never want her to change and morph into a Stepford-esque shadow of herself if she felt trapped here.

But *lord*, did he want to be with her.

A few minutes later, the smell of Bloom washed over Nash like cool water over a burn.

Pearl was helping a customer, so Nash grabbed a bouquet of cut flowers.

"She's upstairs," Pearl called, handing a bag to the customer.

"Put this on my tab," he said, thundering up the spiral staircase. It was like he hadn't eaten in weeks, and Lily was his only sustenance.

He tried the door handle, but it was locked.

"Who is it?" Lily's singsong greeting came from somewhere in the apartment.

"Your husband," Nash replied with the same singsong pattern, a smile instantly on his face.

"Come in!" Lily called from somewhere in the middle of her studio. He slid his key into the lock, still puffed with pride that he had a copy.

He walked into her studio, expecting to see her on the couch or at her sketching table.

Instead, the entire room was in disarray. The table pressed against the wall, chairs stacked near the bed, and buckets of paint were haphazardly placed around the edge of the room.

In the middle of the room, a gigantic canvas was stretched out, covered in bright paint and flower petals.

And in the center of that canvas?

His wife.

Naked.

Covered in paint and writhing on the enormous wall-to-wall canvas.

She looked over her shoulder up at him, ass in the air as she moved paint around the canvas. Her bright smile and happy eyes held that joy that he'd been chasing for so long.

She slithered on the canvas, spreading bright blue paint with her arms as a makeshift enormous paintbrush. Her breasts were bare but covered in paint, and his cock jumped at how they gently bounced against the canvas.

He scratched his head, trying not to stare at them. "I can't even form sentences to ask what you're doing right now."

"Isn't it obvious? Working." She stuck her tongue between her teeth, trying to get the right fanning effect with her paint-covered hands. A paint soaked thong clung to her skin. She was covered in stripes and blotches of white, blue, and lavender paint. "I had some body paint left over from a very sexy art exhibit a few years ago, so I decided to use it up on this."

"It looks good," he said, looking at her ass. She wiggled her butt and looked over her shoulder.

"It does, doesn't it?" she said with a cheeky smile. She pressed herself up to standing, and it occurred to him that she'd moved up and down without any grimacing.

Blood surged to his dick as his hot, barely clothed wife panted up at him from the middle of the canvas. He knew exactly how he wanted to spend the last hour before he'd admit they didn't need to be married anymore.

"I never expected to find my wife writhing like a snake impersonating Matisse." Nash pulled off his tie, needing her body against his.

"Oh, it has Matisse vibes?" She looked over her shoulder, proud of herself. "This is for the KGM print. I needed something bold and big in the real world so I could shoot products on it."

He walked to the edge of her canvas and reached for her arm covered in blue paint. He pulled her toward him, but she resisted.

"I don't want to blue you."

He pulled off his belt in one smooth motion, making a cracking sound with the leather.

"I know what I want," he murmured and pulled her in so his mouth met hers, covering his suit in neon blue paint.

Lily moaned into his mouth as her arms wrapped around his neck.

She tasted like coffee and smelled like paint and flowers and that fucking *magic* she had running through her veins. He tried to memorize her every sigh, the curve of her mouth like he was studying for the most important final exam of his life.

The memory of her might be all he had left after they finally talked.

But that was for later.

Now, he craved his wife. He'd do anything to see her moan over him, under him.

He tossed his belt with a clatter and lifted her up so she straddled him. She licked into his mouth as she giggled, that playful sprite inside of her that he loved bubbling to the surface. The dab of lavender paint at the end of her nose was the cutest fucking thing he'd ever seen.

This woman was an artistic genius, sexy as hell, and cute beyond reason.

He kissed her like a crazed man, wanting to somehow claim her forever.

God, I fucking love her.

He squeezed her harder, cursing his suit that was getting in the way of the feel of her naked breasts against him. He needed her so badly. Wanted to play with her paint covered nipples, sliding around and around as his mouth never left hers.

"Where should we take this?" he said between urgent kisses. "Do you want a blue smeared wall?"

"We could try the shower?" Her voice was muffled as she scraped her teeth against his throat.

His grip grew tighter on her thigh wrapped around his waist, thinking of her getting hurt again. "No way are we having sex in that death trap."

She chuckled against his neck. "Or," she looked over her shoulder to the enormous canvas sprawled over her entire studio. "You could be a paintbrush with me."

Her eyebrows arched in a playful challenge.

He huffed out a laugh as he captured her lips again, hungry for her. *Of course she'd suggest sex on a painting.*

God, he loved her so much. It was getting nearly impossible to keep the phrase in. "What about your knee?"

She slid down his body with a smile, leaving neon blue and lavender streaks across his jacket. He'd memorize this suit. It looked like how he felt when he was around her: bold and unconventional. Messy. *Real*.

She unbuttoned his pants, biting her bottom lip. "If you recall, I do just fine on my knees."

"If I *recall*? Sweetheart, you kneeling with your tits out as you sucked my cock flits through my brain about every forty seconds."

He toed off his dress shoes as he slid his pants down. "I had no idea what I was getting myself into when I proposed to you, did I?" He stared at the sexy wonder that was his wife.

"Less talking, more undressing." She flicked her fingers up and down his shirt as she kneeled in front of him.

He shrugged off his suit jacket and undid three buttons before he felt her tongue along his shaft. He nearly doubled over from the pleasure of it, stopping to close his eyes and get his bearings. *Don't come yet.*

He tortured himself deciding whether or not to look down at her, splayed out in front of him as she took him into her mouth.

He focused on finishing the rest of the buttons and tore off his shirt.

With hands finally free, he ran his fingers through her hair. It was in a messy bun and tendrils had fallen down as she'd worked on her painting.

The hot wet heaven of her mouth closed around him again and he needed to stop this right fucking now so he could have her the way he wanted. *You're not going to come down her throat on what might be your last time together.*

Her hand fisted around his cock as she slowly slid back to lick around the sensitive edge of his tip.

He pulled away from her slowly and bent down, his hand cupping her face. "I don't want this to be over too soon." He kissed her deeply. "Plus, that's not how I want you on your knees."

Her eyes flashed. "Nash Donnelly has a plan? Shocker," she teased. He crawled over his wife onto the canvas and she leaned back. He blanketed her body with his and kissed every paint-free patch as he passed it.

I love this part of her, and this, and this. He kept those feelings bottled in though. It would only complicate their discussion later.

The slick squish of paint under his hands on the canvas barely registered as he sucked on a spot on her neck. H
er body was slicked with paint and he loved the feeling of pressing against her. His hard cock nestled against her heat. Her breasts pressed against his chest. He tried to memorize the perfect torture of them while his hands ran through her hair.

This woman. He'd crawl through hot coals for her. Why wasn't there something he could do to just make this last forever, naked and rolling in paint, not caring beyond this moment in their bubble together?

His hands slid under her, hooking around her waist. He rolled onto his back into splashes of lavender paint, bringing her with him. She rolled on top of him, and their mouths never broke. Her leg swung over his body and she straddled him. They were a sticky sexy mess .

Her hips thrust against him seeking relief and the friction made him crazy for her. He wanted to be in her. He wanted to fuck her for all eternity just like this so they could stay in this moment.

His fingers dug into her skin, territorily grasping her ass because what he really wanted to say was *mine.*

"Fuck, I love it when you do that. Harder," she said, nibbling his ear. He dug his fingers in and gripped harder. He loved that she loved it just a little rough. She sighed out a moan as he jiggled her ass in his hands.

He slid his hands down her paint-slicked hips, rocking her against him as she moaned into his mouth. His cock twitched at the sound. It was raspy and needy and only for him.

He wished there was a way he could tattoo it in his memory so he could think of it anytime he wanted.

He wanted to hear more. His cock begged for attention but he had to make this last. They'd had sex plenty of times in the last few weeks, but there was one position they hadn't yet tried because he'd been concerned about her injury. *She seemed fine when I came in, so maybe this is the time.*

He slowly slid on his back, moving underneath her. Wishing he could suck the blue and lavender breasts over his face.

"Where are you going?" She asked as he slid between her thighs.

"Where I belong," he answered as his face landed directly below her pussy. Her inner thighs and underwear line had stayed paint free somehow, thank god.

"Is your knee okay?" he asked. He swiped the flimsy fabric of her thong to the side and gave a short lick along her opening.

She gasped. "Yeah," she said with a breathy chuckle. "I'll be *just* fine if you keep doing that."

"Good." He kissed her inner thigh. "Then sit." He slapped her ass and pushed her toward his face. Her hips bucked toward him and she settled onto his chest with his hands holding her ass to support her. She sat up, and began to ride his face.

His tongue curved around and around her clit as her nails dug into his hair, gripping it in fistfuls and pushing him closer. *Fuck* that was so hot.

Her clit was plump and begging to be bitten. He nipped it lightly with his teeth. She cried out with pleasure, throwing her head back.

"*Fuck* I want to do that again, but you've got to be quiet, sweetheart. You have customers downstairs." He still had to memorize the taste of her and didn't want this to end.

She bit her lip, her brows furrowed in pleasure. "I'll be quiet." She panted as her hips thrust against his face and he met them with his tongue, swipe for pulse.

She was a cock-hardening vision. Tits bouncing above his face, the most perfect pussy over him and getting taste after taste.

His tongue circled lazily around and around her clit,

enjoying teasing her. He nipped her again and her legs squeezed his head as she cried out again but she tried to stifle it. She'd rattled the windows of their bedroom the last few weeks and he fucking *loved* that she was a screamer.

"Here," he said, holding up a hand that had been supporting her. "Bite this." He couldn't scare off her customers but he wanted to hear her moan.

She didn't think twice. She grabbed his hand and bit down on the heel of it. He nipped harder and harder, and her muffled screams were going to make him come if he wasn't careful. Luckily the pain from her bite was keeping him at bay.

He bit down harder, flicking her clit with his tongue and her cry went higher, near climaxing. As he sucked hard on her clit, she released his hand, panting. "Want you...in me, please," she begged. "So close."

He wasn't proud of the fact that her begging turned him on. She was strong and he fucking loved that. But he also loved knowing that she wanted him. That she *needed* him, even if it was only fleeting.

He nipped her clit again, wanting to hear her moan one more time. To file it away.

"Fuuuuck." Her voice was breathy and needy and perfect. She ground it out as her wetness coated his tongue. Her hands gripped his hair, tugging it, feeling so fucking good. "Please. *Please*, husband."

His hips thrust involuntarily. *Husband*.

Jesus Christ he found a woman who liked giving oral as much as he did *and* they were already married *and* he was in love with her.

He was going to lose his goddamn mind if he couldn't figure out how to keep her.

"Stay there," he said, placing a kiss on her thigh. Her knee must be killing her by now. He grabbed a paint-splattered chair and dragged it to the edge of the canvas. He tossed off his paint-soaked boxer briefs, sat in the chair, and leaned over to grab his wife's hips. He pulled her back to him, lifting her up onto his lap.

She straddled his thighs, her back against his chest. He leaned in to kiss her neck and scored it with his teeth. Her hair fell out of her clip in thick, heavy waves. Her floral scent clouded around him as he nuzzled her and she pressed back against him.

He swiped the paint from his hand onto the suit jacket. He didn't want any of that getting inside of her when he felt how wet she was.

"You're going to ride me while I pull your hair," he murmured in her ear. She sucked in a breath. "You're going to be quiet and you're going to come all over my cock. Is that understood?"

"Please," she sighed.

He pushed her hips up and tugged on his hard cock once, then twice to relieve the pressure in those last excruciating few minutes. He found her slick entrance and rubbed the tip of his cock up and down her. Her moans wrapped around him, torturing him.

Finally, he found her entrance, hot and tight, and pulled her down on top of him. She slowly sank onto him and his eyes went dark at the corner from the pressure of trying not to come.

He breathed out a controlled sigh as she lifted herself up slowly, then sank back down.

"This is perfect," he murmured into her hairline. "You're perfect."

I love you.

Fuck, put that away.

He raked his fingers through her hair like she liked the first time they were together. He grabbed her hair lightly and pulled. It arched her back and the curve of her neck.

"Yes, harder," she panted.

"Harder what?" He toyed with her clit as she slowly bounced on his cock.

She turned over her shoulder and that lovelorn, lost look in her eye connected with his. "Harder, husband." She was melting into every part of his soul.

How could he ever be without her?

She kissed him and he tugged her hair again so her mouth would open for him. His tongue met hers, and his kiss grew hungrier. Her teeth raked sloppily against his top lip. She hadn't stopped grinding against him, taking her pleasure between his cock and his hand. He needed to kiss every part of her. He broke away from her, kissing her eyelids, the center of her forehead, the edge of her jaw and her delicate neck.

More, more, more. He needed more. He needed all of it.

His hand twined around the length of her hair again like a silky rope. He'd buy a thousand fabric swatches until he found one just like this so he could always feel this if he couldn't have her.

He pumped inside of her as he kept his climax at bay.

I love you. "You feel so good," he said against her back.

I love you. "Just like that, you're doing so good."

I love you. "Such a good, tight wife."

She clenched her pussy hard around his cock at that praise.

Oh fuck he was going to come. He kissed the nape of her neck as she tightened around him. Her arms came up over her head to hold him against her.

"I..." she panted.

His heart seized.

"I..." she paused. "I've never wanted someone like this." She said it like an admission of guilt.

"It's..." she whispered as he sucked on her ear lobe. "God I just *need* you, husband."

The feel of her pussy against his hand, her clenching around his cock and the whispered *husband* from her lips were too much.

His balls tightened as desire shot down his spine and finally he came inside his wife as she rippled around him. She started to scream out his name and he captured her mouth as she came around his cock.

One last kiss to savor until they'd have to talk about their future.

∽

LILY

Lily scrubbed the paint from Nash's hair as hot water flowed over them.

"I still don't think it's safe to be in here together." Nash blinked as water ran over his face. He had criminally beautiful eyelashes for a man.

"Eh, the tub's been here for a hundred years. I'm sure it can take one hulking sex-drunk man covered in paint."

A shudder chattered her teeth. Sexy showers always sounded like a better idea than they really were.

"Here." Noticing her discomfort, he maneuvered her against the wall until she was under the spray of water.

"You know I love being manhandled," she murmured as she leaned up on her tippy-toes for a kiss. His hands clamped down on her hips, steadying her.

"No sudden movements in this ancient contraption until I get you in bed," he muttered, and while that sentence should have felt thrilling, there was dread underneath it all.

She could only sex him so many times until they'd have to talk about the board vote that was happening today. *Or maybe already had happened?*

Then she'd have to tell him she was going back to New York for at least a week. KGM had insisted she come to handle the next round of presentations in person with senior management. It would also be a good opportunity to network with people if she was going to move back to New York.

That *if* was feeling a lot bigger these days.

She hopped out of the shower first to start dinner, and a few minutes later, a clean, naked Nash with a towel wrapped around his waist—*yum*—sauntered out of her bathroom. She'd scrambled tofu and made fries in her studio air fryer.

They sat in their towels, knee-to-knee on her fluffy, quilt-covered bed, eating in silence. The twinkle lights wrapped around the overhead beams cast a cozy glow around his face.

Why hadn't they spent more time here together? She loved seeing Nash in her space, big and unassuming. She'd imagined him here a trillion times. First when she was a lovesick girl and he was a cool teenager, then later when she was a teen and he would come home from college, hang out with Rose, joke around. She'd dreamed a lot of dreams under these rafters, and he'd starred in a lot of them, both sweet and X-rated, and now here she was: in the prime position to sit and wait it out.

Could she grow old with him? She wanted to, but that was not what he'd signed up for.

She wasn't the perfect wife. She made fart jokes, enjoyed pissing off his mother. He'd barely blinked when she'd been covered in paint on the floor.

He chewed and swallowed, looking as though he was eating glass.

"Is the tofu scramble bad?" She took a bite quickly to check it.

"No, no, it's fine. I um..." He set his plate down, taking a deep breath, his expansive chest filling as he sat up straight, running a hand through his hair. "The bylaws went through," he said finally.

His arms flexed as he scratched the back of his head, creating an unfortunate dichotomy of looking sexier than ever while telling her the saddest news.

Oh no.

It's over.

The whole thing was done. Mission accomplished.

Sad confetti horns sounded in her head.

His face was pained as their eyes connected, knowing the discussion they had to have next. He tugged her by the hips to him, tucking her into his arms, and they melted back against the bed.

She stared at the ceiling for what felt like ages. "I need to go to New York next week." She blurted it out quickly. *Like ripping off a band-aid.*

This wasn't really running away, right? She had a legitimate reason. She'd tried to stop running away. Tried to deal with the hard and the bad, because maybe if she got good at dealing with the hard and the bad, she'd be happier.

Maybe she'd be able to finally open that damn envelope on the table five feet away. The ultimate boss level: dealing with the pain of reading her dad's last words to her.

Later. I'll be strong enough later.

"KGM asked that I come for at least a week. Maybe longer."

"Where will you stay?" he murmured into her hair.

"There's a hostel in Brooklyn I know of."

"A *hostel*?" Exasperation laced his voice. "Absolutely not. A friend has an apartment that's always empty in Midtown. I'll see if it's available, or we'll get you a rental."

"Nash, that's not necessary."

"You are still my wife," he said firmly.

Those five words rolled over her like a warm bath and settled deep into her.

You. Are. Still. My. Wife.

His thumb ran over her fingers and caught on her ring. "I want you to feel safe. How's your leg? Could you walk on it through New York?"

She rolled over to finally meet his eyes with a jaunty smile. "I mean, I did pretty well on my knees twenty minutes ago."

A slow smile curved his lips, but it didn't meet his eyes. His finger traced the edge of her cheekbone. "I've been happier in the last two weeks than I have been in my entire life." His voice was soft and ragged. "I don't want to stop dating you, wife."

Damn. He was an elite-level emotional stuntman.

She was too afraid to say what she wanted.

That she'd give anything to figure out how to stay with him if he didn't break her heart.

That this was the happiest she'd ever been.

That he didn't have to love her; she'd love him enough for the both of them.

"We don't have to decide anything right now," she offered, her heart beating wildly. This wasn't running. This was just delaying the decision between the career she'd worked for and a husband tied to Fairwick Falls. "We can talk when I come back from New York."

His hand smoothed over her long, wet hair. She liked the weight of it on her head. She felt safe with him.

Wholly herself and safe.

A thundering crash in her heart made her realize that was a new sensation. She was always on edge with the guys in New York because she didn't know them. But she *knew* Nash.

She'd seen him earnestly shake players' hands in high school after he lost a game, his shy smile during his valedictorian speech, how he treated the overall-clad farmers at the bank as well as any board member.

He'd literally helped an old lady cross the street last week.

"Or you could come with me," she said suddenly, sitting up. *Maybe I can have both for now.* "Everything's fixed here, and you love the city. We could visit your favorite places, my favorite places. *Someone* could give me a shopping trip in my favorite art supply stores," she said, rocking him side to side as she got excited.

He groaned. "I wish I could, but things are still touch-and-go here. Everything's not official until next week, despite the vote today."

The swoony vision of them together in New York deflated in front of her eyes. "Yeah, of course," she said, smiling as though she was silly.

"But we'll text all the time. To make sure you haven't fallen into a sewer grate."

"*Nashly* Simpson, I don't need nannying. I lived there longer than you did." She settled back into his arms with a smile.

"What do you miss most?" He tucked her chin under his head as he cuddled her.

"Hmm, all my favorite foods. There's this vegan Chinese place near Bryant Park that was my absolute comfort food. When I had a really shitty day, I'd haul my ass over the Brooklyn Bridge, and simmer my soul in hot and sour soup, crispy wontons, and a mountain of barbecue tofu." She sighed as her mouth watered just thinking about it. "How about you?"

The sound of low, soft breathing signaling Nash was falling asleep sounded in her ear.

"Didn't have a favorite place," he murmured, lifting up to kiss her forehead briefly and pulling her tighter. "Too busy working. Financial District food is crap."

Well, that's true.

He yawned, his hot breath against her cheek. "Mostly, I missed Pop's pancakes."

Right. Of course he would have looked forward to Fairwick Falls. He was destined to be here until the day he died, and she belonged in New York City.

She finally moved, laying her head down in her favorite place on earth: the nook of his chest. He tugged her in tight next to him. They were quiet for the rest of the night, avoiding the looming cloud of the future.

LILY

Three weeks later, a herd of cattle running across pre-war hardwood floors woke Lily from a deep sleep.

Her upstairs neighbor in the borrowed Midtown apartment either had fourteen enormous dogs or gave clogging lessons at 7 AM.

She sat up stiffly, having fallen asleep in a weird position working on her laptop. It was still open, phone beside it. She flipped up her phone and saw it was 9:05.

"Fuck!" she yelled and dove for the shower. Not giving the luxury shower its due, she rushed through and was out the door five minutes later.

As she waited for the elevator, she checked her phone. She'd missed two texts from Nash. She'd fallen asleep finalizing the presentation deck for today's stakeholder review.

HUSBAND

Good night. 🤍

Good morning.

They'd texted constantly since she'd been in New York—almost two full weeks. She hadn't realized how much she'd come to depend on him emotionally since they'd been together.

Her time back in the city hadn't felt like she'd expected. She'd felt busy and lonely and exhausted. Her old friends were either busy or didn't live in New York anymore. She worked crazy hours at the KGM office working on the final product proofs.

Today was the final approval meeting where everything still had a chance to go sideways. She was so fucking proud of what she'd made. It was leaps and bounds better than what she would have done even a year ago. By inventing Bloom from nothing and then pushing herself to get better every day so she wouldn't let her sisters down, she'd inadvertently grown into a better designer.

If this project went well, she'd be known as a creative director who worked with one of the biggest global brands in the world.

She stepped out of the apartment building elevator, feeling expensive and fabulous. Maybe this would be her everyday life in New York if she moved back.

If? When. When I move back. Everything was still just casual with Nash. Just dating.

But she looked down at her lock screen. A hunk with dashing good looks stared lovingly back at her from a wedding candid Gray had snapped.

She unlocked her phone and texted as she walked.

LILY

good morningggggggg

sorry, i was in the zone last night and then zonked.

> and now I am absofuckinglutely late for the biggest day, of course 🫠🫠 (melting face emoji)

She looked both ways before darting across the street. She'd missed this part of city living, feeling like she was really doing something by existing in all the chaos. But she'd forgotten how much it drained her to be here.

Living in New York was its own Olympic sport. Dodging trash, questionable liquid on the sidewalk, going down three flights of stairs, up three flights of stairs, walking half a mile and then another mile and then another mile, all to go to work or get some groceries.

She'd take the subway today since traffic was already crazy. Nash insisted she take cabs so she didn't hurt her knee, so the subway was her dirty little secret.

Her hand buzzed with his response.

> You'll crush it today. 🩶
>
> Also, please tell me you're taking a cab.

She thundered down the steps of the Rockefeller Center to catch the F train with a happy jaunt.

> i'm taking a perfectly safe mode of transport to work
>
> So not the subway?
>
> i never said that. kisses!
>
>
>
> The scrambled vegan eggs aren't the same without you here

He's still vegan even when I'm not there.
The swooniest of swoons.

She caught her goofy smile in the train's reflection as it whooshed by, pulling into the station.

As the doors closed on the train car, performers dressed in rhinestone bodysuits with glittery G-strings ran onto the train, probably on their way to Union Square to perform for tourists. The doors clicked shut, and Lily desperately wanted to share the quintessential New York moment with him.

> too bad you're not here.
>
> you too could be surrounded by glittery banana hammocks at 9am

> Oh god, now I *hope* you're on the subway. 😐

After rushing to the fifth floor of KGM's Creative Operations, she was only two minutes late to her meeting with Rachel. "So sorry I'm late. Train delays," she lied as she ran into the room.

Only Sven was in the room though, the very European man who'd sat in on her early calls. Dressed in all black with a slicked-back, severe haircut and thick black frames, he scowled at her from the middle of the conference room.

He gestured to the chair across from him. "Rachel won't be joining. Please sit."

Oookay. "Should we record the meeting for her?"

"Rachel was fired this morning for poor creative decisions. I am her replacement on this project."

Oh fuck. She knew exactly how this next part would go.

Sven crossed his legs and scowled at her with a scholarly air. "Why should our company work with a small impact brand like Bloom?"

Yep, there it is. "As I explained to Rachel"—*and the three other managers she had me speak to*—"We've had several viral products online. We're also featured in an upcoming show on the Wayridge Network."

"No one remembers viral products from six months ago." He shrugged, his sour face unimpressed as he crossed his thin arms. "The only people who watch that network are wine-drunk moms. We are in the *taste making* business."

She arched an eyebrow, not intimidated by him in the least. "Wine-drunk moms tend to have a lot of money," Lily said with a smile, unable to curb her tongue.

Sven sucked in his cheeks at her barb. He stood. "You'll have to re-pitch if you want to keep the partnership. I suggest you start over or take the Greyhound bus back to Ohio."

"Pennsylvania."

"Same thing." He walked out without a backward glance.

"There is a big difference between Ohio and Pennsylvania, thank you very much." She snatched her laptop up and stalked out after him. "We created Taylor Swift, Tina Turner, and Tina Fey. The queen of pop, the queen of rock, *and* the queen of sketch comedy? Ohio could never."

She was talking to herself, and the entire office had turned around to stare at her.

She smiled with a bright, goofy grin as if she was in on their joke and went to go find a desk to scramble for new ideas.

"I'm dried up." She walked briskly down the sidewalk. "My creative well has run dry. I've hit bedrock. I can't even think of a better metaphor than a creative well."

Nash's deep chuckle washed over her in her ear. "*And* you're talking on the phone like a sociopath."

"See? Who even am I?"

She'd scrambled for eight hours to come up with a new vision. She'd bounced ideas back and forth with Allison for an hour. Rose had assured her that she wouldn't be excommunicated from the family if something went wrong.

The fact that Rose was so calm made her freak out even more. She *knew* how much this meant to Rose. How big of an impact the product line could have on their lives if she nailed this.

"What did bitchy Leona say?" Nash asked.

She loved that he loved gossiping about KGM as much as she did. At this point, he was fully aware of the office drama.

"Oh my god, don't even get me started. She walked behind me as I was working and said, 'Hmm, that's cute,' and then walked away."

"What. a. bitch," Nash said with a teasing voice.

"It is! That's a mean comment. If you were more fluent in girl, you'd know. Later, I made sure to *not* hold the door open for her." Lily huffed in delight.

"Sounds like she had it coming," Nash said confidently.

They talked about their days the whole way to the subway stop, and Lily was enjoying it so much that she said fuck it and grabbed a cab back to Midtown. She was about to offer to video chat to prove she was in an actual cab when a loud sound rang out on Nash's end.

"Are you okay?"

"Uh, yeah. I'm out running errands. I'll call you back in a bit."

"Okay." The urge to say "love you" was on the tip of her tongue, and she swallowed it. Thank god. She didn't need to make their *just-dating-even-though-we're-married-and-I-love-you* situation more complicated.

As she crossed into Manhattan, the cab whooshed past a bright, friendly flower shop she hadn't seen before.

She felt the pull of it with every fiber of her being. She paid the driver and dashed toward it.

She wandered into the bright, friendly space. *It isn't quite as nice as my flower shop*, she thought with a proud smile. But it had that smell she needed. That fresh, floral scent—marigolds and roses and lilies, their perfumes all twined together. She wandered in, wanting to touch flowery things. She picked a small hand-tied bouquet of simple flowers.

She needed to reconnect with what drove her, what motivated her to create. She loved the simple shapes that nature created. Her fingers ran over purple lilacs. They had simple petals expertly shaded from center to edge in a dreamy lavender. It was hard to improve on something that was already perfect, but she'd tried every day for the last year by making centerpieces, events, bouquets, and arrangements. She'd become so used to being surrounded by flowers that she hadn't realized she was withering without them around her.

She bought several small bouquets for herself and walked back home. She checked her phone—still no call from Nash.

It's fine. It's not like I need to talk to him all the time. She'd gotten in the habit of wanting to hear what he thought, though. It felt nice to have the safety of a partner who had your back.

An hour later, PJ's on and two glasses of chardonnay in, the weight of the day finally came bubbling to the surface.

How was she going to turn everything around? Sven hadn't given her a deadline, but the underlying subtext was immediately, and here she was, still creatively dry. She stared at the bouquets she'd purchased as though they held the secrets to the universe.

Oh, fuck it. She needed her best friend. She grabbed her phone and called Nash.

He answered in one ring. "Hey, sorry. I got held up."

"What did you have to grab?" They talked about the mundane now, and she loved it with every fiber of her being.

"Oh, some dinner. Thought I'd treat myself," he said with a happy note in his voice. "So, any big revelations?"

"I had a pretty good revelation that chardonnay would make the bad feelings go away. Turns out, I was right—until you hit the tipping point of two glasses, and then the bad feelings come back with a vengeance."

He chuckled. "Maybe try some water. That'll make the bad feelings go away."

"You're not the boss of me," she spat back with a smile.

"But you like it when I am," he murmured into the phone.

Woof, she did not need to get distracted with her vibrator right now. She needed to fix her problem. "Stop using your sexy voice," she complained. "I need ideas."

"Maybe you should walk around the city."

"It inspired me before, but now it's so loud out there. Oh my gosh, I sound so old," she said, chuckling. "I forgot how the garbage smells in the middle of the day, and did you know people still smoke in the world? And they all walk *right fucking in front of you* while doing it? Last night, I had to jingle my keys when I came home so the rats wouldn't run on my feet."

"So New York is as glamorous as ever. That's what you're saying?"

"Yes, and uninspiring. Didn't realize how much I needed an attic to be creative. And silence. Ugh, glorious silence."

"I'm sure we could find you a moss-ridden attic in Queens."

"But does their shower have fourteen directional heads and room for me and my five best friends to hang out in?"

"Sounds like a fun shower."

"Too bad *you're* not here. You could have been. You could've used your sexy voice in the sexy shower." Shivers ran down her spine at all the things they could do in that shower.

"Well, I do have a surprise for you. I ordered you food. Your favorite. It should be at your place in about three minutes."

She gasped. She'd forgotten to grab dinner on the way home, being too in her head about today's drama. "The soup?"

"And the wontons, and the barbecue tofu."

"Oh my gosh, I"—she bit her tongue; it was *not* the time to say 'I love you'—"I am so excited. I'm starving. Thank you, thank you."

"Hopefully, it'll give you some inspiration back. Oh, it looks like the driver is there, and uh..." Nash murmured to someone. "He'll be at your door in about one minute."

"Oh, great!" She launched herself off the couch, setting her wine glass down. She slowly walked through the enormous apartment toward the front door as the doorbell rang. It sounded like a gunshot going off.

"Holy hell, my ears. Either the food's here or someone just declared war, hold on."

She swung the door open to see a devastatingly handsome, six-foot-five smiling man leaning against her doorway, holding a bag of Chinese takeout.

Her husband had brought her takeout.

From two states away.

Her brain went staticky, and she dropped her phone as she launched herself at Nash, pouncing on him with her legs wrapped around his waist.

He caught her, holding her tight, never losing balance.

Tears lodged in her throat as his arms wrapped tight around her. She hadn't realized how much she'd missed him until right now.

She let herself be wrapped in the nonjudgmental warmth and steadiness of a hug returned. No questions, no pulling away. In fact, he never pulled away first, she realized. She was always desperate to escape him, not wanting to linger, to let her true feelings be known.

But now, she fucking lingered.

They stood there for a minute, then two. Her heartbeat slowed as she felt safe. Finally, she let go and slid down his body.

"Hi," she said, her voice breathy and embarrassed.

"Hi," he echoed. His eyes sparkled with humor, and she moaned from how much she'd missed his face.

"Oh, come in," she said, feeling embarrassed at how much she'd obviously missed him.

She opened the apartment door as he rolled his suitcase in behind him. They stood in the hallway to the front door as it slammed shut.

She stared at him, barely willing to believe he was here.

He'd come all this way.

He'd brought her soup.

"You brought me soup," she whispered, not able to process it all.

He moved in, backing her against the hallway wall.

"Yes, I did." He put an arm over her head and leaned in on his forearm, and all the brain cells left her head in one flushing motion.

"Hi," she sighed out again as the scent of him surrounded her.

"Hi," he said with a slow smile and bent down for a quick kiss, a brush of their lips.

"I missed you," she breathed, and as his mouth trailed down her neck, the garlicky spicy soup scent wafted to her nose. "Oh my god, this is the hardest choice I'm ever going to make. My favorite comfort food or bedding my husband who I've dreamed about for two weeks?"

Nash pulled her against him and lingered over her mouth, kissing the side of it as she stood dazed. The scruff of his cheek burned a blaze as he slid along her jaw, her neck. His cologne and his scent swirled together to pull at her molten core.

Biting her shoulder, he slid his hand from her waist between her legs and gripped her pussy hard enough she lifted onto her toes.

"I can reheat soup," she moaned as she pulled his shirt so his head came back to her lips. He set the takeout on the floor and wrapped his arms around her as he plundered her mouth.

"I needed to see you," he said suddenly, his hand coming to her jaw. They took a break from making out, their breaths heavy as they stared at each other's swollen lips.

"I missed you," she admitted. "I'm just surprised you're here."

"A little spontaneity never hurt anyone," he said as he trailed his thumb along her bottom lip.

He might as well have said he'd acquired a pet bear. Nash Donnelly? Spontaneous?

She needed him like she needed water and sunlight. "I would love nothing more than to throw you down right here and ride you like a Central Park carousel horse."

Nash puffed out a laugh against her lips.

She giggled. "But I'm gross from my panic sweats today. Can I take a quick shower? And *then* ride you like a carousel horse?"

Nash pulled her toward the bathroom. "If I remember right, you said there's room for five of us in there."

NASH

The rush of water sounded as Nash tore his clothes off, only breaking from Lily's mouth when necessary. He peeled layer after layer off her as the bathroom filled with steam.

"I forgot how good you smell," she murmured against his lips. "It's like caffeine to my nose. Addicting."

He huffed out a laugh against her skin as he kissed her shoulder. He loved how funny she was.

Pulling at his belt, he unbuckled it as quickly as possible, and she stepped back from him as he took it off. Her eyes went molten as he unzipped his jeans.

"God really does have favorites," she said as her eyes raked him up and down.

He pulled her in by her hips, hooking a finger under her panties to tug them down. He whispered in her ear as he pulled them past her legs. "*And* cash spurts out of my ass."

She threw her head back in laughter, and he took the opportunity to close his mouth around her nipple. "Fuck, my wife's got great tits," he muttered against her.

He'd missed her curves, this being one of his personal

favorites. Her nipples pebbled under his touch, and he flicked one back and forth with his tongue.

"Unless you want me to drag you to the floor right here, we should move this to the shower," she panted.

He pulled her inside the large shower. Two shower heads sprayed hot water over his shoulders as he pulled her in for a long kiss. Their tongues met as his hands wrapped around her. Sometimes he forgot how small she was with her larger-than-life personality. He picked her up, loving the feel of the press of her as they slipped and slid against each other.

He sucked on her lip, grazing his tongue against it, trying to memorize the feel of her. Could he remember what she tasted like in a week? A month?

He squeezed her tighter, and she moaned against him. "I really should wash off," she said with a smile.

He ran his tongue along the column of her throat. "But I love your taste." *And who knows how long I'll get to taste it.*

He begrudgingly set her down and reached for the body wash, squeezing it into his hands. "Here." He turned her away from him, lathering the soap, and an expensive champagne-and-cashmere scent fluttered through the mist. He dragged her long hair around and started massaging her shoulders with his soapy hands.

The bone deep groan that came from Lily's mouth made his hard cock a bar of steel. Her shoulders were tense, but she relaxed under his touch and sighed back into him.

"I missed you," he ground out as he worked her shoulders. "Your piles around the house. Your arguing with the microwave."

She turned around, kissing his chest, nuzzling her face against it. Her hair was plastered to her face, and he pushed it back as she looked into the watery spray. Swollen, red lips were perfect from his kisses.

"The house is too quiet without you," he admitted.

She raked her nails down his chest, along his abs. "I missed this. You. How solid you are. How caring you are," she sighed as he squeezed her to him.

He pumped more body wash into his hand. His hands moved over her breasts, slipping over and around. His thumbs lingered over her nipples, flicking them as she gasped.

"I missed that." She grinned against his chest as her limbs were turning heavy, raking her nails gently along his waist. "I missed your snoring, how you boss me into taking care of myself. How you adjust the mail after I set it down on the counter so it's perfectly squared to the corner." She kissed his shoulder as he bent down to wash her hips, her legs, running his lathered hands over her ass again and again, loving the *pop* of her curves.

He lathered her calf, savoring in running his hands up and down her thigh. The curve of her hips called to him like a siren in the shower's mist and he kissed it, lingering there. He nipped and sucked as he went along her belly. Lily was toned but had a perfect soft pouch stomach. Since they'd taken their situationship into more, it had become one of his favorite resting places. He buried his face there and moved downward, toward heaven as spirals of hot water rolled over him from the many shower heads.

"I don't want you to drown," she sighed as his tongue found her clit.

"Seems like a good way to go, honestly," he said in between licks. "Fuck, I missed your taste." He pushed her to sit on the wide bench away from the spray.

Her pussy would be his official last meal request. He dove in like a madman, pulling her closer, biting, licking.

She moaned as he swiped his tongue back and forth over

her clit. He was on his knees for this woman, and he'd give everything to stay there.

Her hand raked over his wet hair, scraping down his shoulders. "I..." she started as he ate her, but her back arched in ecstasy.

He slid two fingers into her pussy, needing to feel her. "You what, sweetheart?"

She clenched like a vise around his fingers, and his cock pulsed at what it would feel like to fuck her. He'd thought about it every night. Her tits were heavy and glistening, and he jolted at the thought of fucking her just like this. Legs spread and slippery.

"I worry about you." She threw her head back as he licked her pussy. "When I'm not there. You're too, oh *fuck*. Too serious. Or..."

He wanted to gather her up and run her back to Pennsylvania. This woman worried about *him*?

She'd be the first.

"Or what, wife?" He parted her legs, loving spreading her out for him.

"Or you'll want someone else. Someone right for you." Her big eyes blinked from the drops of water spraying over them, looking nervous.

She'd shown her hand.

He rose up on his knees and grasped her neck, pulling her toward him to capture her mouth. "Sweetheart." He stroked her cheek with his nose and she nuzzled back, eyes wide and nervous. "There's no one else. No one else for me."

Don't say it, Donnelly. It's not the time. Too soon for the three atomic bomb-sized words.

But they pulled at him.

He pressed her to him as he kneeled in front of her, brushing her soapy slick tits back and forth across his chest like some sort of sexual torture. He didn't trust his mouth not to be occupied right now. He slid his fingers down her stomach as he kissed her. Her pussy was swollen and slick.

But he wanted more.

He slid his fingers inside her, and she bucked against his hands. "Fuck, you're so slippery," he ground out. "I want to taste all of you, wife."

He slid out of her, his fingers dripping from her pussy. He teased the tight rim of her ass along the ridges he wanted to lick. She moaned and clenched, urging him on.

"You love being bad, don't you, wife?"

She moaned in answer. Her eyes were wide with surprise as she bit her lip with want. She grabbed her breasts in pleasure.

He wanted to frame this moment. Her legs spread wide on the bench. Breasts clutched in delicious agony. Her ruby red lips panting and open for him.

"Any of those New York fuckboys ever taste you right here?" His finger teased the rim of her ass in slow circles, and her back arched in pleasure.

She sucked in a breath between loud sobs. "No...Too embarrassed...to ask..."

"But you want it, don't you, wife?" He felt her clench around the tip of his finger teasing her ass. "You want it so bad."

She bit her lip and nodded with a tortured expression. "Please," she whispered.

"Good. Eyes on me," he ordered. He slowly lowered, sparing a lick for her pussy, then his tongue landed right where she'd wanted it.

She cried out in pleasure as he rimmed her. "Yes...what... *fuck*," she screamed.

Let's see a New York fuckboy eat ass like a champ.

He'd ruin her for anyone else.

"Eyes on me, sweetheart." He held her gaze as she fought to

keep her eyes open. She'd only think of him, would remember him for fucking ever as the man who gave her the most pleasure.

He swiped side to side, tonguing her where no one else had been, branding it as *his*.

The perfect round ass he'd stared at for months was *his*.

Her fingers gripped the edge of the deep shower bench, flexing in pleasure. Water ran down in rivulets along her breasts, stomach, thighs. He grabbed her ass, spreading her wide and tugging it over the edge of the bench with a quick spank on one side.

Her moans climbed and climbed as his tongue did lazy victory laps around the rim. He spread her cheeks wider to make her feel naughty and exposed. His tongue slid around and around as she trembled, pulsing against him.

"Need you," she panted, reaching for him.

Their mouths met with hot urgency. She held his head with both hands, as if *he* was precious. He stood, picked her up, and moved them back under the warm spray. Her legs gripped his hips as he slid home into her slick pussy. He held her against the shower wall. Just for a moment. Coupled together as her head buried in the nook of his neck and shoulder, he wrapped her against him tighter.

Don't leave me.

How could he make her see? She belonged with him. "Everything is better with you," he murmured against her hair.

She arched against the shower wall. Her breasts had gone pink under the hot water, and his eyes lingered there before they met her face.

"*Everything*, firecracker." He thrust in her, needing to claim her. "I couldn't breathe without you," he whispered, afraid to admit it.

She raked her nails along his back as she held onto him. The fire in her eyes caught him by the balls and wouldn't let go. "Mine," she whispered.

Oh fuck. "Yours." He wanted her to ruin him. Mark him as hers. *I love you so fucking much.*

He needed to see her come undone. Know that it was because of him. He shifted her weight until he could free one hand, rubbing her clit.

"Mine," he growled as he fucked her under the shower's spray. "Say it."

She panted as she clenched higher and higher, her tits bouncing as he fucked her in hard strokes. "Only yours, husband," she panted. "Come in me."

Jesus, I love her. "Fuck," he gasped. His balls tightened at that possessiveness. At needing to stake his claim.

Mine.

A carnal, animal urge to mate and keep her had him fucking her hard.

The sight of her screaming on his cock was finally too much and he emptied into her as she came rippling around him.

He panted as they stilled and the feelings of all consuming love were nearly impossible to keep quiet.

He sat her down on shaking legs, looking into those big brown eyes that were sleepy and sexy.

The woman he'd love until his dying breath.

"I love you" wrenched out of him, whispered into her hair.

He wanted to shove it back as soon as it had escaped. *Fuuuck.*

She was silent as she panted. Never a good sign.

He rushed ahead as he stared into her panicked eyes. "I don't expect you to say anything. I just...couldn't keep it in any longer. It's a gift. Given without expectation. I just want you to know that someone knows you." He gulped and took in a ragged breath. "And loves you."

For fuck's sake, stop saying it. She'll run naked down Fifth Avenue to escape.

She pursed her lips but finally met his eyes, nodding. "I need a few minutes."

He turned off the water and handed her a towel as he stepped out of the shower. He wrapped one around his waist and left the bathroom, mentally berating himself.

You know she's a flight risk.

You know she wants to live in New York.

You know she's terrified of commitment. And still you fucking said the thing.

Nash took the forgotten food to the kitchen. His stomach was in knots, and food was the last thing on his mind.

He'd really just had the best sex of his life and then shot himself in both feet.

"I don't want anything to change."

He whirled around to see Lily in an oversized robe in the archway of the kitchen.

She twisted her hands together, like she was considering skydiving. "You know I'm new at...feelings. But you're the most important man I've ever had in my life."

She was scared. He could see it. He'd frightened her. Too much, too soon.

They'd only been married for seven weeks. Only *together-*together for less than a month.

He gulped, nodding.

This is progress. There wasn't a Lily-sized hole in the wall from her running away.

But was it enough?

Her lip trembled as she spoke. "I obviously have feelings for you, but I'm not sure how it all fits together. You, my work, my future, Fairwick Falls, here. I know you are the best man I've ever met. I just don't want anything to change."

He cupped her cheek and she leaned into him.

A sigh of relief escaped him at feeling her coming into his arms, and he held her as if she were the most precious thing in the world.

Because she was.

LILY

Lily's creative spark had returned since Nash had been in New York.

The fact that it was after Nash said he loved her?

Pure coincidence.

He hadn't said the Big L since the shower, and she still berated herself for chickening out. For keeping her heart tucked safely in her pocket rather than revealing that it had been his for too long.

She couldn't stand it if something happened to him. Or their very new, very real relationship. What if she told him that she'd loved him forever and scared him off?

She had to keep her distance because it would probably end, right? Even people in love still eventually broke up. And she'd break into pieces if he left her.

When he left her. Because love always ended...right?

They'd spent the weekend at the MoMA and the Met, intent on finding her inspiration, but of course it had struck at the most unexpected time. They'd been walking through the cacophonous hall of Grand Central Station, and stopped at a pop-up flower shop that was doing brisk business.

It had reminded her so much of Bloom, she couldn't breathe. The juxtaposition of fresh flowers against the burnished-brass train station background grabbed her by the brain and wouldn't let go.

After buying a taxi-sized amount of flowers, she'd rushed back to the apartment and worked into the early morning for the presentation the next day.

Now she stood in front of Sven, sweating bullets, presenting the revised vision of the Bloom and KGM partnership.

"Upscale classic accents in burnished gold complement opaque matte, floral-inspired colors. Each print is an oversized interpretation of nature's most perfect paintings: petals. Rather than being busy and loud, we opt for timeless elegance that will be investment pieces. The timeless combination of nature and New York."

Lily composited images of Grand Central Station and 1000x close ups of a purple lilac petal, a spring green leaf, and the bold red of a rose petal. She cycled through slides showing her vision, and then how that could apply to a vase, a handbag, home goods.

Sven's face contorted into an odd shape: a smile.

"I like it," he said, looking over her designs. "This feels on market trend, but ahead. Approachable."

"As my sister would say, 'Omaha would love it.'"

His eyes narrowed as he seemed to evaluate her. "This is impressive for only a few days work. If you get tired of Bloom, you could be a good fit here. I'm going on parental leave, and we're looking for a contract backfill for nine months. No commitment after that, but you'd be able to do pretty much whatever you wanted afterwards," he said with a smile. "Just say the word and I'll recommend you to be first in line."

Lily's heart leapt to her throat. Having her name as a contract creative director at KGM, even for only nine months, would open doors that had never been possible when she'd been an independent illustrator and artist. This would be next-level shit.

Plus, it was only a few months, her favorite kind of commitment. She'd worked her whole life to get to this moment, and she'd be in the perfect position to live the life she'd planned for.

No-commitment-needed Lily.

"Yeah, maybe," she said with a nervous smile. "It sounds like a dream come true, but I need to talk to my business partners about it."

And my husband.

This was everything she had wanted, right? To come back to New York, bigger and better than ever? Living the life she'd loved before it had been interrupted by her father's death?

So why did her heart break as she considered leaving Fairwick Falls—and her husband of convenience—permanently?

Chapter Twenty-nine

NASH

Nash walked out of his favorite New York bakery early the next morning, carrying coffee and donuts back to his sleeping wife. He'd extended his stay a few days already and was dreading the flight home that afternoon.

Maybe I'll bump my flight to tomorrow.

No one could begrudge him taking time off for a long-awaited honeymoon.

As he walked down the chilly street, a familiar face turned the corner, jogging toward him.

"Josh?" Nash lifted his sunglasses in surprise. He'd been on Wall Street with Josh years ago.

An athletic man in his late thirties slowed to a walk with a surprised face. "Nash? Shit, you back in the city?" Josh bent over, trying to catch his breath. They gave each other a bro hug.

"Visiting for the weekend."

"Too bad," Josh said. "We should grab a drink to catch up." Which was New York bullshit for 'Nice to see you, but let's not make a habit of it.'

"Yeah, next time," Nash said with a wave as he started to walk away.

Josh stretched as he caught his breath. "Hey, I was surprised you didn't come with your brother about the thing. He was in the office last week."

A chill crept up Nash's spine as he turned around. "Where are you at again?"

"Quantum Capital."

Oh fuck.

Josh stretched his quads. "We're looking to expand into some new states, and he mentioned you as a connection. I assumed you'd be at the meeting. That's why I didn't reach out."

Fury crawled up his spine at his brother, but this was a prime time to do recon. "How do you like it at Quantum?"

"Oh, we're the future," Josh said with a smile. "Our operations cost is rock-bottom, about seventy-five percent cheaper than everybody else's, given our state of the art humanless AI workforce."

Gross.

"Plus, we only hire part-time workers, so it saves on our insurance and operational cost."

It would be a nightmare if they got their hands in Fairwick Falls. Fairwick County Community Bank was a blip compared to Quantum, but it was still one of the largest independent banks left in Pennsylvania.

AKA, one of the only chickens left ready to be devoured by the fox in front of him.

Nash stewed all the way back to the apartment and had already moved his flight to leave earlier. He set the coffees down in the kitchen and immediately started packing.

A sleepy Lily wearing his long-sleeved shirt leaned against the door frame, looking like a decadent French dessert. Sunshine backlit the blonde, wispy curls around her face.

He leaned down for a kiss, trying to savor every moment. "I have to go back earlier than I thought."

"I thought you'd stay a few more days," she said, hurt on her face.

"I ran into an old friend, and apparently Jeremy's still cooking something up, even though everything should be settled. I have to." He ran his hands down her arms and hugged her.

"But can he really do anything? You're the president. The board approved the bylaws."

He tucked her closer, more for his comfort than hers. "I don't trust him as far as I can throw him. He could still persuade the board into pushing for a buyout." He pulled back, hating that he saw her eyes wide and nervous. "I'm sorry. I have to. You know I made a promise and—"

"Your duty, I know," she said, shrugging as she broke away from him. "I'm just"—she spun around, changing her mind apparently—"I'm frustrated you can't be free and choose what *you* want. Even now, when nothing's wrong. You can't take time and know everything will be okay."

"Someone has to be responsible. We can't fly through life hoping somebody else will catch us. *I* am the catcher." His voice had an edge to it, and her eyes got wide. "I didn't mean to insinuate that you... I'm sorry."

He *saw* her put on her shield in front of his eyes. Her self-indulgent smile and a wink. Funny, silly good-time Lily was back. "No, no. I know. I know I'm flighty."

"That's not what I—"

"It's fine," she cut him off with a tight smile.

The day had started out so well, too. They'd made love at the light of dawn, and he'd been too wound up to go back to sleep.

The pull to take care of the potential fire at home warred with his need to keep the woman he loved.

She hovered in the doorway while he packed, looking nervous. "I might need to stay in New York for a while."

He scoured the bedroom, checking to make sure he'd grabbed everything. *Keys, charger, phone.* He'd have to hustle to LaGuardia to make his flight. "Uh, sure. Do you know when you'll be back home?" he asked distractedly as he looked under the bed.

"KGM wants to offer me a full-time role."

Nash stilled and slowly stood.

That was her dream. Only possible in the city.

Nash pulled her into a crushing hug. "I'm so proud of you." He meant it. He held her tight as she sniffled against his chest. "And I love you enough to tell you that you'd be amazing. I love you enough to tell you to go after your dream."

I love you enough to let you go if that's what you want.

He just wished her dreams included him.

He pulled back to look down at her in his arms. She fit perfectly there. "It doesn't change how I feel about you. Or what we could be."

Tears started falling down her cheeks. "But you're there. I'd be here." Her voice cracked through the tears.

"We'd figure something out." Desperation laced his voice.

"For forever?" she asked, as if he was nuts to think they could live in two places.

His reminder went off. Time to leave for the airport.

Goddamnit.

Lily walked him to the door, and it felt like the gallows. Who knew when she'd come back to Fairwick Falls? Her life was picking up steam here.

He had a ticking time bomb at the place he'd promised he'd

protect, and yet something so perfect was slipping through his fingers right here.

Nash wanted to scream, but instead he ran his fingers through Lily's curtain of blonde hair. "I'll call you when I land."

"Okay." Her voice was quiet. No smart comeback, no innuendo, none of his firecracker.

"Do you know when you'll be back home?" He didn't want to pressure her, but he couldn't leave without knowing when he'd see her again.

She shrugged, uncharacteristically quiet. "It depends on some meetings tomorrow about the full-time role. Maybe I'll stay longer. Start looking for a place."

A knife twisted between his shoulder blades, piercing his heart. But she was pliant in his arms, looking up at him with those liquid eyes of longing.

Maybe there was still hope.

He threaded his fingers through her hair, trying to memorize the silky softness. She pulled his shirt and he took her mouth, trying to brand his name there. He inhaled her scent as his tongue traced her lip. Moving her head to take more of what he wanted, he deepened the kiss and felt her arms circle his waist, clutching at the fabric of his coat.

She tasted like coffee, and tart brightness—like his *wife*.

No one else would do.

His thumbs stroked her cheekbones as his phone beeped. His car was here.

He was inches away from saying "Fuck it" and staying here, throwing her in bed, and never leaving.

"I don't want to go," he murmured, pressing a long kiss against her cheek. "I really, really don't want to go."

But he pulled away, remembering the promise he'd made to the man who'd given him everything. To show up for others. To do his duty above all else. "I'll talk to you soon."

She wordlessly held the door open for him, fighting back tears.

And with an echoing click that thundered along the hallway, he realized...

...That might be the last time I'll kiss the love of my life.

NASH FLOORED it down the highway toward Fairwick Falls. As soon as he'd landed in Pittsburgh, his phone had blown up with texts and voicemails from Maria and other staff members at the bank.

The board had convened an emergency meeting.

Without him.

As he took the exit to Fairwick Falls, his mind raced. Would he have the power to block an acquisition? Was there a way to make this work for the community so that it actually was better? He wasn't averse to change, but he felt the responsibility to make sure everyone was taken care of.

A few minutes later, he burst into the conference room where board members sat listening to his brother. A line of suit-clad men stared at him from the front of the room. Heads whipped toward the door as he stood there, panting.

"This is a closed session," Josiah said.

"And I have every right to be here," Nash said, striding into the room. No one would meet his gaze.

"You're out," Jeremy said with a smug smile.

"What lies did you tell them?" Nash bellowed.

Al turned to him. "Jeremy shared that you withheld crucial information to the shareholders and customers of the bank. The investment that Quantum could make could significantly increase profits. It was your duty as the president to bring all offers to the board. And you failed, repeatedly, to do that."

"We'd have online banking," Josiah said.

"We already have that," Nash said offhandedly, still glaring at his brother. "I set it up three years ago."

"But it would be better," Jeremy said. "Quantum has an app."

"We already have an app," Nash said with a tight edge to his voice. The board members looked at each other, confused. What twenty-four-pack of lies had Jeremy sold to them? Were they so unfamiliar with the bank's own products that he had been able to sweet-talk them?

"Our customers would have access to a national network of finances," Al said with a sad smile.

Et tu, Al?

"We don't need it. We manage risk on our own through thoughtful investments," Nash said, running his hands through his hair. He sounded desperate, like he was begging someone not to leave him.

It was exactly how he felt.

"Operations cost for employees will be exponentially lower, which means more of a profit for the shareholders," Jeremy said, looking pleased with himself.

Nash fumed, feeling out of breath in the shrinking conference room. "Did he tell you Quantum doesn't believe in full-time employees? The bank employees wouldn't have any benefits. No parental leave, no health insurance. If they even *have* a job after being replaced by a machine."

"That's not our responsibility," a board member said. "They're welcome to get a job with full benefits elsewhere."

"Of *course* it's our responsibility," Nash yelled, hitting the table. "It is *everyone's* responsibility. The bare goddamn minimum is respect, fair compensation, and equity. Not a race to the bottom of how little you can care about other people." He was disgusted with them. He stared at Jeremy with hatred.

"Destroy hundreds of years of a family legacy all for, what? A few hundred thousand dollars in a finder's fee?"

The board members looked at each other in confusion.

"You can't see"—Jeremy interjected, a panic at the edge of his voice at being found out—"this is better because it's bigger than you've ever thought. You're just a bad businessman."

Nash wiped his mouth in desperation, feeling crazed. "We sponsor Little League teams. We funded the biggest food drive the county has seen in a hundred years last year. Our customers are taken care of and our employees are happy," Nash said, making his voice stay firm and not wobble with the emotion he felt in his heart.

He'd busted his ass, and it still hadn't been enough.

He tried to outthink, outwork, outmaneuver everyone to be above reproach, to think of the community first and himself second, and yet it hadn't been enough.

Jeremy smirked. "I don't think Quantum gives a shit about any of that. Do you boys?" The line of suited white men along the edge of the room wouldn't meet Nash's eyes.

No one would meet his eyes.

"All I ever wanted was to do what was right, and you let this snake oil salesman come in with promises that you'll earn, what? Ten thousand more dollars next year in dividends? I'm surprised your integrity is so cheap."

Al stood. "You should go, Nash. You can collect your things."

Nash's world tilted on an axis.

"Right. I should take my things. Will I be escorted?" Nash said with a laugh that escaped him at the *ludicrous* nature of this whole exchange. "Maybe take the wrought-iron hat rack that my great-great-grandfather installed in the lobby? Or the pee-wee baseball trophy we sponsored last year? How about the chipped section of the front desk where I ran into it when I was seven that's never been fixed? Good thing I have the scar to keep for myself," he said, pointing to his forehead.

"This place is in my DNA and you can never take that away from me." He stormed out of the room, disgusted with them.

He felt like a man in a fire needing to grab memories for his family's legacy. He dashed into his office, grabbed his wedding photo and his father's name placard from his desk.

Holding two things that represented the people that meant the most to him, he walked out of the office in a rage, never looking back.

Nash's vision blurred as he swayed in front of his father's headstone a day later.

Half a bottle of scotch was a bad idea.

He clutched a manila folder of divorce papers as regret turned in his stomach. No need for Lily to stay trapped to him, the guy who fucked everything up.

He had to give her a choice. He wanted her to *choose* to stay with him, not be forced to.

If she doesn't love me, I won't trap her. I love her enough to let her go.

But I'll never sign first.

The manila envelope in his hands felt heavy. The thick stack of sadness weighed him down as he swayed. She wouldn't want to be with a loser, someone who failed at the one job he'd been bred for his whole life.

"I did it," he slurred, looking at the moving headstone in front of him. "Failed. Been waiting my whole life for the one big mistake I'd make, and it turns out I'm really good at it. No job, my wife doesn't love me. I've worked so hard"—he hiccuped, his lips twisting with emotion—"but I failed. Ugh, I feel dizzy.

Do you mind if I...?" He turned around, looking for something to grab before the world tilted sideways. "Sorry, Aunt Ethel," he said, grabbing a headstone in front of him.

He'd always liked Aunt Ethel. She'd had a tickly mustache when she kissed his cheek and had always carried butterscotch candies. "I think you might be having a better day than me, Aunt Ethel."

After texting Mrs. Maroo for a copy of standard divorce papers, he'd passed out after wallowing by himself last night.

He'd tried calling Lily once, but she hadn't answered. He'd let his phone die. No reason to be reachable now.

Who needed him?

He'd decided to comfort himself by allowing himself to slip up, fuck up again, and drink away the shame.

Then when all the bad had still been there when he'd woken up at noon, he'd given it another try. Maybe the bottom of a Lagavulin bottle would be more comforting than the top.

He eyed his dad's headstone. "You know the thing you told me to do, 'Put the community first'? Welp," he said, his voice going loud, swinging his arms wide. "Tried it and it didn't work. But you, you did everything right for thirty years. You were better at making people believe in you or, I don't know, convincing them of shit."

His dad had kept everything the same when he'd inherited the leadership position of the bank from Nash's grandfather. Nash had been the first person in decades to bring fresh eyes to the institution. He'd seen the faded furniture, the old wallpaper, the website that barely worked, and had known he could do better.

"I worked so hard," he said, shaking his head at his foolishness. "I...I wanted to do you proud, and I fucked everything up. Sorry, Aunt Ethel, for the language," he added, turning around, and saw Gray walking through the headstones.

"Hey, man," Gray said with a tentative smile and concerned eyes.

Nash swayed with a grimace. "Oh god, go away."

Gray handed him a bottle of water. "Wanted to check on you. I'm worried."

"I don't need you to babysit me," Nash said through a hiccup, pushing the water away.

"Let's get some coffee in you, and I'll buy you some pie at Pop's."

"I don't deserve pie. I don't want to see anyone. Or their pitying looks." Nash rubbed a hand down his face. "Let me be in this."

"Hey, you were there for me."

Gray had struggled to get sober five years ago. Nash felt like he'd barely done anything to help one of his closest friends. "I could have done more."

"Bullshit. Who stepped in this year when Frank wasn't there for my sober anniversary? Who checked on me when I was at my lowest?" Gray got in front of him, made Nash look at him. "What happened with the bank is not your fault. You said Jeremy's always been an asshat. Why is that your responsibility?"

"Because I was given everything!" Nash yelled finally. It felt good to let his rage flow. "Life isn't fair and I was given the *best* hand. And that's fucked up. I wanted to even out the odds as much as I could. Do the right thing like my dad," he said, faltering for a minute. "Keep his legacy alive. Keep *him*..."

He shook his head, not willing to finish the sentence.

He pushed away from the headstone, wanting to scream in the middle of the silent cemetery. "Why was I saddled with this? Why did I bust my ass only for *no one* to care? And then Lily," he said, looking down at the papers in his hands. "I had to drink half a bottle of scotch to get the courage to print the papers from Mrs. Maroo."

"What papers?" Gray asked.

Nash wiped a hand over his mouth. "It's nothing," he said, realizing he'd said too much. "Just don't tell Rose. I don't want the Parker inquisition."

Gray's eyebrows furrowed. "Is something going on with you and Lily?"

Nash started laughing. *That is an understatement.* He put an unsteady hand on Gray's shoulder. "Look, I appreciate you, but go away."

"Let me at least give you a ride home. It's a mile back to your house."

"Leave me alone!" he roared, letting the beast out to finally show the world how much of a failure he really was.

Gray's eyebrows shot up. At least, one of them did. There were a couple of Grays in front of his face as Nash walked away, cutting across the cemetery, stumbling as he went.

He'd already gotten the hang of this failing thing.

But he'd do one thing right.

He'd let Lily go, not trap her here with him.

Chapter Thirty

LILY

Lily's heart felt like it would burst from happy possibilities as she crossed into Fairwick Falls.

The KGM job conversation yesterday had gone well, but she hadn't made a decision yet. She needed to see Nash.

It had only been twenty-four hours since he'd left New York, but it had felt like days. She'd tossed and turned last night, catching whiffs of his cologne in the bed sheets.

It had all finally clicked when she'd inhaled the scent on his pillow like a goblin.

She'd *never* feel this way about a job.

A job couldn't hold you when you cried, or make you scream in pleasure. She couldn't wake up to a job spooning her on a lazy Saturday morning. A job wouldn't move heaven and earth to make her happy.

She would try to *emotional stuntman* her feelings out before she fucked up the best thing that had ever happened to her.

The fact that I started name-change paperwork?

Definitely coincidence.

Her stomach flip-flopped with excited nerves. Parker-Donnelly *did* have a nice ring to it.

I did always hate choosing.

She drove past Bloom on her way home to surprise Nash. He hadn't answered her calls or texts, but she assumed he'd been busy with the bank.

Rose said the news was bad coming out of the bank meeting, but she didn't know details. Nash was strong, though. The man who never lost at anything probably didn't need his wife worrying about him.

She unlocked their front door with a happy smile. A stack of papers sat on the foyer table, looking important.

"Nash?" Her voice echoed through the quiet house. She'd texted she was on her way back, but her message had gone unread.

The house was quiet.

"Nash? I'm home. I have a surprise for you." Her hands shook with happy nerves, clutching the name-change paperwork.

She walked to the papers on the table and saw her name at the top.

Read the first page.

Read it again again with panicked eyes.

Divorce papers?

She felt sick. The name change papers burned in her hand. He

She hadn't come home with a firm plan, but she'd mostly thought out that they'd stay together, she'd change her name, they'd live happily ever after in this beautiful home together, somehow.

He'd said he'd loved her...and yet?

She called Nash's name again, ran through the entire house, needing to talk to him. Called his phone ten, fifteen times. Needing to yell at him and ask him what the hell this was.

But nothingness answered back.

She shook her head not wanting to believe it as she ended back at the foyer where her purse had fallen to the ground.

The antique wainscoting, the marble floors all mocked her now.

She thought he'd loved her enough to see that she belonged here.

But now? A tear slapped onto the awful paperwork in front of her.

She needed a new plan, and she wouldn't stay here, not where she wasn't wanted.

She tossed the divorce papers in the unlit foyer fireplace and ran out the front door.

Lily bit into a piece of blackberry pie as fat tears rolled down her face, feeling like the biggest cliche on Earth.

"So, it was all fake?" Violet said with a raised eyebrow as she rubbed Lily's back.

"Except it wasn't," Lily cried through a mouthful of pie.

"But...it was initially?" Rose asked, trying to piece everything together.

Lily nodded. She stuffed her mouth full of pie again. "This pie is really good." She hiccuped. "But then after we got married we started to date for real and he said he loved me..."

Violet gasped.

Lily avoided their eyes, gulping down the pie.

"And what did *you* say?" Rose said, with a knowing glare.

Lily shook her head, unwilling to admit her shame.

Rose's mouth fell open in shock. "Lillian Grace, you have been in love with that man since you were twelve years old."

Her very thoughtful, mature response of "So?" came out before she could stop it.

"Put down your pie," Rose ordered.

Lily complied, putting it on the coffee table and then Rose lobbed a pillow at her face. "You are *married* to him, you fool," she said, yelling at her with an exasperated smile. "And you love him."

A watery laugh bubbled out of Lily behind the pillow. "Don't yell at me, I'm sad."

Rose shoved at her hair with an incredulous smile. "For no reason!"

She hated it when Rose made sense and didn't agree with her. "He printed divorce papers, Rose."

"Because he thinks you don't love him."

"Don't yell at her. She needs more pie," Violet said, picking up Lily's plate and handing it back to her.

"You always were my favorite sister," Lily said, putting her head on Vi's shoulder.

"Ugh, I swear I need to shake sense into you half the time." Rose started pacing. "Look, he's had a really hard time with the bank. Gray wouldn't give me the details, but he was worse than Gray had ever seen him. I've never seen Nash anything but perfectly buttoned up and I've known him literally forever."

Violet wrapped her in a tight hug. "I just know you'll work everything out."

Rose sat next to her on the couch, staring her down. "I know it's scary for you to commit. But you can't be a chicken shit about this. If you really love him, you have to tell him even if you know he could hurt you."

Lily's stomach flip-flopped. "How did you know?"

Rose shook her head with disbelief, a slow smile spreading across her face. "Because I know you better than myself, goober." She wrapped her arms around Lily, a rare treat. She nuzzled into Rose's shoulder as she smoothed Lily's hair. "We're only scared of things that can hurt us. Nash leaving you after you've been in love with him forever? That would really fucking hurt."

"I never wanted to be like Dad," she whispered. Violet and Rose nodded in understanding. "I didn't even know dads could be happy until I stayed over at Jenny Meyerson's house in first grade. I thought it was normal for dads to cry and sit alone in the dark." She sniffled, the tears starting again. Her earliest memory had been trying to make him laugh, doing handstands with her goat stuffed animal, Nibbles.

Her Dad's whole demeanor had shifted when she'd made him laugh. He'd come alive, and she'd chased that feeling for the rest of her life.

"But you guys said he was so happy before Mom died. I dunno. When I figured out why he was so sad, I just didn't want to risk it," Lily said.

Rose patted her back. "You can't let his life dictate yours, Lilybug."

No, she couldn't.

"So, what are you going to do?" Violet asked.

"I thought I knew but..." Lily shook her head.

I'm more confused than ever.

Hours later, Lily stared at Violet's ceiling as the clock ticked to 3:56 AM.

As it finally clicked to 4 AM, she tossed off the covers and drove to her apartment above Bloom. She needed to feel grounded again, somewhere that felt like *her* as she figured out how to untangle this mess.

She loved her husband. And he loved her.

But he'd made plans for their relationship to end. Divorce papers didn't grow on trees. He'd printed them for godsakes.

And she'd printed her promise for their future, like a fool.

She allowed herself one big inhale of the Bloom shop as she hugged the prep table. She'd missed it desperately. It was the longest she'd been away from the shop, the beating heart that lived outside of her body, since they'd redone it last year.

She happily inhaled the familiar scent of home as she opened the door into her dim apartment. The incense that she burned, the smell of pencil shavings from her work, the lingering scent of florals from the shop, and the woodsy smell of the beams all combined into something that hugged her heart and made her feel like herself for the first time in weeks.

A snore cut through the silence, and Lily jumped against the door.

Nash was cuddled in her bed over the quilts, clutching one of her sweaters like he'd fallen asleep smelling it.

She crept closer. At least she *thought* it was Nash. His beard was scruffy. His hair was a mess. He wore a stained t-shirt and sweatpants.

The man who never let a crack show looked like he'd been dragged through hell and back.

The tortured pinch of his brow as he slept cast shadows on his face in the moonlight.

Stepping back toward the door, her foot hit a creaky floorboard.

Nash startled awake. He stared at her, wide-eyed with wonder, not moving from the bed. His hand still wrapped around her sweater, clutched close by his face.

"Lily?" His voice was scratchy, like he'd screamed her name a thousand times.

"What are you doing here?" She asked.

"Needed you," he whispered, slowly moving out of bed.

"But you...you gave up on us." She shook her head, trying to get it on straight. "Don't you want to divorce me?"

He wiped a hand down his sleepy face. "What are you talking about?"

"I went home and looked for you. I saw the papers in our foyer and—"

"Hold on." He rubbed his hand over his face to dust off sleep.

She would *not* hold on. She could barely hold on at all. "I'm going crazy, Nash. I came home to see you and then I went into our house,"—she paced, now angry—"and there were divorce papers in our foyer, front and center"

He stood slowly, still looking at her like she was a ghost. "I didn't know you were coming home."

"But you had divorce papers printed in a nice little stack. Might as well have put a red fucking bow on it for me. I tore through our house looking for you—"

He reached for her hand. "Lily."

His sleep-crackled, forlorn voice was an arrow to her heart.

She tried to tug away, but he gripped her wrist. She felt like a trapped animal caught in a web of her own making.

His penetrating stare shot through her. "You called it ours. You called our house *your* home."

A panicked heartbeat hit like a snare drum in her ear, and she couldn't. She *couldn't* open herself up now and admit the Very Terrible Thing.

That she loved him so desperately.

"No big deal. A slip of the tongue," she said, avoiding his eyes.

He released her wrist. "No, Lily." He was awake now, and frustrated. He leaned against the eave of the alcove, crowding her. "I have been waiting for two months for you to catch up to where I was on our wedding day. You said you went home. *Where* is that?"

"My home is with you!" The words burst out of her. "*This* is home because you're here," she said through tears, gesturing around her. "Wherever you are, that's home to me."

She finally met his eyes. He'd gone still, understanding dawning on his face.

"And you want to end it, even though I thought..." Her voice faltered with sob.

"I need you to *choose me*, Lily. Make a choice, for once. I will *never* sign those papers first, but I love you so much...I'll let you go. If that's what you want." His voice was firm and final.

"What do *you* want?" she asked, dizzy at the power he was giving her.

He huffed out a tired laugh. "I *want* to keep you forever. I *want* to build a life with you. I *want* to be selfish for the first time in my life and keep you locked with me like a dragon hoards its gold, because I don't think..." He faltered. "I don't think I can do this without you."

"This?" she asked, hope filling her soul.

He gestured around them. "This. Life, all of it," he said, sounding desperate. "You brought color into a life I hadn't realized was black and white. Like in *The Wizard of Oz* where you didn't know you're missing something until a blast of technicolor wakes you up? *That's* what you do to me. You make my life better by being *you*. So, please, what do you want to do?" His voice was yearning, desperate.

He stepped closer. She didn't move an inch.

He wiped a hand down his face in exasperation. "Lily, just tell me what you *want*," he said, finally, harshly.

"To feel safe," she sobbed. It burst out of her and he pulled her into his chest, his hand on her cheek.

Surprised at her own words, she finally let herself feel just how hard she'd worked her entire life as tears streaming down her face.

To be okay on her own. To need no one and nothing.

She hadn't even known what she was saying until it was out of her mouth. But god, she did want to feel safe.

To feel like she could *finally* rest.

Finally stop running from the love she craved.

The rumble of his low voice was a salve. "You *are* safe here. I will always catch you. I will always, always be here."

She looked up into his pleading amber eyes that were so full of love.

Something clicked in her head.

Love wasn't a trap.

Love was a *net*, meant to catch her from falling.

And Nash would always catch her.

"I'm really scared because maybe...maybe I want to stay. Because maybe..." She pushed herself over that terrifying waterfall to free fall into the mist below.

She grabbed the crumpled paper from her bag and handed it to him.

His eyes scanned the paper with growing surprise.

Lily gulped as deep heaving breaths wrenched out of him as he read the document again and again.

"Maybe?" He asked, finally looking back at her.

She inhaled a ragged breath. "Maybe...I've loved you for longer than I can remember."

He pressed the paper to his heart.

"How long?" he whispered in astonishment.

She soared through the mist free falling, baring her heart.

"Forever," she whispered through trembling lips. "It's always been you. And," she gulped. "It's only grown." She looked up with pained eyes as she stood virtually defenseless. "I'm so scared. What happens if you get sick? What if you die? I couldn't stand it. I'd be like my dad. Hopeless without you because you're my best friend. A shell. I love you too much to ever let you go."

He took her face in his hands, brushing the tears away from her cheeks with such gentleness. God, he smelled like home. His clean cotton and mahogany blend was her permanent comfort blanket.

"Then you will be a wreck, Lily Parker-*Donnelly*, but you will mend yourself back together because you are a force of nature. A typhoon of a woman. You are not your mother or your father. Thank Christ there's only one of you because I can barely keep my head on straight. Now"—he leaned down, wiping a tear away, and hovering over her mouth—"say you love me again, wife."

"I love—"

But the rest of her sentence was interrupted by his impatient lips.

Chapter Thirty-one

LILY

Nash kissed like a man desperate for air that only she could provide.

She pulled away, gasping, and he kissed her jaw. "I love you. I love you," she panted as he wrapped his arms around her. She couldn't *stop* saying it.

A low growl sounded in his throat, and he lifted her onto the counter and stepped between her thighs, taking her mouth again.

She felt the hard length of his cock as he pulled her hips against him. She ground against it, letting herself get lost in what forever would feel like.

Fuck, they hadn't talked about anything. If he really *was* her forever...

Lily yanked her mouth away panting. "Kids?"

He hovered over her mouth, smiling like he couldn't believe his luck. "Whatever you want." He sucked on a spot on her neck that turned her insides into simmering liquid.

"Maybe," she answered, deep in thought. "Yes to kids, I think. With you."

He grabbed her chin with a fierce look, looking like he wanted to get started on them right then.

She raked her hands along his muscular chest that made her clench. She pulled off his shirt, needing to bury her face in the muscles there.

He panted as he came back to her. "Where will we live?"

She buried her face against his chest, kissing along his pecs. "As long as this chest comes with you, I don't care." She was lust-drunk and horny as hell, but it turned out they had more productive conversations about their future this way.

"I'll start looking for an apartment in Brooklyn," he said as he pulled at the hem of her t-shirt.

She stopped him, unable to believe what he just said. "You can't leave Fairwick Falls. This is your forever home."

Their hungry urgency dissipated.

He looked confused. "Your dream job is with KGM. I can't ask you to give that up."

"I don't have a *duty* to work at KGM. I don't even know if that's what I *want* anymore. I'd miss my sisters too much if we moved away." *How bad had the board meeting been?* "Nash. What happened at the bank?"

He dropped his chin to his chest, wiping his face in frustration. "I failed, Lily. I was fired." He couldn't meet her eyes. "I played by all the rules and still lost. My staff will be let go when the acquisition goes through. They'll lose their benefits. It's all my fault."

Her heart broke for him. For losing the one thing he'd worked so hard to keep. She wrapped her arms around him, and he nuzzled in, clutching her to him.

But he wouldn't be the man she fell in love with if he gave up that easily. "I thought your whole thing was doing your duty, right? You can't protect the town's interests if you're not here," she offered.

"I can figure out some way to help from afar. What's important is that we're together. I don't want to leave you, wife." He rubbed his hands up and down her back.

His mouth found her neck again, and as a rain shower of lust drizzled over her, she realized they were *married* married now.

Like, file-taxes-together married. No more pretending. She stilled. "Wait—how much money *do* you have?"

He raised an eyebrow as he kissed her wrist.

She rolled her eyes. "Ugh, fine, how much money do *we* have?" She'd never get over that. That he wanted her to have what was his.

"It's...a lot. Enough for us to be lazy for the rest of our lives."

She raised her eyebrows at the prospect. "Tempting. We could take time to finally perfect the tall guy, short girl sixty-nine position. I know how you love being creative with numbers."

He huffed out a laugh against her lips, but then pulled back suddenly. His eyes darted in the air with sharp movements, thinking.

"Wait a minute..." His eyes sparkled with awareness. "How much would you care if all that money went away?"

"Living off no money? I'd say...that's a regular Tuesday for me?"

His eyes were far away as she saw his mind race. "I don't have to be the president of the bank to protect the town's financial interests. In fact, maybe I was *never* protecting it."

A wild, happy look grew in Nash's eyes. "What if instead of a bank"—an incredulous laugh barked out of him—"what if I started a credit union?"

He looked like he'd suggested they steal all the crown jewels in London.

Lily tried to match his excitement. "That is an amazing idea! One question: what's the difference?"

Nash nipped her shoulder, kissing down her arm. "A bank is for-profit, so they keep their own interests in mind. In a credit union, it's owned by the people. And most importantly, it's not for-profit." He lingered on the inside of her elbow, kissing it as he thought. "The *members* are most important. All the people of Fairwick Falls, as it should be."

"Where do you come into play?"

He licked her inner wrist, and she was having a hard time concentrating. "They need capital to get going." He moved to her other wrist. "It's risky to start one because you're nothing without members. But maybe..." His eyes moved, as if piecing together a puzzle in his head. "Hot damn!" he shouted in happiness as he swooped her up in his arms in the carry they'd gotten so good at. "I think it could work!"

He looked devastatingly handsome with his tousled hair, scruff, and bright smile. If buttoned-up Nash had been her catnip, this version of him was a wholly unexpected shot of dopamine straight to her heart.

He was happy, freer. More himself.

And so, so fucking sexy.

He walked to the bed and tossed her down before shedding his pants in a hurry. "Should we get married again?"

She sat up on her elbows with a smirk. "Depends. *My* vows were real."

He crawled toward her with a wry, delighted smile. "You think you're so smart, don't you?" She laughed, nodding as he pulled off her yoga pants. "Maybe some of mine were too," he said coyly.

"Which ones? 'I'm sure some of you think this is rushed'?" She snorted.

He went quiet. The humor was gone from his face as he

stared at her from the bottom of their bed, his face full of love. A pure beam of heart-shaped light hit her.

He leaned down to kiss her ankle. "I shouldn't have been looking for the perfect wife." He kissed the other ankle. "I should have been looking for the *right* wife." He nuzzled her calf, looking reverently happy.

Wait, what?

He placed slow, open-mouthed kisses on her formerly injured knee. "The perfect wife for me is the gorgeous, spunky woman who loves to do things her own way, who is brilliant beyond measure."

Holy shit. He memorized his vows. He's vowing at *me right now.* Her heart lurched. *He'd meant them this whole time.*

He kissed her other knee, bending it to lick the sensitive skin behind it, and a jolt of desire shot into her core. "She's fierce, and funny, and cares more for everyone around her than they'll ever know." She clenched at the feeling of his tongue against her skin. He kissed her thigh, nipping at it. Her hips bucked in response, wanting to feel him in her.

"I've been falling for you for five years. I fell for your kindness, concern for every living thing, your humor, and not the least of all, your brilliance."

Her core was molten, her pussy a puddle, as she stared in wonder. This man—her husband—was seducing her with his wedding vows.

Very. Effectively.

He trailed his tongue along her inner thigh, leaving hot kisses. Her nipples were hard pebbles under her shirt, and she wanted to pinch them but couldn't break his spell on her.

"Lily Parker-*Donnelly*"—*fuck yes*—"can do anything she puts her mind to, and I wasn't going to pass up the opportunity to see what our life together could be."

His scruff dragged against her skin, sending shivers of

desire into her pussy. He kissed his way to her bikini line, and she dove her hands into his thick hair. "Having a photographic memory is really unfair," she murmured, equal parts impressed, turned on, and jealous.

He smiled against her skin as he kissed the curve of her hip. "You're my own wildflower." Moving her panties to the side, he dove his tongue into her seam, and she threw her head back with a groan at the pleasure.

He licked up to her clit, taking his time. "Rugged. Raw and bright. The most gorgeous thing nature has ever made," he said, staring at her pussy, and sucked hard on her clit as she arched off the bed in pleasure.

He climbed up with slow kisses along her belly. "I am hopelessly in love with you, and I plan to remain that way."

Kisses along her neck felt like small starbursts against her skin, continuing until he settled between her legs.

He whispered as he slowly, *so slowly,* pressed into her. "You have been, and always will be, my wife."

She clenched around his cock, feeling so full. Claimed, body and soul, by her husband. The only man she'd ever loved.

They sighed together at how good it felt.

She stared up into his face, soft with desire for her. "How did I get this lucky?" She kissed his chest right where his heart was. "You're the most handsome man I've ever seen, but the best part of you is right here."

Running her hand over where she'd kissed him, she wanted to stake her claim right here. As long as there was breath left in her body, guarding his heart, protecting it, and making sure he laughed at least once a day would be her sole and happy responsibility.

"Your ass should go down in textbooks to be studied," he said as he thrust into her slowly and pleasure spiraled through her. "But the best part of you is right here." His lips lingered on her temple. "That's what I fell in love with first. Your brilliance, your humor."

He thrust into her again, and she squeezed her legs around him.

She felt a bright burst of lust overtake her body, needing him desperately. She wrapped around him and rolled them over so she was on top.

"Yeah, yeah, yeah," she teased, her hair hanging on either side of her face above him. "When do we get to the good part?"

She ground against him, moved up and down his cock.

He ripped her shirt over her head. "I think I found some good parts right here," he said as he palmed her breasts.

She snorted with laughter as he chuckled. "Look at you being funny during sex, *husband*." She'd already learned where the rocket boosters to his lust were.

He surged inside of her and she clenched, knowing how much he'd love it.

He threw his head back with a curse as she rode him harder. "Looking at you riding my cock. Taking it like such a good wife."

A surge of lust hit her pussy.

But god, she needed more. "Again," she panted.

His hand grabbed her ass as he sat up so they were eye to eye, grabbing her hard enough to leave a mark where his fingers dug in. *Yes*.

"This"—he squeezed hard, then spanked it—"is mine, wife."

She moaned against his mouth as lust and need coiled around her clit. He fumbled for the bedside table and took out her bottle of lube with a wicked smile.

And then she found the single best thing about having a 6'5" husband: long arms.

He licked into her mouth with a kiss as he reached around,

his hand sliding down between her cheeks until his lubed fingers slowly circled her ass.

"Fuck. Yes." She panted, kissing him with desperation. "Deeper. I need it."

A smile curved his lips. "You know how to get what you want, firecracker." She clenched around him. He raised an eyebrow. "Beg for it."

Her three favorite words after *I love you*.

Knowing he'd always, *always* give her what she wanted.

She'd always be safe with him.

"Fuck my ass. Please," she moaned as his finger circled her rim, playing with her. "Please. Please, husband." She loved the edging he gave her.

He wrapped his other hand around her hair and pulled her head back to capture her mouth with a punishing kiss. She clenched as she moved up and down on his cock. His finger still toyed around and around, driving her mad.

"Will you be a good girl if I do?" he murmured against her lips.

"Never." She smirked back at him.

He slapped her ass hard with a steely glint in his eyes.

Yes.

"Such a brat." He kissed her hard with a smile, sucking in her bottom lip and scraping his teeth over it.

He slowly slid a finger into her as she rode him.

Pleasure bloomed at feeling so slippery, so fun. So good. She clenched around him and sobbed each time he slid in and out of her ass, further and further as she rode him.

He'd surrounded her, the wall of his chest pressed against her cheek, her tits, as he slid his finger slowly in and out. "Mine. This tight ass, your pussy that will drip with my cum. All mine, " he growled low into her ear.

"Oh fuck," she sobbed as she rode him harder and harder, his finger and his cock fucking her back and forth.

"So full," she gasped. "So good."

"Such a greedy little wife. You want all of it, don't you?" He caught her earlobe between his teeth as she rode him harder, her tits brushing against his perfect, thick muscles.

"Yes, more," she cried out as she barreled toward the pleasure, grinding, grinding, grinding.

"My wife gets whatever she fucking wants," he growled.

She moaned higher, louder with every pulse, raking her hands through his hair and claiming him. "Husband. Mine. *Mine*—"

"*Fuck*, I'm going to—" He came in a sudden, hot burst. The feeling of his cum dripping down her thighs felt too good as she shrieked, soaking his cock as she came.

They gasped against each other, a sweaty sheen along their skin. He kissed her cheek, slowly sliding out of her.

"Well if we weren't married before, we are now," Lily said as she rested on his chest.

He flopped back with a laugh. She loved seeing his megawatt smile come out.

She let the happiness wash over her. She had a husband who loved her.

And she'd been brave enough to say it back.

He cleaned them both up—she'd married an aftercare king, apparently—and they lay back down in the dawning morning under a mountain of quilts.

"So what will you do," he muttered against her shoulder as he tucked her against him, "now that you admit to being hopelessly and forever in love with me?"

Lily arched her back with laughter.

"I love it when you do that," he murmured against her hand

as he kissed it. "It's like your body is too small for all the joy you feel."

"Eh, you're saying that because you get a good view of my boobs."

"That helps," he said with a wicked smile.

She toyed with the hair on his chest, thinking about his question for the future. "I don't know. I don't want to arrange flowers over and over again, but I don't want to leave what I've created when it's taking off, you know? Bloom is my baby."

He nodded against her hair. "What's made you happier in the last few months than anything else?"

"Well, this new hunky husband that I'm banging is pretty great. Having constant access to really good vegan food, that's been pretty great."

"Two checks in the stay in Fairwick Falls category, got it." He lifted her onto his chest so she lay on top of him.

"I really enjoyed working with Allison. Seeing Bloom expanding beyond this little town. Having a whole other store is more than a high-end knickknack that will be forgotten about after a season, you know? The KGM line is great, but it's short-lived." She shrugged, going dreamy. "I want everyone to experience coming into a beautiful store, having great design at their fingertips. Feeling fancy, and not spending a ton of money to get something great."

She shrugged, at a loss as to what it all meant.

"You're perfect, you know that?" he said, his thumb sliding along her cheek. "It doesn't sound like you need KGM to do that."

"No." She shook her head. "I wish I could keep doing what I did with Allison but all over, you know? Work with people to redesign their flower shops so their business gets better. Make a *lot* of little Blooms."

And then the thought occurred to her.

Why not?

The soaring feeling of possibilities tugged at her hands, whispering to come and play, run toward something amazing.

It could keep her right where she wanted to be: with her people.

"Why not?" he echoed her thoughts.

She slapped his chest in realization. "What's that quote from that guy you like so much? 'Though she be but little, she's fierce as fuck'?" she said with a laughing smile and smacked a kiss on his lips. "I gotta go talk to Rose."

She hopped off the bed as he groaned, holding onto her hand.

She grabbed a sweatshirt and threw it on. "What, don't you have a new plan to set in motion too?"

He sat up, his eyes never leaving her bare ass. "I do; I just thought I got to enjoy this a while longer." He reached for her thighs, tugging her back.

"I need to work on my pitch to Rose. You are not getting rid of me anytime soon, husband." She leaned down with a smile and placed a long, hungry kiss on his lips.

"I could hear you say that word every day." Locks of hair fell across his forehead as he lay in her bed, sleepy and sex-drunk and perfect.

"I plan to, as long"—she kissed his cheek—"as we both"—she kissed the other side—"shall live."

With a growl, he grabbed her hips and tossed her in the bed beside him. "The pitch can wait five minutes," he said, pinning her down on the bed as she giggled under the cage of his arms.

"Only five whole minutes?" She lifted a challenging eyebrow.

"I can't help that you do something primal to me." His

hands dove for the bottom of her sweatshirt as he ripped it off her.

The future could wait for five minutes.

She had a husband to enjoy.

Chapter Thirty-Two

NASH

That evening, Nash heard the door clang at Bloom and went to grab it.

It was after hours, and Pearl must have forgotten to lock the door on her way out. He and Maria had worked nonstop in Bloom's prep room since that morning, game-planning how to launch a credit union in record time.

"Sorry, we're closed…" Nash rounded the corner and reared back in surprise. Gray, Jack, and Violet were walking in with happy smiles.

"Lily said you needed some help, so we're here." Gray shrugged as he walked in with a friendly tap on Nash's shoulder. Violet squeezed his arm with a smile as she walked by to set her stuff down.

"All our hands are on deck," Jack said as he hopped onto the prep counter.

He'd asked Lily earlier that day to start thinking of who could help with his harebrained scheme. "Oh, when I said all hands on deck…well, you didn't have to come tonight."

"We're happy to help," Violet said. "Will there be lots of people? Do you need me to set out some chairs?"

"Oh, uh, no." He wasn't quite sure what to do with them, but he could always practice the credit union pitch. "We should be fine in the back."

Violet held up a bag. "I brought cookies in case. I'll find a plate for them."

A warm pang of happiness hit his chest. He hadn't realized that when he'd convinced Lily to stay, he got to keep the family, too.

He hadn't spoken to his brother since the news with the bank, and he'd ignored his mother's calls after she'd defended Jeremy's actions in a voicemail.

He'd already loved Violet and Rose like sisters for a long time. Gray had become his closest friend in the last few years, and he'd formed a close friendship with Jack. They'd be his family forever, and the realization delighted him.

Nash started to excuse himself to go back to Maria when the doorbells clattered again.

Trisha and two other tellers from the bank came through Bloom's door. He'd asked a few bank employees he trusted to hear his and Maria's vision. "Hey, guys. Come in," he said, opening the door and gesturing inside. "Thanks for coming on such short notice. Maria and I wanted to run an idea past you."

"Oh my gosh, I'm so excited," one of the young tellers said.

Gray walked out with folding chairs from the back. "Maybe we should set up in the main store?"

Trisha grinned. "I'm so excited we get to hang out with everybody."

"What do you mean, 'everybody'?" Nash said, turning back toward the door as it clanged again. Five loan officers arrived together, closely followed by Aaron and Nick.

"Hi guys," he said with a confused smile.

"We heard it was all hands on deck and you needed some

help. We brought leftovers from today," Aaron said, holding up a bakery box.

Nash's eyes went wide. "*You* heard?"

Nick nodded after getting a friendly fist bump from Jack. "Lily said you were thinking of opening something and needed small businesses to move their accounts, so we came to support."

So that's where she'd gone off to. "Well, uh, thanks. We're still really early." He scratched his ear with embarrassment. *This is getting out of hand.*

"Even better," Aaron said as he slid by Nash. "I'm going to put these at the front."

He got distracted by a question from one of the younger tellers and watched Violet prop open Bloom's door, beckoning in four men who were flower farmers in the area. *Gray must have told them.*

Jack's father and his wife popped their heads in, led by Rose. Nash pulled himself away from the tellers who were asking questions about what he planned to reveal.

"Hi, welcome." Nash was surprised to see his brother-in-law's family appear.

His second grade teacher, June McClotsky wrapped him in a warm hug. "Oh, I'm so proud of you, Nashford," she said, pinching his cheeks.

He smiled in spite of himself. "Thanks, June."

"Is there anything we can do?" Rose offered.

"Uh, I'm not sure," Nash said. He was quickly losing control of the situation.

Why did people keep appearing? He'd just wanted to bounce the idea off a few former bank employees. He heard Lily's bright voice outside.

She walked in the front door with a bright umbrella and a brighter smile. "Oh good, we have some people already."

"Is this your doing?" he said with a smile, looking down at his wife in wonder.

"Sort of. I mentioned it to a few people, and one of them told Mrs. Maroo, and then it got out of hand. Everyone just wants to help, honey." She looked up in thought. "Is that the nickname I should go with? Or maybe cutie pie? Oh god, no. Not that one. Eh, we'll take honey for a spin today." She leaned up and kissed his cheek.

He huffed out a laugh, looking around as people filed into Bloom. Friends, acquaintances, and loyal customers all filed in. Pearl brought in several biker-looking guys who Nash recognized from the Thirsty Beaver bar on the edge of town.

Margie, Pop, and Mrs. Maroo handed out coffee they'd brought.

"When did that table get set up?" Nash muttered, looking at the table of coffee urns and baked goods at the front of the store.

Lily grimaced at him. "I'm sorry. I didn't know it would turn into a whole thing. But on the bright side, if you're going to launch a credit union, you need customers, right?"

He'd always wondered if the women he'd dated had only wanted his money. And it was a bigger comfort than he realized that his wife couldn't care less about it.

She just wanted him to be happy.

He shoved at his hair as the hardware store employees walked in, and Christina and her son waved. He waved back, still talking to Lily. "I mean, it's really early. We don't even know where we could have it."

"There's no time like the present to announce it to everybody. Come on, guys!" Lily said, calling outside.

Nash peeked out the front door of Bloom and saw a line of people walking in. Maria's daughters rushed in and Lily hugged them, having designed their wedding flowers last year.

Allison came in with a wave, talking with one of Maria's daughters.

Maria walked up, looking as confused as he felt.

"Hey, boss. You believe this?" he said with a shake of his head.

Maria put a hand on her heart, seeing the stream of people file in. "I'm not the boss yet. We have to convince everyone to move their assets first."

Lily put her arm around Nash's waist. "Well you got their assets in the door. Go dazzle them with all your do-goody-ness."

He'd never felt this nervous in his life. He could fail. Really make a mess of not only his life, but everyone else's. It wouldn't just be his family's legacy.

Margie sauntered over with a tray of coffees on one deft, ancient hand. "I think it's your time to shine, handsome. Or move this to a place that serves tequila." She popped her gum and kept walking.

The showroom was suddenly stuffed with people. He ran a hand down his face and laughed, unable to believe it.

He took steps two at a time up the spiral staircase overlooking the store. "Hi everyone." He waved his arms, trying to get everyone's attention, but they were too busy eating snacks and chatting.

A piercing whistle below him cut through the noise, and everyone turned their attention to the front.

Lily winked up at him.

Fuck, I love her so much.

"Hi everyone, thanks for coming on such short notice. You heard it was all hands on deck and..." He ran his hands through his hair. "I never expected to have this many hands."

A sea of smiling faces laughed and whooped back.

"You know by now that the board of the Fairwick County Community Bank and I didn't see eye to eye."

"Those bitches," Aaron called from the back and everyone agreed.

Nash laughed. This impromptu launch was a hell of a lot different than how he'd approached everything else in his life.

And he was loving it.

"Agreed, Aaron. So I've decided to personally back the first credit union in Fairwick Falls history. This means that we'll be a non-profit member-driven organization, and there's no chance of ever being sold to a large corporate bank."

A shocking wave of yells and applause startled him. He glanced at Maria who looked as confident as ever.

"We're going to need your help. We have to move quickly before people are laid off at the bank if the merger happens. We're going to need every hand we can find to get this going, including employees—"

"Done," Trisha shouted from the back with a smile, and the loan officers beside her whooped.

Nash smiled, full of pride. "We'll need help with the launch—"

"I know a couple who are pretty good on camera. We could do some ads," Jack added, his arm around Violet, squeezing her and smiling.

"And eventually, somewhere to actually launch the credit union," Nash finished.

"I'm moving the hardware store to a bigger location next year. Maybe you could lease the building from us," Christina offered.

Emotion caught in his throat, and he blinked it away, nodding, needing a second.

A few more people shouted ideas, and Lily captured them on the whiteboard she'd rolled out to the front.

"If you need business accounts, we talked. We'll move ours," Gray added, throwing a thumb behind him as the farmers in town waved back.

He rubbed at his lips, having an out-of-body experience and trying to fight back tears. He'd worked his whole life to make sure he could take care of the town.

And now here they were, helping him.

"Thanks," he choked out. "My uh…" He cleared his throat. "My dad would have loved this. I hope you'll put as much faith in the Fairwick Falls Credit Union as you did in his leadership at the bank. But, I won't be the president of the credit union." Nash beckoned Maria up the stairs.

"We all know who really ran the show when my dad was at the bank. And who should have taken over before I got there. I'm pleased to announce that Maria Lopez has agreed to be the president and CEO of the new Fairwick Falls Credit Union."

A thunder of claps and happy shouts lifted his spirits higher than he'd have thought possible. "You can take it from here, boss?"

She gave him a confident nod and started taking questions. He stood off to the side, wrapping his arms around Lily as they watched Maria hold court.

He scanned the sea of faces all smiling. He'd made the biggest mistake he'd feared his whole life, and yet, the people of Fairwick Falls hadn't turned their backs on him.

His favorite people smiled back—from his childhood, his past, his present, and as Lily pulled him down for a kiss, his future.

And it looked better than he could have ever imagined.

∽

LILY

A FEW STRAGGLERS milled about Bloom as Nash and Maria wrapped up their event. It had been an unexpected surprise launch for everyone involved.

Nash was in a deep discussion with Gray, Jack, and Maria on the far side of the store. Her husband looked happy and excited and relaxed despite starting this new journey she knew wouldn't be easy.

Pop and Mrs. Maroo wandered over to where Lily sat by the register. "We are heading out," Mrs. Maroo called.

Lily hopped down and wrapped Mrs. Maroo in a hug. Mrs. Maroo's tiny arms of iron hugged her back fiercely. How could she have ever thought that she could live in New York City and miss this? "Thanks for helping spread the word," Lily said as Mrs. Maroo squeezed her.

"I take my responsibilities as town gossip seriously and try to only use my powers for good," Mrs. Maroo said with a wink. "Well, good *and* when there's a juicy story. Hey kiddo," she said suddenly, taking both of Lily's arms with a serious look. "I'm proud of you. For going after what you wanted." She glanced at the hunk across the room that Lily now got to sleep with.

"I consulted with my heart and my lady parts, and we were all in agreement that I should get over myself and admit how much I love him."

Mrs Maroo pinched her cheek and moved on to Violet. Aaron and Nick walked over, boxing up the rest of the uneaten pastries.

"I think I owe you both about seventeen meals," Lily said, wrapping her arms around Nick in a hug.

"That's what I was just saying," Aaron said with a laugh as she hugged him too.

"Come over and have dinner with Nash and me next week," Lily said, insisting. "You need people to wait on you for once."

Rose wandered over to lean against the register. "Hey," she

said, holding up a photo. "We're in the same positions." Rose flipped the photo so Lily and Violet could see.

They'd left their dad's photo of the three of them and him taped up at the register. It was pretty much the only thing they didn't change when they'd decided to redo the store and relaunch their family's century-old flower shop.

"Jeez. It's almost been a year since we decided to reopen Bloom," Lily said, surprised. Lily looked with pride at the pretty fixtures, gorgeous arrangements that she'd created, the piles of local-made gifts for purchase. How a humble flower shop had unexpectedly changed her life.

Rose chuckled as she leaned on the counter. "Do you remember how it smelled?"

"Awful. And the paint job?" Violet asked.

"Horrifying." Lily shuddered.

"Dad would have loved tonight. All his favorite people in one room, supporting each other. Speaking of support, you looked awfully cozy with your *husband* earlier. All good there?" Rose raised an eyebrow as she and Violet glanced at each other.

Now, do it now. Panic sweats started down her body as she stared at her sisters. She'd worked all day on her research and pitch about what she thought they should do next.

Just get to it, Parker.

"I figured out a way to stay in Fairwick Falls and not lose my mind."

"You realized Nash has a crap ton of money and you can live a life of luxury?" Rose said with a sardonic smile, staring at her from across the counter.

"She'd never be a lady of leisure," Violet said, shoving Rose's arm playfully. "There'd be too many ideas bursting out of her brain."

Lily cut to the chase. "Focusing on home goods is stupid."

Rose and Violet blinked in surprise, glancing at each other.

"We should do what we do best. What *I* do best: creating beautiful experiences for everyday people."

Lily opened her laptop on the counter, showing a slick presentation. "We should focus on bringing Bloom to more towns. We should franchise."

Ha, nice use of a fancy business word.

"Hmm," Rose said, her brows narrowed in thought as Gray wandered over. "A business format or conversion franchise?"

"Uh..." Lily panicked, feeling outgunned. Shit, she should have done more research.

Gray wrapped his arms around Rose with a proud smile. "Isn't it great when she's all businessy and shit?"

Scratch that. Pitch the vision.

"I want to work with people to turn their flower shop around like we did here. Invest in what's there, in their infrastructure, but co-create the vision with them like I did with Allison."

Rose tilted her head side to side, considering. "And we shouldn't do home goods, why?"

"Because it's a flash in the pan. I can make the coolest limited edition candle series designed with our signature scents, but it won't matter six months later. It'll be stuff in people's closets or Goodwill or whatever. That's not why we got into this."

Jack had wandered over and wrapped his arms around Violet. "Didn't you do it to pay off your dad's taxes?"

"Yeah, but wasn't it fun to *make* something together?" Lily said, bouncing on her toes. Violet's shoulders started wiggling with excitement and understanding.

"I'm listening," Rose said slowly with a smile.

"In Fairwick Falls, we've been able to change people's lives. We added a profitable business to the community. We've made ourselves more money, we've supported other small businesses through the gift selection here. Alejandro had to start a second production line to keep up with our lotion order. We're a space for people to have events, and they don't have to travel far away for wedding florists.

"I want to change communities *with* the communities by doing what we do best: making beautiful flower shops full of lovely things for you or someone you love. I would use every tool in my very deep toolbox to do it."

"She must be serious," Gray said, knocking Violet's shoulder with his elbow. "She said 'deep toolbox' and didn't laugh once." Violet threw her head back with laughter.

Lily's eyes connected with Nash's as he stood behind them, listening, a wide smile on his face.

She got a burst of confidence. *Bring it home.* "Rose, we could be the biggest flower shop franchise in the country. Think of who we'd be competing against. Soulless corporate companies with no sense of style, no perspective. You know me, I'm *oozing* with perspective."

"Practically dripping with it," Nash said with a mischievous smile.

Gray raised his eyebrows, impressed. "It's a good idea. I can think of a handful of shops that could benefit." Lily hadn't even considered how Gray's network of flower sellers and farmers would come in handy.

"I like it," Rose said, shrugging.

"Really?" Lily clapped her hands with excitement. "Hot damn, I thought I was gonna have to work on you for at least two more weeks."

"Allison's business has increased over eighty percent since her Bloom-ified reopening. She's getting more walk-in traffic and more online orders. Have you seen all the selfies tagging her *Allison in Wonderland* magic garden in her store?"

"Oh my gosh, they're so cute I can't even handle it," Violet said.

"Plus, franchising our brand requires very little infrastructure on our part. You'd be carrying the whole load in the creative direction. Since we are already making a profit, thanks to the superstars to my left"—Violet and Jack bowed—"we now have the capital to invest in another location. The trick would be finding more stores around here that we could start to experiment with."

"Two steps ahead of you." Lily clicked to the next slide in her presentation. "These are five potential stores that have a good customer base, but their store and arrangements need updating. The next step would be talking to them to see if they'd be interested."

Violet clapped her hands next to Rose as they waited for her verdict. They were a team, but Rose was the boss, it came with the title of oldest sister.

"What would *you* want to do?" Rose said, steepling her hands.

"I'd keep all our stores up-to-date on the latest design trends. Teach classes, co-design their space in a way that works for them like it did with Allison. Not forcing their shop to look exactly like ours, but taking the essence of what Bloom is: modern, timeless, local, fun, flirty, and co-create it with the people we franchise with. You wanted to take over the world, right?"

"That's the plan," Rose said, getting excited.

"Let's do it by investing in small businesses, not with stuff that will wind up in a landfill."

"So, you're staying? Forever?" Violet asked Lily with hopeful eyes.

"As long as I have the freedom to stretch my metaphorical

legs when needed, and not stay tied to the prep counter until the day I croak, I'm staying."

"You are the biggest, bluntest outdoor cat I've ever seen," Rose said with a smile, walking around to wrap her arms around Lily. Violet was already scrambling to join their hug. "I think we need pizza and a movie to celebrate."

Lily let herself wallow for a second in the comfort of her two older sisters being there to support her and let out a sigh at how stupidly perfect she'd unexpectedly made her life.

I need to buy Peaches a thank you gift for making me twist my knee.

Violet and Rose debated the flower shops Lily had identified as they all walked to the front of Bloom to go home.

Nash slid a hand down Lily's back. "You were amazing. But you sure you're OK with all this? A lot is going to change after today. We're going to have a lot less money." He glanced at the whiteboard filled with rows of large numbers.

She threw her arms around his neck with a wide smile. "Nash Donnelly, I'd live in a camper van in Donnelly Park with you as long as I get to work with flowers beside my sisters and kiss you anytime I want."

His handsome face went soft with warmth as a lock of hair fell across his forehead. *Swoon*. "You really are the perfect wife for me." He interlaced their fingers as Lily got out her keys to lock the door. "Feeling like running after everything that's happened today?"

Her mouth quirked. "How dare you act like you've known me all your life, husband."

His eyes heated, and he pulled her close. "You are known, Lily. All the mushy bruised parts, and the sweet and the cynical ones too. I know you to your bones and I love you even more for it."

He pulled her into a slow, melting kiss, his tongue tracing

her sigh as she fell into it. Wolf whistles interrupted them from the sidewalk as Rose, Gray, Vi, and Jack waited for them.

"From now on, I'm only running *toward* you and the life we want. *Not* away." She locked the door with a happy sigh.

Nash nodded his head toward the door as they walked out. "So what do you say? Should we live happily ever after?"

"Only if we get to be there too," Violet shouted as she hop-skipped up to Lily, grabbing her other arm with excitement.

"Who's picking the movie tonight?" Gray asked.

"Vi's turn," Rose answered, her arm wrapped around Gray's waist.

"And for the love of god, my love, not another romance," Jack said as he eyed Violet with a grin.

As the three Parker sisters and those they loved walked toward Pop's to see if he'd make a late-night pizza to-go, a breeze fluttered through their hair, feeling an awful lot like a caress.

But they were far too happy, far too in love, and far too excited about what was to come to notice.

THE END

Epilogue

13 Months Later

LILY

Lily ran across her studio and belly-flopped on the queen bed tucked under the twinkle light-covered alcove on the top floor of the flagship Bloom store.

The woodsy, floral scent swirled around her as she huffed lungfuls of the quilt on her old bed.

It's been a long two weeks away from my happy place.

Well, her second happy place. The first one was with Nash in their hot tub at home.

She'd been in Pittsburgh working on the newest, biggest Bloom yet. It would be bigger than the Elliotsville, Cape Creek, Cooperstown, and Fairwick Falls Blooms put together. A tumble of anxiety somersaulted in her stomach from thinking about the stakes. But that was just part of the job of doing new and crazy things now.

It'll be great. And we'll kill it when we pitch the Philly store next week.

Lily's eyes roamed the space that was now her private studio. *I should take the wildflower watercolors and post them for sale downstairs*. The oil painting next to the watercolors was probably dry now. *Time for it to go to the Elliotsville Bloom where it belongs.*

Her eyes lodged on a simple crinkled envelope still sitting in the center of the table. The reason why she'd come back to the studio first instead of going home.

She'd finally decided that *today* would be the day she'd read her dad's letter. It was the second anniversary of Bloom's opening, and they were hosting a party downstairs to celebrate. The three of them wanted to finally give back to the town that had helped them so much.

She'd told Nash she could stomach the pain if he was with her and there was the promise of cake afterward.

Don't think about the pain, think about the cake.

And the sexy sexy 'I missed you' sex from your husband.

Lily cataloged her busy week ahead as she splayed, starfish-style, on the bed, waiting for Nash.

After the party today, I need to start sketching for Violet's next season. Allison had taken over day to day work for the Fairwick Falls and Cooperstown Bloom stores. Vi was on maternity leave, but the next season of *Plant Parent SOS* would start in a few months. Lily would have style segments throughout the season. *Maybe I'll do a 'how to' on moss art, or a plant wall like downstairs.*

Familiar thundering footsteps on the stairs made Lily sit up with a happy grin. The doorknob turned, and she launched herself across the studio. Her husband never broke his stride and caught her. His arms crushed her to him, and she wrapped her legs around his waist.

Home. That feeling of safety, of being enough, of being exactly where she wanted to be—that was what Nash was.

He crushed his mouth to hers, and she reveled in his taste. Licking, swiping her tongue along his bottom lip as his hands dug into her ass.

"Hi, wife," he whispered against her lips.

"Hi, husband." She smiled back.

"The next time someone convinces me to speak at a weeklong conference and then book back-to-back meetings so I don't see my wife for two weeks...kick them. Hard. In the balls."

Lily laughed as Nash let her down.

"How was the drive back from Cape Creek?" Lily asked.

Nash had a happy, tired smile on his face as he ran a hand through his hair. "Good. Looks like the second location of Fairwick Falls Credit Union might actually be possible. The town is desperate to have another option besides Quantum."

The Fairwick Falls Credit Union had miraculously launched in just under one year. Nash had burned the candle at every end, and somehow also in the middle, to get it ready. He'd already fielded requests for additional branches from underserved communities in the region.

"You excited for the Credit Union's move this weekend?" Lily said, throwing her arms around Nash's waist.

He squeezed her tight. "A little bittersweet. A little excited. But mostly, stressed that it'll all work out okay."

After the mass exodus of the Fairwick County Community Bank employees to the Credit Union, the customers followed. Quantum, unhappy with the developments, canceled the deal and left the bank's board up a creek without a financial paddle. The bank closed a few months ago, and now the Fairwick Falls Credit Union would be moving back into the building that Nash's family had built hundreds of years ago.

And in the happiest news, Jeremy lost his finder's fee. Becky took what little money he had left, and Jeremy now lived with Nash's mother.

Unsurprisingly, the Donnelly family dinners had stopped.

Nash shrugged off his coat, and Lily wanted to paw at the zip-up sweater covering his chest. "You know, I almost miss your fancy suit days," she said with a wistful sigh as she stared at his ass. "But then you look so hot that I can't remember why I miss it."

He leaned down for another slow kiss. "You just miss tugging off my tie." He kissed the side of her mouth. "But I'm always happy to role-play when we get home."

Yes. She leaned into him, wanting to get lost in how good he felt against her.

His muscles were warm and solid as she ran her hands under his shirt. "Or I could straddle you right here, right now."

He kissed and nipped her neck. "That will have to wait. I want to take my time enjoying you, and we have to be downstairs at the party in fifteen minutes." He took her hand and squeezed it. "You ready?"

She gulped in a breath for courage and nodded, already feeling some Big Feelings. She grabbed the letter from the table. The bed creaked with familiarity as they sat on the edge, and she realized this felt exactly like the right time to finally read her dad's letter. She was happy and settled and so, so loved.

With trembling hands, she opened the sealed, crinkled envelope. It had coffee stains, paint splatter, and mushed corners from sitting on her table for two years. It just looked worn-in and perfect. Like her dad.

She pulled the piece of paper out, and as she unfolded it, two small drawings fell into her lap. A surprised sob scratched at her throat.

The first: a bright purple crayon drawing of stick people surrounded by vibrant, wonky flowers and a 'lily + dad' written at the top in her preschool scrawl. The second was a cartoon her dad always drew of an old man with a top hat and monocle, and she'd used her crayons to color it in.

Tears streamed down her face at the forgotten art. "He liked to doodle, like me," she said, getting choked up.

Nash gripped her hand as she started to read the letter.

Hi my Lilybug,

I'm sorry I can't be there with you when you read this. Sort of how the deal goes, unfortunately. But if I know you, you have someone beside you (or some animal) so you won't feel so alone. You were always making friends so fast with your chatter and charm, I never had to worry about my Lilybug being lonely.

I never quite knew how to say sorry for when you were little. Your mom was my bright spark, and losing her extinguished my light for a long time. I'm sorry that the darkness crowded in on you and you had to bear it on your little shoulders.

I'm so sorry you didn't get the best version of me. You deserved it. I tried my best, but in the end you deserved better than my best.

You were the bright light at the end of the tunnel that got me through more days than you'll ever know. I'd be lost in sad memories thinking about your mom, and here my little ray of brightness would tumble in front of me and say the most outrageous things. That you and Mr. Nibbles would be taking the train to Paris, and did I want to come with you? You'd do endless front flips and handstands until I clapped. You were just like your mom that way—always knew how to pull me out of my funk.

Your mother never got to choose her path. She'd been destined to run the flower shop since it'd been passed down in her family for so long. I always wanted you to have a choice. You reminded me so much of her, and I never wanted you to feel trapped.

You have a fire in you like she had. I hope you never lose it. Make sure when you finally settle down and let someone see all the parts of you that we all love that they don't extinguish the fire, but they encourage it. Protect it.

I put in some of my favorite drawings of yours that always made me smile. I don't know if you noticed when you were little, but we somehow never ran out of crayons. I swear you'd use up half a pack in an afternoon. I kept a stockpile in my closet. Never wanted you to stop expressing yourself.

I wish I could see all the beautiful things you'll make in your life. But I'll settle for knowing that the world will have been brighter because your soul was in it.

Love you forever,
Dad
P.S. - Don't wait too long to tell Nash. Life's short, bug.

Fat tears rolled down Lily's face as she finished reading the last words he ever wrote to her. Nash pulled her into his chest and she sobbed and sobbed. Minutes went by until the pain passed. It always felt like she was in an unending ocean of sadness until finally the wave ebbed and she could breathe again.

"He said I should tell you that I love you," she murmured against his chest as his soothing hands rubbed up and down her back.

Nash's rumble of laughter soothed her. "And we could have been married a year sooner if you'd just read the letter two years ago," he said with a smile, kissing the top of her head.

"And miss you sweeping me into your arms 1.4 billion times? No way." She lifted her head as his mouth connected with hers, turning her gooey. His lips had a direct line to the dopamine center in her brain, and happy, warm sunbeams curled their way through her body as his lips nipped and pulled at her.

Meeeeeeeep. Ma-ma-ma-meeeeeeep.

A comically bright car horn sounded outside, and she pulled away with a laugh. "Someone's car horn swallowed a Muppet."

Meep, meep, mahmeep-meep.
Meep! Meep!

Nash's lips twitched with mischief as he nodded at the window. "You better go check it out."

Dawning realization that it might be *her* Muppet-swallowing car horn had her running to the window.

She swung open the window with a shriek.

"You said you needed a fun tent idea for the new Fairwick Farmer's Market," Nash said, coming up behind her.

"Is that...?" Lily looked back at him with surprise.

"The rusted-out VW van you fell in love with six months ago? Pearl's brother fixed it up. I thought you could use a pick-me-up after reading the letter." Nash was beaming. He loved giving excellent presents, and Lily was glad he was so good at it.

The bright and shiny teal vintage VW van pulled to a stop in the parking lot beside Bloom. The side of the bus that had been rusted beyond repair was cut out, and instead of windows, flower buckets were attached to cut out stalls. A hinged roof was pulled back, and Lily could already see the pictures forming in her head. Wedding photos, events, farmer's markets. It would be cute as *fuck*.

She leapt into Nash's arms and yanked his head down for a hard, long kiss. He hugged back, and as the kiss heated, she pulled away with a laugh. "I gotta go see it up close."

They ran down the stairs to the back side of Bloom. Violet and Jack were walking up to the van carrying armloads of baked goods. Three-month-old Frank was strapped to Jack's chest.

"Frankie boy," Lily cooed. "Normally Auntie Lily would cover those round cheeks in kisses, but I gotta go hug a van first."

Lily pressed her arms up to the sides of the van and squeezed as happiness shot out through her fingertips.

"I tried to convince Nash to make the horn a German death

metal song, but he wouldn't go for it," Pearl said behind her. She tossed Lily the keys.

Lily snorted. Pearl was now their delivery driver for all three stores and everyone was happier. She got to listen to endless audiobooks and had to deal with significantly fewer people.

A tattooed man popped his head through the window. "Hey, I'm Luca." He stuck a hand out through the open window, and Lily admired the sleeve of insane tattoos running up and down it. "When you're ready, I can show you how to attach the canvas awning so you can have some shade on the flowers."

"Hey man." Nash shook Luca's hand. "This looks amazing. Thanks for driving it over from Elliotsville."

"Anyone who can deal with my little sister long enough to employ her deserves the red carpet treatment."

Pearl lifted two black-polished middle fingers at her older brother with a smile. She turned to Lily. "Luca's friend might join the party if that's okay. He's renting the shop across the square, and I told him he could stop by. Need help for the party? And more importantly, will there be booze?"

"Yes, yes, and yes. June is setting up now." June McClotsky had taken over as their part-time store help now that she was retired. It was a *little* weird having everyone's second grade teacher as their employee, but they were rolling with it.

Lily turned to Nash after everyone went inside for the party. "Thank you," she said earnestly. "This is fun and fabulous and kind of ridiculous. It's absolutely perfect and I cannot wait to show you my *thank you* panties later tonight. Hint: there's no panties in thank you panties."

"God, I love you." Nash swept her up in his arms with a laugh. "For old times' sake," he whispered as he walked them inside.

An hour later and with many bottles of wine, sparkling lemonade, and champagne uncorked, Lily was flushed and happy. The chatter in the store had reached a din as everyone laughed and caught up.

Rose and Gray chatted with Mrs. Maroo and Aaron. Jack's father told an animated story to Pop, Allison, and Nick. Maria had come by with one of her daughters, and somehow baby Frank was sleeping through it all on Jack's chest.

Rose clinked a fork against a champagne glass. And when that didn't work, Lily let out a piercing whistle that had everyone turning.

"Thank you for coming, everyone. You all have been there for every one of my family members in the past two years, and Bloom wouldn't be anywhere as successful without you. I wouldn't have met my husband, and then Vi wouldn't have met her husband, and then Lily wouldn't have finally wised up and gotten over her lifelong fears—"

"Alright, alright," Lily said as they all catcalled her when Nash bent down to kiss her. She'd never live it down, apparently.

She wouldn't have it any other way.

"So, in honor of tonight, I want to make a toast to the man that kept Bloom going so it would be here waiting for us to live out our dreams when we were ready. Our father was complicated, but so well loved by everyone who knew him." Heads nodded around Rose. "In the end, he was a man who did his very best and whose *interesting* choices—"

"Like making us work together so you'd fall in love with me?" Gray asked as he wrapped an arm around her waist.

Rose rolled her eyes and smirked at her husband as he kissed her cheek. "My father's interesting choices made our lives exactly what they should be: happy. To Frank Parker."

A chorus of "To Frank" echoed in the crowded store.

Chatter kicked back up as Margie walked around with the

champagne bottle, refilling glasses. Right as she got to Lily's, it ran dry. "Oops, sorry kid." Margie winked. "That's the last of the good stuff."

The bells on Bloom's front door clanged. "Hey." Pearl waved shyly to the person who came in and walked past Lily. "This is my brother's friend, Reed Berry."

Lily yelled out, "I hope you brought good booze because we just ran out. Unless you have a secret stockpile somewhere, Rose-the-planning-goddess."

Lily turned to Rose and saw her eyes go wide in shock.

Rose stared straight ahead, mouth open. Her champagne glass slipped from her hand, shattering on the floor.

The chatter died down to a whisper as they all followed Rose's gaze to the young man who'd just walked in.

He was in his late twenties, had reddish-blonde hair, an athletic frame, and wore wire-rimmed glasses framing his brown eyes.

He waved a hand with a confused expression as he registered everyone's shock. Silence greeted him as everyone stared back at the familiar-looking stranger.

His face was clean-shaven, kind-looking, and heart-shaped...

...and the spitting image of Frank Parker.

No one moved a muscle in Bloom as they registered Reed's face.

A million unspoken questions hung in the air.

"How old are you?" Rose blurted out the question with a sort of crazed look. No *nice to meet you*, no *welcome to Bloom*.

Reed quirked his brow with suspicion.

He looked so much like Rose in that moment that Lily almost burst out in inappropriate laughter. "Uh, I'm twenty-seven," he finally answered.

Everyone in Bloom let out a collective sigh of relief.

Four years younger than me. He was born two years after mom died, Lily thought, doing the mental math. She'd just turned 31 earlier that month.

Pearl was from Elliotsville, and if this Reed person was her brother's best friend then maybe that's where he was from too?

"Why do you care how old he is?" Pearl asked with a scrunched face.

"Because," Violet said with a tentative smile. "That was…" She faltered, biting her lip.

"Well, you uh see…" Mrs. Maroo stuttered, trying to jump in to help.

"You look like our dead dad." Lily shouted it out, cutting to the chase.

Reed slid his eyes to Pearl with a "what the hell?" look, clearly thinking her bosses had lost their minds.

"I don't have a dad." He scratched the back of his head with embarrassment. "I mean…I have a great stepdad but, you know. Not…" he cleared his throat.

"He doesn't have a dad," Lily murmured, sharing a heavy look with Rose and Violet.

Lily sauntered over and wrapped her arm through Reed's. "I think you might want to come in and grab a strong drink," she smiled up at him with an arched eyebrow, "so we can figure out what the fuck is going on."

TO BE CONTINUED IN UNEXPECTEDLY BOOKISH!

BONUS CONTENT

For a bonus prequel for Conveniently in Bloom and a look at four years in the future for Lily and Nash, join my monthly-ish newsletter at elisekbooks.com

AUTHOR'S NOTE

Well, hello there friend.

You're probably expecting some sort of explanation for that last reveal, aren't you??

Pull up a seat and let's dish!

As I started to dig into Rose, Violet, and Lily's stories when plotting the series, I realized I wanted to add one more surprise to the mix. In fact, if you go back to Accidentally in Bloom's dedication, there's an easter egg in there...hinting that there might just be four stories in store for the Parker extended family! (Sneaky, huh?) Frank is a mysterious, mischievous character (like pulling the trick on Rose & Gray in the first book!), and I liked the idea that there might just be more of him in the world.

And for those freaking out—don't worry. As I mentioned, Reed is in his late **twenties**...Lily is in her early **thirties**. Lily's mom died when she was 2 years old. Frank adored Ivy so if Reed IS his son *(we'll have to wait and see!)*, there was never infidelity.

Selfishly, I'm also in no hurry to leave Fairwick Falls. I have a lot more stories in me, and I'd love to see all the shops in the town square fill out as Fairwick Falls bursts with new love stories and quirky characters.

OVERDUE THANK YOUS

Thank you to my ARC readers / bookstagram friends / readers who've reached out online. You've all had a knack for sending me a kind message right as I hit a tough emotional roadblock throughout the Fairwick Falls series.

There's something deeply personal and emotional about not being able to figure out a story. Or thinking the story your writing isn't good enough. Or think *you're* not good enough to do the story justice.

When I've had those dark thoughts, inevitably you've been there without me even asking. Please let me know how I can return the favor (I'm taking spicy scene requests 🌶️🌶️ for future books).

Thank you to readers for joining me on my first ever novel earlier this year (Accidentally in Bloom), and my first ever interconnected series. It means a lot that you'd take a chance on a new author. Your money, your time, your friendship—all are precious. Thank you for entrusting me with one or more of those. I wanted to write these stories for 7 years and thanks to you, I finally got to write them. I hope you'll stick around while I take a brain break from Fairwick Falls for the rest of 2024 and write some light, fun, spicy novellas.

In 2025, we'll be back in Fairwick Falls with a new multi-book arc featuring the new bookshop in town, **Bookish**. Make sure to follow me on Instagram or my newsletter for announcements when I have more to share!

Finally, I'd be remiss if I didn't thank the following people:

- The women in my life who inspired the feisty ladies of Fairwick Falls. I hope my portrayals help you feel like you'll live forever this way.
- My writing groups who've provided immense moral support, logistical support, beta reading, advice, and most importantly: cumin-flavored cheese curds. I'd still be stuck on page 1 without you.

- Jennifer Herrington at Fresh Look Editorial. Without your gentle, kind guidance, Rose would have had a surprise baby and the entire internet would have hated me *(CAN YOU IMAGINE, READER?? Horrifying. What was baby writer Elise thinking??)*. Thank you for helping me turn my jumble of feelings and ideas into a great series I'm proud of. Also, I'm sorry for accidentally naming the villain in Book 2 Jennifer. 😬 There are evil Jennifers in my life, but you are not one. 🤍
- My copyeditor Alex and dictation superstar Jordan. Alex, someday...I'll learn—to use, punctuation—I swear. Jordan, thank you for never judging how dumb my first draft sounds or how winded I get when walking my dogs. 😅

And finally...

- To the original blueprint for Nash. The good guy to my chaos demon. The safety net to my nervous fears. The man who absolutely cannot help but do the right thing. The good-hearted man who I fell in love with a long, long time ago. My heart has found its way back to you again and again, and I know it always will.

    With love,
    - Elise

CONTENT WARNINGS

Off Page

Death of a parent due to heart attack (off the page), addiction (off the page), and cancer (off page). Animal cruetlly (off page).

On Page

Knee injury, oral and penetrative sex, anal play, analingus, light spanking, begging, dominant MMC, threat of getting caught in public having sex.

About the Author

Elise Kennedy is an author of cozy, spicy, heartfelt small-town romances. She lives in the midwest with her (very) patient husband and two perfect pups.

Join Elise's private Facebook reader group to chat, vote on future books, and make general romantic merriment the small town romantics or her Instagram channel the small town romantics.

www.ingramcontent.com/pod-product-compliance
Lightning Source LLC
LaVergne TN
LVHW091700070526
838199LV00050B/2230